WHO KILLED SAL MINEO?

"THE ATMOSPHERE IS HEAVY WITH BARELY SUPPRESSED MENACE AND TENSE EROTICISM . . . Sara's sexuality is stunned by a startling, sensual affair with a gay man . . . fast, sharp and deftly written."
—*San Francisco Chronicle*

"A SPELLBINDING WHODUNIT . . . a scathing image of those in Hollywood who rule by whim of iron . . . SHOCKING REVELATIONS . . . A WHOPPING GOOD MYSTERY."
—*Hollywood Reporter*

"THE BEST NOVEL ABOUT THE KINKY HOLLYWOOD SCENE I'VE READ IN A LONG TIME . . . IN THE TRADITION OF NATHANAEL WEST AND RAYMOND CHANDLER."
—*Peter Maas*

"A glib, hard-boiled murder mystery . . . provocative . . . THE READER WILL DEFINITELY BE KEPT GUESSING."
—*Variety*

"Intimate perceptions of life in the L.A. fast lane . . . SCENES OF DAZZLING DECADENCE . . . some of the most erotic writing this side of respectability . . . STEAMY AS HELL."
—*Cleveland Plain Dealer*

WHO KILLED SAL MINEO?

A NOVEL BY
SUSAN BRAUDY

PUBLISHED BY POCKET BOOKS NEW YORK

"Roaming Through L.A.," lyrics by Tim Dorr, copyright © 1981

POCKET BOOKS, a division of Simon & Schuster, Inc.
1230 Avenue of the Americas, New York, N.Y. 10020

WHO KILLED SAL MINEO?

Prologue: Los Angeles

There are two seasons in Los Angeles, day and night. He loved the nights. Easterners complained the climate never changed here. But at sunset the temperature dropped. It became winter.

That evening there was a rich chill in the air. The rain had slowed to a drizzle on the Pacific Coast Highway. Rehearsals take a toll. He'd worked hard all day, and his body was relaxed. He steered the Porsche north past Malibu, and the cars in the next lane spun rainwater at his windows. On his right, dune grass grew on the hills. When he glanced left he saw watery sea and sky.

He grinned suddenly, remembering when he was a kid speeding here. His mind wandered. A week ago he'd watched the last half of *Rebel* on the late movie. He snapped his fingers. Then he pushed his leather jacket cuffs up to his elbows. "Sal on the run, Sal on the run, making it go, go baby, go."

This was his comeback year. He could feel his power returning.

He still got "Hello, Mr. Mineo," "Let me seat you, Mr. Mineo," when he set foot in restaurants like Mr. Chow's, the Old World, or Musso's. And there wasn't a cashier on

Hollywood Boulevard who didn't wave him inside the movie theater once she got a look at his face. He hadn't waited in line or paid for a ticket in years. Twenty-three years. He wondered if they were playing one of his movies somewhere on television tonight.

Sal Mineo didn't need a big bank account. He was getting by on a lifetime fellowship. He glanced into the rearview mirror and pulled on his cheeks.

Money, he thought, what good is it? It can't love you. It can't hug you. It can't even kiss you back.

He rolled down his window and stared at a man in a passing Rolls Royce. The gentleman smiled, and then he and his car were gone. Maybe he'd been recognized. Last week, that masseuse at the Beverly Hills Health Club on Santa Monica said she remembered him playing Plato, the rich kid with no parents. She loved his soft mouth. She loved his crazy eyes.

"That was my youth," she said.

"Lady," he'd laughed, "that was *my* youth."

He turned on his headlights and his tires skidded. Fat raindrops shivered down his front window. He was driving to a beach party in pouring rain because he was Italian and he didn't break promises to friends. If Mark wanted him there, that was enough. Mark had become family, more than the two fat brothers from the Bronx he called every Easter Sunday.

The beach party was a Kate Lyons special. Sal had already driven out to the house once today, but the reason for that little visit was supposed to be a secret. The secrecy crap wasn't his idea—it was hers, and she was the producer who'd been talking about putting Mark in a movie. Sal hated keeping secrets from Mark, or from anybody that he loved. And he had told her so. But she said it was her secret and her scene and he better keep his mouth shut. Or fade away. The woman had real gangster style.

Sal was annoyed. All this movie talk was probably just talk. And anyway, the kid didn't need the movies. He needed to write music. He needed to get back his focus—and he didn't need Kate Lyons.

Two nights ago, he and Mark polished off a quart of tequila and talked until the sun came up. Mark spilled the story about the mess, and it pissed Sal off that nobody'd come to him with it.

That night was the only time he had ever seen Mark cry. Mark worried him lately. He was a star. He was too young to have career problems.

"I don't know what to do," Mark had said.

Sal promised, "I'll make it work."

Mineo felt responsible. Ten years ago he had launched Mark's musical career. When they met, the youngster had been one more talented runaway on the Strip. He had hitched here from his home in South Carolina.

One day at the beach the boy had picked up his guitar and started to sing "Night Work." Mineo loved the words of the lullaby.

> *I'm too light for heavy work,*
> *Too heavy for light work,*
> *And roll me down, and*
> *Tuck me into bed, 'cause*
> *I'm the right weight for night work.*

"Where did that come from?" Mineo asked him.

"I dunno, man."

"I mean, who made that up?"

"Me," Mark drawled. When he was happy his mumble became a drawl that owed more to his adulation of black blues-singers than to his childhood in Charleston.

"Play it again," Sal begged him for months.

He almost cried every time he heard that song, and he heard it a lot, because years later Mark recorded it with Paul McCartney. Mark Loren was an original Southern blues-singer. You didn't have to be a genius to see it. He had his own way of hearing and writing music. The tunes were unforgettable. The words always made Mineo feel he understood things a little better.

A month after they met, Mineo rented that recording studio above the Thai restaurant on Sunset. For two weeks he sat in the sound booth watching the boy lower his head over his guitar and sing his songs over and over.

The two of them had hugged each other when the engineer played the final tape.

"You're a hit," Sal said.

"Thank you," Mark said. "There ain't nobody like you."

Then Mineo had carried the tape right past the receptionist into the president of Electra Records. Before he spoke, he saw the awe on the guy's face. He also saw the gold records hanging on the walls. He counted ten speakers.

He put the tape on the guy's desk and stalked the room, leaning huge photographs of Mark against the walls.

He said, "I want you to see him while you hear him. Remember the name. Mark Loren. It's going to make you ten million dollars."

Mineo waved both arms at the photographs of Mark. At sixteen, Mark had been a lanky beanpole wearing torn dungarees, the green T-shirt, one sneaker untied, and no socks. In those days, the kid never threatened Liberace in the clothes department, but his face was shock enough—the pouty mouth that undercut the scared and scary eyes; the smile that started sweet, and broke your heart while you watched it grow goofy.

"Looks like your kid brother," the executive said.

There was one picture of a gesture that made teenage girls howl—he was always running his fingers through his fine long hair. Mark looked like he was trying to comfort himself or remind himself of what mirrors showed him—he was a beauty.

Sal and the president shook hands on the deal that night. The man was impressed. The production values were the best in the country, and Mark's tunes were close to art. Two months later Mark's first album made him an overnight star.

Quit brooding about the past, Sal told himself. He turned on the windshield wipers and watched for a lane down to the sea. He swung into an opening in the glistening hedges, his headlights sweeping over dripping mustard flowers. A minute later he stopped by a huge redwood house surrounded by flower beds and gunned his motor over the roar of the ocean.

Coming inside the beach house, he looked down at a hundred dancing kids with shining hair and tan faces. He realized ruefully that they were jumping to a brazen copy of "Love, What Are You Doing to My Friends?" which Mark had recorded five years ago on his album with Paul McCartney. The humid air was pungent. He smelled marijuana. A wall of glass faced the sea and the rainy sky.

He looked over the pretty faces for Mark. Ten teenagers were sitting on top of each other on a couch, giggling. He wondered if these kids knew enough to be happy about being in the prime of their lives. Puppy bodies were so beautiful. A girl brushed past him, her arms covered with down. Teenagers had new muscles. They had baby fat.

Several people had stopped dancing to stare up at Sal Mineo. He knew he was a Hollywood legend.

The record stopped and then everyone was staring at him as he stood framed in the doorway. He almost smiled. He knew how to make an entrance. Then he spotted Mark, and did smile as he pushed himself into the crowd of young flesh. Another record started up.

"Hey, aren't you that guy—that kid—from the fifties?" a girl said. He nodded.

"Didn't I read something about you recently?" she asked.

"Theater," he shouted happily over the crashing drums. "I'm doing *P.S. Your Cat is Dead* at the Westwood Playhouse."

The girl wouldn't let him go. "What was Jimmy Dean like? I mean, you two were close, right?"

He rolled his eyes. He usually fielded this question by saying that Jimmy was the first American teenager. He defined the age for millions of kids. But the drums were too loud. He touched the girl's chin before she disappeared.

When he reached his friend, Mark flashed a fast grin, looked at him out of the corner of his eye, and shuffled his feet. Sal decided to nod at Kate Lyons. After all, she was Mark's new "best friend."

5

Three years ago, nobody could open a magazine without reading about Kate's rise to riches as a young Hollywood mogul. She had been a newspaper writer in New York when she pitched a screenplay to Dustin Hoffman while he was jogging around the reservoir in Central Park. She told him that she and her husband had a green light on a three-picture deal with Paramount. There was no such deal, but she knew there would be if Hoffman said yes.

Hoffman liked her spunk. Better yet, he loved the screenplay. He sent it to Barbra Streisand and four months later Hoffman and Streisand went on location with the new producers. They got the top Academy Awards that year and bragged about grossing a hundred million on a three-million budget. Kate and her husband became the hottest independents in the business.

Then she became the trash talk of Hollywood. Since making movies is all about jockeying for power, gossip is a key ingredient and always pretty close to truth. Everybody disliked Kate Lyons. They said she decorated a huge house next to Warren Beatty's on Mulholland by importing the contents of a Bavarian castle. Then she abandoned her husband and castle, moved to the beach, and ran through a series of good-looking boys, all eager to step over her and into the business. Her husband fled to Nepal to fast at a monastery. Kate developed a weird young entourage and a bad cocaine habit.

Rumors about her nervous breakdown started around the time she blew up at an *L.A. Times* reporter: "I didn't get where I am today by being some dumb-bunny wife."

But a year ago in Corsica, on the set of the biggest movie of her career, she made so much trouble that the director shut down the picture and told the studio it was him or her. Everybody knew about it, but it never made the newspapers. Sal had it from the production designer that the director was right. She was trying to steal his picture. She'd decided that she was better at directing. Five studio guys flew to Corsica and ordered her off the island. It was hardball, but she played rough. Although she got the production credit, and the picture made more money than *The Godfather* in foreign distribution, she was in big trouble. Nobody wanted to work with her.

Her husband was a different story. Sal loved him, and most people liked his outrageous style, his religious yearnings. Still a big favorite in town, he got back from Nepal a hundred pounds lighter, and hired Robert Towne to write an extravaganza about the life of Buddha.

But Kate had dropped out of sight. There were rumors of mental hospitals and drug cures. Then, six months ago, Mark met her at a party for Mick Jagger. It turned out that she'd loved Mark when he was a teenager.

"I'll make you a movie star," she told him.

When he laughed, she pinched his wrist hard. "It's my sentimental nature," she said. "I never forget anybody who gets me hot."

She asked Mark to write an original soundtrack for a new movie. It was a screenplay she'd commissioned about a rock singer who hired a double because he was tired of being on the road. It sounded great.

But Sal wondered how seriously she would take it, and for how long. She was known for her short attention span.

Mark didn't need her kind of trouble right now.

She kissed Sal on the mouth. Her lips were hard.

Mark shouted. "I'll fetch you some tequila." Mineo nodded. He had a plan. He hooked an elbow around Kate's neck and pulled her toward the bedrooms in the back of the house.

"You look great tonight," he whispered into her ear. Her short dark hair and tan looked dramatic with her tight white Spandex bathing suit. Her eyebrows were strong. She had small breasts and a good wall of stomach muscles. Her looks weren't the problem. He knew Mark didn't want him to interfere, but somebody had to say something to this woman.

He guided her through the hall and past a line of people waiting to use the bathroom. Two boys emerged, faces flushed, sniffing and rubbing their noses. Sal nodded to them. At these parties, people were always disappearing into bathrooms together to do cocaine. These kids always carried the white powder if they were working. It was their way to forget their problems. They didn't understand how sad it is to lose time.

Inside the bedroom, he closed the door and pulled the curtains against the wet sky. He'd seen a hundred rooms like this one: mirrored walls, white carpet, a shelf of massage oils, and a glass door leading to a sundeck on the sea. He had necked with Marilyn Monroe at one of her last parties in such a room.

Kate turned from him in a low drunken arc—like something she must have seen in a film—and fell on her back onto the fur cover of the bed.

"Sweetheart, I'm getting tired of your face today."

Sal ignored her. "You going to do right by Mark?" he asked.

"I didn't get where I am today by doing wrong," she said.

"Oh, really?"

"You the kid's guardian?"

"No," he said, "but I love him. I'd do anything to stop anybody from hurting him."

"Anything?"

"Anything."

"Well, I have done *everything* you can imagine to get my *way,*" she said.

"Everything?" he asked.

"Everything," she said, and laughed.

Still watching her, he shoved the back of a chair under the doorknob. He was afraid Mark would never recover if this woman got his hopes up and then didn't follow through.

"Nice place," he said.

"Oh, I've owned better," she said, "and I will again."

"How's the picture coming?"

"With Mark?"

"Right."

"It's great," she said.

"Who do you have in mind to direct?"

"Me, baby, the best," she said.

She surveyed him from his dark hair to his Bally shoes.

"You know, you're short, but you look a lot like Mark up close. But you're old and gay, right?"

He had no answer. He walked close to the mirror and almost bumped his nose. He did look like Mark. Both of them had luminous black eyes. People liked the expressiveness of Sal's eyes. He stared fearlessly, and seemed to understand everything. Mark's eyes were timid and almost too intense. They skittered away when people stared at him. He and Mark both had shiny dark hair. Although Mark's face was gaunt, he had sensual curves to his mouth. Of course, Mark was lanky, but he had the same magnetism that Sal had had as a kid. It made people suck in their breath the first time they saw him.

Sal walked back over to Kate. She was lying on the bed and swinging her hips gently, as if she were dancing on her back.

"Mark has great presence," he told her.

"So did you," she said. "and look what happened to your career."

Sal felt anger, but as usual it was anger at himself. It was a waste of time talking to her. He couldn't warn Mark. It would rob him of his dignity. He felt as if he were watching a traffic accident from a distance. He was old. He had seen the beginning and ending of too many dreams.

"Mark shouldn't be pushed," he said.

He didn't say that if she let Mark down, she'd devastate him. He didn't even want to suggest the possibility.

"I can handle it," she said.

"Mark isn't tough like us," Sal said.

"No, he's not tough like us." She sounded sarcastic. She smiled at him. He'd never liked that smile of hers, especially her small teeth. Her tension showed in her mouth. He believed he could see most people's nature in their eyes, but hers were opaque, like those of a fish. She was hiding something, or else there was nothing there.

"He needs taking care of," Sal said.

"He needs to be a star."

"He is a music star."

9

"Right," she said, "but he's too old for that shit. So I'll make him a movie star."

"Why?" he asked. "Why will you do it?"

"Because he's this week's most interesting project, get it?" she said.

He started to tell her what sort of trouble she was making when, as if on cue, a banging started on the bedroom door.

"Hey, Sal," Mark shouted. "I got to talk to you."

Only he could hear the edge behind Mark's voice. He opened the door. Mark blinked too hard and handed Sal the tequila sunrise.

"Don't hit me when I'm not looking," Sal said. He pretended to cower. "I still need what's left of my looks for business reasons."

He tried to catch Mark's eye in that special way that infuriated their friends.

Mark ducked his head and said nothing. Sal continued, "I meant no harm. I just wanted to pitch a movie idea to the producer here. I'm always hustling."

Behind them, Kate was saying, "Hey, Mark, baby, I wanna dance."

Mark shot him a fast glance. "What's going on?"

"I tell you, I'm trying to take a meeting," Sal said.

Mark shook his head. They both knew Sal was lying. He often lied, for sport, to give life more glamour, or to save somebody's feelings. Sometimes Sal told a fantasy so many times he honestly forgot the truth. For instance, he couldn't remember the scene he had had years ago with Marilyn Monroe. He liked to say he had kissed her and then put his hand inside her satin blouse. But maybe he hadn't touched her at all. He had told the story so many times, and he and Marilyn had both been so stoned at the time on rum and Coca-Cola, that he couldn't remember. He might only have smiled when she told him he was missing a lot by not making a pass at her.

Mark himself aspired to follow in Mineo's footsteps as a fantasist. By now they both realized Sal had invented some of the legend of Jimmy Dean's place in his life. Sal liked the

way Mark would hug him and promise him that he'd sometime exaggerate his relationship to Sal Mineo the same way.

Now Sal looked at the younger man with affection and
said, "You're right. I'm lying, but nothing bad happened."

"I didn't feel real good waiting out there, lonely and
bare-ass."

"I get the picture," Sal said.

Kate said, "Let's dance, please?"

Sal wanted to hug Mark, but he didn't want to let Kate
that far into their world. He smoothed the hair off the boy's
forehead, and left.

Outside the beach house, he slid the thick zipper of his
aviator jacket up and down. Nothing terrible had happened,
but nothing good had happened. In the past he would've figured out how to get that woman to do things his way. He'd
have flattered her into telling him what she wanted most
from life. Then he'd convince her that doing things his way
was how she'd get what she craved.

Mind-fucking—it was one way to do business Hollywood
style, and it worked too.

He kicked a clean white sneaker at the sand and wondered
about dinner. He had a yen for Twinkies. Junk food is the
best stuff to eat when you feel strung out from a long rehearsal.

He lowered himself into his Porsche and wondered why
he spent so much time helping kids. It wasn't just Mark. His
mind wandered to Chris. He had his hands full with him.
The kid had to stop trying to outsmart the sharks out here.
He couldn't win. He shouldn't break the law.

The kids were hard to handle. They called Sal "the old
man," because he took care of things, but part of the problem was that he couldn't take care of enough. Of course,
that was only part of the problem.

He listened to the wheels of the car crunch on the sand.
He thought he heard someone who sounded like Mark shout
his name and he looked in his rearview mirror. But all he
saw was bent mustard weeds, so he didn't stop.

He wanted to get home. He started driving fast.

At Ralph's supermarket, he parked the car and suddenly

wondered what a nice Italian guy from the Bronx was doing out here in the desert about to buy dinner for some native Californian who lived on brown rice. He looked around for a pay telephone. He'd better call and make sure they were on for tonight. But the parking lot was rainy and dark.

Tonight we'll eat what I eat, he told himself, as he picked out cupcakes, frozen pizza, and grapes. He had fifty bucks and change in his pocket. At supermarkets and in Vegas he usually unloaded everything he had, but not tonight. At the checkout counter, he read a magazine story about Marlon Brando and a Sioux Indian boy. It developed that Brando was paying for the kid's schooling. That was decent. Out here people didn't generally bother to flex that particular muscle.

He checked his oil at the station and turned down Sunset, past Tower Records and the silver Donna Summer billboard above the Old World. He waved at the boy hosing down the sidewalk in front of the head shop on his corner. A minute later, he drove into the driveway behind his apartment. It always felt good to make that last turn. The pizza would take only twenty minutes. His living room light was on, although he hadn't been home since noon.

He switched off his engine. He almost smiled when he heard a few raindrops on the roof and somebody playing a Spanish guitar. He picked up his brown grocery bags and backed out of the car.

As he slammed the door, he turned around sharply.

Someone who seemed familiar moved forward from the shadows in the empty garage. He heard a soft giggle. It didn't make any sense for somebody to be back here without a car. One of the bags started slipping down his hip. He cursed under his breath and finally let it fall. "Watch it, baby," Sal said. He fumbled for the handle of the Porsche.

Then something tackled him and knocked him back against the car. His knees buckled against strange legs. He saw the knife as he shuddered and tried to shake free. He hugged the grocery bag up to his face. The knife slashed through it. He heard his pulse.

He felt his torn shirt with both hands. He touched the handle of the knife stuck into his chest, and then his body relaxed into the softest pain he'd ever felt.

"Help me."

He was falling backward on cotton covered with thousands of needles. "Oh, oh, my God, no, help me."

He knew he should not speak. He started to pant, but he felt as if he could not bring any air into himself. His skin cried through every pore. He knew he was still alive because he had shouted; he had used words.

His head fell against his car and then he hit the ground on his side, his knees bent.

Would he die? Was he dead already? Was his shirt dead? It was torn like his chest.

What would happen to him if he died?

He did not feel the knife being ripped out of him. Footsteps clattered toward him and then away down the alley. Rain came down on his eyes and lips. A car door slammed. His arms and legs twitched. Moans came from his throat, from his stomach. He was vomiting. The groceries lay scattered on the wet pavement.

Lights went on in the apartment complex. The guitar stopped. Neighbors were shouting from their windows. Two minutes later a neighbor's lips were on his, blowing air into his mouth against a pain in the center of his chest that was mixed with a kind of clarity. The pain in his chest pressed him to the ground. He felt his body age.

"Help me, help me," he said.

No one heard him. Two of his neighbors were crying. "Do something, please," whispered one woman, her hair in pink curlers. A young man wearing only pajama bottoms patted her hands. "How did this happen?" she sobbed. "I see him every day. Always smiling."

"Where're the cops?" asked the young guy.

"My son was mugged last week after his Sufi lesson. Right in front of Holly's Harp," the woman said.

Minutes later a police car and an ambulance splashed through a puddle at the entrance to the alley, red lights flashing. One policeman wearing a yellow raincoat over his street clothes shoved back the crowd. Another stepped over the groceries and the blood to squat over Sal Mineo, who was lying in a fetal position. He nudged Mineo over onto his back, next to the Porsche. Mineo's knees were stiffly bent; his wrist flopped against a tire. His fingernails were outlined in smeary blood. The cop covered Sal Mineo's face with an orange oxygen mask. His partner opened his metal toolbox and inserted surgical scissors under the bloody leather jacket at Mineo's stomach. He cut up, squeezing the wet leather between metal blades. Then he pulled the jacket open and looked at the soggy shirt. The other cop was taking Mineo's pulse. He looked down at Mineo's pants, stained at the crotch, and backed away from the body. His partner was printing in a small notebook. "Case 393, Mineo, Sal, 8567 Holloway Drive, W. Los Angeles, dead, 2155 hours."

By the time the fire engine siren blared on Alta Loma, the rain had stopped. A policeman was making chalk circles on the wet cement around the body, the groceries, and the blood. His partner was picking a Popsicle wrapper off the garage floor with tweezers. He held a roll of plastic Baggies under one arm.

The other cop dragged a yellow waterproof sheet over the corpse. A police photographer was setting up floodlights. One neighbor brought out two umbrellas and a tray with cups of coffee, papaya juice, and Cokes. "I heard he was gay," she told a homicide detective.

Sergeant William Casey was upset. He pushed her and the others back about twenty feet into the courtyard behind the alley. The pages of his small notebook were slick with water, and the writing was smeared. He was sweating under the bulky yellow raincoat. His tie hung loose over his unbuttoned shirt collar, his blues eyes were bloated, and his thin gray hair still showed the teeth of his comb.

"Let me alone," he told the woman, and tapped a damp Salem cigarette down in back of his ear.

The woman said, "Live and let live." Then she laughed hysterically. "But he's dead."

Casey ignored her. He beckoned to his partner, whose navy suit remained fresh despite the rain. "Call Sheriff's

Homicide and tell them to get ready for the pickup. This guy's bought the farm. I need help."

He pulled out his pencil and headed into the crowd. "Lee," Casey was whispering behind his hand to his young partner, "in ten minutes I want you to order these freaks to get home to sleep."

"I'd wait for the coroner's report. They're still testing, Bill," the man said crisply. He had short, clipped hair and the self-important air of a junior executive running a managerial conference.

It was almost midnight. The neighbors seemed tied to each other. They babbled to keep contact. "I phoned KWFM and they put me on the air. Live. I told them about the blond kid running away."

Sergeant Casey shoved the damp Salem between his lips. It jumped up and down while he spoke to his partner. "I can see the goddamn headlines—EX-CHILD STAR KNIFED IN ALLEY, COPS BAFFLED."

"Casey, don't take it so personal," his partner said. "Did anybody dust the groceries?"

Casey inhaled his cigarette. "I got to talk to these people."

Ten minutes later a beat-up white Cadillac convertible turned into the alley under the floodlights. It skidded into the fire engine and ricocheted away. The car's top was down, and the radio blared. The white upholstery was shining from rainwater. A neighbor pointed at Mark as he jumped from the car, tears rolling down his face. Water was dripping from his hair onto his white suit. He waved a ring of keys at the detective in charge. "I got the key to his place." His voice was pitched low, and his words ran together.

Casey cursed and took the keys. "What's your name, pal?"

Instead of answering, Mark wiped his face on his coat sleeve, watching a police photographer fold a tripod into a leather case. The neighbors were straggling out. Beyond the floodlights, he saw three women whispering and staring at him. One arched her back and began fussing with her bathrobe.

He felt the cop's face next to his. Casey stuck another cigarette into his mouth and Mark felt the heat of the match under his chin. He yanked his head away. Casey crumpled the pack back into his pocket.

"What's your name, anyway?" Mark asked.

Casey grimaced and blew smoke. "Sergeant Casey. I'm the sheriff. That guy your special pal?"

"Sal's family," Mark said.

"What about enemies?"

"Anybody knows Sal, loves him." He heard his own voice fade.

"No lovers, ex-lovers, would-be lovers?" The cop had a notebook open and was penciling circles in it.

"Hold on, man, I can't talk." Mark leaned his chin against the car roof. "I'm getting real sick."

Casey flipped his notebook shut. The ash fell off his cigarette onto his knuckles. "You guys get around so goddamn much," he said, "my suspect list is going to look like the L.A. telephone book."

His partner opened the door on Mark's side of the police car and heaved several plastic bags onto the back seat. Mark leaned down and grabbed at a lizard billfold sticking out of one bag. "Shit, his wallet," Mark said. "Where's his address book?"

"What's your name again?" Casey asked, blowing a small round smoke ring.

"Mark Loren." A siren drowned out his voice.

"What's your line of work?" he asked Mark.

"I'm a singer." He swallowed.

Casey flicked his cigarette into a small puddle. "And where you been tonight?"

Mark pinched the skin of his brow slowly with his thumb and forefinger. He closed his eyes. "I left this party right after Sal and then I was—I don't know—riding in my damn car."

"Were you with anyone?"

"No." He started shaking his head from side to side. "I was alone. I like doing that. Doesn't hurt anything."

"Hold the fancy ideas," Casey said. "Sounds like you got no alibi."

Mark clenched his fingers into a fist and shoved it over to Casey's chin. The fist was shaking. He shouted into the cop's face, "Listen, shut up. Let me see him."

Casey punched Mark's fist away, and jabbed him in the stomach with his elbow. He shoved Mark away from the police car and Mark sprawled flat, his palms scraping the pavement. Using Mark's arm as a lever, Casey maneuvered him over to the body lying under the yellow sheet.

"Get down and look at him."

Mark fell down on one knee against the Porsche. Casey picked up a corner of the sheet. The movement blew Sal Mineo's black hair up from his head. Mineo's mouth was open wide, as if twisted around some silent word. His chest was a gummy mass of blood, cloth, and flesh. Blood stuck to his hair, dirt colored one cheek.

Casey held the sheet, muttering, "This mess . . ." Mark bent over and rubbed his shirt cuff on Sal's caked left eyebrow. The blood flaked away. He sat back on his heels and rubbed the cuff across his own mouth.

The policeman hit his arm. "C'mon, pal." Mark stumbled up and the two of them walked back to the wet trunk of Casey's car.

Mark's teeth were chattering, and he kept looking at the cop out of the corner of his eye.

"How you feeling now?" Casey asked.

Mark ducked his head, like he'd been smacked. "You gotta stay alive, even if it kills you," he chanted.

The policeman tightened his mouth. "Look, I'm too busy. I had tomorrow off, but that's a dead issue. I'm not going to mess with you anymore, so where were you tonight?"

"Damn, I told you. I didn't mean anything by it. I was driving around." Mark hit his fist against his forehead. He was breathing hard.

"You sound like a broken record," Casey said. "A broken record." He paused. "You know he carried your picture around in his wallet with your balls showing?"

Mark turned away. "You dungheap," he said softly. "You're lying to me." He hugged himself and then rubbed his hands together.

Casey's face looked red. "You better understand. This case is my personal problem. I just adopted you."

Mark backed against the car. "I got to call my manager. He handles shit like this."

"We're going to watch you day and night," Casey said. "Don't move an inch. Don't even breathe, because my men will be down your throat to check out the action. Don't talk to strangers. Chances are they'll be cops. You can expect a lie detector in your future."

His partner pinched Casey's shoulder. "Hey, c'mere."

"Remember, pretty face," Casey ranted, "sodomy's illegal. I'll bust you for licking a stamp."

"Bill," the other cop was whispering as they walked away, "go easy. What the hell you doing? You check his ID? That kid's a somebody."

"Him?" Casey rubbed a finger between his neck and his permanent-press shirt collar.

"Yeah, he's some big deal in this town. Calm down."

"Look, this is a fucking faggot-murder," Casey said. But his eyes floated over to Mark and then down to his notepad.

Another detective handed Casey two kitchen knives with steel edges. "No prints," he said. Casey dangled the blades between his fingers, and read aloud. "Sabatier." He walked over to Mark, holding the knives. Mark lost his balance and almost fell onto the blades.

"Recognize these?"

"No, I—" Mark's throat closed.

"Look, aah, Mark," Sergeant Casey said, "I got to get work done. I get excited, see, and we're both upset. This is a fucking murder. Come down to headquarters when you feel better. You need rest."

Mark took a step backward.

"Goodbye," Casey said, and walked back to the patrol car, carrying the knives by the blade.

Mark twisted his fingers around the steering wheel and

backed down the alley. His tires rolled a trash can until it crashed into an empty garage. He braked too fast at Alta Loma. The underbelly of the old Cadillac scraped the curb, and the exhaust pipe sputtered. It had started raining again, and big drops cooled his face. He skidded through the red light, switched on his high beams, and turned onto Sunset, almost hitting a curb. Someone shouted at him from a parked van, "You bastard, you."

It rang in his head. You bastard. You bastard. He sagged against his door, and it swung open. The damn latch. He looked down and his guts lurched. He started to slide down toward the white line on the road. Instead, he pulled the car in front of a grocery store, the door swinging. He heard himself make retching noises. Headlights came at him. In a second, he was crawling up a lawn, behind a FOR SALE sign. He puked warm tequila onto the ivy leaves. Then he breathed deep, a mix of fresh air and car exhaust, and sobbed. "You bastard. Bastard."

He dried his face on his sleeve and his eyes darted wildly. What should he do? What the hell should he do? He put his hands over his eyes. He couldn't think. He couldn't stop thinking about Sal's mouth. He never saw that twisted expression before, and he could never forget it. He lay his cheek on wet leaves, listening to cars slowing for the busy intersection at La Cienega and Sunset.

Back in the car, he kept glancing into the rearview mirror all the way up to Laurel Canyon. Headlights kept moving up on him. At the Wonderland Avenue fork, he felt danger. He dropped his face onto the steering wheel. What the hell? What the hell was he doing?

Then he heard the brakes of another car. In a flurry, he accelerated and swerved up the hilly street. His teeth were chattering, and his shoulder muscles hunched. He was soaked. He had to get home. "You bastard," he sobbed. The murdering bastard.

As he turned into his parking lot, the car behind him sped up and passed him in a blur. The car had been tailgating him since Laurel Canyon Boulevard. His lips went loose with terror. I need time, he thought, time to figure this out. I need to think about something else, anything. He almost spoke the words.

He didn't slam the door of his Cadillac before he stepped into his outdoor elevator. He didn't have the strength. It was only when the elevator was halfway up the hill that he noticed the Mercedes parked on the other side of the clearing.

He ran from the elevator to his front door and fell over something inside the living room. He flinched, waiting for a knife between his shoulder blades.

He collapsed on the floor and then sighed. The red fish undulated in the bright blue tank. Down the road, a dog was barking. On his hands and knees, he felt an overturned chair, a pile of books, and some broken plates. His living room had been ransacked. He saw something move in the darkness. "No," he gasped. "God, no." He reached an arm up for the light switch. A hand grabbed his, then a heavy body jumped onto his back.

Fingers squeezed his throat.

"What do you know?" a man's voice whispered.

Mark screamed, but the muscles of his vocal cords were paralyzed. He couldn't breathe.

"You know too much to live?" The man tittered.

He loosened his grip. Mark's heart began hammering in his throat. He swung an arm up to punch the guy's side. The guy kicked Mark's hipbone hard, like he was spurring a horse.

"It's not here, but we'll get it." The man was talking softly and panting. He smelled of sweat and lime cologne.

Mark tried to roll over. The intruder squeezed him harder with his knees. Mark had never been so scared. What does he want? What does this guy want from me? Why is he hurting me? Who hurt Sal?

"You want your throat slit?" The guy scratched his thumbnail across Mark's throat, hard, from one earlobe to the other.

If he could only bluff. "The cops are on their way here now," he said.

"You lying bastard." The man kicked his side again. His breath smelled like old wine.

"Wait a minute," a new voice whispered. "Let's get the hell out of here. We don't need cops."

"He's lying," the first guy said.

"I don't know. Cops." It almost sounded like a woman's voice. She ran to the front door. "I'm getting out now."

The man slid off Mark's back and kicked him in the stomach with the toe of a sneaker. "You tell anybody about this and you're dead," he said.

The door slammed. Mark stood up and rubbed his scratched throat before he fell forward again on his knees. He licked his finger and wet the scratch. Slowly he dragged himself across the foyer to the front door, and twisted the lock on the outdoor elevator leading down from his house. He was soaked from the rain and sweaty from fear. He groped his way back inside his living room and fell on his hands and knees onto the polished wood floor.

Then he rolled over onto his back. He lay sobbing off and on for an hour. His cat rubbed her head against his leg and finally settled down to sleep on his stomach. He pushed her away and crawled to his bedroom.

He turned on a light and panicked again. His mattress hung off the box spring. The blanket was gone and the sheet was ripped. He turned off the light. The bastards.

The telephone rang for a while. It rang again. He picked up the receiver and heard a voice say, "Jim Logan, City News Service. I wonder if I could ask you a few questions. Sorry about the hour, but I'm sending the Sal Mineo story over the wire service, and—"

Mark threw the receiver and the phone as hard as he could against the wall. He lay down on his box spring, its buttons pressing against his face.

The blast of a car horn made him sit up and look out over the empty balcony next to his bedroom. He saw round treetops blocking the rainy sky above the Hollywood Hills.

He rolled onto his back and clasped his hands on his chest. But then he pulled them apart. "Jesus Christ, I ain't lying here like a damn corpse."

He'd spoken aloud. He was crazy. He laughed, but he stopped.

Then he curled himself into a ball, still fully clothed. He was more alone than he'd ever been in his life. He had nothing left. He shut his eyes but did not sleep. Finally, he just lay still with one hand over his genitals like a little kid.

Chapter
One

After five years of riding the subway to work, you get off automatically. I squeezed past a woman wearing too much perfume. Her odor felt like a balloon pushing at my face, and I needed some air. It was bright and slushy on the street. I hurried into the revolving door of the newspaper building and showed the guard my security pass. There were about twenty people waiting for the elevator. I smiled at Allen, one of the copyboys.

"Hey, hi, Sara, nice story."

He was talking about this article I wrote on a senator who died in the arms of his mistress. Personally, I was willing to let the man die in peace. But the editor wanted the story. So I got it. All of it. I do women and politics. My editor has been up to something. He's sending me out on other stuff lately.

"Thanks," I said.

The boy flipped his glove in the air and caught it behind his back. He was wearing cowboy boots stained from the sooty snow and his shirttail hung out below his down jacket. He was gangly and young, and he reminded me of this completely dazzling boy who once sent me a hundred roses when I was at school. But that boy was rich and fast, and it never occurred to me to get mixed up with him.

23

I've been helping the copyboy learn the ropes. I look over pieces he writes on his own time, and he brings me egg rolls for lunch.

Allen always pesters me. "So, how do I get to be a great reporter like you?"

"Listen, it's too early. I'm holding my journalism seminar later."

"Come on," he said.

"All right. Let me think."

The crowd was pushing us toward the open elevator door. "First you imitate reporters," I said. "Practice reporter behavior. You ever see James Dean in *Rebel Without a Cause?*"

"On television," Allen said.

I explained. "Well, it's true I was only a kid when I saw it. But when he opened his mouth and kissed Natalie Wood, it made quite an impression on me."

"Then you tried it?" he asked.

"First I practiced."

We walked inside the elevator.

"How did you do that?" he whispered.

I wondered did I want to tell this kid on a crowded elevator how I practiced necking when I was twelve? Oh, well, why not?

"On my wrist," I said aloud.

He laughed. "Great going."

We got off the elevator and stood in the hall.

"Didn't you?" I asked.

"No—God, no."

"That's the trouble," I said. "Boys don't practice."

"So?" he said.

"So that makes me the only reporter on the *New York Post* who has this thing going with my left arm."

"That's not the point," he said.

"No, the point is that I act like a reporter. With a notebook in my hand, I'm fearless."

"But you weren't always like that?"

"No," I said. "I practiced. It used to be hard for me to ask somebody to pass the salt at a coffee shop."

He looked incredulous.

"You know what's really hard?" I said. "A good reporter never makes friends. You always wind up selling someone out. Joan Didion wrote that."

Inside the city room, I watched the metropolitan editor spill coffee on his shirt. His wife had just bought him three turtlenecks. She wanted him to clean up his image. In a week he would be wearing his old crewnecks again.

When I first set eyes on Martin Burns, five years before, I felt as if I were meeting a movie star hiding behind thick glasses and a puzzled expression on his face. He was thin from working fifteen hours a day. The man smoked and cursed out reporters instead of eating dinner. He rarely smiled, but he always looked as if he might. I had been a philosophy graduate student in need of a part-time job when he hired me, and night work on a newspaper was better than waitressing.

"Hey, hey, Brenda Starr, what's red all over?" The entertainment writer shouted at me. It was the same joke every morning. "Tangerine" is the way some smart aleck described my hair on my press card. Reporters here are used to me now even though I am different from them. I don't drink Wild Turkey at Moochie's bar downstairs, and I'm not planning on writing the hot screenplay of the decade.

I get high on my own adrenaline. Last week I not only covered the philanderings of a senator and a women's march against pornography on 42nd Street. I spent one night with the city's best female lawyer, who confessed that new evidence shows she helped a murderer escape conviction.

It was also my first week living alone in four years. I moved out of the apartment I shared with Joe. The move was a long time coming. I can't talk to him anymore. When we're together I keep riffling through one of my books. I don't want to start fighting with him. Joe insists it is temporary. He wants to get married. I want something more. I'm not sure what it is, and I get sad when I think about it.

Marty Burns was reading clips. He has a mind like one of the wire service computers. Like the news it never stops.

"Pour a little coffee on the left sleeve—you'll get a matching pattern," I said, and then tried to wipe his wet shirt.

"I'm fine," he said.

He knocked a morgue envelope on the floor. I picked it up. "Who's the corpse?" I asked.

"You have a quiet morning," he said.

The envelope was filled with newsclips about murders in Los Angeles. He sat there watching me read them. A good six minutes passed before he explained that he wanted a routine obituary. The death had been posted by the night desk for morning assignment. I had to write it by noon.

"That actor, Sal Mineo," he said. "Remember him?"

"Right."

"Well, over the weekend, he was stabbed in some alley. Near Sunset Strip. He was thirty-seven."

"Killed?"

"Yeah."

"No kidding," I said. "Thirty-seven. I haven't read a thing about it."

He took a look at me. "Well, you've been sunk too deep in that sex discrimination lobby to see anything else. Mineo is a good story. He was out of work. Something happened. The kid was a star at fourteen. You remember *Rebel Without a Cause?*"

"Yeah," I said. In fact I had just mentioned it to Allen. He handed me the morgue envelope with clippings on Sal Mineo, but I didn't look at them.

"I think he was stabbed in the heart," he told me. "Call the L.A. County sheriff. I got the wire report."

"You might find this hard to believe," I said. My stomach started to hurt the way it does when I drink too much coffee.

"Yes?" he said.

"He used to live on 191st Street."

Marty Burns stopped reading. "And, so . . ."

"Nothing," I said. "He was this hood. He lived on my block. He wore a black jacket."

"You knew the guy?"

26

"Well, he was older. I knew a lot of tough kids who knew him." I sat on the corner of his desk and pulled apart a paper clip. "He was just this guy, this punk everybody talked about."

He picked up the telephone. "Don't get hung up. I want it fast."

I turned over the clips and stopped at one photograph. It was taken on the set of *Rebel Without a Cause*. He was sitting at Natalie Wood's feet, pulling on her thick white socks. His front teeth looked brand-new. All the muscles of his face were pulling that grin. It worked. He looked great. Suddenly I remembered the pair of thick white bobby sox I thought were all I needed to make my calves look beautiful. My mom used to say they were cheap looking.

"I think we're shooting for page one for your story. Sara, are you listening?"

"I'm listening. What's the angle?" I looked at the photograph again and thought about Sal Mineo. I should remember something. But I'd stopped looking for his name in the newspapers when I went to college.

"Here it is," I said. "It's a tearjerker. Schmaltz. I don't think the guy worked once he grew up."

"That sounds good," he said. "Play it that way. Make it sing."

"Well, I hope I'm right," I said.

I called the L.A. County sheriff to get the coroner's report read to me.

"Look at the press release, babe," the man said. He covered up the mouthpiece of the telephone to shout something.

"I read it and I—"

"Look, I'm busy, lady," he said to me and hung up.

I called him back. I told him New York again. This time he raised his voice. "Lady, we got laws against crank calls." He hung up again.

I was going to have to write the obituary from newsclips. Any professional can do this kind of thing. But reporters like to see people with their own eyes. It gives a story juice.

So I called my mother. Before my parents retired and

moved to Florida three years ago, she knew one of the teachers at Sal Mineo's school. My mother's allergies were better. She was upset. She'd watched a news broadcast about the stabbing.

"Sara, he was a difficult kid. Remember? He probably had bad friends."

"Mom," I said, "I'm writing the obit."

"Oh," she said, "think of his family."

I agreed with her and explained that I needed the name of the Catholic school the Mineo kids had attended. She was flattered.

"I'll think of it," she said. But she hadn't finished. "I bet he ate junk." A few years earlier, she had been upset to read in *Life* magazine that Elvis Presley's diet was Dr Pepper and jelly doughnuts.

"They don't live right. It's unrealistic. They live for pleasure."

"I know what you're saying," I said. I pulled a Hershey bar out of my pencil drawer.

After a minute she announced, "St. Mary's School." My mother'd been a legendary teacher for thirty years at the public high school in our neighborhood. "Isn't that where you played your piano recital?" she asked with only a hint of reproach.

I didn't remember.

"I think Sister Mary Theresa taught him," she added. "Sara, your father heard he was a homosexual."

"I don't think so, Mom." I licked chocolate from my thumb.

"Well, something was off there," she said.

"Mother, come on," I interrupted. "I'm on deadline."

"You're too busy with that job," she said.

She wanted to know about me and Joe. She wanted me to go back to marry him. They loved doing the crossword puzzle when she visited.

She had never liked the fact that we were living together. Now she didn't like us breaking up. "Sara, think of the future," she said. "You're not twenty-six forever." She thinks she never explained it to me right. A husband, children, a modest career are her requirements for my life.

One of my mother's faults, or virtues, is her refusal to see any point of view except her own. She would make a terrible reporter.

I had to get off the telephone. I told her I loved her. I didn't say anything about Joe.

When I called St. Mary's I had to wait a few minutes for Sister Mary Theresa.

"Yes, hello." Her voice was sweet.

I told the nun I was writing the obituary. I also told her that I had lived next door for years and mentioned my mother. She interrupted. "Oh, of course. Did you go on with your piano?" Then she added, "It must be wonderful for your mother—Florida." She paused. "I can't say anything."

I didn't answer. She filled the silence. "All our boys are good boys. I taught him good things."

I wrote her name in my spiral notebook. People were not cooperating this morning. "I don't mean to bother you," I said.

"You're just doing your job."

I started shading in the letters of her name with my pencil.

"What did you think when you heard?" I asked. For reporters bad taste is not a real issue. But she deserved her privacy.

"I'm trying not to blame myself," she said. "We do the best we can with all our boys." I heard the resignation in her voice.

I asked, "Do you remember anything special about him?"

She was waiting for me to end the conversation. "No, dear."

To my credit, I asked no more questions.

"He was a good boy, Salvatore."

Before I started to write, I read an article from Mineo's file on the movie *The Godfather*. The reporter said that Sal Mineo had camped in front of Francis Coppola's mansion in San Francisco. He wanted Coppola to audition him for the part of the brother named Freddie in that film. Mineo wouldn't leave until a neighbor reported him to the police. He never got the part, but he said that being a movie star wasn't so different from being a vagrant.

I rolled a piece of paper into my typewriter and slugged the obituary: MURDER.

Two nights ago, Sal Mineo was murdered in Hollywood. Born in 1938 in the Bronx, he was thirty-seven years old. Officials report that Mr. Mineo suffered one knife wound to the heart. He died minutes later. His assailant is unknown. Although the Sheriff's Homicide Department declined comment about the murder's motivation, Mr. Mineo was not robbed.

A child star of the 1950s, Sal Mineo was nominated for an Academy Award as best supporting actor for his portrayal of a delinquent boy who is befriended by James Dean. Mineo was an instant star after *Rebel Without a Cause.* He went on to play similar roles in *Exodus* and *Somebody Up There Likes Me,* both starring Paul Newman. Dean once said of him, "That kid's a natural. I love him. I taught him."

At the height of his career Mineo was receiving 5,000 fan letters a week from teenagers. He struck a chord in the hearts of millions of adolescents by playing the young sidekick who acted out the troubled feelings of the male lead. At the age of twenty, he bought his parents a $250,000 house in Mamaroneck, earned a million dollars in two years, dated starlets like Natalie Wood, and threw beach parties in Malibu that lasted for a week.

However, after making such movies as *The Gene Krupa Story, Dino,* and *Tonka,* in which he starred, Mineo dropped out of sight. Friends told Los Angeles reporters that Mineo had become interested in serious local theater. At the time of his death, he was in rehearsal for a Westwood Playhouse production of *P.S. Your Cat Is Dead,* in which he played one of the starring roles.

A friend of the slain actor told the press, "Nobody who knew Sal could have killed him. To know him is to love him."

The man who became a child star overnight once said in another context. "Vagrant or movie star, in show business and life, it's not a question of talent, brains, or looks. It's a question of timing and maybe lighting."

The funeral will be held at St. Mary's funeral home in the Bronx. Mr. Mineo is survived by his two brothers, his mother, and his sister.

——30——endit. . . .

Marty Burns liked the story. It was clear from the way he was nodding his head.

"We'll make the front page of the late edition," he said.

"Thanks," I said.

"Sit down."

I stood. He didn't mind.

"I got news for you. We want a follow-up on Mineo."

"Why?"

"Read the West Coast coverage," he said. "Since last night all the gay bars got nailed shut in Los Angeles. Especially around the Strip. I hear Hollywood stars in and out of the closet are scared for their lives. In California, the gay newspapers are screaming S and M and Satanism. The wire service boys say it's a crime of passion. They flew the body in last night. They're burying him out in some Catholic cemetery in Mamaroneck where the mother lives."

"Hey, it's not my beat," I said.

"I need you to get me something. The funeral, the viewing. It's headlines."

"Why me?"

"I'll tell you once, and then I don't want any fancy intellectual debates." He looked up at me. "I got instincts."

"Marty, you sound corny," I said.

"You're smart, and you're getting bored with the women's stuff," he said. "You're tired of Bella Abzug's stand on lesbian pornography. Soon it's gonna show in your copy.''

"I like my beat," I said sullenly.

"Why?"

"Because I get to write about people trying to make the world better. That's better than headlines."

"Yeah?" he said. "I'm running it down once. That funeral is a headline. I'm giving you your big break. Start with these names." He pushed a piece of paper across his desk at me.

I turned the page around and read:

Robert Stigwood
Dennis Hopper
Mark Rydell
Paul Newman
Desi Arnaz, Jr.
Natalie Wood
Peter Bogdanovich
Warren Beatty
Yul Brynner
Peter Lawford

"What do these people have to do with Sal Mineo?" I asked.

"A pal of mine at the *Hollywood Reporter* gave me the list. They could show up at the funeral. In other words, they're either pals, neighbors or connections of Sal Mineo."

"So I should go look for them there?"

"Not just them," he said. "Listen, if there's a big gangland murder, the FBI goes and checks out the funeral. Every face. Sometimes they find something. Maybe it's what they're looking for. Maybe it's something else."

"So I look for something?"

"Yeah. Go out there and look for headlines. You got sex, dope, cheap thrills, glamour, murder, and American tragedy. Work it."

"Why not lift the story off the wire service or the *L.A. Times?*"

"Instinct," he repeated. "I tell you there's a lot more to it. Mineo left here and went there to get something. He got a

32

knife in the heart. What's really going on? Who were his pals? It'll start with that funeral."

"But it's a Los Angeles story."

"Mineo grew up here. He talked like the Bronx. We'll claim him."

I started to read the clips. Then I said, "Jesus, I lived next door to a gay guy once. But that's it."

"You won't meet gay guys on the women's beat," he said.

"You always impress me with your class," I said.

"I'm no hypocrite," he said, handing me an old fan magazine. "Get to work."

"Send the show business reporter." Maybe I wanted more compliments.

"I think it's easier for a woman to get into that world. A straight man would hate it," he said. "And he might turn the guys off."

"Any more advice?" I asked him.

"Remember every cliché about Hollywood and gays. Gays love gossip. They love talking about sex. They just may be the last romantics. They suffer over broken hearts." He counted down his points by raising a new finger of his hand. "They love you; a minute later, they hate you. Then they love you. They love drama."

He was always on top of the cliché. It was part of being a journalist. First you understand the prevailing wisdom. Then you dig for facts to support it. You try to ignore facts that don't—unless they start piling up.

He was still talking. "Faggots supply women with masculine admiration without danger."

"Danger?"

"Of sexual entanglement."

"Hey, you're sophisticated," I said.

He turned the Rolodex file and came up with a telephone number for the publisher of the slick gay entertainment magazine in town. I had actually been introduced to him once at a press party for John Travolta, who looked that day like a shined-up version of the boy next door. Travolta stayed at the party only ten minutes, hiding from the onslaught of journalists behind a table covered with long French breads and cream cheese dips. The *Post* entertainment reporter had dragged me there when I admitted a weakness for Travolta. It was a joke, because everybody thought it was out of character.

The publisher had said nothing when we were introduced, but had slowly extended his hand to me as though he were Queen Elizabeth and I were a coal miner's daughter. Quite an acting job. Journalists like talking to each other. He was a journalist. But he was an insider for gay culture.

I called him to discuss the Sal Mineo story, and he urged me to come right over. His voice sounded as if he practiced making it resonant.

An hour later the receptionist at the magazine was showing me down a hallway. He was about five feet nine inches, but I'd bet money he weighed under one-twenty. From behind, he looked fifteen.

Unlike the receptionist, Robert Bogart was fifty and looked it. His hair and his mustache had white streaks, but he was lean and well tanned. He wore a three-piece navy suit and no shirt or necktie. On the wall behind him was a photograph of male ballet dancers, muscles bulging, foreheads sweating. The dancers were twice as big as life.

He stood and slowly offered me his hand. It was pink, as though he had just scrubbed it with a brush.

He told me the names of the choreographer and the ballet. I didn't recognize them, but I didn't expect to.

He sat down behind a bare chrome-and-glass table, his desk. I sat on the chrome chair facing him. The room was empty except for the chair, the desk, and the huge photograph. The window was covered with chrome blinds. The temperature was as cold as the decor.

Once I got him talking it would be fine. He raised a hand. The gesture was languid, matching the dancers in the photograph.

"Spare me the warm-up," he said. "We're both professionals."

"I need some background on Sal Mineo. I'm doing an article on the funeral."

He folded his hands on the empty desk and turned his thumbs around each other. "Ask me any damn-fool question you like."

I almost smiled. I had the feeling he was weighing his alternatives like an actor. I asked my big question without fencing. "Who will show up at the funeral?"

"No, ma'am," he said, "I haven't a clue about who will publicly mourn him."

"Why not?"

"Because people are dying of fear, darling. This murder drove two producers whose names you know, but I won't speak, right smack back into the closet."

"How do you know?"

"Don't be pushy," he said. His thumbs stopped turning, and he clasped his hands together.

"You can tell me how you know."

He ignored me. "Sal, poor man, had to get himself murdered to become a headline again."

"Did you know him?"

He ignored this too. "You wrote the obituary?"

"Yes."

"Front page?"

I nodded.

"You wrote that he was a loser, right?"

He didn't wait for my answer. "Last year, he produced and directed a great play. A homosexual play. *Fortune and Men's Eyes*. It wasn't Sal's first gay-rights play. But then theater doesn't count."

I shrugged. "It's not that." The man was making me uncomfortable.

"Did you write about his plays?" he asked, reaching down to the floor. He sat up again, wiping his palms on a white handkerchief.

"I wrote he was doing *P.S. Your Cat Is Dead.*"

"That was acting. Sal was a good director. You didn't know that?" His tone was full of contempt.

35

"No." I hate to be stupid about anything. It's my Achilles' heel.

He continued, "You wrote how he optioned *The Last Picture Show* and gave it to Peter Bogdanovich?"

"No, I—"

"And how he tried to buy *Midnight Cowboy* so he could play Ratso Rizzo?"

"Well—"

"Why didn't they get an arts expert?" he snapped.

"I'm good at my work," I said.

"But you wrote that he was gay?" he persisted. "Sal was a faggot. I presume that's why you're here?"

"I didn't write that," I said. This guy was acting superior because of his sexuality. I wondered how he and my mother would match up. He was a more obvious target. But she didn't have his repertoire.

"Well, now you know," he said.

"Yes," I said, reaching into my shoulder bag. I couldn't find my notepad, so I pulled the bag into my lap.

"Say it," he said.

"What, that he was a gay person?" I looked up at him. I had found the spiral notebook.

"I'm obnoxious," he said. "I'm sorry."

"Why are you sorry?"

"Good reporter," he noted. "You answer a question with a question."

Then he said, "I'm sorry that it pleases me that the *New York Post* has come to see me. Do you follow?"

"Of course."

"May I be discursive?"

"Please."

"Well, it used to be that people only whispered about gays. Oh, maybe there was a gay conspiracy ruining theater. Maybe gay designers were dressing women ugly. Because we hate women, right? But it was a whisper.

"Then it loosened up. A year ago, straights were still dining out on bulletins about the latest closet case. The last fruit story I heard was Winston Churchill."

I must have looked startled.

"The English vice," he explained.

"He was homosexual?"

"Right. It seems that Winnie went to Tangiers for the boys in springtime." He laughed. "But times have changed. . . ."

"How?"

"These days David Susskind squirms with joy on television when Truman Capote pretends he's sorry they never made it. As if Truman is interested in that creature." He was patting the desk.

"On television?"

"Right, on television. Then Susskind begs Truman to tell him how to dress his wife, where to eat, where to live, where to travel." He took a pair of tortoise-shell glasses out of a leather case and held them up to his face to look at me. "And these days the *New York Post* sends some Vassar girl to ask my advice. Not bad."

"Barnard," I said, "and nobody sent me."

"I'm flattered," he said, and put the glasses away.

I watched his face to see if I'd overstepped. The reporter has to keep a low profile. You can't make snappy remarks.

He yawned. "You're going to find people in Hollywood who are bored by the idea of Sal."

"Why?"

"It's easy for you and me to get fascinated by his particular mix of glamour and frustration from a distance."

"They're too involved in the same struggle for success?" I asked.

"Right," he said and added, "don't do anything rash."

"What do you mean?"

"At the funeral, darling. Somebody has just tasted blood, a psychopath. He's capable of killing again, if somebody asks him a stupid question or rattles him or—"

"But not at the funeral."

"Wrong," he said, "and you know it." He slapped the glass top of his desk with anger. "You act like Jane Fonda taking some Vietnam orphans to the beach."

"Look, nobody's going to bother me."

"Why? Because you brush your teeth after meals and

never steal cabs from old ladies in the street? It could be over like that.'' He snapped his fingers. "Fast."

"I should be trembling and shaking," I said. "Then you'd like me better?"

"Actually no, I wouldn't like you any better. I'd just find something else about you to dislike." He buzzed his assistant and asked for Sal Mineo's folder. The receptionist brought in a stack of photographs.

"I can't let you have these," he told me, using his glasses like a lorgnette to look at them.

I didn't particularly need photos, but I asked, "Why not?"

"Why not? You are fast with the questions. Because, my dear, after a certain age . . ."

He handed me a glossy portrait of Sal Mineo. The photograph was out of focus, but Mineo looked handsome. He was wearing a white tuxedo shirt and a black Boursalino. The white shirt set off his dark tan. He looked like a European intellectual, not a tough Bronx kid. His face had no wrinkles. His lips were soft and his black eyes had good laugh lines in the corners and an extra fold in the lid that implied intelligence. He looked shy in the face of the camera.

"Sal was in his Fellini stage," he said.

"He looks great." I sounded silly, but there was no question that he was a fine-looking adult man.

"Too short," he said absently.

"How tall was he?" I asked.

He raised his eyebrows with exasperation. "Too short," he repeated.

"Where's this taken?" I asked.

"Our Halloween bash at Carnegie Hall."

"Who's that standing next to him?" There was a tall young man staring at Mineo sullenly. He was as blond as Mineo was dark, but looked a little too slick, in the way that professionals do who've learned to groom themselves.

"Chris Franklin."

"Who's he?"

He made a noise to show he couldn't pull his lips apart. I smiled, but I didn't stop.

"Where does he live?" I asked. He made the noise again. From the photograph, Chris Franklin could have been Scandinavian, although he had the cheekbones and the introverted mouth of a young Michael York. There was an animal cast to his face. He looked lupine, like a wolf puppy.

"He looks young," I said.

"When he was younger, he looked a lot younger."

I wrote down "Chris Franklin." I don't usually take notes. If I get interested, I don't forget stuff.

"You've heard the rumors?" he asked.

"What rumors?"

"That's why you're here, remember? About the rough trade Sal did."

"Rough trade?"

"Sadomasochism. Marking people with cigarettes, whips, knives, sewing the testes together with surgical thread," he recited.

I forced myself to look at his eyes. "How do you know he was into that?"

"Darling, unfortunately, I know too much. I hear the whole gay crowd in Los Angeles is in danger. One maniac and the whole scene is poison. No cruising tonight. Every faggot in Los Angeles is scared he'll fall in love with the Angel of Death if he leaves his house."

"Maybe it wasn't a sex murder," I interrupted. "Drugs are a problem in California."

"Wrong," he snapped. "Drugs are nobody's problem unless some dumb reporter writes it up. Cocaine is boring, but if the goddamn New York Jewish liberal press starts screaming its head off, that's trouble."

"Somebody murdered him."

"Maybe he wasn't murdered at all," he said. "The gay Mafia in Hollywood are all hiring bodyguards."

"Will they come to the funeral?" I asked.

"Good question," he said. "But you're repeating yourself. It must be what you came here to ask."

He stood up and began opening and closing the chrome blinds. The flashing sunlight hurt my eyes.

Then he said, "You wouldn't believe the people who called and asked me if they should go."

"Famous people?"

"My lips are sealed."

"Well, what did you tell them?"

He closed the blinds. "I told them, 'Don't be a target.' " He sat down, facing me. "Here's something for you." He waved at my notebook. I picked up my pencil.

"It's my last lecture." He pulled a slim gold pen out of his vest pocket and pointed it at me. He raised his voice slightly, as if he were on stage. "Try to understand a little. The difference between straight and gay. Style. Energy. The differences makes us better."

I let him talk.

"Singles bars for straights are"—he shivered—"grotesque, unimaginative, flat-footed. We live better."

"Why?"

"Because it's what we have. Straights have kids. They have families. They have wedding anniversaries. We have hot sex. A shrink would say we're denying like mad."

"Denying what?"

"Denying death. Dropping out of history. Denying our biological chance to join in the chain of life. We do sex for its own sake, in queer, wonderful ways. Alas, we lack the excuse of procreation. We hate our sex objects—much more than straights do. We even call them 'tricks.' "

I thought of something and spoke fast. "What's that joke? Oh yes: 'Sex is only dirty if you're doing it right.' " I was proud of myself, I'm not used to making casual jokes about sex.

"Nice," he said, without really reacting. "So take Chris Franklin. He wants to make it big in theater, Broadway. But sex is his real interest. Hot sex. He keeps himself like a courtesan. He'll go anywhere, do anything, at any time, for wild sex. Wild silver colors. Perfect grooming, flawless body. Oh, the grace of that body. He cooks. He charms. The cultivated wit. He flatters so deftly."

"But?" I asked.

I watched him frown and make a neat pile of the photographs. He sounded irritated. "But right below that gorgeous surface, he hates himself more than you can possibly imagine."

"Well, what about Sal Mineo?" I asked.

"You knew him?"

"Not really," I said.

"Yes, you did." He stared into my eyes.

"What makes you say that?" Like he said, a good reporter answers a question with a question.

"Because you looked funny."

Sometimes things show that I'd rather hide. I've never mastered the poker face. "I grew up in his neighborhood."

"I see. Well, Sal had an odd set of problems. He was still a star. But he hadn't played a really good star role since he was a child. He had a baby face, but he was too old for kid roles. And he was no bathing beauty."

"What does that mean?"

"Well, take the nudes, for instance."

I looked shocked.

"Tut, tut," he said, "you haven't seen the nude pictures, then?"

"Of him?" It was bad enough I was writing his story. I didn't have to intrude even more and look at his naked body.

"We were going to do a nude feature, but alas, the flesh wasn't willing." He pushed a photograph toward me. "Here."

I stood up. "No, no, I don't need to see them."

He laughed. "That, my dear, you never know." He handed me a small card. "That's the photographer, if you change your mind."

I hesitated a second. A reporter should be agreeable, affable. Try to act like somebody the subject knows. So I took the card, but I blinked away from the photograph on the desk. It was just a quick impression. Sal Mineo was standing sideways, his hip forward.

He pointed a finger at me. "You give away too much on your face. You're a prude. It's bad journalism to let it show." He sounded patronizing. "Be sure you never make judgments, at least while you're talking to people like me."

He stood to signify we were saying goodbye, and he walked around his desk to my chair. He made no sound on the shining mahogany floor. His feet were bare and pink. I should've noticed earlier.

I had passed some mysterious test. This handshake implied more equality than his others. "Consider me a loyal contact," he said. "Remember my advice. Don't get murdered."

Chapter
Two

When I opened my eyes, it was dark. I kicked the blanket off and turned on the light. I knew it was six o'clock. I hate alarm clocks. I've taught myself to wake up without them. It was quiet without Joe and our dog.

Today I wanted an early start. I had to drive to the Bronx for the funeral.

I looked down at my body. After a terrible adolescence, when I was too tall and too straight up and down, I am in style. I am built like a fashion model with small hips and breasts that stay round even when I'm lying down. My hair is red and never looks combed. Joe says my eyes are the color of night clouds. Anyway, they are big and dark gray. He says I don't think of myself as pretty—and I don't act pretty. I don't have time to concentrate on stuff like that. I'd rather look at the world around me than worry about what people see when they look at me. That's why I'm a good reporter. I like to study other people, and not think about myself. Joe says I'm real smart, but there are things I don't know yet. The way I see it, I got time.

I drank my coffee and walked into the living room to stare at the bare winter trees of Central Park. They stretched in front of the window as far as my eyes could see. The apartment and furnishings belong to a man who lives in Belgium. When we met a week or two ago, he remembered my articles on foreign women living in Manhattan. He agreed to let me take care of his apartment for a few months.

It suits me. I moved into this space filled with his antiques four days ago. I don't know what to do next, about Joe and everything. Living here on Central Park South, a street of expensive hotels, makes me feel like I'm taking a vacation. I hear all languages. There is no neighborhood laundry or market here, so I can't really settle down.

The best part is that I stare over the park in the morning and think about the day's work.

I rented a Dodge Dart and drove to the Bronx. That's the car I always rent.

I hadn't been in the old neighborhood for a long time, so I slowed down to stare at the neon pizza sign, the rows of brick apartment buildings, and the Rexall drugstore where I drank Coke after school. In front of St. Mary's Church, some kids were pitching dimes in the street next to several black limousines. Sal Mineo had gone to school behind this church. Now his body lay in the funeral parlor next door. I drove by the crowd of mourners and curiosity-seekers.

I parked my car in front of an Italian restaurant down the street from my old apartment building. Last week's snow had melted and turned to ice near the curb. Two waitresses in heavy sweaters stood watching. They had the restaurant door open to keep them warm. One of them was wearing a lot of pink lipstick. Her front teeth were covered with it.

"Hey, Sara," she said, "you get tits finally?"

I knew something about her voice. I stared at her pink mouth until I remembered. It was Eileen, the girl who'd been the neighborhood rebel. She used to bring a radio and dance with boys in the schoolyard instead of going to math class. Her parents never forced her to study, and although she was pretty enough to be a cheerleader, she rarely went to practice. She didn't have to be home in bed by nine-thirty like I did. Always wisecracking in the back of the classroom, she'd been suspended from school several times.

She had also been the president of the local branch of the Sal Mineo fan club. "It's been eight years," she said.

"Right."

"I heard you live with some guy."

"No, not right now."

"I heard about you, fancy schools and everything. You sure used to read and play the piano a lot."

"I don't so much anymore," I said. Years before, she had me pegged as a drip. A boring bookworm. Now she was less sure of things.

"How's it going with you, Eileen?" I asked.

"Great," she said, rubbing her hands on her apron to keep warm. "I remember your dad, a personnel director or something. Right?" She grinned. "Once he interviewed me for a typing job. Said I shouldn't show up with dirty fingernails. Said you can tell a lot about people from their fingernails."

"I used to come here for the salami hero," I interrupted.

"I don't remember that," she said. "You back for the funeral?"

"Yes." I decided to avoid a precise explanation.

"Figures. The family's hysterical," she offered. "His mom runs that health-food store on Arthur Avenue."

I knew that store.

"They hate all the freaks who've shown up for the funeral," she said.

"Who showed up?"

"I dunno," she said.

"You going over?" I suddenly didn't feel like going there alone.

"I dunno." She glanced at the other waitress. "Maybe I can get off. I'm working for my dad." She looked back into the restaurant. The other waitress slipped inside the open door and disappeared.

"I remember the fan club," I said. There was something more about her.

She rubbed one white shoe against the back of her leg as though she had just been bitten by a mosquito.

"Didn't you go to Los Angeles?" I asked.

45

"What's the big deal?"

Then I remembered. Before graduation, she ran away from home. Her father closed down his restaurant and went to California to bring her back.

She was wondering how much I knew. "I even saw him out there. I had a ball for three days." She pointed her thumb down the street at the funeral parlor.

"You did?" I was surprised.

"I called him up. He met me at some restaurant, the Old World. He bought me an avocado salad with bean sprouts. Boy, that was something different—bean sprouts. Natalie Wood, she came in with her husband, Bob Wagner. They hugged and all. He introduced me."

"What did he talk to Natalie Wood about?"

"Nothing much. She told him to come by the house for drinks and a swim in the pool. They joked around about some teacher they had when they were working on the lot. One time Sal locked him in a trailer. She said how it was a shame school is wasted on kids. Sal said back then he only wanted to be in movies, wear sharp clothes, and drink malteds."

"That's it?"

"He mentioned some script he wrote. I forget now."

"Did he give you any advice?"

"He told me to go home and get married."

"He was probably right. You did the right thing," I said.

"Yeah, great," and she yelled behind her into the restaurant, "all right, one second." Then she shrugged. We both knew it wasn't that great.

"Nice seeing you," I said. I meant it. She made me remember that I belonged here.

"Come in sometime. Dad'll make you a salami hero on the house."

"When I'm back in the neighborhood," I promised.

I walked down the street toward the church. It was hard to remember that I had lived here eighteen years. A woman sat on the front step of our brick apartment building. I used to sit there and watch people rushing for the subway. The woman had complained about my practicing piano. She lived down the hall by the elevator. She was always cooking something that smelled like onions and butter. I did not wave. I didn't want to have a conversation about who was now sleeping in my old bedroom that overlooked St. Mary's schoolyard.

The parking lot of the brick funeral home was full of people. Old women in black huddled on the sidewalk. A group of children stood on the icy lawn watching. One man bent to pick up his keys. He was wearing a navy suit and an open tweed coat. I saw something curved in his trouser pocket. It was dark wood and attached to dull black metal.

The skin on my shoulders flushed. The gun in the crowd reminded me. These people had all known a man who was savagely murdered.

A movie scene flashed in my mind. It was a man screaming, kneeling over a body and stabbing at it. It was terrifying. A murderer was here with a corpse, as Robert Bogart had predicted.

I wanted to sit down, but instead I kept looking at the man with the gun. He rubbed some Chap Stick on his mouth, looked over the crowd, and started to walk around the back of the funeral home. He stopped once to look back over his shoulder. He was tall and had a businesslike appearance. I didn't want to forget him. He was wearing horn-rimmed glasses. His beard was dark, or else he hadn't shaved recently. He didn't look like a local.

Then he sneaked off behind the funeral home. I didn't know what else to do, so I took off after him.

I ran six steps and bumped smack into a policeman. I was scared to death. I shouldn't run before I think things through. That's how I get in trouble.

"Excuse me!" I said. "But this guy with a gun—"

"Hold on," he interrupted, and stepped away. I had touched his arm, maybe to steady myself. Anyway, it didn't help. We made white steam in the air with our breath. It was cold.

"He was young, tall."

He fingered the nightstick hanging from his belt in a holster. I pointed to the back of the funeral home. "He headed back there."

The cop looked over his shoulder and then back at me. "You family?"

"Press."

"Got a card?"

I pulled off one glove and groped in the bottom of my shoulder bag until I came up with the press card.

"He had a gun," I repeated.

He read every word on the card and turned it over twice. His hands were bare and shaking. He must have been freezing. "You got quite an eye there, Sara. How old are you, anyway?"

"Twenty-six."

I put my glove back on and took a few steps toward the back of the funeral home.

"Hey, hold it," he said, without looking at me.

He was giving somebody else some kind of signal, waving. "Off limits back there. And don't try me."

I had no time to argue. He began moving people away from the curb, clearing a path for an old woman who'd just stepped out of a black Cadillac. Her face was covered by a veil. Two men held her arms. She didn't seem to move her black orthopedic shoes as the men walked her inside the funeral home.

"The mother," I heard.

I began pacing the parking lot. Old people were standing around, stamping their boots to keep warm. They wore sober overcoats and dark hats. But I stopped when I saw two guys wearing camel-hair jackets over wool sweaters, no topcoats, no gloves. The tall one was weeping, his head on the other guy's shoulder.

He raised his face, pushing his hair away from his eyes. I walked nearer. I couldn't help it. He reminded me of Sal Mineo. Maybe it was his suntanned coloring. But he was too lanky in the legs to be a member of that family. His jaw muscles jumped, and his mouth was trembling. His face was all emotion. He looked as if he were standing inside a special spotlight in the thin gray air.

I figured I had seen him on the screen. He was that good-looking. There was something familiar about the way he combed his fingers through his hair. He didn't look like a real person, more like he'd been drafted by an architect's pen. I bet he knew people loved looking at him.

From about three feet away I watched him pull a gold cigarette case from his pants pocket and stifle a sob in his hand. "It's not you," he was saying to his friend, "don't worry. I can't sleep either. Jesus, this sure turned me upside down." There was a Southern lilt to his voice. His nose was running. It was narrow, but almost too big.

"Mark, baby, keep it quiet," the other young man said. He had a theatrical English accent. Two fat teenage boys were gawking at them, eavesdropping like me.

"I can't eat. I can't make it," Mark continued. "I keep on forgetting what in hell I'm doing. I keep wanting to ask Sal who died, him or me. The old things aren't working for me."

I didn't get it. The English guy was a study in pastel parchment skin and silver-blond hair. I jumped. He looked like Chris Franklin, the man in the photograph with Sal Mineo. I was annoyed I hadn't recognized him sooner. But daylight didn't suit him.

Mark kept tapping one foot on the pavement as though he was trying to pump energy from the ground into his body. I was hypnotized by him. He mumbled, "Remember how Sal hated funerals, hated them real bad? I remember Sal saying, 'When I go, have a party, have the best stinking party.' " He had a wonderful voice. All the words ran together in new ways.

He laughed, but it sounded like misery.

His friend Chris looked over at me. "This celebration isn't his style, actually."

Mark shot a wild glance in my direction. I held my breath and kept my eyes on him. But he didn't see me. He was checking out the crowd.

"Hey, over here," one fat kid shouted. "It's Mark Loren."

Of course, I thought, what a reporter. They should've sent the copyboy to cover this. Then I almost flushed. I love Mark Loren's music. Not that I tell everybody about it, but I bought his *L.A. Frost* album before anybody called him an American troubadour. He wrote songs about death and love and sunlight. I used to hear his guitar licks on every cab radio.

Nothing pleases a reporter more than stumbling over a celebrity. He was the best kind, one who shuns the press. A challenge. He was also totally gorgeous, roughly a hundred times more magnetic here in the daylight, in person, with his hair short and wearing a suit, than on my record album cover.

Mark took a deep breath. It sounded like a moan. "You reckon he was praying here every Sunday when he was little?"

"He might have done," Chris said.

Mark squinted at him. "I feel robbed."

A girl wearing a white dress and a sweater moved in front of me, edging around a black car. She faced him, her back to me. It was Eileen. She'd shed her apron and her waitress hairnet, and added more pink lipstick.

She leaned her hip against the car door, inches from Mark. Her lower abdomen was directed forward. "I was at the Garden when that girl jumped the stage—the way you hugged her."

Mark twisted his head from side to side fast as if he wanted to escape. He stepped backward, one arm on the black limousine.

She swayed toward him, still leaning against the car, her shoulder inside the curve of his arm. From a short distance, it looked as if he were hugging her.

". . . and you never showed at Dylan's concert," she said.

She was bold. But how many pop music stars come to the parking lot down the street from her father's restaurant? She glanced over his shoulder at Chris, who was scowling at her. "Oh, he thinks I'm pushy, right?"

Mark was trying to control his anger. "We got to go," he said stiffly.

Eileen's body sagged. "You think I'm nobody," she said.

He leaned away from her, grabbing the side of Chris's jacket for balance.

"I'm too pushy," Eileen said.

Chris cleared his throat. "Lady, you've got bloody cheek, and—"

Mark pulled on his friend's jacket and said to her, "Let me be, or join us in silence."

Eileen rubbed her shoe on the back of her leg again, and looked around to see if anybody had witnessed the scene. I avoided her glance. It was better for her dignity that way. A second later, she was gone.

Chris handed his pal a folded white handkerchief. Mark blew his nose hard and then wiped his mouth. I was watching him from behind the trunk of the limousine.

"Ah, Mark," Chris said. "About your place—"

"What?"

"I mean the guys that broke in, you've heard nothing further?"

"Yeah, two junkies were working the canyon."

"You've told the police?"

"They told me."

"I wish I could get it all straight," Chris said. He scowled at Mark, as though he had a lot on his mind.

Mark squeezed his shoulder. "Only thing he ever did wrong was try to help out."

Chris struggled to look calm. "What does that mean?" he asked.

Mark wasn't looking at him. "Oh, you know, man, his whole life—he was so close to God in his own way. He'd walk a mile to put a bug outside and not hurt it. If he'd just taken better care of himself."

"Oh, right, he should have done." A certain kind of English person loves the full subjunctive.

Chris reached into his breast pocket. "Toot?" he asked Mark.

"No, man, I'm going through this straight," Mark said.

Chris stuffed a silver bullet inside one nostril, closed one eye, and inhaled.

I was irritated to see cocaine at a funeral. People who cut their feelings with drugs leave me cold.

A minute later, I followed them up the path to the funeral home and inside a small chapel filled with folding chairs and people. It smelled of soap and incense. People stood in line waiting to kneel in front of the brown casket in front of the room.

The box sat on a metal table surrounded by wreaths.

I took a seat in the back of the room. The woman sitting next to me was pressing her pocketbook into her lap and speaking to someone behind her. "They sent my nephew flowers. Movie stars sent flowers. Some producer sent gladiolas. Robert Stigwood sent tulips. The yellow roses are from France. Yul Brynner. I hear his son is here. This is some affair."

A nun sat down in a pew near us and crossed herself. It had to be Sister Mary Theresa. I walked over and sat next to her. The black wimple framed her freckled face. Her eyelids were red.

I told her my name. "I'm sorry I bothered you over the telephone."

"I'm sorry I lied to you," she said. "You're Claudia's daughter." She started to cry.

I grabbed her hand. "How did you lie?"

"I knew Sal. He was my boy. I got nothing to be ashamed for. Sal was my special boy," she repeated. "I loved him but I should have said something to the father. They wanted so much and they were so poor. I never said a word to them and now this," and she closed her eyes.

"You think they pushed him too much?" She didn't seem to hear.

"I saw him two years ago," she said. "He came to visit."

"Here?"

"Yes. We talked for hours. He said he had recovered."

My face questioned her.

She explained, "They took a little boy who was afraid of things; those roles he played all came from inside him. He was tense and he saw too much and he felt too much. They blew him up. He was so fragile that he exploded. He never had time to grow up."

She crossed herself. "Everyone who knew him loved him. I remember once some big boys got him to hide stolen tires in his father's caskets. The father was a carpenter. Salvatore came to me for help." She wiped at one eye. "I told the authorities that Salvatore was a good boy. Fragile, but he was good."

"He was lucky to have you on his side."

She patted my hand. "My best to your mother. She was a strong teacher."

Her skirt brushed my leg as she stood. "I have to get back to my children," she said, and she was gone.

Mark was waiting in line at the front of the room. I stood in line about six people behind him to pay final respects to Sal Mineo.

There was a shout from the doorway. A girl wearing a floppy black hat ran into the room on high-heeled sandals. She dashed right up to the casket and, holding her hat on her head, she climbed up on the stool.

"My darling," she said, "it's you and me." She reached over and grabbed a metal handle on the top of the box, and a gasp went through the crowd. "Sal, I'm going with you," she shouted, pulling on the lid. She looked drunk, and I knew she was an actress. I recognized her face, but I couldn't place it.

She teetered on the stool and heaved the cover off the casket. I glanced at Mark's stricken face. He was pressing the back of his fingers against his lips. For no reason, I felt tears behind my eyes.

Sal Mineo's head was propped up by a pink satin cushion. His hands were crossed on his chest. The hands and the face seemed coated with orange color. His black hair was greased back like an elderly Italian banker's, plastered in an upsweep off the orange forehead. He was wearing a loose black suit. It reminded me of the jackets the Russian Tea Room keeps for men who come in without one.

His eyebrows looked as if they had been shaved and then drawn in with a pencil. Not the way I remembered from the movies. His eyes were closed and his mouth was arranged in a loose smile. The lips were set together, and someone had put red shine on the cupid's bow, the full center of the upper and lower lip. The gloss was too red, and lighter than the dark purple Mediterranean cast of his mouth.

I will never forget the thick flesh falling away from the nose bone, the soft skin at the sides of his face that looked as if your finger would leave a round dent if you were to touch it. He didn't look like a movie star. He looked like a bloated man who had just fallen into a drunken sleep.

I backed away from the casket, while the girl reached for Mineo, her stool sliding. She sprawled forward, and everyone was yelling at her. Mark dropped his head into his hands. Her black hat fell onto Sal Mineo's face.

A funeral parlor employee and the policeman rushed up front to lift her off the body. She dangled between them like a doll. Mark grabbed her hat out of the casket. I watched him touch her mouth with his forefinger. "Let her be," he said.

"Shame, shame," a woman's voice sobbed. Everybody was on their feet, cursing in English and Italian.

"It's a shame he's dead," Mark shouted.

I saw the girl kick the cop in the knee. He grimaced. "She's fine," Mark said to him. "I'll take her out. We're fine, you bastards."

"You freaks," the cop muttered.

Mark flinched, and opened his arms. "C'mere, sugar." He clutched her against him and planted her hat on her head. The girl huddled against Mark, and both of them sat down next to Mrs. Mineo. But five minutes later, another shout paralyzed everyone. It was Mrs. Mineo, and she was glaring at Mark.

"Shut up," she shouted.

"No, wait," Mark said. "Look, it's just pictures." He was waggling a billfold.

The woman spit in the direction of Mark's shoe. Nobody else in the room was talking. "Blood," she yelled. "You don't know him. I knew him. His sister knew him. My husband knew him. Not you, fancy man."

Mark didn't answer her. The girl in the black hat ran out of the chapel. Mark was crying again. Something fluttered out of his hand. He hunched his shoulders and took long loping steps down the aisle past me and toward the door of the chapel. I reached over and grabbed what he'd dropped. It was a snapshot of Sal Mineo in a white bathing suit, holding a red beach ball. Behind him stood a boy with a mop of white-blond hair. The sun's glare blotted out his face.

Several people rushed by me to comfort the old woman. "God help us," said one man. "From children comes suffering."

I followed Mark outdoors.

In the parking lot, a television news reporter was interviewing the girl in the black hat. A group of disapproving Italians and curious kids watched the scene. The girl was talking into a microphone and looking at the camera.

Then I remembered her. I'd read nothing about Nell Fields in years. The funeral was bringing people out of the past. She'd been Sal Mineo's costar in a television movie of an F. Scott Fitzgerald story around the time she and Mineo had announced their engagement. The two of them had been posed nose to nose on the cover of *Ladies' Home Journal* when I was a kid. Her hair was still the same black color as Sal's.

The newsman nodded at her. "Well, I have a new agent," she said. "I'm doing voice-overs for shampoo commercials. It's my transition period."

She was out of work.

"How well did you know the deceased actor?" he asked. He signaled his cameraman to come in for a close-up.

"I know what you're getting at," she said slowly and loudly. "Sal was straight, straight as you and me." She was shouting into his microphone, but not loud enough to destroy the sound. She seemed annoyed. I wondered if it was the murder or the fact that she'd been in love with a gay man. Suddenly Nell lunged at Chris Franklin. He had been watching her out of camera range. "Follow her," the interviewer shouted at his cameraman.

"Watch out for him," she said, locking both delicate arms around Chris's chest and back. He twisted loose in one sinewy movement.

She shouted at the crowd. "He lies about Sal. He never knew him." She addressed the lens. "The old man told weird stories on this dude. I knew Sal. He never did."

It was obvious that at least two women here believed Sal Mineo left only them.

Mark strode in front of the camera lens, his jaw muscles jumping with anger. But he said politely, "Please shut this machine off. We're no circus."

He threw one arm around Nell and another arm around Chris, pulling them together. They looked frail, elegant.

Sal Mineo's mother limped out of the funeral home, leaning on the arms of two old Italian men wearing hats. Mark glanced back at the old woman, shook his head, and muttered, "Chris, you tell her goodbye. We're hiding out until the service," and Mark guided Nell down the path to the street.

I wanted to give him his snapshot. It would be useful to connect to him. I almost slipped on the icy curb. He held Nell's elbows while she stepped into the dark limousine.

"Could I ask you something?" I said to Mark. He was leaning against the car, his legs spread apart, his chin down. I forgot about the snapshot. I looked down at my notepad.

"I'm getting out of here. Gonna get smashed."

"Is she okay?" I asked.

He stuffed his hands in his back pockets and stared down at the icy pavement. "You a buddy of Sal's?"

"I wish I wasn't a reporter doing a story—" God, I sounded dumb. I didn't know why I'd said anything at all.

He jerked his head up. "What's with you people? Let me be. Go on away."

I started babbling. "I didn't want to upset you. I didn't mean any harm."

"Harm, harm," he said as he crumpled back against the car.

The look on his face made me want to kill anybody bothering him. I held out the photograph mutely. He turned and disappeared into the car. The door slammed and the gray window rolled up. I felt frantic.

A moment later Chris walked past me and banged on the car window with his knuckles. I held out the snapshot. But Chris ducked down and disappeared into the car.

The engine started and the tires spun, whipping the ice into slush.

Chapter Three

The city room was deserted. It was past dinnertime. I told Marty in a big rush about the funeral. I gave him the snapshot of Mineo at the beach. He just grunted and sat there writing subheads. He believes the reporter's excitement makes the story. But he was excited too.

When I sat down at my desk, he was watching me. My mind raced.

"What else struck you?" he asked.

I spoke slowly. "That English boy, Chris. There was this funny look on his face when he asked Mark Loren about somebody breaking into his house. He pretended he wasn't scared."

"Eagle eye," the editor said. He sounded sarcastic. But that's his style. "What else?"

"Well, he did cocaine, right there."

"So?" the editor said. "That's Hollywood. What else did you see?"

"That rock singer, Mark Loren, he—"

Marty's eyes gleamed behind his strong lenses. "What happened to him, anyhow? Didn't he go to London and write music with the Beatles?"

"Hibernating," I said, "according to the morgue files, for the last four or five years."

"My daughter says he was studying composition at Juilliard under a fake name," Marty mused.

"I read he got blocked."

Marty shook his head. "The doomed-artist type. What the hell dragged him out to that funeral?"

I shrugged. "Love."

"How does he look?"

"Amazing," I said.

"Listen to her," he said.

"Wrong," I said. I know he likes it when I act spunky. I told him about Nell Fields grabbing the dead actor, and how it made sense to me.

"A naive intellectual." He laughed to himself.

"What's so funny?" I asked.

"I was thinking about that lecture you gave me last month."

"What lecture?"

"Oh, about women and gays being sexual outgroups. Right?"

"Right."

"Run it past me again," he said.

"Both groups break the patriarchal code."

He looked up at the ceiling for some help from that great Patriarch in the sky. "How do they break the code, again?"

"By asking for the kind of sexual pleasure that procreating heterosexual men take as their God-given right."

"You equating faggots and the female orgasm?" he asked.

I looked meaningfully up at the ceiling. "Well, everybody knows about Him," I said.

"What about Him?"

"Well, He ain't no faggot and He ain't no woman." We both laughed. He likes a good argument.

He sharpened his pencil and the shavings floated over his desk. "There a horde of faggots at that funeral?"

I didn't answer.

"Well, did you see them?"

"I don't know," I said.

"Were they swishing around?"

I spoke right up to him. He likes that. "I hate to sound like the liberal of the month. But the crowd was Italians from the Bronx and beautiful people from Hollywood."

Five minutes later, I was typing my lead, and it hit me.

"Hey, Marty," I shouted, swiveling my chair around, "send me to Los Angeles. That's a world I want to see."

"Get lost." He didn't look up. He was making a long slash through somebody's story with his copy pencil.

"Send me. I'll dig up names, anecdotes, gossip. Knock your eyes out."

"What names?" he asked, and then he did look at me, squinting as though that would help him see what I was driving at.

"Mineo names. People who knew him. It's a good story. He went from street crime to street movies. The child star who never got old. Who did he love? How did he live? Why didn't he work?"

He looked at me without blinking. "What do you really want?"

"Seasoning," I said.

"Too glib," he said. But he lit a cigar. That meant I had three minutes to talk, until it went out.

So I started to sell him on the trip. "I'm so fucking curious," I said. Rough language gets his attention. "I liked those people," I said. "I want to know why."

He laughed. "Feminist to fag hag in one day."

Sometimes he grosses me out. But I put up with him. He's smart.

"I never said I was a feminist."

"So you can write Hollywood smut better than the hacks?" He poked his cigar in the ashtray. I had to talk fast.

"With your help," I said. I considered a speech about how much he'd taught me. But we don't talk like that. "Let's ask the publisher," I coaxed.

"I'm thinking," he said. He narrowed his eyes again and stared at his cigar.

"Send me tonight," I said. When I make up my mind,

nobody can stop me. Stubborn isn't a strong enough word for it. I'm lucky it doesn't happen to me that often.

The entertainment reporter walked by.

"She wants to go to Hollywood," Marty called out to him.

That was unfair. Hollywood was this guy's beat. He gets press lunches and press junkets at the studios' expense. He writes only good news.

The reporter laughed. "Warren again?"

He ducked when he saw the look on my face. He was joking at my expense about the fact that Warren Beatty had once talked to me for two hours at an ERA party, and that I found him smart.

"Beatty turns her on," the reporter said.

"That makes me a freak," I said. But I remembered something. "Actually, Beatty made a good point about Hollywood gays."

"What?" they both asked.

It's been a pet theory of mine that Warren Beatty intrigues men more than women. Men are awed. They believe he's got some magic touch. They wish they had the secret of his success with women.

"What?" They were real casual, but they had both asked again.

"I think he said something about how gays are now defining Hollywood style."

The reporter was frowning. Ordinarily, he'd agree with anything Warren Beatty said about Hollywood. "Beatty was putting you on."

"She wants to go out there and cover the Mineo murder," Marty told him.

"Didn't you get my memo on John Wayne?" the reporter asked.

"What?"

"He's licking a drinking problem, beating cancer." The reporter was picking at the eraser on the end of his pencil.

"Now, Harry, we need you cityside, and you hate hanging out with faggots," my editor said.

"They aren't faggots," the reporter said. What he loved

best about movie stars was the idea that they were just like him, only more masculine, rich, and happy. "Anyway what does she know?"

My editor scratched his head. He wasn't used to prolonged conversations about John Wayne or anybody. He is terse. That's why he's good at headlines.

"She knows she's ignorant," Marty said, shoving a Xeroxed page into my hands. He nodded at me. "It's called an open mind. She also knows how to keep her mouth shut like she knows something. Sometimes."

"Any other instructions?" I asked. Fast. Things were going my way.

"Yeah, no fancy theories," Marty said, "no intellectual bullshit."

I looked down at the Xeroxed paper, and my mind blotted out his voice.

. . . AT APPROXIMATELY 2130 HOURS 2/12/76 CRIES FOR HELP WERE HEARD BY TENANTS FROM REAR OF 8567 HOLLOWAY DRIVE W LOS ANGELES FOUND DECEDENT ON HIS SIDE IN DRIVEWAY BETWEEN CARPORTS R7 AND R6 WITH STAB WOUND TO LEFT CHEST FIRE RESCUE UNIT 7 TURNED DECEDENT ON HIS BACK CUT JACKET AND SHIRT AND ATTEMPTED RESUSCITATION DECEDENT PRONOUNCED DEAD AT 2155 HRS . . .

I glanced at Marty. He was sharpening another pencil and registering the shock on my face. My eyes fell back down to the crudely typed police report.

. . . DECEDENTS WALLET CONTAINED $21 IN BILLS IN LEFT JACKET POCKET COINS IN LEFT PANTS POCKET 85 CENTS IN CHANGE FOUND ON PAVEMENT UNDER DECEDENT WHITE METAL RING NOTED ON DECEDENTS LEFT INDEX FINGER AND LEFT ON BODY RESTAURANT STUBS TWO CARDS WITH NAMES AND TELEPHONE NUMBERS FOUND IN DECEDENTS POCKETS DECEDENTS HANDS BAGGED AT SCENE FOR SHERIFFS CRIME LAB . . .

My stomach lurched. I sat down, feeling an unfamiliar horror. Marty was watching me like a hawk. He said casually, "Like I'm saying, this isn't *Partisan Review*. You promised me headlines, famous names."

"Two weeks?" I was bargaining, but my voice sounded squeaky.

"Eight days." For a second there, his eyes were wide, excited, watching what I was going through. But then his phone rang. "Remember, I'm paying your bills," he said, and his face settled back into the familiar melancholy like an old dog finding his favorite spot on the carpet.

The story conference was over. Things happen impromptu around here. I hear the best meetings take place in front of the urinal.

"I'm packing my bags," I said.

Marty Burns was reading wire service reports. Worrying about something else. He looked up at me blankly.

"That's it?" I asked.

"Surprise me," he said. "Act smart when you get back." He watched me shove a stack of copy pages into my desk drawer on top of a poetry book and a jar of bouillon cubes. I had no time to file now. One of the great things about the job is the way you get thrown into things—fast. This was the best assignment I ever got. It showed that he respected me.

"I am smart," I said. He likes the sound of confidence.

"I'm not talking book-smart," he said. "Sophistication—it's like sex." He shook his pencil at me like a teacher. "When it happens, you'll know what I mean."

"Right," I said. "In ten days I'll have a coke spoon around my neck."

He laughed. "Not in ten years."

I smiled and shut my mouth.

My phone rang. It was Joe. He wanted to set up joint custody arrangements for our dog, though Spike had been staying with him. He asked me how I liked the new apartment. He'd make a great husband. I didn't ask how he felt living all alone after four years. I'd been working around the clock but I knew something was missing.

I told him about the Sal Mineo assignment.

"So you're leaving," he said.

"Yeah, well, it's a good story."

He was happy to keep Spike, the dog, for eight days while I was away. A friend of his in political theory at Harvard was camped out in our spare room. Joe was studying night and day for his Ph.D. orals in medieval history.

"Good luck," I said.

"Hey, Sara, stick around and let's talk."

"Getting away will be good." I wanted to hug him and tell him everything would be all right. I would do anything not to hurt him. But everyone suspects himself of at least one of the cardinal virtues, like the narrator of *The Great Gatsby*, Nick Carraway, said, and I'm compelled to tell as much of the truth as I know.

"Don't go," Joe repeated.

"Maybe you'll fall for that new graduate assistant."

"Fat chance. Maybe you'll miss me the old way." He did sound hurt. "Hey, didn't your mom teach Sal Mineo?"

"No, but he went to school on my street. I used to think me and him were the only kids to get out of the neighborhood."

"Don't make too much of it," he said.

"What?"

"Researching his murder, walking around in his footsteps."

"Don't worry."

"I don't like it," he said. "This isn't some women's seminar with coffee and danish."

"That's the good part."

"Sara, you're walking into a strange world. You don't know a soul in Los Angeles. There're probably still bloodstains on the ground."

"You sound like my mom." In fact, that was part of what had gone wrong.

"Wait a few days," he said, "until the police arrest the killer."

"The point is to get the story now, before the cops."

"You're not scared?"

"No."

He sighed. "I hope you're lying."

"I'm not scared."

Then he said, "I miss your noises and smells around the apartment."

"I know what you mean."

Spike barked in the background.

"The dog's depressed," he said, before he hung up. "He misses you."

Chapter
Four

When I woke up, I knew we were about to land in Los Angeles. My shoulders felt tight from sleeping so long. My knees were numb. The man next to me was dying to talk.

"You got nerves of steel, miss. You slept the whole way." He kept smiling at me. In fact, I'd woken up every time he had ordered a whiskey sour and asked the stewardess about the Rangers game.

I'd asked the stewardess to let me sleep through meals. I needed the rest, and if I didn't eat I wouldn't get jet lag. It was Warren Beatty who told me that digestion causes jet lag. I bet this secret gets him through life a little better.

"Can I buy you a drink?" the man asked me, waving at the stewardess. He was tan, and he wore a bright madras jacket over a yellow shirt open at the collar. He was dressed for the West Coast. His voice had a forced cheery quality.

"No, thanks."

"You work or anything?"

I told him about my job. He turned in his seat to give me his full attention.

"You write about movie stars?" he asked.

"Yeah."

"Who?"

"Sal Mineo," I said.

"Christ, that's murder. You own a gun?"

"No, do you?"

"I'll put it this way," he said. "Both my neighbors have rods."

I didn't respond. "I think fags are sick," he said. "I don't care if they stab each other in alleys, as long as they stick to their own kind."

He took a long sip from his whiskey sour, and chewed some ice. "You'd think they'd send an expert," he said. "It's way over your head." It seemed to make him feel good to put me down. I didn't mind. I am used to people—men—who don't believe I'm good at my work because I'm young and female. This works to my advantage. People are disarmed.

"What do you do?" I asked him.

He was grinning. Nice teeth. "I'm head of West Coast space sales for *Newsweek*. I'm on my way back from Germany."

"Oh, a traveling salesman."

He stopped smiling.

He was making me claustrophobic. I shifted forward in my seat and looked over the top of his chair. People were sleeping under small airline blankets. Behind us, one guy had four blankets on him. He was sprawled across three seats. His head was propped up against the far window. My stomach twisted. Something about him bothered me. He was wearing horn-rimmed glasses and he looked like a million New York office workers, except that he needed a shave. His eyes were closed, but I had a sudden irrational fear that he would open them. My brain clicked. He was the guy who had been running around the back of the funeral parlor with the gun in his pocket.

I unbuckled my seatbelt, stood up, and spotted several magazines and a long leather case on the floor under him. It wasn't golf clubs. It was too narrow.

The man sitting next to me smiled broadly. "Listen, let me show you Los Angeles tonight. You're going to get plenty sick of faggots."

"I'm all work, no play. Sorry." I sat down, opened the window screen, and pretended to look out at the transparent sky. It was a color between blue and gray. I felt as if somebody were pressing on my chest. It wasn't just that we were hurtling toward the Los Angeles airport. I couldn't think straight.

The salesman touched my arm, and I turned around to watch him wiggle his eyebrows at me. "Come on, you don't know what you're missing."

I knew what I was missing. I kept turning my head to see the guy sleeping behind us. He finally opened his eyes, took off his glasses, and began rubbing them with a beige silk handkerchief. He was losing hair in front, but he cut it short and neat. He had thick eyebrows that grew together.

"Thanks, but somebody's picking me up at the airport," I told the salesman.

I ducked when the stranger put on his glasses and stretched.

When the stewardess came by to pick up the whiskey bottles, I tugged on her cuff. Then I looked around. The stranger with the gun had put a pillow over his face to block out the morning light. I pointed at him.

"Is he famous?" I asked her. "I know him from somewhere. I interviewed him once for my newspaper."

"I couldn't tell you."

She pushed a small cart ahead of her.

The salesman winked at me. "You should've let me handle her."

When we filed off the plane, I stepped on a woman's tennis racket, apologized, and kept elbowing my way forward. I wanted to get behind the stranger.

I followed the back of his tweed overcoat down the steps and into a long corridor filled with children's paintings. He was tall and walked briskly. His hair was thin in back. I hesitated before stepping on the moving floor, and three children pushed ahead of us. I almost lost him. I had never seen a horizontal escalator before. Nobody walked. They stood and waited for it to move them. I felt restless. I could move better on two legs. I pushed past somebody and tapped the man twice on the shoulder.

He whirled around as if I'd punched him. Sometimes when I get scared, I get aggressive.

"I know you from someplace," I said, and stared up into his brown eyes magnified by the horn-rims. He got a dreamy look in his eye, or maybe it was just the way the glasses magnified them. I saw tiny hairs in his nostrils.

He twisted the shoulder I'd tapped. "I don't like getting hit from behind," he said in a high, hoarse whisper.

The escalator was carrying us sedately. "I'm sorry, but I think I met you someplace."

The long leather case stuck out from under his arm.

"Butler Library at Columbia?" I smiled broadly.

"Lady, don't make trouble," he whispered, turning and bumping my ribs with the point of the case. It jolted me.

"At a funeral?" I asked.

We were almost at the end of the moving floor. I spotted a policeman laughing with an airline stewardess. "Police—hey, police!" I shouted, and ducked my face into my elbow.

I saw something coming at me from the corner of my eye. I reeled back, coughing, and fell against the railing. He'd hit me hard in the stomach with his fingers. I stumbled and slipped down. In a split second the escalator deposited me in a heap. People stepped around me. The stranger pushed his glasses up high on the bridge of his nose and broke into a run. His long leather case jutted out behind him.

The cop was still oblivious. I had no time to think. I pushed through several generations of a kissing and hugging Mexican family and ran right after my assailant. At the exit he was working his knee against the door. I kept my distance. He turned and found my face in the crowd. He had a scared look behind his glasses. "Don't get yourself killed." His words ended in a thin scream.

"What're you talking about?"

He dropped the straw suitcase with a loud thump. Then his eyes got more vacant and dreamy. He flexed the fingers of his right hand. I took one step backward and tripped over somebody's feet, twisting my ankle under me. He grabbed his straw suitcase and kicked the door open. I rubbed my aching foot until it went numb.

From between people's legs, I saw him knock over a pile of suitcases outside the terminal as he ran across the sidewalk to climb into the open door of a dark Mercedes. His car disappeared into acres of symmetrically parked automobiles.

I sat on the floor in panic. I wasn't sure my foot would hold my weight. My brain jammed. A boy in tennis shorts asked me, "You stoned?"

I shook my head and tried to stand up. My ankle wobbled and I fell back on my buttocks again.

"I been there," he said, and held out a hand. I gave him my arm, and he pulled me up. I leaned against the glass wall of the terminal and tried my foot. If I didn't wiggle the ankle, it held my weight.

I stood at the luggage conveyor for fifteen minutes rubbing my sore foot before I noticed my brown suitcase circling the crowd of people as if it was lost.

Then I realized my whole body was sweating. I was wearing my Salvation Army fur coat—mouton, according to the label. It was the wrong climate. I took off the coat and folded it over my arm. I picked up my suitcase and dropped it. A woman with a bare tan midriff smiled and handed it back to me.

I gawked at the crowd for the first time. Their tan faces looked bland and foreign, like guests at a Caribbean resort. A lot of painted toenails and shorts revealing trim bare legs. Unlike a crowd at La Guardia, they didn't look as if they were working, or worried about it.

I dragged the suitcase to the Hertz counter, and my fingers shook when I signed for the rental car. When I saw the *Newsweek* salesman across the booth, I picked up my keys and turned away.

Outside the terminal, warm winds tickled me. I was surrounded by porters, cars, and piles of suitcases. I almost relaxed. A second later, my head snapped to duck a skyful of screaming metal. It was shaped like a shark. I saw black wheels protruding from the silver underbelly. The engines sounded like thunder in my body. I dropped my suitcase and smashed both hands against my ears.

From where I stood, it sounded as if the world were breaking apart. Tons of metal smacked down on a runway about a quarter of a mile away. The black tires screeched, smoking.

The engines reversed and raced louder. Behind me a terminal door opened and I heard a flight number announced. I straightened up and watched the airplane skim the ground like a solitary skater. Tiny cars, carts, and a staircase began to approach it.

My nerves were shot.

I ran for my gray Dodge. Inside, the heated air was close. I smelled gasoline fumes. I knew it was crazy, but I locked all four doors, and leaned my head against the vinyl seat. In a minute the back of my neck was sweaty. I cruised uncertainly around the parking lot on a horseshoe-curved street, then I opened a window and looked way up to the yellow sky. The scabrous trunk of a palm tree swayed in front of me. I got a kick out of it. High above me, the leaves stuck out like a cowlick on the head of a giant.

On an overpass, I came up behind a dark car and slammed my brakes. But the Mercedes was packed with boys. I had to calm down. The stranger'd been dying to escape me. It didn't make sense that he'd be lying in wait.

I stepped it up to sixty and started enjoying the drive. The license plate on the Volkswagen ahead of me read ELVIS. I leaned back and rolled down all my windows. I saw cars, blacktop highway, more highway, telephone wires, and sky. I passed six stunted skyscrapers that looked deserted, air freight depots, and an old olive-green airplane factory. I wondered where people in Los Angeles saw new faces besides restaurants and movie lines.

I drove under strange green signs: LA CIENEGA, CENTURY CITY, VENTURA, WILSHIRE, BEVERLY GLEN, WESTWOOD. I was actually approaching West Hollywood.

I liked the look of Los Angeles, even from an elevated highway. It was glamorous and tacky and filled with buildings painted in garish and tropical colors. I whizzed by a salmon-colored stucco shack, surrounded by sandy terrain. Its handpainted sign spelled DISCREET RETREAT. I felt as if I'd stumbled onto the outskirts of the northern capital of Mexico, a series of dry towns with lots of breathing space and sky. The midday sun was strong, and there wasn't much vegetation, except for a few patches of bright, tense green.

On the Santa Monica Freeway south, the traffic stopped. No lanes moved. Sitting on the roof of a gas station off the freeway was a fifty-foot replica of a whitewall tire, made of papier-maché. I saw the red lights of a police car careening down the shoulder of the road. Twenty minutes later I nosed past sparkling bits of glass on the black pavement. A motor-cycle was lying on its side like a dead bird.

I swung down an exit ramp and onto a lazy street. The billboards looked terrific, the architecture of the roads. I admired one portrait of a long gleaming Cadillac in sun-drenched, super-realistic red. I turned left around another big one, a white monument advertising a graveyard in Century City. I sighed aloud. The funeral, the murder.

The mansions on Sunset Boulevard had curving drive-ways, thick expanses of walls and windows, pillars, and balconies. They looked fake. Back east, I wouldn't be able to drive by houses like these. They'd be hidden on estates behind fences and green acres.

Five miles more, and I was on Sunset Strip. It looked like a toy compared to the malevolence of Forty-second Street in Manhattan. It was sleepy, slow, and sleazy, and I had a feeling people slept away days, crawling out at night when the sun went down. I tried to read unlit neon signs advertising empty massage parlors, dance halls, and something called the Institute of Oral Sex.

I knew I was in Sal Mineo's neighborhood, because I'd circled his place on my book of street maps. He lived at Alta Loma and Holloway.

My hotel was high on a hill above Sunset Strip. It was a huge castle that dwarfed everything around it. I noted that its orange spires would've looked good in the Spanish Pyrenees. The building was topped by a Gothic sign, CHATEAU MARMONT. Behind it were the peaks of the Hollywood Hills.

In the lobby, I recognized a woman who plays a mother of six on a television series. The desk clerk was asking about her coach and hanging on every word. "No kidding," he said, as he flashed a glorious smile at her. "He runs you six miles every day. You must be rich."

I plopped down my suitcase, and he winked at me. He was young, Central American, I guessed, and he had a soft mustache that was really some black hairs on one side of his upper lip. I liked his eyes. They jumped with enthusiasm. I signed in and flipped my press card at him. His teeth glowed. "I bet we could swap some stories."

In the hall, I saw trays of half-eaten breakfasts. I bumped into somebody carrying a guitar case. He had long blond hair, frizzed like Rod Stewart. He was Rod Stewart.

The room was clean, the furniture new and ugly. The brass bed looked garish. Behind it was a small kitchen that looked unused. There was no clue to the hordes of human beings who'd unpacked their bags and stayed here. I wondered if Sal Mineo had ever put up friends at this hotel.

I walked out onto the balcony and touched the yellow spines of an old cactus chained to the railing. Below me were huge billboard portraits of pop music stars in lurid colors.

I watched the rooftops of cars on Sunset. They seemed to travel in swirls of dust. Far below, I saw a nude massage parlor. The sun shimmered in the heat. There were no trees. There were no pedestrians. The murder had taken place near here on another empty street. At least in New York streets there was safety in crowds.

It's funny, but when you're put into a room that's not your own, you get more condensed. You tend to think about yourself more. And that bothers me. I'm afflicted with a disease that hits journalists. I'm allergic to brooding.

I kicked off my boots, peeled off my socks, and threw myself down on the bed. Despite my elation, I was exhausted. Suddenly I wanted to hide my head under a pillow and not face a murder story on unfamiliar ground. But I didn't have time to pamper myself.

I rubbed the crystal of my grandfather's old gold watch. I never did get it fixed. Even the band is burnished yellow eighteen-carat gold. It's way too loose on my wrist, like a bracelet.

It always reminds me of my grandpop, who's dead now. He wore it under his starched shirtcuff every day until I was fifteen. We had a routine. I'd ask him the time, and he'd close his eyes, think real hard, and put both hands behind his back. He'd pull in his lips until they were the size of a prune. I'd say, "Grandpa, just look at your watch." That was our little joke. Then he'd tell me the hour. He was never off. The watch hadn't run right for years. It was slow. I think he disciplined his mind by guessing the time. I do the same, and I'm never off either.

I sat up. I figured it was one-thirty. I pulled out a pair of sandals and a light-green cotton shirtwaist. My legs looked pale. It was odd, dressing for summer in February.

I called the Sheriff's Homicide Department. "Lady, I'm just walking out of the office," Casey said, and hung up.

It was about two o'clock. I tied a sweater around my neck, went to my car, got in, locked it, and consulted the street map book. The motor kicked over and died. I had read up on Dodge Darts in *Consumer Reports* magazine at Butler Library. The motor kicked over and died again. I knew this Dodge had an engine that had to kick over three times.

I set out for downtown Los Angeles. I didn't mind Casey's abruptness. It comes with the territory. Reporters find a story more exciting if it's hard to get. We cultivate the skill of placing our feet inside doorways where they're not wanted.

Sometimes I forget myself and use this skill in real life. Once Marty's father suffered a heart attack. I took the call from his wife, and then took him out of the office for a drink. I was rattled. When the headwaiter refused to seat us immediately, I walked past the guy, pulled two chairs over to a window in the corner, and ordered a bottle of house wine.

The waiter was so surprised he obeyed.

It's something like knowing you have a steel fist. You rarely use it, but it makes you feel strong.

Chapter
Five

Downtown Los Angeles resembled a deserted space station. Big skyscrapers that looked abandoned were encircled by highways. I saw one or two people climbing stairs up to a courthouse building. A line of tired Mexicans was waiting for a bus.

The Sheriff's Homicide Department had a green linoleum floor and was filled with metal desks. The walls of prefabricated wood paneling reminded me of courtrooms and motel lobbies. One other person across the room sat at a reception desk. He wore a trim khaki uniform and a gun.

I walked through a low swinging door to get over to him. I told him who I was and that I wanted some information about the case. "Where's Sergeant Casey?" I asked.

"Out. You wanna wait?" he said. His telephone rang, and I sat down at a desk behind him. I pulled open a drawer. It was filled with copper bullets. Then I heard him talking.

"The guy heard what? Wait, wait, what's his name? Cleon W-I-L-S-O-N? Okay, hold him." He hung up.

He transferred three calls to the police station, and spoke to a hysterical father about a daughter who'd eloped with her second cousin.

The phone rang again. "No, lady." The receptionist

was trying to hang up. "Okay, so you did his chart. . . . Capricorn, huh? You predicted trouble with the upper torso? . . . That right? . . . You do? . . . Next door? . . . You heard it. . . . All right. Annie Harmon on Holloway. We'll get back to you."

I wrote down her name. I would find her.

The receptionist hung up and neither of us spoke. He started typing something.

I walked back over to his desk. "Let me leave the sergeant a note. I'll come back."

"Suit yourself."

As I wrote I glanced over the report he was typing. He didn't figure I could read upside down.

From what I could make out, some guy named Cleon Wilson who lived in Watts was being held at the police station. He wanted to trade some information about Mineo's murder to the cops in exchange for letting him go free. He claimed he'd heard a guy at a shooting gallery brag that he had killed Mineo to fill a contract for a drug syndicate.

The cop glanced up at me. "Write your note over there. Sit down." After a while, he said, "You live in New York?"

I nodded.

"Where? In the city?"

"Midtown."

He whistled softly. "I don't know if you should be here. The sergeant will probably like you, though."

"Is it his only case?" I asked.

"No, last night they gave him another one. Some kid was murdered, a little girl."

"Also in West Hollywood?"

"The county area," he said. "We have jurisdiction along Sunset down there. But these things always lead to Watts."

The door slammed, and a fat man with a pink, fleshy face strolled into the homicide office. Either he had been running or he did some drinking. "Afternoon, Sergeant Casey," the receptionist said.

The sergeant looked from the receptionist to me and back. His eyes were like milky blue marbles. Then he pointed his finger at the receptionist and said, "Pow, you're dead."

77

He smiled at me. "Want to go get a milkshake?" The receptionist froze. Casey asked, "She work downstairs?"

"No, Bill," he said.

Casey turned his back to me and twisted off his huge suit jacket. He had one of those bodies that was fat in front, but his legs were skinny and his behind was small. Handcuffs and a pistol holder hung from his belt. He wore street clothes. His hair was gray and there were lines where he'd just combed it.

"I wondered," I said, "if I could talk to you about the Sal Mineo investigation."

"Frank—hey, Frank," Casey said to the receptionist, "didn't I tell you about the press?" He raised his voice. "You know what? You don't look like a reporter. You look like something out of a fancy finishing school. Why don't you just fly back to New York and tell everybody how bad Sergeant Casey—that's C-A-S-E-Y—was mean to you."

"I'm reporting a murder," I said. "It's what I'm paid to do. I'd like to ask you some questions."

He walked away.

I watched Casey dial his telephone. He was too far away. I was about to wander back within hearing range when the door opened. I saw someone smoothing his hair with one hand, and there was a flash of gold chain at his wrist. It took me only a second to see that he was Mark Loren.

I pushed aside the hinged door and walked over to him. Before he could guess what I was doing, I pulled him out the office door and into the marble hall. In the corridor, I tried to think up some kind of apology.

He took off his sunglasses. "What's going on?"

It was clear he thought I was some kind of official.

"I'm Sara Martin. You were at the funeral."

"If it ain't the lady reporter."

He shot several jumpy looks at my sweater. He seemed to be assessing the shape of my body. He didn't bother to lift his eyes back to my face.

"Did they get the guy that broke into your apartment?" I asked.

"Who told you that?" Now he was looking at me. His eyes were very black, and stunned. He was holding a camel wool jacket over his shoulder with two fingers. He wore a fresh cotton shirt, tight and beige.

"I heard you talking at the funeral about somebody breaking into your house," I said.

"Forget it," he said.

"You think it had nothing to do with this murder?" I asked incredulously.

"Forget it," he said. "Understand?"

"I know how you feel," I said. "Robbed." I tried the old reporter's line. "You don't have to talk to me."

He blinked as if somebody had hit his face. "I don't want to talk to you."

Then two tears rolled down the side of his nose. "Charming." he said, and wiped them away with his sleeve. Then he was talking fast.

"I can't go anyplace in this town without somebody saying something and me remembering something. I mean, in ten years, we went lots of places, and I saw him damn near every day for breakfast or a drink, and talking and talking. This morning I go to the Old World for pancakes, and I start crying, and I don't eat, and I got to get out the door. People keep coming up and saying, 'I'm sorry for you,' and I break right down again. But it doesn't help. And my manager says to go away somewhere like London. I say no, no, and then I say, 'You're right, I got healing to do, and I'm getting myself out.' "

He pushed at the door. I had that flushed feeling about him again. "Wait a minute," I said.

"I'm mixed up, fucked up, and shut down," he said. He looked angry. "I'm here to see a mean cop I met the night Sal"—he paused—"the night it happened.

"But I don't need cops," he continued. "I know folks in secret places and I can dream up reasons no cops could ever find."

"You could find the person who did it?" I asked.

I could not imagine how bad he felt. Hunting the killer of a close friend was like nothing that had ever happened to me. "I know things because I'm a reporter. I could help. I could also write your friend's story."

It was too soon for me to ask. But I had to start somewhere.

He rubbed his eyes. "You hunting thrills?" he taunted. He was hitting his consonants hard with his tongue.

"Look, I don't mean any harm," I said. I sounded like a stiff.

He raised both eyebrows at me. "Really."

"Let's negotiate," I said, assuming a professional attitude.

"First, you promise me some things."

I tried to catch his eye, but he was looking at the floor. "First off, you write nothing about Sal being some sick faggot."

I pictured Marty Burns listening to this. Nobody gets in the way of a story.

"Second, you don't use us to sell newspapers and you don't try to pin a murder on anybody that loved Sal. In fact, you don't write about anybody without running them past me first." He paused. "Anybody you mention won't work again in this town.

"How's that strike you?" he asked, giving me another one of his jumpy looks.

"What if something's true?" I asked.

"It's not the truth that worries me. It's the goddamn lies."

His answer was evasive.

"I'll try to cooperate. I don't write sleazy stuff, anyway."

"And you'll check stuff out with me?"

I gave a little nod and watched his face. He looked suspicious.

"I mean, I'll check quotes," I added quickly. "But if we're in this together, you better promise to tell me everything."

"Okay, sugar," he said, but he was shaking his head. "Meet me tonight at ten. I want to check out a bar. And you might learn something about something. I say the word 'might' because I hope your ass isn't as tight as it looks.''

I wondered if he felt as uneasy about the bargain as I did. He probably figured I was lying. He was writing with a fountain pen in a matchbook. ''Here's the address. It's on Santa Monica.''

He put his hand on the door to the Homicide Department. ''I doubt either you or me knows what in hell we're doing.''

Suddenly, the door swung open by itself and there was Sergeant Casey.

''You,'' he said to Mark, ''get in here.'' Mark clenched his teeth hard, so that his jaw muscles knotted. He didn't make one move toward the office.

''You,'' he said, and pointed his thumb at me, ''get out,'' and his blue eyes watched Mark disappear inside the door. Casey said, ''You're running in tough company, sister. Don't blame me if you turn up with a knife problem or something.''

I opened my mouth to tell him he was a jerk, but he shut the door in my face. Anyway, I'd scored. Mark was a key connection.

In the street, I asked a Mexican woman how to get to police headquarters. Inside I watched two cops behind the counter answer telephones, open drawers, and ignore me. Finally I asked one of them about Cleon Wilson.

''*L.A. Times?*'' He stood and pushed the typewriter table away.

I showed him my press card.

''All the way from New York,'' he said. He disappeared and came back holding a card with some writing on it.

''Wilson—we let him go. He's a loser, dangerous look in his eye. Purse-snatcher bragging he could connect to the Mineo thing. Bullshit.''

''How old a guy was he?''

He checked a card. ''Twenty; said he was black, but his color was more of a yellow.'' This cop enjoyed talking to a reporter. He would tell his girlfriend about it.

''What's Wilson's address?'' I asked.

"Forget it, lady. Some policewoman was raped down there in broad daylight, over the weekend. Just got her tooth cap put in yesterday. Too thick, sticks out funny. She told me she never saw what hit her. Watts looks like nothing's doing, but it's murder."

"Just tell me Wilson's address."

He rattled off some numbers and then he said, "Stay away from him. He's a bad character."

I closed my mouth.

"Hey, you ever go to Yankee Stadium?" he asked after a while.

I shook my head.

"How they doing over at the sheriff's office?" He kept trying.

I shrugged. "You know."

"Well, it's tricky stuff, fag murders." The cop was dying to talk. "West Hollywood's full of it. 'Boys' Town' we call it, and 'the Swish Alps.' "

"Have you heard about any signature to the murder?" I asked. I knew police often link murders by methodology—kinky or sadistic ways in which the killer worked on his victim.

"No," he said. "We never hear a thing. Those county guys are competitive."

"No rumors?"

"No, but I could tell you plenty of stuff about the Hillside Strangler." Then he looked embarrassed. "Maybe not. I mean, he did some terrible things to women, you know."

"Yeah."

"Cut them bad. What we used to call 'primary and secondary sexual characteristics.' Mutilates them."

"Where's the coroner's office?" I interrupted.

"Let me draw you a map." He checked his watch. "Get there early tomorrow morning. They're closing now."

Chapter
Six

I felt jittery. Maybe it was just jet lag. It was near midnight and Mark was almost two hours late. I was waiting inside my car in the lot behind the bar. The red neon sign above the door was blinking.

My mother never set foot in a saloon. To her that means she's respectable. I am not opposed to sitting in a booth at Moochie's bar downstairs from the paper a couple of times a year to celebrate a newsbreak, but that's it.

I wasn't surprised that my stomach started to hurt the way it does when I drink too much coffee. But this was the trail of my story.

The door of the bar opened, framing a boy and a man in a rectangle of light. I heard jukebox music. The boy looked Midwestern; he was blond and thin. He wore a T-shirt. His older friend was tall, and looked like a television actor. The man draped his arm around the boy as they walked by my car in the parking lot.

"Baby," he said, "hey, please?"

The boy ducked and said, "I thought you were different from the rest."

"Oh, really," the man said. "I wanted everybody in

there to see you do it to me—my toes to my nose. I wanted you to eat me alive.''

''Well,'' the boy pushed at his hair with his hand in imitation of a movie vamp, ''as Bette Davis once said, 'I'd like to kiss you, honey, but I just washed my hair.' ''

''Nobody told me you were a one-way guy,'' his friend cooed.

''Now, now,'' the boy said, ''that's the trouble with you, Harry.''

''Well, Harry's going to get some good candy kisses,'' the man said, and the two of them fell against a car. They hugged. I couldn't believe their conversation.

''You know, don't you,'' the boy said, ''that I leave a little piece of ass everywhere I go?''

''I always knew you were more than just a pair of buns,'' the man said. ''Let's go back in and have a nightcap.''

''Surf's up,'' said the boy.

I wanted to drive away. I was having another attack of nerves. The two men had seemed very sure of themselves. I could not remember playing that way with Joe as a part of making love. Without warning, I thought about myself hugging another woman. It has never felt like sex. If Mark invited me here to show me how little I belonged, I conceded the point.

I turned the key in the ignition. The grinding sound of the starter jolted me. I couldn't quit. I turned off the motor, opened the car door, and walked around to the front of the bar.

The jukebox was playing a Judy Garland song about painful love. The dark room was half empty, and about twenty men were talking, hugging, laughing, and drinking. Very good-looking men, showing lots of skin and muscle. I felt a flicker of revulsion. They had flat stomachs, tight asses, and they wore short shorts and T-shirts, beach fashion. They had the look of California actors. The atmosphere was male, but I smelled sweet perfume.

Most of them were crowded around the bar, and most of the picnic-style tables around the room were empty. Photographs of Garland, Dietrich, and Marilyn Monroe hung on the walls. The ceiling was high and black. A few track-lights showed cigarette smoke whirling up to the photographs. The two guys who had been playing in the parking lot were seated near me at the bar, kissing each other on the mouth. Behind them a sign read, FLIES CARRY GERMS, SO KEEP YOURS CLOSED.

I couldn't take my eyes off the two of them. The boy's small buttocks pushed against his tight dungarees. He kept shifting on the stool. Anal intercourse must hurt. I felt queasy. There was an alien male energy here.

The boy on the bar stool now turned and stared at me. His face had sensitive beauty, purity, with an aureole of blond curls, a small mouth, and a nose covered with a wash of freckles. At his left, an older woman in a black dress sat drinking alone. She looked like a prostitute from a gangster movie. She was talking to three guys who looked as if they'd all gotten the same short haircut that day.

The bartender leaned over to kiss the woman in black, and then approached me. I sat down quickly on a bench by a table. I fingered a glass of water. I needed to claim a piece of space.

The bartender came around the bar toward my table. His face resembled an aging Tab Hunter, but his body looked hard as a rock, like a weightlifter's. He wore blue plastic sandals, blue satin shorts, and an open black jacket without a shirt.

"What in hell are you doing here?" he asked. He had a contralto voice, like an opera singer, and he projected it like mad. He spoke so fast I could hardly understand the words.

"I'm waiting for someone."

"You aren't Vice, are you?" He was talking from someplace high in his throat, like he was imitating a dowager.

I shook my head.

He smoothed his ash-blond mustache. "It's not against the law, but I can't have it. Sorry."

"What?"

"Women," he snapped. "Out."

I said nothing. Of course, I felt like an intruder.

He turned on his heel.

I saw myself reflected in a mirror behind the bar. I looked tense. I tried to stop biting my lips. I felt warm. I hadn't taken off my sweater. The boy got off his bar stool.

He ambled past me, stopped, backed up, flipped out his elbow, and knocked my glass of water onto the floor.

I jumped up as the cold water hit my leg. He looked me in the eye, licked one finger, and hit his buttocks with it. It was a burlesque gesture to show how adorable he was. He ran his tongue over his lips, looking mean, and went back to his stool. The other man smiled. Nobody else moved as I bent down and picked up two pieces of glass. A sharp edge nicked my finger. The pain brought tears to my eyes.

I looked around for the bartender. He hustled over to me, and plucked the broken glass from my fingers. "You're upsetting us."

"What about her?" I pointed at the woman in black at the bar.

"I'm sorry," he said, "that's not technically—or should I say in the Biblical sense—a woman."

"I was invited to meet somebody here," I said.

"Ah, well, madam," he said, "to put it rudely, we don't serve women."

A man behind me made a long wolf whistle. "We don't eat them either."

"I'm waiting for Mark Loren," I said.

"Oh, my dear." The bartender wiped an imaginary spot off the table with his napkin. "You might have said something—anything—before. You couldn't drop a heavier name."

Relief flooded my body.

"How well do you know him?" I asked.

He said quickly, "Watch out, that boy's not on perfect pitch anymore. He's a raw nerve."

He walked away abruptly, and a minute later came back with a champagne glass full of fresh orange juice which he banged down on my table. A little wave of it spilled onto the tablecloth.

"Does Mark come here a lot?" I asked.

"Prince Charming doesn't pull star numbers, and nobody hits on him here. You realize what it would mean if people knew? I mean, we'd be *très* hot, hotter than Ma Maison and Chasen's."

I tried to relax a little. These guys all looked so American, except that their clothing was so precise; no shirttails, no messy fraternity clothes.

When Mark finally arrived after midnight, he sat down without greeting me. I was happy to see him. For a split second, I felt like we were on some kind of date and he hadn't stood me up after all. He wasn't wearing the beach uniform. His hair was clean but uncombed, and he wore a silk shirt and pants.

He looked me over as though the set of my shoulders would tell him if he could trust me. "I can't recollect why in God's name I invited you down here."

He was mumbling like a shy Southern kid. His sunglasses fell out of his pants pocket and he reached under the table for them.

I figured Mark Loren had invited me here for lots of reasons. Most important, to show me what I could learn from him if I cooperated. And he had the advantage here. This turf was his protection against the possibility of my contempt.

"Hey, Alvin, let's get some eggs rancheros over here," he said to the bartender. "It's nearly breakfast time. I'm real sorry I'm late," he said to me, "but something came up."

"Something came up," the bartender said. "Momma bear envies you—lucky, lucky you." Mark ignored him. Alvin didn't leave. Finally he said, *"Mon* prince, a word, please?"

Mark stood up and the bartender whispered something to him, his eyes darting in my direction. I saw the silk shirt stretch when he raised his arm to pat Alvin's cheek.

"Special case," Mark mouthed to him.

Alvin pulled out Mark's chair for him and left.

Mark sighed. "That old queen loved Sal, called him

Sally. He hated charging him for drinks. Sal called him 'the old movie queen.' "

"Why?"

"Oh, because he's queer for the movie business. He's obsessed with it."

"Was Sal Mineo broke?"

"No. But Sal spent every cent in his pocket. Clothing, tabs in restaurants—if he had a dime, he'd spend it on his friends." Mark looked morose. "I want to know what you want," he said.

I ignored the question. "Why were you late?" I asked.

"The cops," he said.

"They suspect you?"

"No. I was driving all around helping them. They want to meet anybody who was jealous of Sal." He sighed.

"Sexually jealous?" I asked.

"Yes, ma'am." His jaw muscles knotted again. "Now, about you."

I folded my hands and leaned forward. "I told you at the police station—I want to write a story."

"But he's gone. It won't help none." His voice was low.

"I want to write the real story about your friend." He was making me nervous, so I looked away from him. Over at the bar, several men stared at Mark.

"I know the real story," he said. He paused, then asked, "What do you think about Sal being a faggot?" Mark relished his question.

"I don't know. The fact he was gay doesn't bother me the way it might bother some men." I didn't like being on the defensive.

Mark laughed and put his sunglasses on the table. "Yeah, well, you-all probably don't know your own limits. You probably don't know how to go to the edge."

"Limits?" I asked.

"Sex," Mark said triumphantly.

"Oh."

I had to keep him talking. He leaned his head close to mine.

"They made my eyeballs hurt, looking at mug shots all

day long. Glossies of suspects. Christ, the scarfaces these cops were flashing hurt my eyes.''

"Who were they?"

He shrugged. "Sal never knew anybody ugly as those guys. They snuck a bare-ass photograph of Chris in with them just to rattle me some.''

"Chris?" I was entranced by the Southern sound of his voice. He ran words together, like notes of a song.

"Yeah. Sal brought him over from London and set him up fine in New York. We helped each other get through the funeral and he's been out here driving one of my silly cars. The door handle broke. Sal was always fixing stuff we broke.'' He was looking down at the floor.

"Why'd you have to look at those ugly pictures?"

"They're up a date-palm tree. Stumped. No weapon, no clues, no motive.''

I wanted to catch his eye. I figured he wasn't telling me the full story. But he was looking around the room.

"They don't suspect a jealous lover?"

"I can't think about it.'' He twisted his upper lip and shot me another of his fast, jittery looks. "You and the cops got the same idea.'' He banged his palm on the table. "Fuck you, whoever killed him. You didn't know what you were doing to me.''

He put on his green aviator sunglasses.

I tried another tack. "You look like him," I said. I missed seeing his eyes. "You stare like he did in the movies—intense.''

"Well, you are a noticer," Mark said. "Folks said we were related—or else lovers.''

I didn't have the nerve to ask if they had been.

"You didn't recognize any other police pictures?" I asked.

He shook his head no.

"Why did Chris pose naked?"

"He's got no shame, like Sal said, because he's got the makings of a great actor.''

"But they loved each other?"

"The week before Sal—I mean, before, it happened—Sal told me Chris was staying on out here to live with him."

I bumped his head with mine. "Oh, excuse me." I winced. He'd shocked me with a real clue. "That's tragic. Do the cops know?"

"I'm not sure," he said.

"You didn't tell them?"

"No." He rubbed his eyes under the sunglasses with his knuckles. It looked like a gesture he had been making since childhood. "I'm tired and old today," he said, "and I know you're thinking crime of passion. Believe me, knowing Sal was the same as loving him, and nobody who knew the old man could kill him."

A drag queen walked into the bar. A few heads turned, but soon nobody paid attention to the chubby man wearing a long skirt.

He pulled off his sunglasses; his eyelids closed. "If only I hadn't let him go driving home from the beach all alone."

Now he was talking more openly. "We were always going to room together," he went on. "Sal never had the bread. I should've gone ahead with it."

I wondered how they could room together if Chris Franklin was moving in with Sal Mineo.

He picked up my hand. I almost pulled it away. "What's that?" he asked. A film of blood had formed on the tip of one finger where the glass had cut it.

"It's nothing," I said. He gestured to the bartender. "Warm vodka, straight up," he said.

He dipped my finger into the vodka glass when it arrived. It stung for a second. "Sal always said this stuff has medicinal value," he said. I was silent, addled by the attention and relieved when he let my finger go. I noticed his wristwatch. Its big face was black, and it had no hands or crystal. It looked dead. I touched it boldly. "Why is it like that?"

He poked his finger into the watch face and tried to smile. "It's a thing we all have, Sal and me and Chris. When Sal broke his crystal in a motorcycle accident about ten years ago, he kept on wearing the watch anyway. It was quirky, and it appealed to him, and he said it kept him thinking in the present, and like his life was timeless. I liked the idea and I bought me a pawn watch and wore it broken, like him. The old man set the style."

I liked the way he told stories, and I wished I could say so.

"That's a coincidence," I said.

"What is?"

"My watch hasn't worked right in over thirty years," I said, holding my wrist up to show him.

"It belonged to somebody in your family?" he asked, rubbing a finger on the smooth links of the band.

"Yeah, how'd you know?"

"Well, you're not thirty, and by the sound of your voice, I figured you got it from somebody close to you."

I smiled.

But then his face changed. He couldn't stay on a feeling very long. "Hey, Jonathan," he shouted. "How's it going, son?"

Mark waved toward the bar, and said in an undertone, "Sal had some kind of a date with him the night it happened. The cops been searching high and low for that boy."

I couldn't see anyone responding.

The bartender placed hot fried eggs covered with tomato sauce and cheese in front of Mark. "Eggs rancheros," he announced.

Mark unfolded a napkin in his lap, paused, and then pushed the plate away.

"You know, I could blow my brains out," he mumbled. I stared hard at him, trying to guess how serious he was. He was still mumbling. "Why I hung around that beach party, fighting with some woman, and then driving the freeways singing songs, I'll never know."

"How did you first hear about it?" I asked.

"On the radio, and then I was all over the road, driving like a lunatic down to his place. I hit a garage wall, and I made the acquaintance of that damn cop."

He sucked his lips in hard. "Oh, dammit, I got troubles. I

got no alibi, and I'm scared, and you're scared of me, right?''

I shifted in my chair. "I don't know."

Then he looked down at the tablecloth and whispered, "You're damn scared of me."

"Why did you lie to me?" I asked, answering him with a question. I wondered if he'd notice, like the gay editor back in New York.

"You mean about being a goddamn suspect?" he asked.

"Yes."

"Because I reckoned you'd see me as disgusting or something."

I did not find him disgusting, but hearing him admit he was suspected of murder got me. "I'm not scared," I lied.

"I loved him better than anything." I strained to hear him. His voice still sounded like music. "I never got that much pleasure from any man, woman, member of my family, any cause, trip, tune, belief, any damn anything. I rate him a mile ahead of myself."

I was bewildered by this man, but I understood a little of his pain. It was less alien to me than homosexuality and murder.

"What happened to the people who broke into your house?" I asked.

"I told you, forget it."

"Was anything taken?"

"Just a few joints."

I didn't get it.

He said, "You're scared of me, all right, and I'm too freaked out and fucked up to sleep in my own bed. I'm even scared of you. It's not you. But you make me say things."

"What did you and your friend do at this bar?" I asked idiotically, in an attempt to change his mood.

"Oh, the old man would chat and cruise," Mark said. "I'd go home early. But I'd always call him first thing the next day."

"Why?" I asked.

"He needed love outside the chase. I gave him comfort, no questions asked."

"Were they—I mean, were they prostitutes?" I asked, and looked over at two trim athletic guys walking up to the bar. One of them could've murdered Sal Mineo.

Mark looked angry. "He never paid, and he never had to. Look, you know many gay men?"

"Oh, a few, maybe."

"Hey, Jonathan." He waved at the bar again. "Well, that kid Jonathan was one of Sal's last tricks."

Oh, damn, I thought. The boy who'd knocked over my glass sauntered over to Mark's side of our table. His hair and eyelashes were pale blond. He was frail, and the spidery lines on his forehead hadn't come from age. He looked like a Christmas tree angel, months after an exhausting holiday.

"You eating right?" Mark asked him.

"Oh, fair." Jonathan didn't look at me.

"The cops want to talk," Mark said.

"Look, I don't need it," he said.

The camp attitude in the parking lot was gone. Now he was behaving like a sullen child.

"This is Jonathan Simpson," Mark said to me mechanically. Then turning back, he explained, "She's doing some research on Sal."

"Yeah?" Jonathan turned his back to me and sat on the picnic table. "Well, I'm not talking to cops and I'm not talking for research."

Mark said, "But you and me got to put our heads together."

"Right, Mark. I got three minutes." Then the two of them started to whisper.

I felt excluded. I pushed my bench away from the table, crossed the dark room, and saw a man in a T-shirt waving a beer mug and telling a joke about a motel. I found the door marked LADIES, and pushed it open. Of course, I was alone, and it felt a little better. I splashed my face with cold water while I stared at it in the mirror. It did not look familiar. The eyes were small. The mouth was tight. The shape of my face was boring. I had no planes or bones in my cheeks.

I realized I had been studying Mark's face.

The door opened, and I tensed up. It was Mark, and he

hadn't bothered to knock. His shirt clung to his body. Despite his shoulder muscles, he was thin. In the dim light he looked naked.

He stretched his arms over his head. I was holding my breath. Our images looked away from each other in the mirror.

"Excuse me," he said, and disappeared into a stall.

Boy, this was one strange situation. I was sharing the ladies' room with a reclusive music star, who was probably gay, at a male gay bar in Los Angeles. I wished I could enjoy the humor of it.

The graffiti on the wall was written in purple lipstick. "Edith Head gives good wardrobe." "Reality is for people who can't face drugs."

"You know, this was his mirror," Mark said a minute later. He held his wrists under the cold water. "He talked to it a lot."

"What did he say?"

"Sometimes he'd stand here shaking his fist, begging the damn mirror for luck."

"What did Sal look like to you?" I asked.

"Sal always looked like a growing boy. It shot down his career. But it never hurt his love life. He'd always be here checking out his eyes. He had these black, hungry, movie-star eyes."

I watched Mark in the glass. Then I turned and looked him in the face. It made me feel a kind of claustrophobia.

"Let's go, ma'am," he said.

We returned to our table and sat down a few inches away from each other on the bench. Mark gulped a green cocktail from a brandy glass, while I raised my voice over the sound of Johnny Mathis on the jukebox.

"Where's Jonathan?"

Mark pulled the glass away from his mouth. "He split."

"What were you two talking about?" I asked.

"He's a worried man," Mark said, still looking straight ahead.

"What's he worried about?"

"Well, sugar, his lover got murdered the other night, and they had a date. Once he threw a crowbar at an opera student in Sal's house, and the cops know it." He sounded sarcastic again. "Oh, shit, who knows what he worries about."

I wondered whether Jonathan had thrown anything when he found out Chris was moving out here permanently.

He stretched. "I got to go. This was a dumb idea."

I tried to add the violence up: Jonathan, the murder, the guy who hit me at the airport. "I told you I want to write a story," I said. "We could track down the murderer too."

He winced, and I felt the picnic table shaking. He was bouncing his knee against it. It seemed that only he could mention the word "murder." It didn't jolt him if he knew what was coming.

"You're hurt," I said, "but I can help you."

"Whatever do you mean?"

I shifted my weight and our arms bumped. I flushed, but I kept talking over the music. "I think we should trust each other. I want a story. You want to find somebody."

Mark raised his chin, and his face looked almost perfect, like a posed photograph.

I kept talking. "Listen, it's simple. If Chris was moving here, somebody could have gotten jealous. You're ahead of the police. You know all his friends. You probably know the person who did it. You can put the pieces together."

"So I should accuse Jonathan?" he asked. He was on a second green cocktail. He chewed a tiny sprig of leaves between his front teeth. I smelled it—mint.

"Well, he should account for himself."

"It's been taken care of," Mark said.

"Why the hell are we sitting here?" he suddenly asked.

I felt my head twitch with surprise. "We can leave anytime," I said, wondering if he was getting drunk.

"What're you doing down here?" he said, twisting away from me on the bench.

"Where?"

"In hell with me," he said.

"You need me." I was trying to sound confident. I

wanted to lower the level of hysteria. "Look," I said, "we already have one lead."

"Shit," Mark said, turning to me again, "It's just a brick wall. You don't understand. My brain's dying on me. I can't close my eyes at night. And you want to play games. It's like Sal. He loved games. When he wanted to pick up the best-looking guy at a bar, he kept a mental picture of himself and the guy in bed and worked the conversation around to that picture. But it was just a game."

I drummed my fingers on the table.

"It's like Sal always saying the big break was coming." Mark's voice was low. "He talked a great game, but you don't get it. You don't understand nothing. You think you're real serious." He stood up, his drink in his hand, and looked at the red light above the exit.

"That's right," I said, grabbing his arm. "I'm serious. I mean, I don't know the city. I don't know Sal Mineo's friends, except for you. But I'm smart. And I'll just go on asking questions." I paused. "And something'll happen. It always does."

Mark sat down and almost spilled his drink. "Right, right. What the hell—I got the time, and I'll turn in circles with you forever. I got nothing but time, and I'm waiting to get old."

Then he started to tell me more about Sal Mineo.

"I never knew how he managed. Oh, yeah, I did, kind of. He had residuals from television work. He always got by. People were always givin' him stuff. I gave him shirts and one time somebody gave me a loan car for a year. I gave it to him. He sold a little grass years ago, but he didn't collect on it. He never hustled enough. He never asked for what was owed him. That's Sal. He never got nothing but good reviews from directing those plays."

"Did he ever get unemployment?"

"He called it 'the Polish Embassy.' He went there once, took one look, and left. He had pride. He never so much as touched a form, and he never went back again."

Mark hiccupped. "Sorry ma'am," he said and continued. "So if he turned up with something like—I don't know—a new car, you'd ask him and he'd say, 'Hey, I got it in the mountains.' " Mark swayed to one side. "That meant he got it by magic, and don't ask.

"Look, I got to get out of here. Right away," he mumbled. "I got to see about something."

"What?"

"It's private."

"Does it have to do with what we've been talking about?"

"I still got a private life," he said, tilting his glass high for the last green drops.

"Well, I'm just doing my job."

"Look, I ain't saying how much of this I can take. But tomorrow I'll meet you at his place, if you like, and you can see it for yourself, the scene of the crime." He looked away from me at the bar. "I got to get over there. I'm looking for something, and with you, maybe I'll get it."

I opened my mouth to question him more, but he said, "Stop, don't ask me."

"I'd like to interview Jonathan," I said as we made our way to the exit.

"Well, that's gonna have to wait."

At the door, Mark said, "Are you surprised Jonathan isn't some nelly fag?"

"Nothing would surprise me," I said.

Mark said, "Well, that's no answer, babe. It's too bad you didn't know Sal. He had pride and he knew how to answer smart. I remember him telling some reporter, 'No matter who you get in bed with, you're a man.' We called him 'the old man.' He was the oldest person we trusted."

Chapter
Seven

The next morning I heard cars and a bird singing when I woke up. The room service operator laughed when I asked for a toasted bagel. She suggested herb tea. I declined, and I called the coroner's office. "No," a man said, "nobody here can say one word about the crime. It's classified."

I asked him his name.

"Bob Candida."

In the lobby I spotted Francis Coppola talking to Al Pacino. "Honest to god, Al, I saw them a week ago, all silver and running together."

"No shit," Pacino said. He looked short to me. Obviously it hadn't ruined his career. It made me wonder about Sal Mineo.

"Excuse me," I said.

"Hush," Francis Coppola said, and then he reached over and put his palm on my mouth.

I moved his hand. "What are you doing?" I asked.

"Working," he said.

"Well, so am I. I'm writing an article on Sal Mineo, and why didn't you—"

"I can't talk now. I'm busy," he said, and turned away.

He put his arm around Pacino and they walked toward the door.

"Al, I saw them with my own eyes. They run down from the hills and take over the Strip at night. In packs. They howl." He howled to demonstrate his point. "I tell you," he continued, "we're temporary here."

They made no sense at all to me. I walked over to the desk clerk. He was sorting mail, but he felt me standing in front of him. I could see his lips curve into a grin.

"Does he stay here?" I asked.

"Who?"

Those white teeth made his skin look even more like caramel. No leathery California suntan. His skin was young and almost succulent.

"Francis," I said. It felt weird, but I'd already noticed that's the way they refer to stars in Los Angeles.

"Yeah, sometimes," he said, looking over his shoulder and out into the lobby. "It's fun. They love it, y'know."

"Say," I asked, "where you from?"

"Panama," he said. "I'm seeing America first."

I laughed.

"You're from New York." He put out his hand. "Call me Jay."

I shook it. "Sara Martin."

He tapped me on the shoulder with his pencil. "Nobody knows this," he said, "but Francis tried to buy this place a year ago. Two million dollars."

"You're kidding," I said, looking around the lobby. The floor was marble and the Spanish colonial lobby was unusual, but I wouldn't rate the hotel high on ambiance.

The clerk lowered his voice. "At the last minute he bought a vineyard in the Napa Valley. He'll do anything for his mother, and she likes vineyards better. They remind her of Italy."

"How do you know?"

"The things I hear," he said.

* * *

Twenty minutes later I almost hit a bus on the freeway, while I was changing lanes to get to the exit ramp near the coroner's office. The driver hit his horn. I sped away. I was going to see the man who had turned me down on the telephone. People who are not used to reporters are flattered by pursuit.

At the office Dr. Candida grinned at me. "I can't believe it. You can't do this. I could lose my job."

He was fresh out of medical school, with acne scars on one side of his chin. He wore a white jacket and black-rimmed eyeglasses that were popular in the fifties.

I swore to him that I would never tell anybody that I had met him. "Take me to the cafeteria and I'll buy you a full cup of coffee on the *New York Post*," I said.

He laughed. "Why?"

"Good question," I said. "Nothing in it for you but good conversation about your work."

He looked around his empty office. It was early in the day. It looked slow. A buxom woman wearing a short skirt was reaching high for plugs on the switchboard. "Cover for me if Dr. Noguchi comes in," he said.

She tried tugging her skirt over her chubby knees. "Now your girlfriends're showing up here?"

He blushed again. He was not tan. He wore a plaid shirt that looked as if he'd bought it in Camden, New Jersey. On the elevator he told me he was living in Van Nuys.

He studied me. "I bet you haven't met anybody who isn't from Beverly Hills or Hollywood or the beach since you been out here."

"Why?"

"It's the way you look." He didn't seem particularly humbled by the observation.

In the cafeteria, I spotted a few men who looked like policemen eating greasy doughnuts. They wore wrinkled suits and looked flabby, as if they shouldn't eat doughnuts. Otherwise the place was deserted.

"When did you first hear about the case?" I asked him.

"Wait a minute," he said. He took out a pencil. "Write me a statement that we never talked about the case, and how I took you out for a cup of coffee, trying to get rid of you."

I was surprised. No one had ever asked me for this before. "What good does it do you?"

"Not much," he admitted. "But if you're ever tempted to break your word, this'll be one more thing on your conscience."

I wrote the note and he folded it and put it in his wallet.

"Now tell me about the case," I said.

"What do you know about my office?" he asked.

"Not much."

"Okay. Well, we do autopsies. We try to match wounds and weapons. We got twenty guys running all over L.A. trying to buy the knife that fits Sal Mineo's wound."

I grimaced. "How can you prove it?"

"Well, we got the wound on the sixth floor," he said. My mouth twisted as if I'd sucked a lemon.

"We cut it out of the body," he said. "People figure the dead man can't testify, but that wound, it'll be plenty testimony some day. Sal Mineo will testify about the murder. His body is testimony, and it'll nail the jerk."

I watched him put a napkin in his saucer to absorb spilled coffee. He continued. "The blade tore the wound, and we figure it was serrated. We're working over at Farmer John's packing house. We stick hundreds of knives into hog material and compare the cuts to the wound."

"What's hog material?"

"Freshly killed animal."

I gave up the idea of drinking my coffee. "Do you think it could have been a mistake?" I asked.

"What do you mean?"

"Couldn't it have been somebody who just wanted to scare him?"

"No," he said. "I think the guy meant business. I think he hated Sal Mineo a hell of a lot."

A shiver went through me. "Why do you say that?"

Candida punched his fists together. "He hit his chest so hard that he shoved an inch of the handle into the wound. He knocked Mineo like a linebacker. The wound is six inches long, and it's an eighth of an inch thick."

"I guess the police think it was somebody who knew him," I said.

"I know they do," he said. "They ruled out robbery. It was too violent. Nothing was taken. The police have Mineo's address book. They're going to hypnotize his friends. They told me all his buddies are suspects."

"Can you tell me more about the weapon?" I swallowed hard.

He smiled at me. "We say it's a standard fishing knife. Five inches of blade. It's got little teeth. And it's missing, along with the murderer."

It sounded awful, but I had to keep up the questions. "Why couldn't it be a failed robbery attempt?" I asked again.

"Because no money was taken," he repeated. "The murderer just plowed right into Mineo."

I didn't want to hear anymore, but I asked, "There a lot of witnesses?"

"Neighbors," he said. "Four neighbors."

"What kind of neighborhood?"

"I went over that night. A block down from Santa Monica Boulevard. Gays sort of stand there. They call it 'cruising.' " He raised his eyebrows as if he'd call it something a lot worse. "The apartments look run-down. A lot of gays live there. Across the street, the buildings look like cheap motels. The cops call it 'Boys' Town.' It's not a place for people who want to put down roots."

"Roots," I said. "I didn't think they were big in Los Angeles."

"They big in New York?"

"No."

"Los Angeles's more American than New York," he said.

Before I paid for the coffee, I said, "Hey, maybe you can help me. I heard something about silver animals coming down from the hills and running loose on Sunset Strip at night. What local wonder is that?''

"Coyotes," he said cheerfully. "People say they eat pets. Nature's still strong out here." He bit down on a toothpick. "We got Santa Ana winds making fires, rock slides squashing houses down the canyons, earthquakes, floods, and coyotes that aren't afraid of people anymore."

Chapter Eight

At sundown I pulled into a fast food joint at Melrose and La Brea in Hollywood and ate two chili dogs. Slick red sauce dripped down my arm while I watched clogged lines of cars poking by.

Inside the small dining area, actors and poor blacks ate at wobbly Formica tables. The floor was littered with plastic spoons and straws. But the walls were plastered with autographed movie-star photos. Smells from the kitchen grills drifted past. I grinned at the faces of Frank Sinatra and Karen Black amid the glossy photographs on the wall. All the pictures were signed with flattering remarks about chili dogs. But the unknown actors' smiles looked tense, their eyes angry.

There was the same picture of Sal Mineo, age fourteen, that I'd seen at the newspaper office. It annoyed me that nobody bothered to replace it with an adult picture. It was as if nobody knew he grew up. I wondered how Sal Mineo felt about it. It wasn't as if he were Peter Pan.

Sal Mineo's neighborhood was two blocks off the Strip, but it was clean and residential. The new apartment buildings were garish, decorated with signs advertising swimming pools and saunas. I parked on a slant next to a highrise covered with orange and turquoise balconies. Cars flew by me. Up the empty sidewalk, a man was walking a white poodle whose fur was cut to resemble a lion's.

I walked down a shadowed alley behind Mineo's apartment. The sun was setting, and it was that time of day when things look almost too clear, like they're outlined in black. I peered into empty garage spaces and at some parked cars. There were gasoline stains on the cement.

To my left was an empty courtyard between two low apartment complexes. I saw a fruit tree, red canvas chairs, and a striped beach umbrella over a metal table. There was no one around. The emptiness was creepy.

Near the other end of the alley, I saw someone standing inside a garage smoking.

"Hello," I shouted, and waved.

I looked behind me. It was twenty yards back to the street where I'd parked the Dodge. It was getting dark. The figure took a few steps. I recognized Mark's long-legged gait. "I wanted to make sure you didn't bring the cops," he said, stopping a few feet away.

"Thanks for trusting me," I said. He shrugged and looked down at the dark cement, inhaling on his cigarette. I peered over his shoulder into the dark garage, wondering where Sal Mineo'd been killed.

"You're standing on it," he said, reading my mind.

"What?"

"His car space. The place where it happened." He shook his head hard like a dog shaking water from his ears, hunched his shoulders, and said, "Let's go, Nancy Drew."

His shirt was unbuttoned and the sleeves rolled up. I felt overdressed in a long coat. I found myself admiring the lines of Mark's back, as he loped ahead to the courtyard.

I followed him over the small path, bending to avoid huge rubber-tree leaves. Behind me a leaf hit the ground with a small crash. A roar of motors told me I was walking toward Holloway Drive. He swerved left, crossing a lawn, and approached a low apartment. Each apartment had an outdoor entrance with two white columns. I stepped over a redwood barrel filled with gigantic geraniums.

Mark stopped near the round iron table and the torn beach umbrella. Sal Mineo might've tossed the Coca-Cola bottle into the hedge. The deserted courtyard was a poor man's paradise in Southern California.

I stepped on something soft and alive. He watched me pull a small fruit off my shoe.

"Green peaches," he said. "I was waiting for them to get ripe so I could make him peach cobbler."

I smelled the sweet peach.

"The stems are too weak or something. The fruit falls off before it ripens," he said.

Mark walked down a path, up four concrete steps, and rapped his knuckles on a door between two white columns.

"Who is it?" a woman asked.

"Mark Loren."

She opened the door a few inches. I saw part of her face, small and overpowered by black eyeliner.

"You real busy?" he asked.

As I followed him over her doorstep, I stumbled into a clay pot filled with blooming cactus. I smiled at the woman.

"I'm Annie Harmon," she said. The eyewitness who'd called the sheriff's office. I liked the way she looked. She was wearing a green leotard and green tights and she was breathing hard. She wore a short sharp haircut, and she was about forty-five and small-boned.

"What's your sign?" she asked me. I was tempted to say asparagus or Valium, but I didn't. Her small living room was littered with brushes, canvases, and twisted tubes of oil paint. Big paintings of wildflowers were hanging on walls, leaning against chairs, and sitting in windows.

I listened patiently while she told me that a Cancer woman like me is emotional and hides her feelings from herself. I stared at a picture of glorious bluebells. Astrology always reminds me of clinical psychology books in college. Every symptom you read about sounds as if it belongs to you.

"You'll fall in love out here," she told me, lowering herself into the lotus position in the middle of the living room.

"Right," Mark said, and he suddenly sang a blues line in a tight falsetto: "Love, what are you doing to my friends. . . ." He stopped abruptly and a second later disappeared out the back door of the apartment. It sounded as if this visit was too hard for him. I finally asked Annie Harmon about Sal Mineo.

"He was so special," she said, and stopped, biting her lower lip.

"How?"

"He had this way of helping you like nobody else. You know what I mean?"

"I'd like to understand."

She hesitated. "I go to work now, the Old World. I'm filling in; mostly I work days. Come over later. I'll take good care of you. I'm senior waitress."

"Did he go there?" I asked.

She looked surprised. "Yeah. I talked the boss into inviting Sal, four squares a week on the house. It made us look good."

"You liked him?"

"I loved him. I been here longer than even Sal. My dad, he was a stunt rider. Before he died he rode in posses for Gene Autry. I was dialogue coach on 'I Love Lucy' for ten years. But I got eased out, and Sal gave me money."

"How close were you?" I asked.

"Honey, there's a lot more to relationships than fucking every night. It was good. Okay?"

She thrust her leg high, grasping her ankle with one hand.

Mark wandered back inside the apartment. He patted her foot. "Annie, baby, you still got the key?"

"No, I don't," she said without moving.

"Yes, you do," he said quickly. "I have the right to go in there." He looked over at me. "She shares Sal's back hallway. He left a key with her for safety's sake."

Mark squatted down and kissed the top of her forehead. "Give it to me."

"What good is it?" She lowered her leg and leapt lightly to her feet. But she didn't produce a key.

"Didn't you do his horoscope?" I asked her.

She said, "I saw trouble with his upper torso. It's a bitch, isn't it?"

"Did you tell him?"

"Sort of," she said, looking up at Mark's face. He towered over her. "I saw the kid running away, the pig."

"What'd he look like?" I asked.

"It was too dark. I saw the side of his head. I think he was blond."

"You didn't recognize him at all?"

"It was dark. I was just walking out back." She jabbed a thumb over her shoulder. "I thought Sal was home—his living room was lit up, and it was past dinnertime. I was carrying my garbage down to the bins. I probably walked right by the bastard hiding in the garage unless he was driving with Sal in his car."

Then she grabbed Mark's wrist, and her voice shook. "Oh, Jesus God, it's shit, isn't it?"

Mark kicked at a tube of oil paint on the floor. "Don't talk about it anymore."

"Wait," I said. "Let me ask her one question. Did you hear anybody say anything?" I did not want to say "the murderer" in front of Mark.

"You gonna give me that key?" he interrupted.

She untied a narrow black ribbon with a key hanging on it from around her neck and handed it to Mark. "When I got back to my door, I heard Sal pull up." She folded her hands in front of her flat stomach. "I heard somebody screaming, saying something like 'No, no, help me, please, God, help me.' " She recited the words without particular emphasis. "I didn't hear anything else, just something falling against a car and the screaming. I went running back to the garage. I didn't recognize Sal's voice. I just figured somebody was in trouble."

"What did you see?"

"Stop it," Mark said. "Stop talking about it."

"Go try the key," Annie said. He walked out.

She glanced at my face and sat down again on the floor. "I saw Sal lying there making terrible sucking noises like he was drowning. And I saw somebody running down toward the street.''

From the hallway Mark shouted, ''Hey, Sara.''

''Do you think the police can find the man?'' I asked. Every once in a while, you find somebody you can pester with questions—check your hunches out—and you hate to give them up.

''You never know. There's justice somewhere.''

''What's Jonathan like?'' I asked.

''Oh, he's a wild kid. He'll settle down.''

''How does he make a living?''

''He's a studio musician. Banjo.''

''How did he get along with Mineo?''

''With Sal? Well, it was stormy.''

''Was he jealous of Chris?''

''Is the Pope Catholic?'' She added, ''No offense, miss, if you're Catholic or anything.''

''No, no.''

I said goodbye and left through the small kitchen. It was white, spotless, with no sign of food. But she probably ate meals at the Old World.

In the back hallway, Mark was standing next to an open door to another apartment. ''I'm going in,'' he said.

''Not me,'' I said. It felt indecent.

Mark disappeared and began clumping around inside the dark apartment. He knocked something heavy to the floor. From the doorway Sal Mineo's living room smelled like old air and dust.

''Don't do nothing till I find the light,'' he said.

Suddenly I felt something strangely like nostalgia. Sal Mineo had come home to this room for years. I'd never seen him in it and I never would.

He found the light switch. From the hall I said, ''Mark, I don't feel right.''

''I invited you here,'' he said. ''But you're on your own.''

I stepped inside the apartment. I felt a kind of craziness, rule-breaking.

"Don't touch anything," he said. "You could be ruining fingerprints or making new ones."

The living room was small, and the brown squared sofa looked comfortable. There was one expensive piece against the white walls, a leather and rosewood Eames chair. The place looked as if somebody were moving out. Cartons of books and kitchen utensils sat in the middle of the room. On the coffee table were a few pennies, a paperback copy of *Lolita,* and a brass incense burner with ashes in it. The only thing in the room that clearly marked Sal Mineo was a magazine called *Film Comment,* addressed to him. For a moment I wanted to take it with me as a souvenir. But I didn't have the nerve.

I peeked into the bathroom. On the sink was a silver toothbrush with smashed bristles, an old tube of fennel toothpaste, and a bone china shaving mug. A week before these things had been part of this man's morning ritual. Now they were debris. I smelled floral shaving soap.

Mark was sitting on a carton and looking around the living room. "Whenever I'd knock on the door, music was playing real loud. He loved early Beethoven and Wagner. Then the door'd open up and it'd be him and music and I always felt good."

I tripped on something. It was a yellow plastic bowl with "Dov" stamped on it. "For the collie," Mark said. "Jonathan's caring for him now. Sal named the dog after his character in *Exodus.* He liked to call him 'Starfucker,' because when he was a pup he was running away all the time to Jack Benny's house. People are dumb. Some reporter once asked Sal if he did it with his dog. Sal said, 'Sure, and he even wears a leather collar.' "

Mark stood up and closed his eyes. I still could not believe that I was here. It had happened too fast.

Lying on the floor was a theater poster for a play called *The Carnival* that showed Chris Franklin dressed up as a matron in a platinum wig and a sable coat.

I turned to Mark. "What's *The Carnival?*"

"A play Sal produced. For old Chris," he said.

"What was it about?"

He flopped down on the carton and shook his head slowly from side to side. He was staring at the floor between his knees. "It's about a guy who picks up a boy, takes him home, and the boy stabs him." He laughed. "It ain't like life, right?"

Mark looked as if he were listening to something far away. I ran one hand across the scratches in the coffee table.

"Don't touch things," he said, shooting me one of his fast glances.

I had forgotten fingerprints. Now three long smudges from my fingers ran down the dust of the coffee table.

But I kept on looking. I knelt down and pulled paperback books out of a carton. The titles amazed me: *One Night Stand, Bad Little Boys,* and *The Cocksure Rock Star.*

"His paperback porn collection." Standing above me, Mark kicked at the carton. "Damn things."

"Did he like them?"

"Well, he was writing a movie script out of one of them. Take one. Nobody wants them." He snorted and handed me *The Cocksure Rock Star.*

Inside the book was an *L.A. Times* clipping, three months old. The article announced Sal Mineo's plans to star in *P.S. Your Cat Is Dead.* I read one paragraph: "Mineo says that he has no qualms about playing a bisexual. 'This guy is lonely. He's looking for love. It's like if you needed food, it doesn't matter whether it's breakfast, lunch, or dinner.' "

I shoved it into my shoulder bag. Someday the book would prove to me that I had seen this small apartment.

I pulled a screenplay out of the carton and read: *Fortune and Men's Eyes.* A small card fell out of it, from a Miss Chasin at Canyon Loan Company. No date. I put the card back inside and opened to the title page. It was covered with handwritten notes.

"Sal wrote in books when he got excited." Mark said. He picked up a huge mask of an ape. *"Planet of the Apes.* Sal got great reviews as a monkey."

"I never understood why he took that part."

"Well, he wanted to act in films again, and he got star billing. It proved his name had marquee value."

"Did he mind that nobody saw his face?"

"He laughed about it."

I figured Sal Mineo minded.

Mark held the mask over his face. I didn't like it. He took it off, saying, "Roddy McDowall gave him this at the wrap party."

Just then the telephone rang. After the second ring I ran to answer it, but I put my hand on the receiver and stopped. I was scared. I watched Mark's face to see what he would do. His head jumped with each ring.

It stopped, and then started again. It rang eight times.

"Do something," I said. I wanted to scream.

Suddenly, the bedroom door opened. I knocked the receiver off the telephone and threw myself across the room at Mark. His hands were cold. I think I screamed. The screenplay fell out of my hand, and Mark picked it up.

"Stay there," a man shouted at us, and grabbed the telephone. It didn't make me feel better when I recognized him.

He spoke into the telephone. "Casey here, it was them. . . . Oh right, you did? . . . They came inside. Good work."

Casey slammed down the telephone, sat down on the couch and spread his knees. His pale blue eyes were tired. He yawned, and I saw he was eating a piece of white candy.

"This is the last warning." He slapped his palms on his knees. "Tell your girlfriend to stay out of it, or I'll book you as a material witness. We'll see your standard of living go down in the slammer."

Mark lit a cigarette. It was a silent show of bravado. Casey stood, grabbed the cigarette from Mark's lips, and stamped it out on the brown wool rug. It smelled like burning hair.

"Now get the hell out," he said.

Nobody said goodbye.

Outside, Annie Harmon was standing in her doorway between the two white columns. Mark loped past her and disappeared down the path toward the garages.

I thanked her and walked out back to find him. It was dark

in the alley. All the empty concrete made me shiver. It was quiet as a graveyard.

"Over here," he said. He was sitting in his car, the top down and the lights off. "I got to get on home," he said.

"Why'd you come here?" I asked.

"Never mind," he said, and started his motor. His white Cadillac looked at least fifteen years old, and had chrome tail fins, a dented silver fender, and a weird black door.

"Can I see that screenplay?" I asked.

He handed it back to me.

"I'll take good care of it."

He was staring at me appraisingly. This time I looked away.

"I'll cook up some dinner for you tomorrow night," he said.

"Okay."

He twisted his neck and backed the wide Cadillac down the skinny alley. I opened the screenplay. I realized I was looking at ripped edges. The title page with the handwriting had been torn out. I held the spine of the thing, flipped through the pages, and shook it hard. The loan agency card was missing too.

Chapter
Nine

I drove to Cleon Wilson's neighborhood at noon the next day. There was a harsh white quality to the sun. It made me clench my teeth.

I cruised down a network of streets in Watts, feeling white and sad. I stared down empty alleys between bungalows, then got out of my car to find a house number. It was hot and still, and I smelled smog. A dog nosed over a trash can and licked orange rinds. I smelled frying bacon. Disco music pounded from an open kitchen window. I heard a man humming along. The strangled backyard was dust brown. I couldn't find any house number. I wanted to get out as soon as I could. White girls don't go chasing assignments in Watts unless they're ambitious to a fault. I couldn't remember any smart reasons for being here.

A police siren wailed. Then I saw three teenage boys hanging out near my car. One guy's arm was inside my front window. He smiled at me, pulled it out, and waited. I cringed when the black and white police car blared past. The boys backed away, leering at me, "Hey, lady, better take care of your stuff."

I drove two blocks before I saw the black boy in white sneakers running behind me. I ignored him and tried to park between two empty trucks. Four tries and I gave up. The kid was still chasing me when I passed a bus stop with a bench painted with an advertisement for "El Dinero."

I checked him out again in my rearview mirror. At least it was daytime. He was grinning, and he terrified me. I didn't know how to read danger signals in this neighborhood. In Harlem, 125th Street is crammed with people. I slowed down to peer at more ramshackle houses with television antennae. It was hard to believe this was an urban black ghetto. Except for a bombed-out no-man's-land feeling.

A fat woman stopped pulling stiff dungarees off a clothesline and shook her head at me. Behind her a gnarled cactus, and a patch of scarlet bougainvillea was climbing the brick walls of a liquor store. Two guys stood in a parking lot piled with beer cans. I saw too many pawn shops and second-hand clothing stores. There were no shade trees here, lots of bright sky and no white people.

I rode down a side street past a shack with a broken front window and a white picket fence. Next door, the Wilson house was unpainted brown stucco and had a screen door and a chicken wire fence.

I parked the car against a low curb littered with newspapers. The black boy leaned a bare elbow on the Dodge door. "Watch out," I said.

He banged the door with his fist. "For one buck, let's say I guarantee the car."

"Beat it," I said. He looked about nine.

"Lady, don't get weird. I got lotsa time," and he laughed.

"Pick on somebody your own size and intelligence," I said.

"Hey, lady." He looked over his shoulder. Unfortunately for me, the coast was clear. "Don't lose your cool."

"I was implying that both your size and your intelligence are inferior to my own," I said.

He punched the door again. It rattled me. "You some kind of crazy teacher?" he asked.

In fact, I was imitating my mother. I was also imitating

Humphrey Bogart, who could take a gun out of a bad guy's hand by just convincing him he could do it.

I decided to negotiate. "I'm no teacher, but I'll give you the dollar when I leave."

"Shit, you better," and he kicked at my tire in a proprietary manner. We had a deal.

I walked up the cracked cement path and rang the doorbell. It made a harsh cawing sound. I was standing on a wooden step that hadn't been painted or washed in years. I jumped when a man yelled, "Who's there?"

"You get it," a woman shouted.

The screen was hanging off the wood door frame. "I'm Sara Martin," I said into the crack. "I'm looking for Cleon Wilson."

"Why?" I heard the sound of bolts unlocking.

"I'm from a New York newspaper."

A guy opened the door and I took an involuntary step backward. His face looked Negro, although his skin was a pale ash yellow color and he also had freckles. His brown eyes were puffy from sleep, lack of sleep, or drugs. His hair was weird. He had peroxided some of it to a brassy orange color and braided small tufts all over his head.

"You from New York?" He sounded puzzled.

"Cleon Wilson?" I asked.

"I ain't, and he ain't here." He shifted his weight. Under his workshirt he had the huge arms and shoulders of a weightlifter. He wasn't tall; his legs were short and bowed under the dungarees. He looked about nineteen.

"Well, where is he?" I stepped back toward him.

"Gone," he said.

"Where?"

"To talk to the devil about some deal. What do you want from brother Cleon, anyway?"

His curiosity was equal to mine. "I'll tell you if you tell me where I can find him," I said.

"Ain't nobody knows where the dude is now, but I can get him," he said. "I can get to anybody."

"Does he live here?"

"Oh, sometimes. What do you want from him, again?"

"Well, I'm a newspaper reporter and he told the police he knew something about a story that I'm working on."

He stared at my legs. "You married?"

"No." I stepped up further onto the doorsill to block his view. "Does he have another address?"

"Look, he's some blood dude that crashes here when I say okay."

"What's your name?"

"Johnson, Jerry Lee Johnson," he said. "Come on in."

He didn't move. I didn't want to act scared so I squeezed past him. His muscles were hard. He smelled like garlic and sweat. His palms and fingers were fat. His wrists were wide.

"You live in the valley?" he asked.

I didn't know what he meant.

"Yeah, you know, Van Nuys," he said.

"No, I told you I'm from New York."

Although his mouth didn't change at all, I felt the tension in his eyes. His lids widened. He seemed amazed and suddenly alert. He bolted the front door behind us. I was locked in with him.

"What's your name again?" I asked, sitting down on a green couch in the living room. I was pretending to be a routine guest. There were some color pictures of Jesus Christ and Bruce Lee on the walls. A punching bag was nailed in a doorway.

"Jerry," he said.

"Jerry what?"

"Jerry Johnson, that's what my friends call me."

"This your house?" I asked. "It's nice."

"Yeah, my parents got the papers on it, but I live here," he said.

We were both jumpy. I wondered why I was making him nervous.

He said, "You going up against brother Cleon? You ain't scared of the devil?"

"No." My voice was loud.

"Well, he's one tough son of a bitch, but he no tougher than me, Jerry Johnson."

"What does that mean?"

"Well, I think he could off a dude like that." He snapped a wide thumb and forefinger in the air.

"You talking about murder?" I asked, and concentrated on looking him in the eye.

He started to whoop with laughter. "That's what I'm talking, baby." He sprawled back, laughing, a series of gasps that were part explosion and part shriek. The guy gave me chills. He sounded like a catfight.

"You work or anything?" I asked. It's the way men phrase this question to modern women. It was probably the least offensive way to ask it of this man.

"Oh, off and on."

"Doing what?" I asked.

"Well, I make things happen."

I gave up on him. "Look, will you give a message to Cleon Wilson?"

"I'll put the word out on the street."

"Thanks," I said. I told him that Wilson could call me at the Chateau Marmont.

"You gonna make him famous as Lucifer or something?" Jerry Johnson asked. He had been concentrating before he asked the question. I could see it meant a lot to him. He still had not figured out what I was doing in his house.

"Maybe so," I said.

"Why?"

"Well, he may know something about who killed Sal Mineo."

He stood up and stretched his body. He cracked his knuckles. "He told me some stuff."

I heard the attempt to get attention. "What stuff?"

"I guess he and my old lady stopped off at a shooting gallery and some dude was bragging about killing a famous guy in Hollywood."

"What did the other guy look like?"

"Blond dude."

I tensed up. "The famous guy was Sal Mineo?"

"Yeah," he said. "The dude claimed it was a contract

hit. Some heavy cocaine dealer bought it. They paid the guy heavy bread.''

"How much?"

"Oh, about twenty-five hundred bucks." He stretched his arms high above his head, pleased with my undivided attention.

"Did Wilson know the guy who did it?"

"No, man, he don't know," he said. "But then he don't say everything he knows."

Jerry Lee Johnson was a con artist, and my instinct was not to believe him. But I couldn't ignore him.

"You go to discos?" he asked.

"No."

"Oh, yeah." He sounded angry. I looked over at the locked front door. He seemed to take my answer as a personal rejection.

"That Mineo dude was some bigtime cat," he said.

"Right."

"The cops are pretty dumb."

"What makes you say that?"

"I hear they didn't give a shit about brother Cleon."

"I'm interested in him."

"I'll find him for you."

I heard another door slam. A girl walked into the living room. She had the same ash skin color as Jerry Johnson. They could have been siblings. I stood to show my respect, but she didn't look at me.

"Get out," Jerry said to her. She put her fists on her hips.

"I'm Sara Martin," I said.

"Well, you been sitting on my furniture," she said.

"I'm here to find Cleon Wilson," I said.

"What's happening, big mouth?" she asked him.

"Lay off," he said.

"That's my husband, girl," she said.

"What's your name?" I asked.

"I'm not stupid," she said. "I keep my mouth shut."

Abruptly he ducked behind her, twisting her arm. It was too sudden. I couldn't believe my eyes. She pitched forward at the waist and screamed, "You stupid—" I moved toward them to help her. But then I stopped. I am not always as brave as I'd like.

She kept screaming while he dragged her out of the room. "Let me go, let me go, I'll kill you for this one."

I ran six steps to the front door, listening to the smacking and thumping. I unlocked it and opened the screen door.

"What was her white ass doing here?" the woman shouted.

"I'm telling you—lay off."

She screamed, "You jerk. You wouldn't know trouble if it came up and punched you in the mouth."

Then she screamed louder. "Fuck, you're hurting me."

I doubled up my fists and shouted, "Stop it or I'm calling the police."

The house was silent. Then she ran out of the kitchen, swinging a wood-handled hammer with both hands above her head. "No cops, no white ass in my house."

There was no mistaking the fact that she was dying to use the hammer. I ducked when she threw it. It hit the door behind me and then bounced off my right shoulder blade. I backed out the door, my fingers pulling at my stinging muscle.

"You come back here and I'll kill you and him," she shouted.

As I ran to the Dodge the boy stuck out his palm. "Pay up."

My legs were shaking. "Let me inside the car." My voice was harsh.

I opened the door, got in, and locked it. I tried to get the key in straight. My fingers trembled, and I heard myself panting. I passed the boy a dollar bill through a small opening in the window.

Just then the woman ran out of the front door. She was still screaming and swinging the hammer above her head. The boy ran. I turned the key and started the motor just as she hit the back window a terrible blow. The sound went through me. Glass sprayed through the car, and I kicked the gas pedal to the floor.

The car screeched and wobbled for the next two blocks. I

jammed the brakes at the red light. My hand went to my hair. I stared at tiny bits of glass on my fingers.

I was shaking. I wanted to call my editor. The woman had been a freak accident. But I'd survived. She'd missed my face and all I'd have would be a bad bruise on my shoulder.

I drove a mile before I convinced myself I had lost her. On the outskirts of Watts, I pulled into a gas station with pay telephones. I checked out the back of the car. The seat was covered with glass. I put through a collect call to the newspaper. I needed to talk to Marty Burns.

I didn't just want comfort—I had news to report. The tow-headed blond kid in the beach snapshot with Mineo came back to me. I wished I'd taken the photograph back from Marty. Then there was Jonathan's jealousy of Chris. Annie Harmon saw a blond kid running from Mineo's body. Why was Mineo's apartment lit up while he was on his way home? Maybe somebody was in there waiting. And I wondered if any of this connected to Jerry Lee Johnson's talk about the blond dude who bragged that he killed somebody famous in Hollywood for some cocaine dealers.

But the switchboard was busy.

I called Joe in New York, collect. I was surprised how much I wanted to hear him telling me everything was all right. I figured he'd be happy I escaped harm, but he'd ask why the hell I had gone to Watts alone in the first place.

That was what I was wondering myself. Once Joe told me, "You run too hard. You tried too hard to be a student. Now you overdo the active life because you want to make up for lost time. Take it easy."

The operator let the phone in the apartment ring ten times. "Your party doesn't answer."

Then Joe picked up the telephone. "Oh, hi. I can't talk," he said.

I almost said something mean. But that wasn't fair.

"Sara, I'll ring your hotel later," he said.

It sounded as if he weren't alone. "Yeah, sure," I said. I hung up and frowned at a boy hosing down a Triumph in the sun. Water dribbled along the cement toward me.

Then I called him back. "Joe, I'm scared," I said, closing the folding glass door to the telephone booth.

"Yeah?" he said, and I heard clatter in the background. Somebody was there.

"Maybe you were right about this story," I said, swallowing. "Two people have tried to hurt me, and—"

"Sara, what's that mean?" He sounded scared.

"Well, some guy hit me at the airport out here. He's got guns—"

"Where'd he hit you?"

"In the stomach, but it's okay."

"Jesus Christ, what else?"

"A woman in Watts chased me with a hammer."

"Did she hurt you?"

"Not that much," I hedged.

"Don't go near them again." He sounded mad. "You hear me? If you do, I'm telling that city editor of yours to find another fool to run his errands." It felt good hearing him get angry on my behalf.

"Sara, you listening?" He sounded scared again.

"Yeah, thanks, thanks."

Before he hung up, he said, "Call me later, and take it easy tonight. You got to live to type another article, right?"

"Right."

On the second try I got Marty Burns. "I got a lead," he said. "Got a pencil?"

I always have a pencil. This was a little joke. He was saying, "Mineo left a party right before he was murdered, at the home of Kate Lyons, somewhere at the beach. She's that big-deal producer. Here's her private telephone number. I hear nobody's listed out there." He gave me the number, shouted something, and then asked me, "Everything fine?"

I wanted to run down everything but it was too early. Instead, I said, "Lots of pieces floating around."

"Talk to you tomorrow," he said.

So I called Kate Lyons. Three male secretaries put me on hold until she got on the line. It was impressive. I put some more change in the telephone.

"He didn't know me very well," she said. "We talked once."

"I'd like to talk to you." I emphasized the word "you." It sounded like she needed that.

"Well, I always accommodate the press. I'll tell you about my new rock picture. You can have twenty minutes tomorrow afternoon. But call me first, so I can make sure I'm on schedule," she said, and hung up.

Chapter Ten

Before I went to sleep that afternoon, I called Mark and told him I was too tired to show up for dinner.

"I got some red Dexedrine," he said. "Pumps lightning in your brain." His voice was soothing.

"I run on my own speed," I said.

"Okay, Dinner'll wait, later, whenever. On your own speed," he said, and gave me directions to his home in Laurel Canyon.

I woke up two hours later, showered, dressed, and drove my Dodge up Sunset, watching the neon lights of the burlesque shows. I sniffed at my wrist. I have this idiosyncrasy. Sometimes I wear Joy perfume. There's something about the way it reminds me of a single rose in a crystal vase. It's known as the most expensive perfume in the world. I have a tiny vial, and when I spray it on my skin, I feel chic. Dowager chic. Women who wear it are over fifty-five and rich. But the vial doesn't cost any more than a fancy meal at a French restaurant. And it lasts longer.

I turned on Laurel Canyon Boulevard and left the flatness of Hollywood to drive up into the hills. Trees and plants grew wild and messy. I saw small mountain houses lit by front-door lights. Barefoot kids and dogs played on knolls in front of open garages filled with pickup trucks, tools, and boats. I'd stumbled on a rural mountain town.

At ten-thirty, I parked my car next to his old white Cadillac in a dark, paved clearing at the foot of a hill that loomed against the panorama of city lights. It was a relief to stop and rest. This place was calm and close to the dark sky.

I locked up the Dodge. Stupid, considering the back window was gone. It was so dark I couldn't see the ground. I walked two steps on the pavement and then stopped.

I heard something that made my skin crawl. Somebody else took two steps and then stopped. I took another step. I heard another step. I put an arm out in front of me and cleared my throat. "Hello?"

Nobody answered. I heard two more steps, and then a car door opened and closed. I turned and looked behind me. There was another car somewhere in the clearing. I finally saw a dark shape on the other side of Mark's lumpy Cadillac. There was no motor sound, but I heard tires crunching on the cement. The car was rolling downhill.

I heard brakes and the sound of a door opening. A light went on inside the strange car. From a lot of practice straining to see if taxicabs were available, I thought I could see two people sitting there.

"Lady, what's this street?"

I jumped at his voice. I couldn't see his face. I wondered how long they'd been parked there. It was fishy. Then I saw only one person inside the car. That meant the other one was near me in the dark clearing. I directed my voice at the car, and measured the distance between me and the path up to Mark's house. "It's Wonderland Avenue."

"Yeah?" one voice said. "What's your name, hon?"

"My name is my business," I said.

"Lady, you in trouble?" he asked, and then I saw him standing next to the car. He looked tall, but I couldn't tell much. The car was a Mercedes sedan.

"No, are you in trouble?" I asked back.

"Very, very funny," he said. "I'll remember that one."

My heart started to beat fast as I watched him get inside

the Mercedes and slowly back away. Without headlights, I couldn't read his license plates.

I listened to the sound of his motor grow and then blend with the crickets, birds, and far-off cars of Los Angeles. My nerves were shot, but I got inside what looked like a small waist-high cage at the foot of the hill. It was a cable car that traveled on a diagonal up the mountain to Mark's house. I felt like a lost tourist.

I closed my eyes and felt the outdoor elevator sway as it climbed. When it stopped, I stood there alone, facing his front door. I looked down the steep hill. I couldn't see my car. I needed time to think.

A door slammed and there was Mark in dungarees, his hair wet. With his hair flattened down, his eyes looked bigger and his face more gaunt. "Make it up here okay?"

"Lucky thing I learned to read road maps in junior high school." I followed him into his house.

"I got back ten minutes ago," he said. "Took a quick shower."

"Oh, listen," I said, "who uses that parking area down there?"

"Why? What happened?" He shot me a fast look over his shoulder.

"I just wondered."

"Nobody but me," he said, his voice cracking. "Why?" He didn't bother to close the front door. I stopped and slammed it.

"What's going on?" he asked, smoothing his hair.

Instead of answering, I walked past him into his living room and flopped down on a leather sofa, trying to look calm. I didn't want to upset him more.

"Tell me everything," he commanded, and sat down facing me on the edge of his wooden coffee table.

I pulled my chin away. His face was too close.

"Some guys down there." I pointed my thumb over my shoulder.

His eyes jumped away.

"In a car. They scared me."

126

"Where?"

"In your parking lot."

"Hollywood types?"

"No, not really."

"Cops," he snorted. He paced away and turned down the red gas flame in the fireplace.

"How do you know they're cops?" I asked abruptly.

"They been tailing me all week," he said, walking toward me. "Forget it."

My shoulders got tight. He could be wrong. The guy who slugged me at the airport had disappeared into a Mercedes. I couldn't tell if the guy in the Mercedes tonight had the same voice.

Through the windows I looked down on the lights of Los Angeles, and felt vertigo, as though I was flying toward the city in an airplane. The ceiling had wooden beams. The soft light in the room came from a tank filled with red and orange saltwater fish. Candles glowed around the room.

"Why do you live up here?" I asked, after a minute.

"You want the bullshit response?" Mark sat facing me again on the coffee table. I turned my knees to one side to avoid bumping his.

"Yeah, then the real answer," I said.

"First, because I'm a country boy, and second, because there was a time I hung out with lots of musicians, and they live up here."

"But you don't hang out with them now?"

"Nope, I like my own company." He was resting his chin on his palm and staring past me at the fire.

"How many rooms do you have?" I asked.

"Twelve, not counting bathrooms," he said, walking away again to put a Beethoven quartet on the record player.

He walked around the room, lighting candles on the floor against the walls.

"I thought the place was torn apart," I said, watching him move in the shadows.

"The cleaning woman comes every day." He picked up the telephone. "Forgot to call my service. Sal and I used the same service, Kelly O'Toole, and sometimes I got his messages for him because we had the same operator."

I felt like I might fall out the windows into the city lights.

Mark was listening to the operator and writing. "Oh, yeah, at Universal? . . . Right, I'll call Kate at Burbank."

I got a brainstorm. "Mark, listen to me." I jumped up and pulled on his loose shirt cuff. "Find out if there are any messages for Sal Mineo."

He sat down slowly and we locked eyes. "Alice, babe," he asked, "got anything on 659-2032? . . . Right. Sure, I'll report them to the cops, and it's cool. Just check Serpentine Productions." He covered the receiver with one palm. "That's the company Sal formed to develop properties."

He scribbled for a minute, hung up, and handed me a list of messages:

2/11, Jim at the Westwood Playhouse has all your house tickets. (11 P.M.)
2/12, Mark Loren says maybe dinner at Lucy's after the beach party. (12:15 P.M.)
2/12, David Lyons. (1:30 A.M.)
2/12, Chris, call as soon as you get home. (6:10 A.M.)
2/12, Kate Lyons says to meet her at the beach today after lunch. She's not going to the office, so don't bother calling Burbank. (10 A.M.)

"Let me see the time on that," he said, pulling the paper out of my hand. It was the morning of the murder.

"That's funny," I said.

"What're you thinking?"

I didn't tell him that Kate Lyons told me she'd met Sal Mineo only once.

But then Mark said, "Sal didn't say he was meeting with Kate. It doesn't make sense. We didn't keep things from each other. That's the way I saw it, anyway." He frowned down at the page.

"How do you know Kate?" I asked.

"She's this producer," Mark said.

"Who's David Lyons?"

Either David Lyons and Mineo were awful close or he had problems—late-night problems.

He shrugged. "Big producer. Used to be married to Kate Lyons," and he walked out of the living room.

I found him in the kitchen, grating cheese into milk steaming in a double boiler.

I leaned my hip against the butcher block table. Watching somebody cook puts me in a trance. It's calming. The concoction looked like baby food.

I folded and unfolded the messages. "What's Chris like?"

"The interview begins," he said. I couldn't see his expression, because he was bent over the stove, his hair bouncing down on his face as he rubbed the cheese against the grater. "Well, I got close to him at the funeral. I saw what Sal saw."

"I saw you and him at the funeral."

Mark changed the subject. "I told you how I was always cooking for Sal. Black-eyed peas, candied yams, and French stuff too. Otherwise he ate junk food. It's sure nice to cook for somebody again."

"I like junk food," I said. "It's my vice."

"I bet." He laughed.

"What's so funny?"

"Nothing," he said.

I asked, "How did you meet Sal?"

He covered his eyes. Then he went back to beating the cheese and milk in silence.

"You feel okay?" I asked him.

He threw the whisk against the wall. The eggwhite splattered and hissed on the stove. "I'm real tired." His voice shook. "Maybe you better go."

"I want to stay," I said.

He looked strained. "You don't know shit. It's so fucking hard, and I can't do it solo. Sal and me, we tell it together."

"Well, you're not by yourself," I said.

"Oh, yeah," he said, "right. I'm with you and you're wrapped up in cellophane. I see you looking down your nose at me." He was cleaning the eggwhite off the wall with his bare hand.

"It's the opposite—"

"Shit," he said. "I know much more than you do."

"About what?"

"Sex, feelings."

"Maybe," I said.

"You think sex is dirty." There was a harsh sound to his voice. "You think gay people are disgusting. Sal said some people are special—everything about them is attractive—and to everybody. But you don't get it. Why am I wasting my time?"

"Stop it," I blurted out. "I like you. I get high around people who will be the key to a good story. It hits me like an infatuation or a bad cold."

"Sure, sure enough," and he stopped talking.

Dinner was silent, and over in ten minutes. I ate fast, sitting at a coffee table. Mark unrolled his linen napkin, poured wine into his goblet, ground pepper into his fettucine, and then he looked at his lap. He said nothing and ate nothing.

Afterward he walked over and sprinkled dry food into his fish tank. I watched the fish wriggle for it, and then I opened a photograph album to a picture of Sal Mineo glowering at the camera, his collar turned up, his hair greased.

"That's not really him," I said.

"Hey, you're right," he said, and sat down next to me. He reached over and turned the page. There was Sal, sitting on Mark's leather couch, a book in his lap. He wore wire-rimmed glasses and a tired, soft smile.

"That's him," I said.

"That's right," he repeated. "Sal played a lot of hood parts, but you like him right, the way he was."

Another picture showed Nell Fields aiming a wineglass at the camera. "Her favorite way of getting attention," he said. The next picture showed Nell, Sal Mineo, and James Dean, barefoot, in rolled-up dungarees, at a beach barbecue. They were laughing, with their arms around each other's backs. Mineo's hair was blowing in the wind. Nell wore pigtails.

"She was in love with him," Mark said, "but possessive, and that's why he broke it off. Because of her, he couldn't have his cake and eat it too."

I must have looked confused.

"I know what you're thinking," he said. "But Sal knew how to turn folks on. Man or woman. He made folks feel special, because he made them love themselves."

"How?"

"Well, for him seduction was a daily act—oh, I don't mean only sex—but see, an actor needs to feel the heat of people loving him. It was Sal's talent. He listened to you like he had a goddamn third ear, and once he learned what it was you loved, he'd become that. He changed colors like a lizard in the circus."

"Was it like a game?" I asked.

"It was dead serious. For him, it was just natural, like some folks are good at making you laugh."

"How did he do it with you?"

Mark raised both eyebrows. "We were easy. It wasn't anything like work. We'd just please each other because we hated the same stuff and loved the good stuff."

I asked, "How did he feel about you?"

Mark looked angry. "Sara, no matter what you think, I hear a million things from a million people about how I look. But it was Sal who taught me my looks belong to me. It was like freedom."

"So he made you special," I said slowly.

"Look, you got to be wondering about Sal and me." Mark hooked his thumbs in his dungaree pockets and paced around the couch. It sounded as if he'd thought about it a lot. "Rudolph Valentino is a hero to us, and was he gorgeous-looking. But in his hometown they'd've locked him up—the local pervert. He broke the rules, with great style." He was steaming. "You tell me all about Rock Hudson, Janis Joplin, Errol Flynn. The public doesn't know how they've lived. Everybody loves them. We know all about them and we don't give a shit."

"So you have different standards?"

"We got no standards," he said. "We don't need them. Take Ramon Novarro. He died in bed right smack between two brothers. He's a hero of the silver screen. Elvis Presley didn't particularly like anybody touching him or having sex. But he liked two ladies tucking him in at night."

"So what's the point?" I asked. I noticed he hadn't mentioned many musicians. I wondered if his lecture was about Sal Mineo's life more than his own.

"The point is, these people are loved. Folks love them. They love themselves. We don't put them down. We envy their sexiness. We figure their vices are part of their thing."

"Well, now what are you trying to say?" I asked.

"Jesus, I thought I said it," he said shortly.

"What?"

"That if something is beautiful, I want to touch it. If something is peaceful, I want to contemplate it. If something's cold, I want to make it warm. It isn't bad. It isn't good."

"I try not to pass judgment," I said.

"Really?" His tone was smug. "Anyway, you're about twenty-six, right?"

"Yes." I guessed he was twenty-three.

"Well, you're still growing, girl."

"Look, tell me about Sal Mineo and I'll try to keep my mind open." I sounded too formal. I was sitting up too straight on the edge of his couch.

"Beauty is its own excuse," Mark said distractedly. He paced to the other end of the couch and looked out over the lights.

"In a way," I said.

He cleared his throat and spoke more firmly. "So why's it more disgusting for people of the same sex to be touching each other than for really ugly people?"

"It's not aesthetics," I said, and sprawled back on the couch.

"What is it, then? Masters and Johnson say it's no big deal who you make love to," Mark said in the dark.

"I don't know."

"Why put down Sal because he made love to men?" Mark said.

"It leaves me out," I said, looking down at my fingers and flexing them. This conversation was embarrassing. "Anyway, it's biological. We got permission to have sex from our parents, but with the opposite sex."

"Did you get permission?" Mark turned away from the window.

I folded my fingers in my lap. "But it's just not right," I said suddenly. "Gays don't have kids."

"Maybe enough folks are making babies," Mark said.

He looked back at the lights. "Let me tell you something. I was fourteen when I met Sal. I hitched out here to get somebody to listen to my tunes, and it's a long way up here from down in South Carolina. I was born in Louisville, but we moved when I was little to a beautiful place with pastures and woods near Charleston. You're funny, because you remind me of my mom—determined. She always stood up for me, but Dad wanted me to sit home and read. I slept out in the woods in a hammock. Then Mom died and Dad gave up trying to keep us a family and shipped me to this depressing boarding school. I ran away with this kid Jeffrey and lived with his folks in Bel Air, and we roamed around like we had all the time there is. His folks let us be, so afternoons we went to the beach and nights we hung out on the Strip. I was a show-off on my guitar, figuring I'd get myself discovered." He laughed quietly.

"I'll never forget the first time I saw him sitting there on a motorcycle outside the Old World. I was so excited. It was Sal Mineo. I followed him on down the Strip to a club called the Interlude. It was a jazz club. Lenny Bruce used to play there. I'd seen *Rebel,* and I was the right age. I drank five Cokes, just so I could stay there and watch him." He laughed again.

"Then one day down at the beach I was playing this lullaby I made up and I looked up and he was standing there staring at me."

"What were you playing?" I asked. I wished I could see

133

the expression on his face. But he was hiding by the window.

"I don't know. I'll tell you about Sal. It's like some people have a spotlight wherever they go."

That was something Mark had—a spotlight. "What did you look like then?"

Mark slid across the couch and started thumbing through his photograph album. "I had a picture of myself. When I showed it to Sal last Christmas, he said he'd do anything to meet the kid in the picture."

"He was kidding," I said, watching his face tighten in profile over the album.

"I guess."

"After the beach you made friends?"

"We hooked up when I was fourteen and he was twenty-six, because we didn't belong to anybody." He blinked hard, and handed me the photograph. Mark had been a completely winning boy. His hair hung down to his shoulders, but he had the same scared black eyes, sweet mouth, and thin face with planed cheekbones. I liked the way he looked today. His shoulders and arms were filled out.

He stared at the photograph, his voice straining. "I'd give anything to find him again. I'm twenty-five and I'd give my life to be fourteen again."

"No."

"Yes, dammit." He folded the photograph down the middle until the picture cracked. Then he folded it again. It was ruined.

"I'll never forget the night he asked me back to his place, and I went, scared as a jackrabbit. But in my whole life, nobody ever made me feel so special. He wanted to know every damn thing about me—my music, my family—and he said maybe I wrote lullabies because my mom died when I was real young, and how they were about missing her. He asked me if I was scared girls would disappear on me like my mom did. He said my songs made him feel better about living or something, and he asked me about my old man, so I told him how he teaches legal philosophy and doesn't talk a whole lot to me or anybody."

"My mom's a teacher."

"She talk to you?"

"Not really," I said, looking at him curiously. I'd never thought of it that way.

He stood up, tossed his hair off his face, and said, "Sal was in a phase, working on that play *Fortune and Men's Eyes,* about boys in prison. He showed me his house, and it was one weird place. He had prison bars on one wall. Sal lived in about ten different houses since I met him. Further and further inland."

"Where did he live the first time?"

"On a cliff above the sea, in Malibu colony next door to Peter Lawford and the Lyonses. He loved the beach. He didn't have any furniture, just this huge Harley Davidson. He didn't like leaving it outside because to him it was a real pretty piece of art. He was rolling high. A year before, he'd made a thousand dollars a day doing *The Greatest Story Ever Told.* I think he worked ninety days. That adds up to ninety thousand."

I picked up the folded picture of Mark and put it in my pocket. Mark reached for a twelve-string guitar lying on top of the mantle, and strummed it. In the light from the fireplace I saw his black hair, dry now, curling down his forehead. He kept plucking the same melody, walking around in the shadows.

"Today I'd know better. But I was thrilled because we were going to stay up and talk. I thought. 'Oh, damn, my first real conversation with a famous guy.'

"When I asked him how it felt, being a movie star, he said, 'It's better than being a telephone repairman. All you need is a relationship to your aspirations and you got it made.'

"He asked me did I want to see his house. I said okay, and he followed me into the bedroom, and the bed was huge, man.

"He told me, 'Go on and try it.' So I sit down and bounce a few times and we smoke some joints, and I feel dizzy and real special. It's like being in the best damn movie ever made, starring Sal Mineo and me. I start giggling and sing-

135

ing, 'When you wish upon a star,' a Hollywood movie star, and he loved it, and nobody ever liked me like that.''

Mark was standing by the window, and I saw his silhouette against the gray night sky. He sounded unsteady, but he kept talking.

"He sits down next to me on the bed. I want to hug him because I'm having a swell time, and he hands me a guitar, and I tune it, and he asks me to play a song of mine he liked.''

"Which one?'' I realized I was holding my breath.

" 'Desert Places.' I look up and Sal's staring in my eyes and he looks real kind, and he's saying, 'Mark, I like you a lot, and it's a shame you don't swing.'

"I jump off that bed, because I'm sure he's saying I'm boring him. But I want to spend time with him more than anything.

"So I say, 'Oh, but Sal, I do swing, I really do, and when I get to know people I can be real crazy. Honest.' ''

Suddenly Mark took his guitar strap off and laid the instrument back on his mantle. He walked over to me, knelt down, and put his face next to mine. He touched my cheek with one fingertip and then looked from my mouth to my eyes over and over. I felt a current shoot over my body.

"Sal's talking to me and looking like this, like he's taming a kitten. 'Swing with me,' he says, 'Swing with me.' ''

Mark rocked back on his heels. "I feel this buzz running all over my body . . .''

"And?''

"And fadeout, sugar.''

I waited and asked, "Then you two saw a lot of each other?''

"No way. I freaked. I ran far away.''

"Then what happened?''

"You sure like to keep a conversation moving.''

"I want to understand,'' I said.

He rolled his eyes, ambled over to the fireplace, and turned the gas jets off. The flame disappeared, and Mark's voice quickened in the darkened room.

"Well, Jeff, this kid I was staying with, said Sal called a couple times, and I didn't call him back, but one day I answered the phone and it was him. He was real upset, kept saying he wanted to talk, and I said flat out I never wanted to see him again.

"I told him I never did sex before. He sputtered and said, 'But Mark, you said you swing.'

"I told him I thought *swing* meant being fun, and then he was quiet for a long time. Finally, he said we'd had a bad misunderstanding, and he told me he'd arranged for me to put my tunes on a record. I figured he was jiving me."

"Was he serious?"

"He was, and the tape Sal made was a hit, and a lot of folks got rich, but he never took a dime."

He sang, a little quickly, under his breath, in the husky Southern voice, a song from his album "Desert Places" that I heard over and over on cab radios: ". . . love, what are you doing to my friends?"

This time I was really intimidated. His voice was too famous. I wished he would keep singing, but I couldn't ask. It was like demanding a gift.

Instead, I asked, "What did Sal say when you both told your friends about how you met?"

"Well, it's going to freak you out."

"Try me," I said.

"Well, Sal said I was like hot butterscotch and poetry, but I don't know." Mark ducked his head, embarrassed.

"How did you feel?"

"Well, I felt like dying from pleasure. I mean, I was getting new feelings, and it was my first time."

"What feelings?" I was sure he wouldn't answer me.

"What feelings?" His voice had a mocking sound. Then he flopped down next to me on the sofa, his legs straight out in front of him. He recited in a dramatic monotone, "Oh, please, more, to the left, higher, harder. It hurts. No, it doesn't."

Then he stopped, and without turning his head in my direction he said, "Okay?"

I'd never heard anybody speak so much about sex. It made me a little frantic. "Then what happened?"

"An hour later I felt like I was more dead than alive. I ran away."

I kept thinking that the whole thing wasn't fair. Gay men pick out the best-looking boys. Mark needed somebody to protect him.

"Hey, girl," Mark said, still looking straight ahead, "where's your tape recorder?"

"I can't forget this," I said.

"I'm making a dumb joke," he said. "This isn't for publication."

I opened my mouth to argue, and closed it.

Most of the candles around the room had burned out. Mark got his guitar off the mantle again and was playing another melody line. Then he combined it with blues licks. Then he was singing the last verse. I loved his voice.

> . . . *don't talk, my love,*
> *give me your mouth*
> *to soften love.*
> *Listen to my fingers*
> *on your mouth.*

He hesitated. "Keep me company. Stay the night. I got extra bedrooms."

"Thanks, but I better get back to the hotel."

"I'll make us a hot-oatmeal breakfast."

I shook my head. It wasn't the kind of thing I do. I sure looked up to him. I was so curious. But staying overnight would make me feel like a groupie. I didn't figure him to be making a pass. I read books on sexuality. I wasn't his type, although everything in his life seemed topsy-turvy. He looked lost. I don't know why I started nodding yes. Maybe it was because I am so snoopy. Maybe it was because my day had almost killed me. I was tired.

My bedroom was filled with electronic music equipment. I touched the polished wood of an electrified cello. There was a Moog synthesizer, something that looked like a switchboard, and walls of metal boxes covered with tubes and dials.

Mark gave me a blue silk shirt from the closet.

"This is supposed to be the composing room," he said. "But it doesn't get a whole lot of use."

I had a twinge of sympathy for him. He was out of the room for a few seconds before he knocked and came back in.

"I want you to know," he said, looking down at his hand twisting the doorknob, "I want to be your good friend. We're not alike, but you're steady, and you won't lie and get tricky on me. I can't take any of that right now."

"Friends?" I said.

"What's wrong with that?" he asked.

"Well, the truth is, we could be friends, but . . . well, there's always work, and it comes first." My voice sounded too defensive.

He gave me one of his fast looks. "Don't expect miracles."

It sounded as if he were talking about sex or something.

"I expect a good night's sleep," I snapped.

He smiled for the first time. "You're an honest soul, and I appreciate it."

I sighed and thought of the whispers that had passed between him and Jonathan at the bar and between him and Chris at the funeral, and of the two threatening guys in the Mercedes. "Then why're you hiding things from me?"

He shot me another intense glance, and then he was looking at the floor and running his fingers through his hair.

"I do the best I can," he said.

"Listen, tell me one thing—what was on the page you ripped out of that screenplay?"

"Nothing much. Want to see it?"

He disappeared and handed it to me when he returned a few seconds later. I tried to decipher the handwriting. "Why did you rip it out?"

He was chewing on his lower lip. "I didn't want that damn cop to get any closer to Sal."

"Do you remember a card from a loan agency?"

"No, ma'am."

"It probably fell out when I dropped it," I said. "I hope that cop didn't get it." The notes on the page looked as if they'd been written in a car. I folded it and put it into my purse.

After he left, I felt too tired to take a shower. So I threw my clothes onto the cello case and buttoned up the silk shirt he gave me. It smelled of cologne. It hung down to my knees.

Then I heard a scream of pure terror, like the cry of an animal. I heard him through the door of the bedroom. I heard my name.

I dashed like a lunatic through hallways and into one room filled with musical instruments. Mark seemed to be screaming from somewhere both inside and outside the house. Finally I ran back across the living room and past the fish in the tank, and kicked over some warm candles with my bare feet. I found him sitting in the dark at the foot of his bed. Half-naked. He was doubled over as if there were something wrong with his stomach.

He kept moaning to himself. I bent over to look at his face, but he pushed my arms away.

"What's wrong?" I asked.

"Look at this place," he said. I turned on a lamp.

"Jesus," I said.

It was a shambles. Dresser drawers had been pulled out. The telephone cord had been yanked from the wall. The bottom half of his curtains were burned and spread out against the rising winds blowing through the open window. A table lamp had been thrown against the wall of mirror. The overhead light had been smashed. The blanket and bedspread were ripped.

There was a knife stuck in the headboard. I reached to pull it out and something fell down onto a pillow. I fumbled for it and felt something wet. It made my fingers sticky. When I looked down at the pillow I saw the knife had been stuck into a distended condom filled with a dark red liquid.

I gagged and wiped my fingers on the sheet.

He jumped up, strode to the closet, and wrenched the door open. "Who's been here?" he mumbled. "Who's here?"

He circled his room twice, kicking at the charred curtains, pulling open other dresser drawers. "It's my house," he said. "It's my goddamn house."

He kicked the bedroom door open, and I jumped at the noise.

Then he sat down on the side of the mattress.

I sank down on the floor in front of him and put my arms around his knees. He had to calm down. Then I was embarrassed because I was wearing only the blue silk shirt and underpants. But he didn't notice.

"When did this happen?" I asked, checking the buttons of my shirt. They were secure, but my fingers weren't working. "We were here."

"I was out before," he said.

He broke away from me and lay down on his bed. "You shouldn't be here. It's just too dangerous."

"I'm worried about you," I said. "Let's call the police."

"Call the police!"

I picked up the telephone. "It's dead."

"Hang it up, then," he shouted.

"Maybe it was those guys in the parking lot," I said. Mark wasn't listening.

"Are you okay?" he asked.

"We have to go to the police."

"No way."

"Mark, does that Sergeant Casey know about the other time this place was torn apart?" I wondered if he was trying to figure out how much I knew about his problems.

"Answer me," I said.

"No," he said.

"What's going on?" I asked. "Does it have something to do with Sal planning to visit Kate Lyons out at the beach?" It was just a guess, but he got the same puzzled look on his face as when he heard the message from Sal Mineo's answering service.

"No," he said, "and it's nothing I can't handle myself."

"Let me help," I said. "You told Chris something about it that day at the funeral. You can tell me."

I couldn't help but snatch a second or two of pleasure from the way he looked at me. He did seem to respect my ability to piece stuff together.

"Well, I don't want you writing this."

"Tell me," I said, "trust me."

"Two people roughed me up and said they would kill me if I told the cops."

"Oh, God," I said, "did they hurt you?"

"No."

"Well, who were they?"

"I don't know."

"What did they want?"

He gestured around the room. "They must be after something."

"What?"

"I don't know."

I believed him and I didn't believe him. "What about the cops? Maybe it was them," I said. I didn't say that someone could have come from murdering Sal directly to Mark's house. Annie Harmon said Sal Mineo's lights were on. That same thief might have been looking for something inside Sal Mineo's house the night of the murder and in here earlier tonight.

I followed him to the front door where he walked outside and did something to lock the elevator. The hallway was dark. I didn't know what it looked like in the light. I wished I'd had a better look at the guys lurking in the Mercedes. I heard a bolt snap. We were alone in the house—I hoped.

I led the way back into his bedroom. Behind me, he brushed his hand along my shoulder as if to reassure himself that he was not alone.

I stopped short and hugged him lightly after he touched me. He felt so thin. I closed my eyes when we got to his bedroom. I didn't feel like looking at the mess around us. He sat down next to me on the bed. His leg was touching mine. It was as much from shock as anything.

I took his hands. "Mark, who's doing all this to you?"

"I don't know. Don't ask me." He slid his hands away. "Sara, you have such red hair. Did you always have red hair?"

He touched my hair. It was a soft pat. He was tentative. I heard a new intensity in his voice, but it was just a breath.

"I'd better go," I said, but I didn't move.

He was stroking my head. I wanted to arch my back like a cat and push my head against his hand.

He said, "The old man is dead. I can't believe it, sugar. I can't even say it in words. Somebody has broken into this house twice. I got me some trouble."

He was looking at me and not seeing me.

"He was the first person I loved, and now I'm fucked. I could always talk myself back to sanity with Sal."

I put my hand on the back of his neck to comfort him.

He grew still. I closed my eyes against the guarded expression on his face. His elbows were locked against his body. I wondered what he looked like naked.

He wiggled his arm behind me and pulled me close. "What is it we're doing here?" he asked.

I pulled back, but he held me. I wondered if this was the first time he thought about making love to me. It was terrifying. I stood up and put my palms over my eyes. It was one thing to hang around here because I was a reporter. That was my invisible shield. But I didn't need to neck with a frightened and famous musician who was probably gay. Reporters don't judge, they just ingratiate and soak up facts, feelings. But people in my family judge. I judge. And this was stupid.

He asked, "Do you want me to make love to you? Do you? Say it to me. Tell me how you're feeling. What do you want me to do, Sara?"

I started toward the bedroom door.

"I want to think about it." He wasn't my boyfriend. He was a stranger.

Mark laughed dryly. "You don't want to stop and think about it," and he pulled me back toward the bed.

My knees collapsed and I sat down again. He ran his fingers over my face, stopping to make a circle on my mouth.

* * *

It made no sense, but whatever he said sounded right. I felt as if he were touching me all over. I could not believe it. I was so curious. I wanted permission to touch every part of his body. I felt something change. It felt large and far away, like the movement of an ocean. But it wasn't far away. I wouldn't be the same again. He was right. I wanted him to keep going. But I never do anything that might turn out badly. I wanted to feel his skin. I knew it would be smooth. I wanted to see the curve of his buttocks. I wanted to see if he had an erection.

I couldn't tell him. I was scared to death. I felt ashamed.

"What about you?" I asked.

"No, I want you to tell me."

I didn't think men who made love to men wanted women at all. Maybe he was bisexual. He probably didn't want to make love the normal way. This was some awful tease.

I was like two different people. On the one hand I knew what I wanted, and it was something new. I wanted to watch him and feel him making love to me. On the other hand, I wanted to escape him. I didn't move.

Then I wanted something else. It was so huge, I didn't know how to negotiate for it. I'd always been polite. I'd always felt good when Joe had a good time. Now I was unnerved, caught in overpowering feelings. I closed my eyes and almost moaned. The ground was unsteady. "You know what I want," I said.

"What?" He lowered his eyes with a small smile. He knew his power. "What is it?"

"I want to be with you."

"Not unless you tell me how."

"What do you mean?"

"I want specific instructions."

"What instructions?"

"I want you to talk to me about sex—'harder, more, over there'—stuff like that."

"That's crazy." I covered my ears. I shouldn't hear this.

"Well, then, too bad." He stood up.

"Why should I?" I asked.

"Because it'll make you feel good and it'll make me feel good to make you feel good."

He was right. It would be amazing for me to ask. I'd never done it before. I pulled him back on the bed. "Take my clothes off," he said, lying down behind me.

Instead of speaking, I stood on my knees and pulled off his dungarees. Mark had long swimmer's muscles, narrow hips, and sunbleached hair on his thighs and calves.

He wore no underwear, so I pulled his pants over his erect sex organ, and stopped. He still lay on his side, his lips in a trembling smile. He looked beautiful. I saw pale skin, the triangle of soft hair, the place where his bathing suit had blocked the sun. There was no hair on his chest. I leaned over and touched the smooth gold skin of his pectoral muscles. I pulled my hand away.

He guided my hand back and rolled onto his side, facing me. I had never touched such a perfect body. I sat up and tentatively stroked him. His shoulders were full. I reached over him. The muscles of his buttocks were hard and I traced them down his thighs.

I lay down on my side and we looked at each other. I couldn't stand the tension. I was still dressed.

He was smiling gently. He was giving me permission to play games I had never thought of.

I was trying to hold back my breath. I felt as if I'd been running hard. I didn't want to frighten him with the ferocity of my feelings.

"Now what?" He was teasing me.

"What?"

"What-all's going on?" he asked.

"I have these feelings," I said, and curled one hand around the other.

"Tell me where to touch you," he said, patting my fingers until they relaxed.

I opened my mouth. The words never sound right. "Vagina" sounds like my gynecologist.

"Where?" he said.

I rejected "clitoris."

"There," I finally said.

"The words are beautiful because we're beautiful," he said sternly.

I couldn't speak.

"Take my hand and put it there," he said.

I don't know what it was that made me trust him enough to obey him. I surrendered, in a way. Like he was a swimming teacher who could make me believe I wasn't going to drown when I dived into water over my head. So I did the unimaginable. I put his hand under my underpants.

Then I heard myself moan. I had never been touched so sensitively. He knew what caused me pleasure better than I did.

Then he stopped. "Kiss me," he said.

After a moment, I kissed his mouth lightly. I was holding back. I wanted him too much. It seemed wrong. I hadn't thought it out. I almost laughed when I thought of Marty Burns. Then I forgot everything else. He hadn't moved. His lips were relaxed.

"Come on," he said. "More."

I strained against him, holding my breasts a few inches away from his chest. I felt awkward.

Then he rolled onto his back and pulled me on top of him. I felt his chest, his mouth, his thighs, his knees pressing back against me, and we rolled over again. I no longer felt awkward. I tried to lie still under him. But my mind took over again. He was a fantasy I hadn't dared to have.

"This is my cock," he said.

He put my hand there. The hard flesh trembled.

"Oh, God," he said.

It was hard to stay embarrassed in front of him. He showed no shame.

"You have to express what you feel." I heard the impatience in his voice. "Tell me to take your clothes off," he said. "Tell me to put my cock inside you."

"I want—" but my voice went away.

After he undressed me he touched me all over with both hands as though he was a blind person who was learning me through my body. He took a long time with me. I was out of control.

146

Then he kissed me all over with his tongue. I had no secrets left. I worried that he was too calm. I told him. I was babbling. He put his head between my legs and teased me with flicks of his tongue—hard and soft—until my body was thrashing around.

"I want you to make love to me," I said. "Come up here."

He tossed his hair and put his head down again. His voice was muffled against my body. "Good," he said. "Tell me again."

"I want to watch you. I want to feel you."

All I felt was his tongue on me. It was as though the rest of my body had floated away.

I started to cry and then stopped. He lifted his head to see why I had become so still. He was crying too, and when I saw his tears I began to sob. I felt we were moving forward on a single track, locked in tight symmetry.

When I finally felt him move inside me, he forced me to stop and look at his face. His mouth was shaking. I shook, frightened at my feelings.

"It's okay," he said, and cradled my head with both arms.

Then we started to move together. The friction we made was like a song. It was pure pleasure.

I began to worry that this would end. Then I forgot I was worried. I was moving all over him. I became one long spasm until he moved with new urgency. A soft electric current shot through my body.

I wanted to watch his face. With both hands, I pulled his head up so I could see him. His eyes were glistening, and he looked from my mouth to my eyes and back to my mouth. I was so pleased.

He murmured, "I love the way you smell. You smell like the wind at the beach. You're new to me."

"I know—" I said, and lost my voice again.

"Most girls smell like shampoo," he said, "but you're special." He stared into my eyes, his pupils shaking. "You love this."

I hid my head in his shoulder. He pulled my chin up.
"Say it," he ordered me.

"I love this," I said. I grabbed his shoulders and almost
shook him.

Then he shook me back and groaned, his breath harsh in
my ear. Then he relaxed.

I lay still under him. I was waiting to see what he would
do next. My body was wet where it touched him. He kissed
my ear and grunted. Then I relaxed, because he was relaxed.
He lay still inside me and folded up on top of me, limbs, fingers, cheeks touching.

I was unsure of what to say. "I didn't think—"

I looked over his shoulder at the mess in the room. I kept
staring at the draperies, unable to look at him.

"Oh, I knew," he said, turning my chin back with his
forefinger to face him.

"You knew what?"

"I knew you liked me. I felt it right down my spine."

"How?"

"Like a tickle," he said, turning me over on my side so
that we faced each other and he was still inside me. Then he
ran his finger down my spine.

"Tickle," he said again. My body floated out of control.

"That's not what I meant," I said. "I didn't think I could
feel like this."

He rubbed his fingers across my forehead as though he
could feel what was going on inside my head, and then he
looked at my eyes warily.

"You know, anybody else, I'd figure they were bull-
shitting me," he said. "But I believe you."

"You should."

"I do," he said. "Didn't you know what was going on?"

"What do you mean?"

"Didn't you sense something beforehand?"

"No—well, I don't know." I didn't need to flatter him. It
would be good to see how much of the truth he would toler-
ate from me and how far we could go on it.

I could look at his intense dark eyes as much as I wanted.
After all, he was looking at me. I touched his mouth. I could

touch him now. I felt awed. He kissed my fingers. I ran my palm down his side, stroking the long lines. In clothes, the strength of his torso was concealed. If I were a painter I'd paint a body like his. He had the grace of a boy who had just grown up.

He kissed me hard on the mouth and pulled our bodies apart. He sighed and his lips brushed mine as he spoke. "I feel a little closer to life right now. I'd never die if I could make love forever."

We both looked at the ceiling, until he touched my breasts lightly.

"Now you feel the tickle?" he asked.

I nodded.

"Remember this feeling," he said sternly. "It happens when you make love to me."

"Right," and then I got upset. It was idiotic to be lying here admiring his body. God only knew what he had done with it in the past. Maybe I'd get a Pulitzer for research above and beyond.

"Your breasts," he said, "are so beautiful. They stay the same shape no matter what you do."

I was touched he noticed. Nobody else ever had but me. Then he disappeared.

When he came back, he pulled me by both hands into the bathroom. The tub was sunken, overflowing with pink bubbles. A window opened to palm trunks and dark sky. Steam smelling of jasmine bath salts blended with fresh air.

"I'll inhale until I float away." I said. I stood on my toes and stretched my arms high, yawning. It was hard to stay upset when Mark was trying so hard to please me.

He bowed low. Rituals and elegant details had kept his life going before. They would work for him again.

"Hey, get in," he said.

"It's hot." I held his hand and dropped into the tub, sending a wave of pink bubbles onto the marble floor. I lay back and he soaped me with a huge sponge. He moved his other hand slowly over my skin.

Afterward he dried me with an enormous towel as though I was a child, and spread me out on the bed, kissed me, and opened a new box of bath powder. He hit me with a big puff, raising perfumed clouds.

He sprawled down on me, his mouth near my ear. "The night after it happened, a buddy of Sal's came up the hill, saying, 'You shouldn't be alone. I'll spend the night in your guest room.' But I couldn't sleep. I kept thinking, suppose it was him. He could've murdered Sal. And at the funeral too. I'd look around me and say to myself it could be anybody, anybody in this room."

An hour later, I woke up. I didn't know where I was until he began kissing my mouth in small brushes with his lips. I touched his face in the dark. I would take any excuse to touch him.

"What's going on?" he asked.

"I been through a lot today," I said uncertainly.

He began to talk through a yawn. "Lookit, we are safe up here in the clouds. This is the highest damn house in all of Laurel Canyon."

He was tired, and talking slow, with more of the South in his voice.

"Why are we safe?" I didn't point out that his home had been broken into twice.

"When I first planned this house, Sal kept on laughing at me for drawing blueprints, but I broke a path uphill, and shoveled out dead roots as thick as your leg. I cracked two axes. I put on a pair of big gloves and transplanted a hundred-year-old prickly pear. That cactus blooms every night."

"You sound like a pioneer," I said.

"It was back when we were all doing that number about working on the soil," he said. "I moved in here, proud of my hacienda and my poor excuse of a path. Sal said I was Greta Garbo, wanting to be all alone up here. But I told him no, I was living in an aerie—that's an eagle's nest."

"I know," I said.

He was still telling his tale. It was a nice change. In New York people talk facts and ideas. I read somewhere that Southerners tell stories.

"But one spring the earth was damp and soft and Sal and

me cut steps in the path and laid bricks between the rocks. We got blisters and sores on our palms.

"But then, two nights later, Sal tripped about a hundred feet from my door, and fell six feet before he grabbed onto the trunk of an old date-palm tree. And a week later I heard this scream. It was the wrong key, and it kept going."

"Not Sal?" I asked.

"Nope."

"A burglar?"

"Worse," Mark said. "I quick walked up and down that path for one whole hour. It was a poor skinny dog huddled under a rock. I figured she must've fell down off the path some fifty feet."

"Did you get her?"

"No. I got cops up here. They said she was a coyote and she had broke two legs, and she had a house cat in her mouth. One cop raised his gun and shot her dead.

"The whole thing made me sick to my stomach, and I took it as a warning. So I got some engineer to design me this modern cable car. It's an elevator."

"And that path, it's still there?"

"No. I tore the path away, and now nobody climbs up my cliff, and nobody climbs down. You can dive backward from my swimming pool three hundred feet and land on Wonderland Avenue, but that's the only way down without the elevator."

We were both quiet for a while. My fear wouldn't go away. "What about people who break in?"

"Well, they didn't really break in."

"What?" I was shocked.

"There's one weak point in the whole system," he said. "Me. If I forget to lock the elevator, it's no damn good. Like tonight, I left it wide open."

I interrupted him. "How do you know we're safe now?"

"Because I locked the elevator and the front door once I saw the mess, remember?"

"No."

"Too much going on?"

"Mark, could I just go out and make sure?"

"I'll go right now. Just call it Southern comfort," he said, and jumped out of bed.

When he returned, I almost asked him to come back to the Chateau with me.

"All safe," and he leapt up on the bed, one foot on either side of me.

"You look like a statue," I said.

" 'You can fuck a statue, but you can't have children,' " he recited.

"Is that your line?"

"Allen Ginsberg wrote that. Dylan's always horsing around with his lyrics. It'd be great to write songs like his poems." He fell adroitly next to me on the bed. "I'm happy you're here," he said. "I'm playing make-believe."

"About what?"

"I'm making believe that we're living in the best of all possible worlds. What a joke. Probably on me."

He pulled an edge of the sheet up over his body and his head.

"It must be pretty up here," I said, patting his arm under the sheet. "Tomorrow I'd like to look around."

I tugged a corner of the sheet away from his face. "What are you thinking about?"

"Living too dangerously," he said slowly.

"Like Sal Mineo?"

"I don't know. I don't know," he said. His voice was tired. "I feel like a planet that was taking the same path around the same sun for a thousand years. Then last week somebody up and hit me hard from behind and now I'm spinning all over the solar system."

"I'm here," I said. But I was jolted. I didn't know what he was really saying about Sal and his old life.

"Look," he said. "I'm lucky you're here. But you're strangest of all."

"I am?" I was shameless, begging attention like that. I wanted to ask him if he'd been with a woman before. The crazy part was how little it bothered me.

"Yeah, but that ain't all bad," he joked. "I mean, you

didn't do anything perverted, sick, or weird, did you, now?''

"That's not the best way to describe it," I said, "in negatives."

"I love your body," he said quietly.

"And?" I asked tartly.

He grabbed me and tickled me under my arms. I couldn't stop laughing.

" 'And, and,' " he mimicked me.

I extended my curved wrist. He lowered his head, kissing my hand, and then pulled me back to him, and we were pressing each other from head to feet, as though we were trying to occupy the same space with our bodies.

Chapter
Eleven

At dawn, I rolled over to Mark. But the bed was empty and I lay there feeling afraid. Pictures overlapped across my mind. Unnatural pictures. The orange paint on Mineo's corpse at the funeral, the wild, dark woman banging my car in Watts, then Mark raging through his house. That last picture stuck. I scanned the bedroom. The curtains had been torn off the rods, and sunlight poured inside through gashes in the shades. Small bits of wool poked through a hole in the bare mattress. Today my fear had to do with Mark. If I felt close to him, the murderer was close to me.

The condom was gone. Above me there were three red smears across the headboard. Since the streaks hadn't turned brown, I knew the condom hadn't contained blood—just red paint. After all, I was waking up in Hollywood, where people get awards for inventing illusions. But I shuddered involuntarily, grabbed a sweatshirt from the floor, and held its nubby softness against my bare body.

Yawning, I opened the glass door to the balcony and squinted into the bright blue sky. I felt an odd elation.

The deck was swept bare, except for one sinewy brown vine that had forced itself through the floorboards and crawled up the rough plaster walls of the house. Below me in the hills I counted different shades of green leaves; blue fir, chartreuse palms, and gray eucalyptus.

The wood floor was hot. It drove me inside.

Mark had left a note for me on the bathroom mirror. I read:

Ladybug,
By the time you open your gray eyes, I'll be walking down the mountain. I got to think. I left blueberries on the kitchen table. Soak in the hot tub, and play, don't worry. I locked the elevator. I'll bang the car horn three times so you'll know it's me. It's a boss B-flat horn. Nothing makes sense today except you.

XX Mark
P.S. This note gives you permission to open drawers and closets.

I smiled. He knew me already. I'm addicted to other people's secrets. I'm a snoop. My editor says it comes with the profession. But I go overboard.

In the kitchen, I scooped a handful of blueberries from a copper bowl. They spurted sweet between my teeth. The blue flowers of morning-glory vines stretched past the small window above the sink. Inside the wood breadbox, I found cartons of weird herbal teas. I opened the refrigerator. Unpasteurized milk, vitamin pills, and some brown liquid labeled SECRET SOUP STOCK were the sole contents.

In the trash can, an ant crawled under empty vodka bottles and the remains of marijuana cigarettes. I managed to boil some water in a pan and make coffee.

The kitchen floor was slate gray, and cool on my feet. At first, I didn't look down at my naked body. But I did feel different. It's the way I get on a solitary vacation, where no one knows me. I wondered if it was him or Los Angeles that made me feel like a perfect stranger.

I walked outside on a white gravel lane past skinny bamboo trunks, bougainvillea, and swaying palm trees. Believe me, I don't usually stroll around naked. Then I stepped on hot brown tile steps past huge Mexican pots overflowering with cactus and succulents. The steps curved around and down onto a large plateau carved out of the mountain. I walked under a wood arbor overrun with lilac blossoms.

Under a willow tree, the hot tub was steaming. Made of redwood planks. Hot tub. A California joke-object. Instantly I pictured cartoon people splashing in it. Above the tub, the willow leaves blew. A white towel hung from one branch.

I dipped my palm in the hot water. It was hot. Jets splashed deep inside the tub. As I lifted a bare leg to climb inside, a bird with a white wing shrieked at me and then took possession of one willow branch above my head.

I lowered my body into the hot steaming water until I felt a soothing tingle of heat up to my shoulders. I sighed a few times. It was a shock of sensations. I was in a dream. The bird shrieked at me again. He did not know that I was immobilized by sensuality and torpor and wouldn't bother him. I shifted my hips in front of one jet and watched air bubbles form on my skin, while I felt water hurling itself against my back.

I tried to remember a time when I had paused, alone, to see myself naked like this, outdoors, surrounded by birds and trees and flowers. To see my body in the sunlight was to see the work ethic die.

It was a perfect day, buoyant as a butterfly.

Despite the steam rising from the tub, I did not sweat. The dry winds took care of that.

I broke a eucalyptus leaf and smelled the fresh camphor of the resin. I closed my eyes and breathed the steam of the tub.

Then I heard a car below on the road. It stopped, and I waited to hear horn blasts that would announce Mark's return. Instead, a door slammed. The outdoor elevator whirred, its gate clicked, and the motor growled as it started to climb up the hill. Something was wrong. He'd forgotten to lock it again.

I began to panic. I realized I was caught here, unarmed white flesh in a shallow pit of bubbling water. My face was sweating now from fear. I was in danger.

With a thump, the elevator motor stalled, and started

again. It rode up the hill, closer and closer. I would bluff. I would be cool, extremely nearsighted, and a little jerky.

When the gate slammed at the top of the hill, I called out, "Hey, I'm out back."

Nobody answered. I heard the front door slam. They were inside the house. I kept quiet. Then I heard the back door slam. Footsteps crunched the gravel path, and then I pictured the intruder on the cement steps, under the lilac arbor, and walking across the lawn to the hot tub.

"Yeah, in the back," I gurgled, dumping my head in the water, covering my face with wet hair.

"Oh, hey, listen," I said. "You better give me a hand. I can't find my glasses. Took 'em off to clean the pool. Then my big feet kicked 'em around someplace. Whew, that's dumb, hey? I can't see good enough to find them. They got red frames."

Still, the place was silent. But somebody was listening. Somebody dangerous was judging my performance.

"I swear I used your wet mop, your Hoover vacuum cleaner, and your garbage disposal," I said. "I only been in this tub for five minutes. The agency said I'd clean your house in five hours and I will or you can keep the twenty-five dollars."

I don't know where I found reserves of energy to keep on. I was trying to sound like IQ zero. But the words wouldn't come out of my mouth. Instead, my throat closed up. I had played all my cards too fast. I surprised myself. I started to cry.

Then a figure stepped out to one side, pulling off huge sunglasses. Like me, he was posing. He closed his eyes against the sun and the sight of me. He was the essence of disdain. I was so surprised that I forgot I was naked. I stood up in the hot tub, and then, with a rush of shame, I crouched down again. Water flooded over the edge. I bent my knees to get my breasts under the water level.

He laughed at my clumsy efforts at modesty. It was Chris Franklin, Sal Mineo's English lover. It seemed like a hundred years ago that I'd seen him at the funeral.

"Didn't know Mark had hired a blind maid," he said. He

sounded extravagantly English, cool and supercilious. It was a voice that told you it was hot stuff.

I was furious. He looked better than he had at the funeral. Physically, he was a knockout. His silver-blond hair was disheveled and his green undershirt torn. Somehow his blue eyes and sullen mouth looked very James Dean.

"Just how did you get up here?" I said.

"Me?"

"I thought the elevator was locked."

"I, love, am a proper guest." He held up a key.

"Well, you're new to me," I said, trying to match his disdain.

"Well, if you last, love, at whatever your duties, then maybe the master of the house will give you a key as well."

I was tired of crouching. My face must have looked numb.

He spoke without smiling. "I'll turn my back, and you can step out. I don't fancy watching you."

I reached up for the white towel hanging on the willow tree. Then I heard the sound of Mark's horn from below.

Chris caught my eye and held it. He was adroit at creating drama. Too adroit. We stared at each other the whole time the elevator motor labored down and up the hill.

Still staring, he walked past me toward the turquoise pool, reached down, and turned a round handle in a patch of English ivy. Music poured from the earth, rising from behind him. It was an old black man singing "I Got A Woman," an early Elvis Presley song. But hearing this guy made me realize Elvis sang it too fast. This old man was singing Memphis blues in a sly voice, tired and easy.

Chris's eyes stayed on me, saying this was his territory and he knew every trick.

When Mark loped into the garden, he whistled at the sight of us. I noticed the two of them were dressed alike. They wore faded T-shirts tucked into old jeans, and silver cowboy buckles on their belts. They trimmed their sideburns the same way, high and boyish.

Mark nodded to the music. He walked over to the ivy and

turned the handle. The sound went way down, and, with his back to me, he faced down past the pool to the city and began scat-singing. His voice leapt above and below the old black man's. When the old man began to sing against the melody, Mark did the tune. It was lovely and natural, like a choirboy singing a solo hymn.

Then the music stopped. I said, "Didn't you say nobody else could get up here?"

"Sorry," Mark said. "I forget he's got a key."

"How quickly you forget," Chris said. "She's a girl, darling. What's going on?"

I felt exposed, and a thrill of fear went through me.

Mark said, "Why don't the gents retire for some cigars while the lady steps out of her bath?"

It sounded as if he were protecting me. I liked that.

They turned toward the house, ignoring me completely. I started to lift myself out of the hot tub. I was listening intently. Chris whispered something.

"I don't reckon I know anybody by that name," Mark said.

"Oh, he's seen you on the bar scene," Chris said.

Mark laughed. "A lot of folks on the bar scene. Maybe I know them. Maybe I don't."

Chris tried once more. "Jonathan Simpson's his full name and he knew Sal."

Mark said, "A whole mess of weird folks are going to start saying they knew Sal."

I wanted to see what Mark's face looked like when he was lying.

Chris laughed sourly. "The police seem to fancy the whole lot of us as suspects." They were standing ten feet or so from me in a bamboo grove.

"But they haven't mentioned a lie detector test and your alibi?" Chris asked.

"No, I got my manager to call some lawyer. I'll tell him about you too."

"Actually, they tried to book me last night."

"They got laws against mourning in peace?" Mark said.

"Bloody hell," Chris said.

The next few minutes passed slowly. I got out of the tub, wrapping the towel around myself. My knees were shaking under the weight of my body.

"Her name's Sara," Mark said abruptly. "You two meet?"

Chris shot a glance at Mark and then knelt down to tie one of his sneakers. "It's pushing it, isn't it, to force me to chat it up in your garden with a naked member of the distaff side?"

I tried to think of something cutting, but the fight was between them.

Mark said, "I'm going to ask you to say howdy to her one more time, and that's it."

Chris folded his arms against his chest. "Good show."

Mark didn't turn around.

Chris put both hands on his hips. "What would Sal say?" His voice was mocking. "I mean, his favorite prince in all the world, Mark Loren?"

"Sal loved both of us," Mark said quietly, not moving.

"We know Sal loved what he couldn't have."

"It wasn't like that."

Chris's voice was full of anger. "It's easy for you to sit back while everybody admires you, and you can tell yourself you're not hustling your sweet ass. 'Oh, Mark's just in it for the refinement and the fucking beauty.' "

He raised a fist, as though he wanted to punch Mark's face.

Mark turned toward him, pouting. He seemed almost flattered by the outburst. That made me angry. "Don't try to make everything ugly," he said. "I make my own moves on my own time."

"Mark," I called out, "is this part of the package?"

"What package?" he said, raising his eyebrows at Chris.

"What you were saying about pleasure and loving beauty," I said.

"What do you think?" he said, looking meaningfully at Chris.

"I think it's a catfight," I said.

Chris snapped. "Oh, oh, I see now. You're throwing

your lot in with that." He nodded his head at me. His voice was at a fevered pitch. "I'm sure the guys at the bar are going to be heartbroken to hear you're retiring your princely ass. No more admiring looks for Prince Mark, no more hustling. Just the little woman."

Mark said slowly, "Don't take it out on me."

"That's not what we're talking about." Chris's mouth made a smirk.

I wondered why Mark didn't throw Chris out, or at least mention the possibility of punching him in the mouth. But he didn't.

"He's dead," Mark said abruptly. "Quarreling won't bring him back to life."

"It stinks," Chris said.

Mark took a step over to Chris and put an arm around him. "I hear you," Mark said. "Remember that hymn about the whispering of the trees?" He waved one hand disparagingly around him. "That hymn about how nature proves God is love and all? Well, today it don't and He isn't and that's a fact."

"Today you're sour on religion?" Chris asked.

"They say death is the reason for religion," Mark said. "It's always things you can't control that kill you."

"Mark, I must see you alone," Chris interrupted. "Don't make me beg."

"Mark, can I say something?" I said.

"Sara, I'll be right back."

Chris and Mark strolled away in step, their eyes down, their elbows still against their sides. They disappeared up the flagstone path without saying another word to me.

I leaned against the willow tree. I was pink. My body'd been cooking too long. I was pretty like a baby after a bath, soft and weak. And I was angry. I'd stumbled into somebody's life and I was on dangerous ground.

Then Mark came running down the lawn. At least their private moment had been brief. He was in a different mood. He pulled his shirt over his head. "Last one in the pool buys me a hot meal, a drink, and another pool," he yelled.

In the daylight, his skin was taut, poreless. I saw that he

was brown except for pale shadows under his eyes, between his fingers, and in his armpits. His nipples were the same brown color. I forced myself to stop looking at him.

"I'm leaving," I said. "Got work to do."

"You were in that tub too long," he said. "Let's swim."

"But what about the guys at the bar?"

He lowered his arms. "Sara, I'm sorry you heard that. My friend is bereft. I'm apologizing for him and for me."

"What about hustling at that bar?" I repeated.

"It's not like that. They like me." He shrugged.

"What about me?"

"You treat me good, and"—he hesitated—"I like you." A look of surprise flashed across his face.

"I don't feel like swimming," I said.

He knelt and turned the music on again. "You need to get the blood moving, and then, I promise, you'll feel better. You'll love it." From somewhere in the ground, his voice came up, pure and melodious. I recognized a hint of the blues the old man had been singing. He learned well.

"I don't feel like playing."

"Life is short," he said. "Trust me."

At the edge of the pool, he kicked off his dungarees, thrust his arm high above his head, and sang out, "Lord, keep me from sinking like a stone." He grinned for my benefit, jumped high up in the air, arched his body down, touched his feet, and disappeared underwater.

I had never seen anybody do anything so graceful.

I dangled a foot in the pool while I watched him glide past me underwater. He looked like a marine creature with the water rippling off his bare body. He surfaced near me, snorting.

"Hurry, hurry," he shouted over the music. "Jump." He put a cold hand on my ankle. Ordinarily I take my time. I wade into lakes and pools. I kicked at the cold water, held my breath, and jumped feet first.

The underwater speakers shocked me. My body seemed to absorb the vibrations of his guitar and his voice through my pores. Waves of sound bounced off the tile walls and floor of the pool, like in an echo chamber. When I came up I heard him singing in the air.

I felt high. The music was all around me, and inside me, and making me stretch and swim clean and hard. I let myself be carried along by it. There was no real purpose, no product to all of this, except that it was fun. The water kept surprising me, tingling my breasts, my thighs, and all the parts of my body that are usually covered by a bathing suit.

Whenever my face broke the surface, I felt the heat of the sun, and the fresh winds, and the smell of the camellias, and then I was back inside the cool, dappled darkness being touched all over by the wet and the movement of the water and the music.

We were two naked bodies, gliding past each other, sometimes flesh showing at the surface, splashing, shouting, playing, singing lines of his songs, turning on our faces, turning on our backs, to the sound of his tunes.

There is a way in which strobe lights transform the most inept of dancers at a discotheque into split-second pictures in graceful poses. The two of us had the grace of dancers. I felt beautiful.

At the shallow end, he grabbed my hand above the turquoise water and then I waved goodbye and kicked down and swam along the bottom of the pool to the other side.

When the record ended, we both climbed out of the pool. We flopped down on dark green ivy, sunning ourselves.

"I was lying before," he said.

"When?"

"Before, when Chris was here. I love flowers and trees, and I want to believe nature and life have an order," he said.

"Pantheism?" I asked, spellbound.

"I don't call it anything special."

A few minutes later, I stood up and rubbed myself with the towel. It was as much out of habit as anything; I was already dry. Mark surprised me by throwing himself into the towel and my arms, so that I wrapped it around him and we laughed and fell over in the towel together. We untangled, and several minutes passed while we sunned ourselves, and then I said, "I don't understand Chris."

"What do you mean?"

I didn't know where to begin. "Does he work?"

"He's an actor, classical training at Cambridge. Sal flipped when he saw him do *Hamlet* in London. He's done Broadway, arty stuff with Joe Papp, porn flicks; he was the voice of a zebra on a Beech Nut commercial."

"Is he good?"

"Depends on his mood," Mark said. He lay back supporting himself on his elbows and squinted against the sun. "But you mean acting, right?" He snorted. "Sal loved his work. Of course Sal would've bought him the *Queen Mary* to keep him happy."

I wondered how dangerous it was to make Chris unhappy.

"What work are you planning to do today?" he asked suddenly.

"I'm driving out to see Kate Lyons. Why do you think she saw Sal Mineo?"

"We don't know if they ever had that meeting," he said. "No."

Then he said, "But you'll figure it out, won't you, baby?" There was a cold tone to his voice. It sounded as if he wasn't sure he wanted this stuff figured out.

"Why do you think he wanted to see her?" I asked.

"Sal was worried about this rock movie that she wants to get me for."

"You?"

"She wants me to play the lead and write the score," he said.

"What's your part?"

"Some burned-out musician who gets tired of life on the road and hires a double to do his act, then the double gets knifed in front of a live audience. Sal didn't like the plot. He was afraid it might make me a live target."

"But he never told her?"

He watched me for a second before he said, "Well, maybe that explains her message on the service."

"What's she like?"

"Only thing I know is she's rich," he said. "Oh, people talk about the star system, but money makes movies."

"Why did you lie to Chris about Jonathan?" I asked.

Instead of answering, he said, "Don't tell anybody you saw Chris here today."

"Why not?"

He pulled the towel over his body. "Tough-girl reporter."

"That's why I'm here. I'm not some mermaid," I said.

"I ain't either, but I don't owe you. I'm not proud of everything I learned out here. But just because somebody's smart enough to hit you with good questions don't mean you owe them the answers. That's what Sal always said."

He picked his head up and watched my face falling apart. Then he said to me in an almost impressed tone, "You mad?"

I stood up, naked, and grabbed for the towel. "I have work to do." I had to control myself. People often refuse to answer reporters' questions. I shouldn't whine and run away.

He stood up, pulled my towel over my shoulders, and smoothed it there. "Coffee and homemade orange juice?" he asked, bumping his nose on mine. "Don't go away unless you have to, and don't do it mad."

Chapter
Twelve

Sunset Boulevard is a canyon road. In another era, water must have spilled here from the hills and made a river flowing into the sunset and the ocean.

Sitting at a red light, I noticed other cars flashing their turn signals. I looked up. I had arrived at the sea. The sun was shrouded by a cloud. The ocean was gray, with waves that crested like icing near the shoreline. A green sign read "Pacific Ocean," as if there could be any mistaking it. The water smelled fresh, not pungent like the Atlantic.

Driving toward Malibu made me lightheaded. The winds whipped sand across the highway, beige snakes wiggling over the black road. Somebody—Sal Mineo—said there's no smog down here. I was driving between a wild desert area on my right and a row of beach houses facing the ocean with their backs to me on my left.

I was high. It was new, and I'd gotten here on my own steam.

I slowed down to see the addresses on silver mailboxes that looked straight out of suburbia. But soon they were hidden behind fences, wild grasses, and flowering hedges. The houses became bigger, farther from one another, and drenched by growing things.

I passed LYONS painted on a white fence swarming with sunflower vines. I braked on the shoulder.

I turned the Dodge toward the lane, while other cars whizzed by. The beach house was set back from a road. A field of yellow mustard flowers bordered by a green hedge ran down to the house. Black and Mexican men bent over the hedge with pruning shears.

I parked behind a silver Rolls Royce in front of the long, low redwood house, nestled in gardens of yellow tulips, pink daisies, and orange poppies. Somebody here had a green thumb. The building took possession of the coast like a motel on a tropical island, reflecting a bright and gray light from the sea.

I had to get inside this house. It was the last place Sal Mineo was seen alive, and I wanted to ask Kate Lyons about the message she'd left him. These people's lives might be tangled in ways that could take years to understand.

The wind whipped my hair while I climbed the polished black marble steps. A black maid opened the door. She was wearing a black chiffon dress under a white apron, and she was almost six feet tall. With her round face, breasts, and hips, she resembled a Gauguin painting. A gardenia bloomed in her black hair.

"Yes?" Her voice was soft, modulated.

"I'm a reporter with an appointment."

She nodded. "Come in. Mrs. Lyons wants to see your press card."

This rarely happens on routine assignments. It's not a friendly sign. I flipped open my wallet and handed her the card.

The entire front wall of the living room had been torn out and replaced with glass. I walked over and stared at an endless horizon and sky. The room was filled with pink and white furniture. In fact, it looked like a boudoir, down to the huge pink daisies from her garden that filled the antique silver vases. It occurred to me that it had been created to appear in a magazine.

The maid raised her long fingers and indicated a white wicker loveseat, with dainty white linen pillows. I sat down on the edge of the sofa, and she left for a moment. She returned carrying a tray of Georgian sterling tea service. I was sure the teapot, sugar, and creamer were polished daily. On a small silver dish were four hot chocolate-chip cookies.

"Mrs. Lyons loves to bake cookies," she said, bending one knee and holding the tray while I poured some tea and ate a cookie.

I sat on the edge of the wicker sofa, sipping the tea.

When she left, I popped another cookie into my mouth. I touched the old pink and white American quilt on the wall. I picked up a photograph of a baby in a heavy silver frame.

The room was too ordered. It was hard to imagine the fertile chaos of a baby. It made me uncomfortable. I don't think I was reacting to the money, but nobody's perfect.

I dropped the silver frame when the maid announced, "Mrs. Lyons will see you after her daughter's swimming lesson."

I sat down again on the tiny sofa and watched the room change color when the clouds moved away from the sun. The light bounced off the water into this pink and white space.

Somebody slid open the glass doors facing the beach and came in. She was about five feet tall. "Welcome to the end of America," she said, extending a small hand and my press card.

Her voice was nasal and flat, and she was wearing a floor-length white velvet bathrobe, open to show a skinny body under a skimpy black bikini. The bathing suit was more gold chains than fabric. There were lines around her mouth. She was dieting too hard to keep her body thin; it made her face look drawn and old. She gave the last chocolate-chip cookie a furtive look as she gripped my hand. "Your series on women and porn was something," she said. She talked like a New Yorker, fast.

I dropped her hand, pleased that she recognized my name. She must have read my stuff in the *Post* about real-estate owners and feminists banding together to get rid of porn theaters.

"Beautiful poppy garden," I said, returning the compliment.

"I love tending flowers," she said. "I only have two men helping me out."

A blond-haired child about two years old followed her, clutching a small handful of her white velvet robe. Kate sat down on a small white wicker rocking chair, and tucked her bare feet under herself. The child climbed up into her lap and closed her eyes.

Kate smoothed the baby's hair and rocked her as we talked. "Your first trip out here?" she asked.

"Yes."

"You have big eyes like a tourist," she said. Her eyes were blank.

"Your daughter is great," I said.

"Nothing pleases me so much," she said, and her voice broke. "I love her so."

I listened with one ear, waiting to work the conversation around to Sal Mineo. Her mouth was stretched into a smile, but her eyes gave nothing away.

She was saying, "Motherhood is the answer to life. Look, we've all lost our way. We don't want to grow up. What's the answer, a big house? A husband forever? Money? Fame? Freedom? Each answer is a trap. The sixties didn't work. I did the picket lines at Columbia. But things are still happening in California. There's hope out here."

I didn't agree with her. "How are you Californians different?"

"We haven't given up. We didn't roll over and accept mediocre lives in Ourtown, U.S.A. We want more. We went west. Out here we're still looking. We make the fads, the trends that sweep the country. For me, the answer is motherhood. I belong to a group called MOM. Dedicated to getting women into the maternity scene."

Sometimes disagreement works in interviews. "You have tans, motherhood, self-help, and exercise groups. What's new about that?"

She pressed a brass button on the floor with her bare toe.

The black maid appeared and took the sleeping baby from her lap.

"How long you going to be out here? We can talk later. I got a screening now."

So today's interview was over. She'd presented *House Beautiful* and *Good Housekeeping* to the reporter.

"A week or so," I said, watching her open a huge address book covered in white leather. Her name was written in gold on the front.

"Where you staying?"

"The Chateau. When can we talk again?"

"I'm having a party tomorrow night," she said, writing my name with a gold pencil. "You come. You'll look. You're wrong. It's a different place. The problems we got out here are typical for paradise. It's different. It's about after dreams come true."

Instead of asking her about dreams that come true, I hit my forehead with my palm.

"You're, you're . . ."

"Yes?" She preened, running her fingers through her short damp hair like a bird, feather by feather.

"I know you from before." It was all that sex last night. I'd probably lost six IQ points. I was dazed.

"Yes, dear." She closed her eyes and smiled. I noted that she had very small teeth.

"You're from New York," I said, sitting forward.

She ran her fingers through her hair again, and I saw that her nails were bitten down. She stretched, and yawned slightly. "Honey, it shouldn't have taken you so long. I didn't get where I am today by forgetting—how can I put it—people like me."

I blinked. *"Women's Wear Daily,"* I said, sitting back.

"Six fucking years," she said, and twisted her mouth like she had just tasted soap. "I made more money taking one pissing meeting yesterday than I made breaking ass for six years at *Women's Wear.* "

Then I remembered her. Under the byline K. R. Lyons, this woman'd made incredible controversy as an entertainment reporter. She covered domestic lingerie and show business for *Women's Wear,* the trade newspaper for the clothing business. For years she was that paper's star.

It was rumored that she invented the term "BP," beautiful people, for celebrities. Everybody in the news business said that back in the first hectic days of *New York* magazine, Clay Felker got some of his best feature ideas from her *Women's Wear* pieces.

It was also said that she made Jackie Kennedy Onassis into legend. For years Lyons paid salesgirls to call in Mrs. Kennedy's purchases and boutique haunts. Since the former first lady was the country's primary clothing consumer, the newspaper of the retail and wholesale garment business made mythology of her buying habits.

I had only seen K. R. Lyons once, at an ERA fund-raising party. I never forgot her moves. At any point, she was always in animated conversation with one of the most famous people in that room, smiling, and looking as though she was honoring them with her attention. After years of watching her small dark head bobbing next to the celebrity of the hour, people stopped calling her a cheap hustler. She became a beacon. She always knew the latest chic restaurateur, dungaree designer, or hot actor. So it seemed perfect to find her in Hollywood where stakes are bigger.

"What's the most interesting thing you remember about me!" She almost batted her eyelashes.

What I remembered was how she broke one of the major rules of journalism.

"It was that story you wrote about the governor," I said.

One night at Elaine's restaurant, a distinguished governor told her how he'd been seduced by a fading Hollywood star. She put down her pencil when he told her she couldn't use the story. It was "off the record."

" 'Off the record' is a big deal in daily journalism," I said.

She smiled without pleasure. "A stupid gentleman's agreement."

I didn't agree. I telephone and telephone people to confirm facts I get off the record without mentioning anything I'm told by my original source.

I'll never forget *Women's Wear's* banner headlines over her story about the governor's dalliance, along with a graphic description of his pinching technique. Lyons's piece was accompanied by a photograph of the governor whispering in her ear at Elaine's. She was smiling directly at the camera.

She was reviled and didn't mind admitting that she never told her editor about her promises to keep things off the record. She was written up in the *New York Times* and quoted on her love of expensive jewels, famous people, and the right of journalists to print anything.

"It was my farewell move," she said. "I decided that 'off the record' impeded the process of getting news to the public. Do you agree?"

"Well, the best stuff is often what people don't want other people to know about them, but—"

She interrupted me. "A do-good lawyer from the ACLU defended me and talked up the First Amendment."

I remembered hearing how she'd stood on a chair at Elaine's to read aloud the *Columbia Journalism Review* article praising her courageous stand in favor of the First Amendment.

"I won every fight on that case," she said. "Don't bet against me."

I never heard any woman talk with this kind of swagger. "Are you still indestructible?"

"Don't you ever read the trades?" she snapped. She began nibbling at one fingernail. It was either nerves or plain hunger. "I made a hundred million before I hit thirty."

"But money doesn't buy indestructibility."

"I haven't come across anything better," she said.

I was about to open my mouth and remind her about the power of motherhood. She cuddled a pink telephone on her shoulder, dialed, and made urgent sounds of dissent. "Absolutely not," she repeated. A man dressed in bathing trunks and a T-shirt entered between sliding glass doors. He sat down on the white rug at her feet, widened his hazel eyes, and stared at me with the assurance of someone who was convinced that he was wonderful to behold.

I had a hunch his character'd been ruined because people told him he looked like the young Robert Redford. He had a strong jawline. His fine hair was bleached in front by the sun. His hair, eyebrows, and eyes were the same gold color. The effect was heightened by a small stubble of beard.

After a moment, he threw back his head and laughed soundlessly. Probably at my discomfort. Then he turned away to stare intensely out the glass doors. He'd been practicing on me. Nothing personal.

I tried to make sense of the phone conversation. She saw me looking at her and said, "I'm taking this in the master bedroom."

He waved one hand languidly at me. "I'm not her husband."

Boy, conversations didn't exactly flow drawing-room style out here. She held her bathrobe up like a train and ran out of the living room. He sat in her chair, staring at me again. He didn't replace the telephone receiver. We both heard the babble of angry voices coming from the instrument.

"That's the husband," he said to me, inclining his gold head toward the telephone. "You're the girl reporter from New York."

"How do you know?"

"I was looking through your clippings all morning," he said.

"Where?"

"At the morgue, the *L.A. Times* morgue."

I was annoyed that Kate Lyons had flattered me so easily.

"You ever do television commercials?" I asked.

"Aftershave lotion," he said. "Guess which one."

"Any of them," I said.

He stiffened. "Watch it, darling."

"Well, what are you so angry about?" I was trying to imitate his tone of idle curiosity. I failed. I'm the earnest type.

"Nothing, babe. I got my place in the sun." He pointed his thumb back at the door Kate had exited through. "She's producing this idea of mine. An original screenplay."

"Oh, really?" He sure didn't look like a writer.

"Yeah, *Rock Star.*"

"Sounds familiar," I said. "What's it about?"

"This big rock star. He sits in the audience and sings along with his double."

A version of the script Mark had told me about.

"Great." I didn't feel bad about lying.

I was about to ask him about Mark when Kate came back into the living room. Her eyes narrowed. "Up," she said to him, and they both laughed like it was a joke. He stood quickly at her side, almost at attention. Then she sat and tucked her feet under herself again, whispering behind her hand, "It scares me how much he loves me."

I wouldn't have been surprised if the next sentence had been delivered in baby talk.

"Tell her, tell her how we met and how much you love me." She hit him playfully on the leg.

"I love her a lot," he said. He was looking out at the ocean. "I came here with a net and a truck one day to clean the junk out of the swimming pool, and I stayed for—well, dinner."

"A pool cleaner." Kate laughed. "Everybody out here is really somebody else."

She stopped smiling. "Can I help you with anything else?"

"Well, about Sal Mineo—"

She interrupted. "He was somebody else too. He was a kid star who disappeared from the screen. He was dead in this town for fifteen years before some local faggot took a knife to him. He couldn't act. He was nowhere. Who cares about those kinky faggot plays? He was a big nothing. He owed money in this town."

"He was a star," I said.

"He was a joke," she snapped. "Didn't you hear the old Nichols and May record where somebody says Sal Mineo will play Ernest Hemingway in a play about Gertrude Stein? And that was the fifties, for Chrissake. His image was bent."

"So you didn't know him that well?"

"Who'd want to know him?"

I stared her in the face. "Well, there was a message from you on his answering service."

Her boyfriend, whose name she hadn't told me, laughed. "She's not that hard up."

"Shut up," she said.

"What about the message?" I asked again.

"What'd it say?"

I couldn't tell if she was stalling. "It said something about meeting at the beach and not at Burbank, and doing it after lunch."

Kate sighed. "Darling, I was calling Mark Loren to break the bad news. They must have shuffled my message into the wrong box. No wonder Mark never got back to me. In this town people return my calls fast."

"What bad news?" I asked.

"Oh, Sal had some lame idea that Mark would be good for a movie I'm developing."

"We're developing," the boyfriend said. "Remember me?"

"As long as I do remember you, we're developing," she said.

"Do you know Mark?" I asked.

"Barely," she said. "He gets me hot."

I shot a glance at her boyfriend. He yawned.

"But he won't translate to the screen. Except for Presley, singers don't. Remember that bomb, *Two-Lane Blacktop?* James Taylor looked like a zombie. It was a mystery how he made little girls cry for him."

"Well, who're you using?" I asked.

"Not Mark Loren," she said.

"He's a good musician," I said.

"There's something wrong with him," she said. I flinched. "Anybody who'd pal around with Sal Mineo has lost it."

She had brought up Sal Mineo voluntarily. So far, he hadn't been her favorite topic of conversation.

"He's got no drive," she continued.

"For what?"

She was rubbing the fingertips of her left hand with her

thumb in the peasant gesture for money. "Success—for success."

"You're tough," I said.

"I'm a businesswoman."

"Well, who will you use?"

"Mick Jagger," she said. "He needs a commercial movie. Those arty things get him nowhere. He's going to be a family man in my film."

"You're the producer?"

"Yes." She sounded impatient.

I've got some of the fan in me. "What's he really like?" I asked.

She turned her wrist around and stared at it as if she were wearing a watch. "I got work to do."

"Doesn't Nicholas Ray live around here?"

"He directed Sal too long ago," Lyons said absently.

"But I want to hear about Sal Mineo and James Dean. That's the only movie they ever did together."

"*Rebel Without a Cause* is old news," she said.

"Where does he live?" I asked again.

"Way down the beach." She pointed a thumb over her shoulder.

"Could you show me his house?"

"You run into Chris Franklin?" she asked as we walked toward the glass wall and the ocean.

"No." I'd promised Mark not to say anything.

We walked out onto a white wood balcony. The sun was so bright I saw red whirls when I blinked. I followed her down about fifty marble steps to the sand. Her bathrobe dragged the black steps.

"You ever meet Chris?" she asked over her shoulder.

"Yes."

"Where?"

"At the funeral."

"How was his mood?"

I stopped ten steps above the sand. The beach below me was deserted except for three white gulls walking on long legs.

"Do you know Chris?"

"Too well," she said shortly.

"You don't like him."

"It's business."

"What business?"

"Mine," she snapped.

I almost sighed. We were down at the sand. Two steps, and my shoes filled up with it. The wind smelled like seaweed. Except for her, it was a calm setting.

I looked her in the face. "When did you hear about the murder?"

"Don't remember."

"Were you here at the party when it happened?"

She twisted her mouth. "No, darling, I was creeping down behind Sal's house holding a dagger in my hand like Lady Macbeth."

Instead of saying goodbye, she spread her bathrobe open and put her hands on her bare hips. "The woman's thing, it's just an excuse for girls diddling girls, right?"

"No." I haven't argued about that stuff for years, but she was exasperating.

"Yes, it's just a way for girls to do it to girls in the least erotic, most boring ways—legislation, meetings, moral theories."

I stifled myself.

She added, "And, darling, I'd bone up on my Hollywood if I were you. Read *Hollywood Babylon* or *Variety* or something. You're all wrong for this story. Too uptight, too prudish."

"I'll get the story." My voice sounded cold, almost bored.

She said hurriedly, "No hard feelings," and squinted toward the horizon. In the sunlight I saw more lines between her eyebrows and around her mouth.

"Just joking around, darling," she said, looking up and down the beach.

"I'll see you tomorrow night," I said. Her head shot up, and she stared at me blankly.

"The party."

She tried to smile. It was partly the lack of flesh on her face, but her mouth looked mean.

"Your friend inside, he's a writer?"

"He's Hollywood born and bred." She laughed. "I mean, he's born in San Diego and he's fighting his way to the top through me. I mean, the motto here is 'Always fuck up.' You always fuck somebody who's more successful than you."

"How can both people fuck up?"

"Don't be so analytic," she said. "Some people do it out of lust or affection. You know that already, I assume."

I nodded like an idiot.

"The ambitious one has to offer something."

"What does he offer you?"

"Guess," she said shortly.

We were both watching a naked little girl run down the beach to the water's edge. She was plump and dimpled, a great spot of pink flesh against the sand.

Kate turned from the child to look at me. "I don't mind you as much as I thought."

"Thanks."

"No, I mean it. You got that New York thing. Out here they come bold, but they're short on curiosity."

"Women, you mean."

"You noticed it?" she asked. "You would."

In fact, she was the only woman besides Annie Harmon I'd met out here.

She added, "I like you because I don't scare you—yet." And then she twisted her mouth.

The little girl screamed and we both turned. She was running at the waves on chubby little legs until they started to flow toward her, then jumping away.

I tore my eyes reluctantly from the child. Kate Lyons was looking the other way down the beach at some houses bunched together. "That's the colony. Nick Ray's staying at a white house. Next to Paul Newman's. It's about fifteen houses down, and it's got Italian designer furniture out front."

I stuck my hand out to the woman. "I'll see you tomorrow night."

She looked confused. For such a smart cookie, there was something funny about the way she kept forgetting.

"Your party."

She tried to finish off our interview with a compliment. "You got one thing," she began.

"That's interesting, Kate," I said in my new cold voice. "What is it?"

"Innocence—it could go over on limited engagement."

"What do you mean?"

"We've popped every pill, fucked the wrong people at the wrong times. We've done it all. We can't go back."

She climbed the stairs to her huge house, and I set out for Nick Ray's bungalow. The heels of my loafers kept sinking into the sand. I stuffed them into my pocketbook.

I gazed out over the ocean to the horizon. The sea was dense and silver like wrinkled tinfoil. It was too bright to look at for long.

I pulled some damp seaweed off the bottom of my foot. I've always liked what Homer called the sea—"the many-voiced roaring." I closed my eyes to hear the surf building hundreds of waves that swelled and crashed down into gentle tides.

My mind went back to Sal Mineo. I suddenly remembered something that happened as a kid. I'd been practicing piano when I heard loud cheering up the street. I ran down to the sidewalk and saw a whole parade of girls carrying a sheet with writing on it: WELGOME HOME SAL MINEO. It was his local fan club, and Sal Mineo was somewhere in that crowd, but I couldn't find him. I felt left out.

Walking along the ocean started me thinking about the last frontier. This was it. Maybe movies were the last American fantasy. Sal Mineo must've had a dream about movies. A fantasy that the screen could make him more than himself, more than human. I wondered if the movie screen was the biggest mirror we'd produced for personal vanity. It was the biggest reflecting pool in the world. Under the shadow of my hand I stared at the sea again. It looked as hard and silvery as a mirror. Small waves washed over my feet on the damp sand, and I turned to look for the little girl. But she'd vanished. The tide had smoothed away my footprints. I remembered that Sal Mineo once lived here in Malibu near the Lyonses, and now he'd vanished without a trace.

Chapter
Thirteen

Sun beat down on the cars in the parking lot of Schwab's Drugstore on Sunset. This was a big afternoon hangout, but I wasn't going to play tourist. I needed a phone to find Nick Ray, and I had to buy some batteries for my miniature tape recorder. Normally I rely on memory and a few notes, but I was starting to feel wary.

I looked at a huge cactus in the flower shop next door and shook sand out of my shoes. I bumped the hot hood of a car with my elbow. At least I wasn't still back at the beach looking for Nick Ray. I'd swallowed my terror and trudged up from the waterline to a white bungalow with Italian furniture. When nobody answered Nick Ray's door, I turned the knob and wandered in, nervous as hell. But I found a message he'd left near the telephone from his office at Burbank Studio.

Half of Schwab's was as empty as a small-town drugstore, filled with sleepy pharmacists and analgesics. The other half was packed with women and men in sunglasses smelling of suntan oil. They were all reading *Daily Variety*.

I walked past two schoolkids licking ice cream cones and thought about the murder. Sal Mineo's world was beginning to take shape for me. I wanted to hunt out Jonathan, that bitter kid from the gay bar who didn't have an alibi. He must hate the idea that Chris came out here to join Sal. I had a million questions for Chris Franklin. I could use my tape recorder to scare him. It'd be my bodyguard. I'd have physical proof if he threatened me.

Also, I wanted my editor to hear some of these flaky and sadistic conversations. Kate Lyons told a quick story about her message on Sal Mineo's answering service. But she claimed she didn't want Mark for the movie, and that wasn't the way he told it. I'd bet that she was lying, but I didn't want to say it in print without her voice on tape.

I'd promised Mark to work on solving the murder. From now on, the tiny Sony recorder would be hidden in my shoulder bag.

Schwab's dining area had a bland smell like warm cardboard. I squeezed onto a stool at the counter next to a woman with tawny skin. She was the color of honey, with sun-dipped hair that resembled Kate Lyons's boyfriend's.

I felt around in my pocketbook for my purse. The guy on my other side dropped his grilled sandwich back on the plate and shook his fingers. "Too hot." I asked him about it. "Tuna melt with cheese," he said.

"The same," I told the counterman, my fingers feeling the edge of a folded paper. I peered into my bag. It was the page Mark'd torn from Sal Mineo's play, *Fortune and Men's Eyes*. What a detective. I'd forgotten it.

The handwriting was uneven and slanted in several directions. Sal Mineo'd written it in pencil. Some of it was illegible, but I started to make it out. It was a message to himself: "I must . . . Christopher, and he has to get it. There are many different ways of . . . We're . . . each other. I must be kind . . . life friends." I folded and unfolded the page. I wished he could tell me more.

I was eating too fast. My tuna melt tasted great. It had a middle-American gourmet quality. Somebody like me decides to get brave, and what do I do? I order a new kind of tuna sandwich.

The note kept going through my mind. ". . . I must be

kind." I had a hunch that Sal was trying to break up with Chris.

After testing the tape recorder batteries, I paid cash for them. It was easier than worrying the woman in the pink uniform with an out-of-state check. But my money supply was running out.

I went to the pay phones in the back and dialed Chris Franklin. He answered the phone after six rings. I licked the tiny rubber suction cup of my phone tape and smacked it onto the receiver.

He sounded rushed and very important. "Darling, you see it's not just me." He intoned like he was speaking in iambic pentameter.

"I mean, really, dear, it's family. When the time comes, and the best—and I mean the best—writer approaches me, I'll tell my story. The only bloody story. I am the only one in the world who knows what he went through. Where were you when Sal was opening his play last year?"

If all an actor needed was a silent audience, this man was a hit.

"I must ask you something," I insisted. "There's this note in his copy of *Fortune and Men's Eyes* about how he's got to tell you some bad news. What was that all about?"

"I must ring off," he said.

"Did it make you mad?"

"Sal never made me angry."

"Well, I heard he had a date with somebody else the last night of his life." I hated myself. This was dirty pool.

"Darling, I haven't time for your vulgar chit-chat."

"I'm going to write my article no matter what you say."

"I must ring off." He sounded distant.

"You should contribute—" The phone went dead.

When Nick Ray answered the telephone at Burbank Projection Room 10, I heard old movie music, upbeat and static.

"I want to hear about discovering Sal Mineo," I said.

"No, no," he said, and paused. He stopped, as though time had literally slowed down his brain. "There's no point."

"Well, it would set the record straight."

"What record?"

"I'm writing the piece whether I talk to you or not," I said. "If we talk, I'll be closer to the truth." This is an argument I often use.

"What is it you want?" he asked after another pause.

"I want to write how you found him."

"It's too painful," he said at last.

I tried a different tack. "What's that in the background?"

He pronounced each word slowly, as if he was reading a sad poem. *"Rebel Without a Cause."*

"Why are you screening it?" It was touching to think of him watching the film that he directed Sal Mineo in twenty years ago.

I heard a long sigh. "I never look at it. But the French government invited me to Cannes . . . in the spring for that festival, and I thought I'd speak . . . about Sal. Today, I'm holding my own memorial service. I'm getting . . . smashed for it."

After a silence I asked, "Can I come see it with you?"

"No."

"Please?" I said.

He cleared his throat. "I'll do what's best for Sal."

"I can be right over."

He didn't answer.

"Thanks," I said.

"Oh, if you come—"

"What?"

"Last week at the funeral I told that singer friend of Sal's he could watch the film sometime. . . ." He hung up.

Mark sounded exhausted when I called. "Okay," he said. "Maybe I'll come on by. Maybe I won't. Don't wait for me, now."

I drove up Laurel Canyon and over the Hollywood Hills to the valley. It was hot and dusty. I missed the Burbank exit and swore.

One end of the movie lot was fenced with chicken wire like a secret military base set against the San Bernardino hills. I slowed down at an entrance for the uniformed sentry. He leaned into the Dodge and walked around to the trunk to check out my missing window. Then he returned to his sentry station, called Projection Room 10, and waved me through.

Inside, the lot was the size of a village, with dirt roads, a long brick office building, wood barracks, and workers driving open electric carts. It wasn't what I expected to find at the dream factory.

I parked my Dodge outside Projection Room 10 and was mollified to see Robert Redford's name painted on the parking space.

The projection room was cool and black. I groped my way to a velour theater seat. When the projection light went on, I turned and saw Mark slouched down in a seat behind me. "Just made it," I said, holding up my broken wristwatch. I couldn't see his face, but I thought he nodded.

"Roll," somebody said.

I had a rush of nostalgia when Sal Mineo's face came up on the screen. What a great-looking kid. His soft face was vulnerable, loving. And then I got a glimpse of something. He had gangly limbs, but he walked with a bounce at the knee like Mark. I loved his hurt black eyes that looked inward. I went back to being thirteen. I fell in love with his black pompadour again. I remembered going to Woolworth's and smearing on pink lipstick and spraying my hair into a pompadour to get my picture taken in the twenty-five-cent photo booth.

He played a rich WASP kid named John Crawford, nicknamed "Plato," and he had a deep voice. He wore a suit, a sweater, and a tie. He adored James Dean, also an intense, misunderstood kid. But Sal Mineo is more extravagantly lost. Dean keeps trying to care for Sal Mineo and Natalie Wood, but he fails Sal the way the real parents in the movie fail.

As a kid, I saw this movie twice with my best girlfriend. We were awed because Sal was from the neighborhood, and afterward we followed his mother from the bakery to their house. We argued about the way Jimmy Dean opened his mouth when he kissed Natalie Wood. I said he put his tongue inside. She said they would taste each other's lunch. It made us giggle.

But watching the movie now made me wish I'd sat next to Mark. I wanted to share his memory of Sal Mineo. I didn't dare turn around to him. I watched Dean playing the loving friend. Sal didn't act effeminate or corny, and he suffered and loved for himself and Jimmy Dean. I watched his mouth tremble while he refused Dean's offer of a coat when they met in the police station. His black nurse explained that his parents were always away, and that he'd shot a puppy on his birthday.

There was something truly touching about the way Sal slowly opened up to Jimmy Dean. He gave him long, loving looks. When Dean fought with a switchblade, it was Sal Mineo who caught my eye. His hands were clasped, his body contorted with terror. His eyes snapped after Jim won. I loved the way he loved his friend. I wondered how Mark could stand watching Sal's face glowing like that.

It seemed to me that Sal played the doomed parts of Dean and himself. Plato was too damaged. His fantasies would never come true. He wanted Dean to take him hunting and eat breakfast with him like his Dad used to. But Dean saved his charged, loving glances for Natalie Wood. I shivered when Sal Mineo crouched under a chair in the planetarium and asked James Dean in his low urgent voice, "Do you think the end of the world will come at night or at dawn?"

When the lights went on, Mark had gone. Nick Ray stood up slowly, rubbing the back of his neck. He wore an eyepatch and his thin face was covered with lines. His yellow cotton polo shirt stretched over skinny shoulder blades and the bones of his spine. His hair was a shock of electric white fur, like a dog's coat. With a small orange scarf tied around his neck, he looked like a cowboy-style French artist. He was a compelling Hollywood director, down on his luck but not on his legend.

"It's good, your movie is still good," I said.

"You're here about Sal." He drawled like John Wayne,

his voice raspy. He lit an unfiltered cigarette and coughed out smoke. His movements were as slow as his words.

"That movie is about a kid who wants one day in his life that's not confused," Ray said. "Sal's the rebel, like in the title."

He paced the slanted aisle, grasping the backs of the chairs for support. "You're not asking me about Joe Smith who worked his whole life in a hardware store in Newark, New Jersey. Sal was a complex man. I don't think he had one unconfused day in his life after he met me."

His words sounded somehow veiled, as if he was a poet or a minister. I wanted to ask him why he blamed himself, but he continued drawling. "You're talking about a moral man . . . dined by royalty, nominated for an Academy award . . . he made over a million dollars."

"A moral man?"

"Yeah, but to do art, you got to be ruthless," he said, and coughed again on the smoke.

"He wasn't ruthless?" I already knew the answer.

"A star needs the steel of a Joan Crawford . . . but Sal, instead of taking, he gave away." He drew his eyebrows together. "I doubt Sal knew when he was getting ripped off."

After a while I asked, "When did you last see him?"

"Not long ago," he said. "He stopped by to thank me for something. I did a screen test for one of the boys, Mark. You could see Sal all over him. Chris Franklin too. Sal was a good director. He was going to direct a hit film one day."

"It doesn't sound so bad," I said.

"What doesn't?"

"A life where your flaw is you aren't ruthless."

"No, but he fell in love with being a boy and a star. He'd never be back there again, and these boys got to be his obsession."

"Why was he obsessed?" I asked.

"Back when he was a boy, the world turned upside down just for him. His dreams came true faster than he dreamed them."

"So he wanted to be a child star again?"

"He wanted that feeling of sudden change, when he went

from being just a boy to somebody that strangers loved—not just liked, but loved.'' Ray opened his arms wide at the small movie screen and almost fell backward. Then he sat down and rubbed a finger around his eye.

"Who killed him?'' I asked.

"Sal drank five cups of coffee a day. I don't think he smoked cigarettes. I made him espresso when he came by. He wasn't self-destructive like that. He wasn't a serious user of anything.''

Ray stopped rubbing his eye. "He got murdered because he liked little boys. He lived in Westwood for a while, just to look at kids. That's what he said. I think some little boy got emotional. Sal wasn't about to be tied down. How many astute conversations can you have with little people? But it wasn't sadomasochism.'' He pronounced the word as if he'd wanted to spit.

"What about Chris Franklin?''

"What about him?''

"He wanted to move in with him,'' I said.

"That fellow came out here to build a career. He's going to be a star. He's got the steel. The reason their lives worked for so long is they were never together.''

"He didn't get too emotional over Sal?''

"I couldn't say.''

"How'd you meet Sal?''

"He played the young prince on Broadway in *The King and I*, the King's son. He tested great with Jimmy.''

"How great?''

"He looked at Jimmy with love. It hit you between the eyes. He was the same age and coloring as my own son, but Sal had the vulnerability.''

"What was the test like?''

He heaved himself to his feet. His dungarees were tight, his brown boots scuffed. "We cut that scene . . . . It was after Jim drops Nat off and drives Plato home. A siren wails. Then Sal looks at him, shy, making friends, 'My mom's in Hawaii.' Jim giggles, 'Hey, don't tell me she going bongo, bongo with the coconuts?'

"Sal can't stop laughing and Jim can't stop laughing.

Then Jim says, 'Buzz exploded, he blew up, boom' or something like that, and Sal loves it. He keeps laughing. They start screaming and laughing. They never laid eyes on each other before. It happened in a minute.''

He lit a cigarette and coughed smoke. ''Now I'm going to ask you to give some sympathy to an old man. I don't talk about this much. But some things bear saying on some days. I find myself guilty. I helped Jimmy make that kid what he became.''

He turned his back to me and kept talking. ''Sal never seemed gay. No limp wrist, no swish—there was nothing like that.''

''How could Jimmy Dean do that, make him gay?''

''I'm getting there. Love. Love was necessary for the role. Sal had to explore that part of himself that would love Jimmy. Now, Jimmy was an easy person to love, and to hate. A child plays naturally. An actor lives in a world of fantasy and play. There's no bad child actor. The sad part is how a child can't tell the difference between games and real life. Those games Jimmy played twisted him up.''

''Why did he do it?''

''Jimmy fell in love with the kid. He knew it, and I knew it. I didn't stop it. . . . It was helping the film.''

''What was he doing?''

''Well, we were on location at Griffith Park. I heard him explaining things to Sal. He was saying, 'You know how I am with Nat'—that's Natalie Wood—'Well, why don't you pretend I'm her and you're me.' He got Sal to look at him and rub his shoulder a certain way. Jimmy'd say, 'Pretend you want to touch my hair but you're shy.' Then Jimmy says, 'I'm not shy like you. I love you. I'll touch your hair.' . . . Jimmy was an easy man to hate . . . and I hated hearing him talk to that boy.''

''But you didn't do anything.''

''I took one look at that kid's face . . . he was transcendent, the feeling coming out of him. You saw the film. It was something to cry from, so I tiptoed away. Then the next scene Sal did, he broke the sound barrier. It was that same scene where he asks Jimmy to go hunting and sleep over his house and eat breakfast.''

Ray clapped his hands. "If I can sing on the way back from work at three in the morning, well, I feel good. That night I started whistling and thinking, hey, they're going to like my film in Paris, France.''

"You were ruthless enough,'' I said.

"You see what I'm saying.'' He sighed. "Think of what Sal Mineo was up against. Jimmy had power. Every kid in America was mumbling his words, combing his hair back, and looking intense. Think of how Sal felt close up to that, and then later on kids got the same thing for Sal.''

I was starting to sweat. The air conditioning wasn't working anymore. After a while, Ray slowly pulled out another cigarette, and while it dangled in his mouth, he asked me, "You going to accept an old man's confession . . . you going to grant me absolution?" He lit his match and laughed his dry laugh. It made his arm shake the match out.

Then he said, "I remember the Academy Awards that year. He was nominated for best supporting actor. I sat him down and said, 'Sal, go home, forget this town. Go to Syracuse business school.' I wanted to see him untouched.''

"But he didn't do what you said.''

"Too much guts." Ray was rubbing the top of his head. "I remember that award night. He brought his whole family out here to Hollywood. Simple peasant types, rolling in his new money. He got such applause. Nat cried for him.''

"Well, he was good.''

"Nobody ever pushed him further as an actor than Jimmy and me.'' Ray started turning up theater seats, preparing to leave.

"When did you last see him?'' I asked, watching him move slowly around the room.

"Oh, he stopped in when he was out at the beach visiting some producer couple. He liked the husband. Million-aires.''

"Lyons?'' I asked.

"Yeah, maybe so.''

"How long ago was that?''

"The day he was murdered, I saw him out there."

"Oh, you mean for the party," I said.

"They throw afternoon parties?" he asked, and turned off the projection light from the back of the room.

I felt my way up the aisle. "Wait a minute. You mean he was out there that afternoon?"

"Yeah."

"Visiting that couple?"

"Well, look, I can't remember why he was out there, but that was the only reason he ever did come all the way to Malibu. So maybe I just assumed."

Kate Lyons had lied to me.

"Did he say anything?"

"Yeah, something about one of the boys. He was worried about that kid Chris, wanted to talk to some producer about it."

"Mark," I said, wincing as the sunlight hit my eyeballs. "He was worried about Mark."

"No, I don't think that was it," Ray said. "If you were to ask me, I'd say it was something about Chris being in trouble."

He tripped on the front step of the projection room. I grabbed his arm. I felt bone right under the skin.

"What kind of trouble?"

"I never asked Sal," Ray said.

No wonder the cops wanted Chris for questioning. But I had no clue what Chris's trouble might have been, or why Sal thought he could help. Or why Mark had led me to believe Sal's dealings with Kate Lyons involved him rather than Chris Franklin.

"Why did you fly east for the funeral?" I asked.

He made a gesture of dismissal with his free hand. "This is it. After this, nothing more." He stepped away from me. We were both fighting the sun. It made me feel out of breath.

"Usually I go to funerals to lament myself." He lit a cigarette and exhaled the white smoke. "Everybody does. I didn't feel that way about Sal. I went to applaud. I admired his guts. He stuck to it. He wasn't some quitter. No Syracuse business school for Sal." I watched his yellow jersey disappear as he walked down an alley between two long shacks.

A minute later, I pulled a note from Mark off my car window. He was waiting for me at the commissary. I asked directions of two women wearing nineteenth-century crinolines and twirling parasols. I didn't gape at them.

A hundred feet away, the commissary was a bungalow with a front porch. It had a faded linoleum floor, and a fan circulated hot air smelling of soup and disinfectant. It could have been an employees' cafeteria at a Minneapolis department store. Two salesgirls behind a card table wore inexpensive cotton blouses. They were selling piles of felt pennants stamped HOLLYWOODLAND.

In the back of the dining room, Mark was drinking club soda from a plastic cup under a huge photograph of Marlon Brando. He was playing with the salt shaker. Next to him was a table full of young people sketching on napkins and arguing. They looked like graduate students in engineering.

"Film editors," Mark said. He read my face. "This place isn't what you'd expect." He pulled out a chair for me. "Too many things in life like that."

Although his eyes were hidden by aviator sunglasses, I knew he'd been crying. "You walked out of that movie," I said.

He shivered. "Reality is weird. I kept seeing his face, remembering the last time we ate supper, the way he talked with his hands. Now, you tell me, he doesn't look like a dead man up there on the screen, does he?"

I touched his arm and took a swallow of soda from his straw. The film editors were passing around a napkin with a drawing on it.

He pulled an ice cube out of the glass and rubbed it on his forehead. "Boy," he said, "it's fucked up. The police pulled Chris in last night for lie detectors and shit."

"But they let him go."

"Yeah, but he says pressure's on to arrest me."

He pushed a knuckle under his sunglasses. "It's one bad dream," he murmured. "Wake me when it's over."

"Don't worry," I said automatically. But this was terrible news. I finished his club soda and said, "They are probably trying to trick Chris. He's the one they're after."

I looked at Mark to see if he believed me. "They're afraid to arrest somebody well known," I added.

He pushed his chair back from the table. It screeched against the linoleum. "I can't breathe right," he said. He stood up and the film editors stared.

Outside on the porch, I caught up with him. "Look, don't sit back and take it," I said. "Let me tell you something—"

He loped away. I saw the bounce to his gait like Sal's. I hurried after him. "Kate Lyons says her telephone message on Sal's service wasn't for Sal, it was for you—" I began.

He turned, still stepping away from me. "Not now, sugar, I respect what you're doing, but I'm going home and holing up."

He strode away three steps, turned, and came back. I held out my arms. He rested his elbows on my shoulders and bent one knee against mine. "Okay, how about me helping shut out the whole world?"

I stretched up and kissed his ear. "But we have to talk."

He pulled his head back. "Not about cops and murder, because I can't take any more."

We fell into step. "James Dean was something," I said.

"It's a funny thing about Jimmy."

"What's funny?"

"For Sal, Jimmy never really died. He was always in touch, and that's the way I feel about Sal."

"You don't mean literally?"

Mark gave me a fast look out of the corner of his eye. "Don't forget, sugar, this is California."

"What's that mean?"

"Many's the time Sal talked to Jimmy's spirit."

I didn't want to know about this. It gave me the creeps. But I was a reporter, for God's sake. "What did his spirit tell him?"

"Many, many things," Mark said, "about being a director, about life.'' He opened his car door and felt around near the gas pedal for the keys. I wondered why he drove a car that was such a wreck. The white leather seats were torn. The trunk and one big chrome tailfin were smashed.

"The last time he asked Jimmy for a sign was the summer of 1967. I was sleeping at his place at the beach.''

"You saw it?''

"No, I felt it. It was noon and the temperature of the house dropped twenty degrees. Not a window open. It was a visit of something.''

Now Mark did seem weird. It sounded like a fantasy, as though both of them had flipped.

"I don't know,'' I said aloud, and leaned against Mark's door. The handle was wrapped with silver tape.

"Sal thanked Jimmy for coming,'' he said. I was remembering Jerry's babbling about the devil. It was probably just an unpleasant coincidence.

"Sara, don't be such a bigot. Some folks won't deal with black people, some folks won't deal with Orientals. They draw lines. They make judgments. Sal never went on like that.''

"There's a difference between being a bigot about Orientals,'' I said contemptuously, "and talking to Jimmy Dean after he's dead.''

"Well, you can't say why folks get born and why they die,'' Mark said. "I ain't as sure of things as you.''

"Do you plan to talk to Sal Mineo?''

Mark whistled something fast.

"Well, what did Jimmy Dean tell him?'' I asked.

He wrapped his arms around himself and shivered. "He said Brandon DeWilde was going to die, and he told him how it would come about.''

"Did it?''

"Yeah.'' Mark twisted his head to watch the film editors strolling past. "And that's when Sal stopped trying to contact Jimmy ever again.''

This was too much. "Look, I don't get it,'' I burst out.

He sighed, and leaned over the steering wheel. "I don't

expect it of you. I expect you to listen for a while. Get in. I'll drive you to your car."

I slid into the hot leather seat. "This Cadillac's seen better days," I said.

He pumped the gas pedal, flooded the engine, turned it off. "It's a 1962 Eldorado. It's got eighty thousand miles, and the dealer insignia says GRACELAND."

"Elvis Presley?"

"Right."

"You got this car from Elvis Presley's hometown?"

"No, Elvis buys folks new Cadillacs, hundreds of them, the way you'd hand somebody a stick of gum."

"He gave it to you?"

"No, Elvis bought this baby for a black kid from Memphis who sold it to me." He got the motor going.

"The top doesn't work?"

"Never has," he said. "Sal called my car 'white trash'—"

"Mark," I said, "I need to understand things."

He hit the steering wheel lightly with his fist. "I know," he said. "I hear you."

Chapter Fourteen

I sprawled back on Mark's leather sofa. The sky was cloudless. When I picked up my head, I saw treetops and curves of distant mountains. The room was cool. At my left, a slow-moving red fish in Mark's tank was hypnotizing me. I felt drowsy.

Then his knee nudged me. There was something like heat transmitted every time he stared at me. He plopped a silk pillow on my chest and I hugged it. He sat down, his back pressing my side. I struggled to sit up.

"No," he said, "you look real comfortable," and he swung his long legs up along the edge of the sofa. "Tell me," he whispered sweetly, closing his eyes, his head in my lap, "tell me something that's happened to you on the subject of love."

I took a deep breath, shy, feeling his body. "Is this a game?"

He nodded. "Sal's game, and he loved asking things. I called him 'the erotic politician,' and he knew parts of *Lolita* by heart. Just by watching somebody dance, he'd know what turned them on."

"How'd he dance?"

"He was shy. He hated folks watching him. But Lord, he loved watching them."

"That means something," I said, leaning over to see him.

"He watched over us," he said, and reached his fingers up to trace my mouth. Then he said an amazing thing. "I want you."

I couldn't read the expression on his face. He was smiling shyly, his eyes closed. He murmured, "It's your mind—your brain makes you real special."

I laid down next to him on my back.

He poked my head. "Your mind's like an acrobat. I just wish it didn't work overtime."

I hid my face in his shoulder.

"First I'll tell you a story about love," he whispered, "and then you tell me."

Instead I rolled away, facing the back of the couch. I didn't relish hearing about his past love affairs. He tried pulling me toward him. But I went stiff.

"I'll tell you what I do best," he said. "Okay?"

I didn't answer.

"Sara, I listen good, real good."

"That's your best thing?" I twisted my neck around to see if he was kidding me.

"It's half the story when it comes to sex," he said.

"What's the rest?"

"Attitude," he smiled at me. "You need a great attitude."

Then I let myself feel his breath on the back of my neck.

I heard him whistling. I had the feeling he always heard music in his head. I faced him. "What's the difference between making love to a man and making love to a woman?"

He answered in a monotone, "I guess deep down you despise men who've been with me."

I hated to hear his voice so flat. Jumping up, I straddled him and his body made a new heat between my legs. "Mark, you're special," I said. He pulled my face down and brushed my lips with his mouth. "Why ask me about women?" he mumbled.

"I'm sorry," I said. "It worries me, the whole thing."

He put a palm on each side of my face and turned my head so he could whisper in my ear. "I don't remember—I swear I don't remember making love to anybody in the whole damn world but you."

His voice set up a friction in my ear that alerted my whole body. I flopped back down flat. "No memory at all," I teased. "It's a medical tragedy. The war—you lost it in the war."

"Yes, ma'am," he said. "A rare and tragic case of sexual amnesia."

"You need surgery."

"I need an answer to my question," he said.

"I can't remember your question," I giggled.

"Tell me a filthy story, something you reckon is real wild that has some mystery to it, and I'll do the judging."

I sat up on the edge of the couch, crossed my legs, the plump silk cushion on my lap. "Well, it was midnight, and I was surrounded. Bank robbers to the right of me. Bank robbers to the left of me—"

He hit the pillow in my lap with his palm. "Now, sugar, I said erotic."

"Oh, okay, then listen to this," I said. "It was my birthday a few years ago. I got standing-room tickets, me and the entertainment reporter, to the hot play in town, *The Cherry Orchard*. Well, in the back, leaning against the wall, was this man. Thin. Too gorgeous, like a god or something."

"Too gorgeous, now?" Mark asked politely.

"Let me tell it my way."

"Oh, good Lord, yeah. Too good-looking."

"His shirt was unbuttoned. He had this sultry smile."

"Oh, no. Sultry—that's disgusting."

I saw myself in his eyes, and I knew I could fall into them.

"Will you let me tell my story?" I asked tartly.

"A thousand pardons."

"Well, this man was staring at me. Giving me those

love-me looks. He put his hand inside his shirt, and then he started to flush.''

''Hey, now—an actor,'' Mark said. ''Who in hell was he?''

''Not yet,'' I said.

''Wait, wait some more,'' he interrupted again. ''These looks, they didn't get you?''

''I don't respond to strangers.''

''That's because love is your scene. You are no kin to erotic politicians,'' he said.

''But you haven't heard my story. I grab this entertainment reporter and say, 'Hey, look at that fag. Why is he staring at me?' I mean, he was wearing tight Italian clothes. And straight men didn't act that way, at that time in New York anyway.''

''What way?'' Mark asked.

''I don't know. Flashy. Like they can do anything because they're great-looking.'' I glanced furtively at his face. He hadn't taken offense when I said ''fag,'' but he was hard for me to read. ''Meanwhile,'' I continued, ''this reporter did a double-take. He acted like I'd just pointed out the Grand Canyon. He said to me, 'Sara, you overeducated jerk. That's no faggot, that's the biggest heartthrob on the silver screen.' ''

Mark snapped his fingers several times. ''Actors make gays look like monks.''

''I wasn't so dumb,'' I said.

''Dumb isn't the problem,'' he said. ''So who was he?''

''That's the mystery,'' I said.

''Lloyd Bridges?'' he asked sarcastically.

I ignored him. ''Anyway, the guy disappeared. The play started, and I sat down in the aisle. Then somebody bumped my shoulder. When I turned my head, I nearly died. It was him giving me that love-me look.''

''But you didn't think anything of it,'' Mark said.

''Well, I kept my eyes on the play. If I moved my head, I could've touched his mouth.''

''That made you feel bad?''

''No, but I heard stories about him chasing women.''

"Oh? Then what?"

"The lights went on, and I looked over, but he had disappeared."

Mark winked at me. "Cat and mouse."

"This other reporter was babbling about how the guy couldn't take his eyes off me. I told him it had nothing to do with me."

"Scared as a jackrabbit," Mark said.

'Well, but out in the lobby, there he was, sitting in a telephone booth. He waved like we had known each other for years. I almost fell over."

"He really turned you on?" Mark said.

"Not him, just the attention."

"Tell it your way," Mark said.

"Well, afterward, I drank two brandy Alexanders, like an idiot. My pal drank bourbon and made a pass at me. It was ridiculous. Of course, it took me weeks to stop seeing that man every single minute. I dreamed about him."

"Finished?" Mark sat up and threw himself against me. "Walter Matthau?"

I laughed and I lay back. It felt as if we'd been touching for years. He kissed my neck, moving his face slowly down inside the neckline of my shirt. I was getting goose bumps.

"I'm not done," I said.

"Good," he said, "because that story sucks."

I brushed his hair out of his eyes. "This is a saga," I said, "covering five years."

He nodded solemnly and threw himself back down on the couch. "Burt Reynolds?" he asked suddenly.

"Not telling, but a couple years later," I recited in a singsong, "in fact, last month, I was trying to get to interview a drinking buddy of his who hates the press."

"This all passes for erotic back East?" Mark closed his eyes and folded his hands on his chest.

"Don't ruin my story," I said.

"Do it," he said.

"Well, I heard that my movie star had hired the pal to write a screenplay, so I called his office at the studio. The entertainment reporter said he always calls people back."

"That's classy," Mark said.

"Why?"

"Out here the rule is you don't bother calling folks back who might be less important than you."

I remembered what Kate Lyons said about sex. "So you only call *up*."

He laughed, "You catch on quick."

I said, "But listen, my guy did call me back to have lunch. Also, believe it or not, I forgot the way he made me feel at the theater. Don't ask me why."

"I don't have to," Mark said.

"Why?" I asked him.

"You're scared silly."

"Well, anyway, at lunch, when anybody ogled him, he looked at me. Me. He seemed fascinated. He kept asking me questions."

"Right, because he's into seeing himself in your eyes. That's real seduction," Mark said.

I raised my eyebrows. "Yeah, well he wanted to know why I thought Pauline Kael liked his movies."

"Damn right," said Mark. "A real star's into big-time gratification. Mind-fucking's an art. In exchange he'll show you a great picture of yourself, getting you high on you, and stuck on him."

"But nothing happened."

"Well, he gets what he wants," Mark said.

"That shows how much you know. He didn't even flirt with me. I kissed him goodbye on the cheek. He flushed. I was flying to Chicago for an ERA celebrity bash and so was he, so he asked me to fly with him."

Mark yawned. "He was studying you, figuring why you were going to love him."

"Well, two days later on the plane, he changed. He grinned at me until I wanted to hide, but I stared back. He asked about me."

"Like how?"

"Well, how long had I been faithful to my boyfriend."

"How long?"

"That's not part of the story," I said. "Four years."

"When're the good parts coming?"

I ignored Mark's sarcasm. "Then I told him he had to answer my questions."

"Like what?"

"Oh, about his relationship to his mother and his first sexual experiences."

"He sure doesn't sound like Paul Newman."

"I'll never tell."

"Okay, what'd he say?"

"He told me that in the third grade he hated school, because the girls would pin him against the schoolyard fence and kiss him."

"You believed him?"

"I guess. He told me how good he was at making love."

"In graphic detail?"

"Yes, for hours."

"What'd he say, sugar?"

I twisted my torso around, "I can't remember it. But I told him what the entertainment director heard from some starlet."

"What'd she say?"

"That first he courted her, made all the right moves. It was perfect except for one thing."

"What?"

"Something was missing."

"What?"

"The man himself. He just wasn't there."

"Smart starlet," Mark rolled his eyes. "She's right, and you were all alone in that airplane too."

"No, he was there. How many women get a movie star like him making eyes at them?"

"Seven hundred trillion," Mark said.

"You're saying he wasn't there for me because he's running from girl to girl." I narrowed my eyes. "He's not really looking to love another person, he's looking for a better view of himself, like Narcissus in the myth. He's trying to find his image in each girl's eyes."

"Lecture me tomorrow." Mark patted his mouth over a

yawn. "Anyway, I bet your friend had something snappy to say about the starlet's reviews."

"He laughed and said, 'Poor girl, she's right. I guess I just wasn't there for her.' "

"He wins," Mark said. "He's not there for anybody. He's just viewing himself in action."

"That's what I meant."

"Okay, so what else did he say?"

"That he wasn't sure about making love to me, anyway."

"Why?"

"Because he said it'd be great, but I'd be upset after four times."

Mark looked interested. "Covering himself. Why?"

"I'd get hurt because his feelings wouldn't change."

"Good move." Mark laughed.

Something slipped into my mind, and I stopped smiling. I wondered how long Mark would stick around for anybody.

"Hey?" He ran his finger over my eyebrows. "What else did he say?"

He had me talking again. I loved telling this story.

"Well, he kept scrunching down in his seat and talking and describing sex in this low, teasing voice. I knew it wasn't real life. I told him he was the best movie."

"He didn't try anything?"

"Not really. I told him that I liked him and that was enough. But he raised his voice and said, 'Fucking is scoring. Fucking is scoring.' I told him he was wrong, and we didn't talk like that outside the bedroom in New York."

"Then what?"

"Oh, well, here comes the kinky part. He stood up to go to the bathroom. I was so giddy. I wasn't myself."

"Who were you then? Bette Davis?"

I ignored his question. "So when he teased me, 'Wanna come with me?' I jumped. He was already climbing over my legs."

"So what was the big move?"

"I said, 'Please, let me come and just watch you. It's like

a legacy. I'd love to tell my grandchildren how I watched you pee on an airplane.' "

"And then?"

"Well, he got this worried look. Then he pushed me back into my seat, and said, 'Don't be silly. I couldn't do it.' "

"You wanted to score off him your way, but he didn't go for it," Mark said. "Power freaks, the both of you."

"Not me." I was indignant.

"Okay, okay." Mark grabbed me from behind and pulled me down on the sofa. He buried his face in the nape of my neck. His breath was like a warm massage.

"Okay, you're no power freak. You're just kinky," he said.

"I'm not kinky," I said.

"Really?"

"So when we got off the plane, I asked when he was going to introduce me to his friend, and he laughed like a scene in a comedy. 'What's in it for me?' "

"I came up with ten things, but he kept saying, 'What's in it for me?' Then he dropped me off at the party in his limousine and that was it."

"How did you feel?" Mark asked.

"Lonely, like the movie projector broke down and left me in the dark.

"But a week later, he asked me out to dinner. He said that it was off the record. I got there early. When he walked in, people swallowed their wineglasses. He had his writer friend with him. He really delivered. I was stunned."

"Did you get the story?" Mark asked.

"No way. I tried. The friend hated me. He had a coughing fit. I never saw my actor again."

"You get depressed?"

"Well, yeah."

"You might've learned something."

"And got my feelings hurt."

"But you can learn from hurt feelings."

"Well, it's not that unique to have sex with him," I said.

"With one of the most beautiful men in the world? How would you know?"

"Oh, journalists gossip. I hear stories."

Mark started tickling me. I rolled off the couch and onto the floor out of his reach.

He laughed down at me. "So that's the closest you come to letting your work into your life—" He opened his arms and I sat up and threw myself at him.

"The lady is a voyeur," he continued. "That's why you wanted to watch a Hollywood mystery star in the bathroom. You don't live. You watch."

I started to unbutton his shirt, but he stopped me.

"Come on," I said.

"Well, I'm worried," he said, buttoning his shirt. "You'll get the story and split for home, become a virgin again, or whatever act you do in New York. I'm not real life. I'm work. Somebody's paying you money to hang out with me."

I was touched. But I bantered, "If I was getting paid for this, it would cost somebody a lot more than my salary."

Then he asked, "What do you want from me?"

"Pleasure. I want pleasure," and I started pulling on his buttons again.

"That'll take some work," he said.

"Teach me," I said.

"Promise me you'll do what I say." Mark extended his hand like he was making a pact.

"No way."

"Then forget it," he said, and rolled away from me. After staring at the red fish darting around the tank, I said, "Okay, promise." But I waved my crossed fingers at him.

"You don't mean that promise, but you will," Mark said, and he pulled up my skirt and buried his head in my thighs. All the muscles in my body tensed and then relaxed.

Then something new happened. A sexual fantasy. In my mind I saw him lying on top of me making love. I heard him breathing hard. Then I saw him licking my mouth, his hair falling around my face. My legs began to contract in spasms.

"What's going through your wonderful mind?" he asked.

"I'll do anything," I said.

He lay still, his breath on my thigh. I tried to stop the shaking in my legs.

"Don't tense up," he said. "I love it when your muscles go crazy. Sara, give up on that newspaper story and move right in here with me."

He was joking, but I didn't laugh. "I don't think it's right."

"Virtue," he interrupted, "is its only reward."

He sat up and pulled off my underpants.

"Okay," I said, "humiliate me. Take me. Use me."

"Jesus, you've seen too many filthy movies."

"None," I said proudly.

"Too bad," he said, and unbuttoned his silk shirt. I picked up my head to find his mouth and pulled him to me. I licked wet skin inside his lower lip. His lips trembled. Then I kissed him hard, and pushed my mouth inside his mouth. I slid my palm down his stomach and started to pull on his belt. I wanted to lick down inside his pants, touch him, swallow him everywhere with my mouth and both hands.

I wanted him to want to make love to me.

He pulled his pants down his legs and then threw them over the coffee table. I reached out to him, but he said, "Wait," and slowly unbuttoned my blouse, taking my arms out of the sleeves as though I was more delicate than flesh and bone.

He stood up naked on the couch and lifted me to my feet. Then he knelt and took my skirt down my legs, slowly, as though he was unveiling a work of art. He held my hand while I stepped out of the skirt.

Still kneeling, he moved his lips slowly over my body into secret places. A frenzy was building inside me. He turned me around and around, slowly, searching for the places where sensations begin. He caressed the skin of my neck, ran his tongue down my back, pausing to kiss me wetly as he moved his mouth over my stomach, pressed his hand between my legs, listening for my breaths, flicking his tongue deep inside me, exploring every wrinkle, teasing every nerve ending.

I felt wanton, and my knees buckled. My body was crying for him to touch me more.

He licked tendrils of my pubic hair, caressed under my breasts, and rubbed his forefinger gently on my mouth. Then he picked up my hand and, still looking into my eyes, he kissed each finger and licked my palm.

We lay down facing each other on our sides, my breasts touching his chest. He took my hand, kissed it again, and put it between my legs. I felt the soft hairs and the moisture and then the slick wet skin of my sex. My clitoris was a tiny miracle, a dot disappearing into the smooth flesh.

"What're you feeling?" His voice was soft like he'd been sleeping.

I didn't know. But he put my hand on his hard cock. He groaned and squeezed my fingers around him.

Then he teased me with his fingertips until he was holding my sex, his hand curved over me. I bent forward and kissed the tip of his cock, and the skin felt soft, wet, and smooth as the inside of my own mouth. "Later," he said, in an urgent whisper, "I'll show you how to drive me crazy."

He started to move his fingers between my legs and within a minute my body was moving in ways I had never dared imagine.

Then he took his hand away and I felt a flash of anger. I closed my legs against the loss of his touch and the tension of squeezing the wet and warm places inside me made me go into spasms.

"Do it yourself," he said softly, watching my face. He put my hand between my legs again. The folds of my skin felt loose and wet and strange. I had never touched myself when I was this aroused. I shivered and jerked my hand away.

He forced my hand back. I felt so powerful and so confused. It was up to me to make the feelings build, and I couldn't.

"I'm here," Mark said, "and I adore you. Come on, you

know what to do. Drive yourself crazy. You know what to do.''

I hesitated. ''But you make the rules.''

''I'm telling you the game,'' he said. ''Play it.''

Still my hand did not stir. He guided it in a long delicate caress from my knees up inside my thighs. I felt my skin jump with a pitch of sexual excitement.

He was kissing my ear and saying over and over, ''I'm here. Do it. Do it.''

I pressed myself, searching for the way he'd touched me. His hand hovered above my fingers, flicking at my wrist. I felt skin, wet, slick, and unfamiliar. Beyond all control or sanity, I understood that I could make my legs and sex contract and shake and feel a tension that was better than anything.

It was hard. I was still too self-conscious. My hand was turning slick with my own juices. But then my body felt graceful like we were swimming together again.

I became more sure of myself. My caresses lengthened, my spasms deepened and spread down my legs and up my back.

I felt his mouth traveling in gasps over my body. I faltered, but his lips found the muscle spasms, driving them further and making my flesh prickle with a hundred new sexual openings instead of one sexual core.

I screamed, and all I knew was this great feeling and sound of sex everywhere. Then I heard an odd silence, as if someone stopped singing. I stretched long and supple.

''Here's another game,'' he said.

He spread my knees wide and put his head between them. Then he burrowed his face deep in the folds of my sex. A new rush shot between my legs. He murmured, ''We're at a formal dinner, sugar.'' His voice made music start again. ''The maid has just filled the wineglasses. Now close those eyes. Pretend there's gleaming silverware, candles, and pretty flowers. You're sitting next to an art critic. Your knees are hidden under a yellow linen tablecloth. Nobody but you knows that I am kneeling under the table, between your knees, pressing my tongue into your underpants, begging you to pull them off so I can do this to you."

He rubbed his wet face against my thigh. "Wait," he said, sitting up. "The point of this drama is that you got to pretend nothing's happening. You have to keep a straight face and say, 'Pass the salt,' and, 'The peas are excellent this spring.' "

He looked at me for a minute. I licked my lips and tried to think. I could barely control the muscles of my face. I watched the smile start at the corner of his wet mouth. I wanted him back between my legs.

He laughed in a husky undertone. "Okay, we'll wait on this one." And he disappeared between my legs again to drive me toward the unbearable tension of orgasm. My whole body leapt and jumped, taking off wonderfully, over a long, slow minute. I lost all sense of time—me, Sara Martin. I was in a dream that never ended.

Unaccountably, I burst out crying. I felt so happy, lightheaded, as though I was floating weightless above the brown leather. Mark was holding his breath, concentrating and staring intently at my face. Studying me. Meanwhile, I was snuffling like a jerk. "Hey, what about you?" I said. "You're too self-sacrificing."

"You don't know anything." His voice croaked with fatigue.

"So teach me."

I stopped worrying about my tears. It felt great to cry from sexual release. Another new experience. I kissed him.

"I love making you feel good," he said. "Back home in Charleston, we learn that stuff before we learn how to eat hot cereal with a spoon."

He was lying on his back, his arms under his head and his cock straining in the air. I crouched above him and kissed the tip of his cock and felt it tremble against my lips. I rested my cheek on the white skin of his hip where his bathing suit covered him.

Talking in a rhythm, he said, "It's yours, babe, love me there. Love me."

I took a soft tendril of his hair into my mouth and pulled it. Then I began to take him.

"Aah, uum, no," he said, and grabbed my head gently. "It's time for lessons again. I'm the expert." He pulled me to him, and kissed me hard to keep my feelings from getting hurt.

I would probably have agreed to anything. My body was still ringing from his hands on my skin. I wanted to make him come as badly as I'd ever wanted anything.

"Now, just wet it all over."

I licked at the soft skin until it was slippery against my lips. "Good," he said, "you're getting real close to giving me pure joy. I wish I could describe it." He almost lost his words in a groan. I was rolling his hard flesh around in my mouth.

"Tense your lips and keep them over your teeth," he said, "and grip me hard with your lips."

I felt his quickened breath and a small movement beginning in his hips and buttocks.

"Now take me deep into your mouth and suck on it with the inside of your cheeks and the back of your tongue." My mouth was tired. But I didn't mind.

Mark was patting me erratically on the head. "Now relax, relax your throat," he moaned. "Take me deep inside, don't let it close up, and flick your tongue on the front part." He curled my hand around the slippery base of his cock. I gagged as my throat contracted around the firm skin, and my eyes filled with tears.

"Relax. It's good," he said, and cleared his throat. "It's great. It's a matter of training your throat. Just don't do that this time. Concentrate on this." He took my hand and made a circle of my thumb and forefinger around the base of his cock, and he closed my fingers tight, pushing them into a stroking rhythm.

He wiped the tears off my cheeks tenderly with his thumbs. I wanted to make him shake and tremble more.

He squeezed my fingers again around the base of his organ. It was slippery, and it was hard for me to remember all the different movements at once. I kept my mouth taut and full of him, following the rhythm of his hips and pushing him further and further into it. I wanted to keep flicking my tongue around the tip because it made him gasp every time. I gripped him hard with my fingers, sliding in the saliva and the wet to create more friction and feeling.

I found his rhythm, coming harder and faster. When I felt him tremble inside my mouth, he whispered, "Is it okay to do it like this? I mean for you?"

I loved being so close to his pleasure. I was still sucking him in slow strong movements, and the slippery wet skin was like my own flesh inside my mouth. Then I quickened the tempo, my mouth drunkenly pulling and licking, trying to unlock the sensations exploding inside him.

Suddenly my whole mouth was shaking because he was thrusting and I forgot to suckle and cover my teeth with my lips, and my tears became part of the mix of saliva and wet. His liquid rushed through my mouth, and my lips went slack. I swallowed the soapy fluids. He was trembling, still hard and in my mouth. I felt as if he were part of my body now.

Then he went soft and smooth. He sighed and pushed the wet hair off my forehead. "You'll get good, real good at this, and guys will be lining up at a hundred bucks a shot. The barber pole must be worth that much in New York."

I slid him out of my mouth. "The barber pole?"

He smiled drowsily. "Sugar, the way your tongue goes around from top to bottom like those red, white, and blue lines."

I'd have a hard time explaining the barber pole to anybody in my life, even Joe. For four years, Joe and I got each other aspirin in the middle of the night. Sometime we must have gone crazy together. But I couldn't remember it. It had happened when I was somebody else.

I drifted into sleep, woke up, tangled with him. The room was gray. The sun had set. I wanted to look at him sleeping. I snuck my knee out from under his thigh, listening, matching my movements to his breathing rhythms. He sighed once, and clasped me tight, his right arm around my waist.

His hair was curling, sweaty. His lips were full, more

childlike. He was a mystery to me, a stranger. I had so many doubts.

But I wanted him. I felt like an explorer who'd just stumbled on a new range of mountains and then, over the knoll, on a new uncharted ocean. Balboa at the Pacific must have thought something similar. It was a whiff of possibility, the idea that life might satisfy me more. I didn't want to think it. I didn't want to sense the future breathing down my neck. If I wanted it too badly it would turn sour. I live my life cursed by diffidence and decency. I believe the big sin is catching myself really wanting something.

I couldn't eat less, work harder, be kind to the unfortunate, and assume I'd be rewarded. Mark had shown me too much pleasure. It didn't make me grateful. I was scared of what I might lose.

"What's happening?" he whispered through a yawn.

I stared at his bottom lip, caked in one corner.

"Answer me." He threw his arm heavy from sleep back across me.

"Nothing."

"Come on, babe," he said, rocking my hips a little with his hand. "Don't be scared."

"Well, you're different. It doesn't make sense."

"You're afraid," he said, closing his eyes, "because you want to be happy."

"Maybe," I whispered.

Suddenly I craved something sweet, a Hershey bar, Coca-Cola, or chocolate-chip cookies. I put my thumbnail in my mouth and sucked it.

He was asleep. When I closed my eyes to sleep I coughed and jerked up on one elbow. The living room was dark except for the city lights below and the glowing aquarium. I felt like I was on a night flight. It was ridiculous to sleep away the whole evening. I felt defeated. I lowered myself back and frowned in the dark. It was okay for him. He had an excuse. His best friend had been murdered. He needed to distract himself. He could afford to fritter away time.

Chapter Fifteen

Nobody was awake inside the lobby of the Chateau Marmont but Jay, the desk clerk. He looked at me curiously when I asked for my messages. It was seven in the morning, and birds chirruped in some invisible courtyard. I smelled freshly brewed coffee.

"Been gone two days?" He flashed his wide smile.

"I been away," I said. Let him infer I was staying with relatives. I wished I had the guts to tell him some fancy cover story. But my reputation wasn't worth a lie to Jay.

Usually when I'm out of town on a story, I take care to get to sleep before midnight and eat protein in the morning. I make myself work twice as hard as anybody else might, and be much less reckless. That's why I do well.

"You know Jimmy Breslin?" Jay's teeth flashed white, and he handed me another telephone message.

"Yeah, a little."

"When he comes out here, he never sleeps. Lives with his subjects around the clock. I bet you're that good." He winked and hit his old brass cash register with a flourish.

I thanked him and looked over my messages. Two were from Joe, my boyfriend, or former boyfriend. He had called twice around midnight, last night, when I was with Mark.

My editor had called the previous afternoon. The remaining three calls were from the guy in Watts, Jerry Lee Johnson. His last call came in at five A.M. this morning.

It was irritating. That call would've scared me to death. I didn't need to hear from a troublemaker in the dead of the night. I resolved to call him after breakfast and tell him.

After I showered and flopped down on my bed, the telephone rang. I thought Mark'd just woken up. But it was Jerry again. At eight in the morning. I hit my pillow with my fist.

"We got some talking to do," he said. "You don't get much of a story without me."

"I'm doing fine, thanks," I said.

"Hey, I'm not looking for trouble," he said. I doubted if he did anything else.

"Come on over," he said. "I'll make it worth your while." His self-importance was annoying. But I had to talk to the guy.

"Don't call me again in the middle of the night," I blurted out.

"Lady, I got hot news—"

"I don't do business that way," I interrupted. I could've kicked myself. He slapped his wife around. She tried to kill me with a hammer. It wasn't smart to push him around.

His voice was tight with fury. "So you want me to fuck off, right? I ain't good enough to talk to you."

He scared me. I swung my legs around and sat on the side of my bed.

"I'd like to see you," I said, in what I hoped was a pleasant tone. "May I invite you to breakfast?"

"That's more like it."

"Please meet me," I went on saying as though he was doing me a favor, "at the Old World restaurant at Sunset and Holloway. You've a way to get there?"

"Lady, I got wheels. I ain't that kind of loser. But why don't you come to my place?"

"I have a bad headache."

214

"Yeah?" He didn't sound too interested in my problem. "You buying breakfast?"

"My pleasure," I said, and sneered into the telephone to make myself feel better.

The Old World was filled with people. The man next to me was drinking carrot juice on crushed ice. The cashier had red fingernails as long as her fingers. She hit the register with her knuckles. I walked through the place fast, worrying about Jerry. I saw Annie Harmon in the back, pushing ice cubes into a metal ice crusher.

"Come here," she waved. "Pina coladas," she told me, keeping an eye on the machine. "I do the setups, fresh, every morning. It's all natural, from the ice cubes to the rum."

She took a look at my face over the top of the machine. "That's a joke about the rum," she said. I described Jerry, but she hadn't seen him.

Then I recognized him walking around the back of the restaurant from the direction of Holloway. He was bent over, and fiddling with door handles of cars parked out there. It took him ten minutes to wander to the entrance of the restaurant. He stood by the cash register, cracking his knuckles and bobbing his head until I waved at him. Then he sauntered over, slow, like he had ten million better things to do.

The guy had a lot of problems. He stood at my table and tried to give me the eye before he sat down.

Annie Harmon dropped two menus on the table and looked dubiously at Jerry. It was amazing how he'd developed the muscles of his torso and his arms. His legs were short and thin and looked like they could barely support the huge weightlifter's body.

"I don't like it here," he told me, shifting in his chair like it was a small cage. His skin was an unhealthy ash yellow.

"Aren't you hungry?"

"You're payin', right?" he asked, picking up the menu. While Annie Harmon tried to catch my eye about him, he ordered three hamburgers with bean sprouts, two chocolate milkshakes, and a side order of french fries. To be congenial, I ordered a cup of coffee.

While we waited for the food, he picked at a sliver of skin next to his thumbnail.

"Breakfast or lunch?" I asked him.

"What? Oh, breakfast. I'm a growing boy," he said and stood up quickly.

Without explaining himself, he ran through the restaurant and out the front door. I followed him and watched him disappear into a car. A minute later he closed the car door behind him and ran back toward me.

"What's that for?" I asked.

"Forget it," he said.

He was swallowing some things that looked like yellow capsules.

I followed him back to our table, but he kept looking over his shoulder as though he expected somebody to walk in and make him leave. He gave me the creeps. When the hamburgers came, he lowered his face to the plate and wolfed them down. I almost said something about his manners. But he was a man who hit women. He made a lot of loud noises with his straw in an effort to finish the second chocolate milkshake. Then he snapped his fingers at Annie and ordered another one.

"I was walking around here," he finally said.

"Where?"

"Oh, I went and looked at the place where Cleon told me it happened."

"What else did Cleon tell you?"

"Cleon's a heavy dude," he said. He couldn't stop glancing around the restaurant like he expected to be menaced any second. I was curious to hear what he'd say next. I tried to remember our last talk. His friend Cleon Wilson overheard somebody with blond hair brag about killing a famous Hollywood person, and his wife heard the murderer talking about a cocaine contract.

"How heavy is Cleon?"

"Well, he's into Satanism."

I nodded.

"He thinks he can buy his way out of his problem if he gets enough souls and sells them."

"Who to?"

"The devil. Then, come Judgment Day, Cleon goes free. Let somebody else pay."

This Satanism talk reminded me of Sal's seances with Jimmy Dean. It gave me chills. "How does Cleon collect souls?"

"Oh, you want me to rat on a blood? No way."

"Well, what about the other guy, the guy who was bragging about stuff?"

Jerry leaned forward. "Cleon drove shotgun."

"What do you mean?"

"He was waiting in the car for the blond dude down at the end of the alley."

"What alley?"

"Where the dude got Mineo."

"Whose car was it?" I asked.

"Oh, I don't know. It was some yellow compact. That's it, lady. No more on that."

"Why not?"

"I could get in legal trouble, and I don't need it."

I tried once more. "Does Cleon get along with the other guy?"

"They understand each other. He had the same feeling, that if he offed somebody, like an animal, it would be collecting souls for Lucifer."

"Did your wife hear about this also?" I asked politely.

Jerry looked enraged. "Who said anything about that bitch?"

"You told me the other day that she was with Cleon Wilson when he met the other guy."

"I was mixed up or something. They weren't together that night. Anyway, she ain't my wife. I mean, she split. And she was just living there, that's all. But she's split now."

"Well, you have anything new to tell me?" I asked.

He glared at me but restrained himself, and said, "I told you Cleon was riding shotgun, and I got lots more—don't get me wrong." He was rolling up the sleeves of his workshirt as he talked, admiring the inside of his huge fleshy, muscled forearm. I saw that he was tattooed. "Brother Cleon is something. The dude knew some big-shots in Hollywood."

"What people in Hollywood?"

"Some big movie guys out at the beach."

I stared at his tattoo. It was a picture of a knife drawn in blue and green ink about ten inches long. It had a straight edge, and the veins of his wrist ran into the blue of the knife.

He raised his arm between us and flagrantly admired the knife on his yellowish flesh. "Cleon said his buddy was shook. He killed the Hollywood guy, and that famous dude was running around in his head."

"What else did he say?"

"That the dude was a hit man who feels better if he goes out and hurts somebody when he feels down on himself."

"Who are the producers he knew?"

"Don't remember." Jerry was staring at his forearm, clenching his fist, pumping up the muscle.

I had to try things out on him. "Lyons?"

"Could be," he said, still watching the knife on his arm. "It does damage," he said suddenly.

"What does?"

"The knife." He twisted his elbow and raised it to my face.

"I want to meet Cleon Wilson," I said, flinching, but trying to look him square in the eye.

"You call me up," he said.

"Did he know Sal Mineo at all?"

Jerry stood up so fast he knocked the table toward me. "Listen, babe, how would he?" he asked.

Somebody came running over to our table. I turned my head and almost bumped my face into a wrinkled suit jacket stretched over a huge stomach. Sergeant Casey grabbed Jerry by the sleeve of his workshirt. "Get out," he said. "I catch you talking to her again, and you're a jailbird."

Jerry ran for the front door. He stopped, looked around the small restaurant, and raised one thick arm. Nobody but me noticed he was giving us the finger.

Casey smirked at me like he remembered a dirty joke about girls and newspapers. "You'll have to sit still for some questions," he said. He lowered his girth between the chair and the table. His eyelids were pink, and his pale blue irises were dominated by patches of red veins. His tie was hanging unknotted. He had the tired, sprawled look of an office worker who'd overeaten at lunch and now wanted more than anything to lie down and sleep it off instead of going back to work.

Opposite me, he kept pulling his coat forward to take the strain off the buttons. He moved with fatigue. "What the hell are you doing?" he asked, in a voice that convicted me of crimes.

I straightened my spine in the face of his contemptuous authority. He shook his head dubiously, and tossed a crumpled pack of Salems on the table.

"I'm working," I said.

"Yeah?" he said. I didn't have much credibility in the work department. "What at?"

"I'm a reporter," I said. "I'm not breaking any law."

"That's my job, lady. What do you know about the law, anyway?"

"Well, I know about newspapers," I said.

"What about them?"

"They're protected by the First Amendment, for one thing." I hate anybody to obstruct my work. The problem was that he saw me as horning in on his territory.

"How'd you find this joint?" he asked.

"Research." I turned the corners of my lips up in a fake smile.

"You probably get paid more for your articles than we get for solving the whole fucking case," he said.

I ignored his crack. "Are you working on any other cases?"

"Yeah, some guy killed a teenage girl. I got called out on it the other night."

He waved a hand at Annie Harmon. She walked over, dragging her feet. Nobody loves cops, even when they're on your side.

"Coffee, very black," he said.

"Banana and yogurt," I said, "with fudge."

He rubbed his eyes until the red patches spread onto the whites.

"Have you had any cases like the Sal Mineo one?" I asked.

"Lady, it's my job."

"What's the strangest murder you ever solved?" I was looking for an opening. I dug into the frozen yogurt.

"Nothing under the sun is strange to me," he said, and he slugged back his coffee.

"Have there been gay murders out here?" I asked.

"I didn't say gay," he said. "Don't quote me."

"Well, there've been gay murders?"

"Well, there was the guy who'd pick up a trick, kill him, and put him in a plastic bag, all cut up."

"God," I said.

He almost laughed. "The press boys called it a case of 'a fag in the bag' or 'a flirt in the dirt.' Unofficially."

I looked at a spoonful of bananas, vanilla yogurt, and fudge sauce, and had a new double sensation. While my taste buds were watering over the fudge, my stomach tightened and turned over. I put down my spoon.

He was reviving for a moment from the coffee. "Last good case was the Skid Row Slasher."

"He killed bums?"

"Eleven of them. Slashed their throats and then had sexual relations. Then he spread salt all over the place to keep the smell of the blood down."

My stomach did a flip like a beached fish.

"Yeah," Casey said, "that guy had some signature. We had no physical evidence except for a shoeprint in the blood."

"Blood?"

"Yeah, and two drinking glasses filled with blood that he left because somebody surprised him." He put a long cigarette between his lips and didn't light it.

I wished the woman next to me would finish her hamburger because the smell of the onions was killing me.

"Yeah, lots of guys that work in packing plants get a taste for blood. That was the guy's signature, a taste for blood, and we knew it. It made a good story."

"Did somebody write it up?" I asked, swallowing against the feeling rising from my stomach.

"Yeah, I write these penny dreadfuls under a fake name," he said, and finally lit his bobbing cigarette.

"You do?"

"Yeah, I write my cases up for *Argosy* crime magazine at about a hundred a shot." He exhaled.

No wonder the guy felt like competition. He was my rival. I had several things I was dying to ask him, but it was his interview.

"So, doll, tell me why you were talking to that small-time con artist." An ash flaked into his coffee cup.

"Who?"

"Cleon Wilson. We been staking this place ever since the murder went down, because this was Mineo's hangout. Then you show up. We figure it's one of them flukes. But then Wilson shows. So I get my fat butt over here. Lady, I just sat down to last night's boiled potato and pork chop. Twelve hours late. It was sunrise, and I hadn't hit my bed. But for you, I broke speed records. I drove in from the Valley."

"Cleon Wilson?" I almost blurted out that he claimed his name was Jerry Johnson. But I clamped my mouth shut. It was very interesting. If the guy was in fact Cleon Wilson, he had lots to explain about the murder. I wanted him to explain things to me, not to the cops. This was my story. I had a chance to break something ahead of them.

Maybe Wilson drove the killer away from the crime and was scared to say so because he'd be implicated in a murder. Or maybe he was just a lost soul, trying to fantasize himself connected to Mineo.

"How do you know his name?" I asked.

Casey coughed out a small, dense smoke ring. It hovered over the salt and pepper shakers. "Identification cards. We booked him. Oh, look, lady, don't play so dumb," he said. "I was eating a whole-wheat bagel out there, inhaling car fumes with my face behind the *L.A. Times.*" He pushed his thumb in the direction of the front porch. "And I'm warning you, I ain't nobody's private protection service. Cleon Wilson's too much for you. And I bet you're obstructing justice. Maybe you don't even know it."

"Why's he too much for me?"

"Lady, he's small-time and scared. He might do anything to prove he's important."

"How did you find him to book him?" I asked. I knew he'd make a minute or two of conversation that he figured had nothing to do with the case. Maybe he was right. Maybe he was wrong. I knew he wouldn't tell me anything he thought was really relevant.

"We picked Wilson up one night," he said, "outside Gucci's on Rodeo, the night after the murder. Some lady and her husband were window shopping, tourists from New York. They'll walk anywhere."

"What about Wilson?" I asked, while he put out his cigarette in his coffee saucer. It was going to be interesting to find out which name was the real one.

"He was holding four dollars in one hand"—the cop raised one huge white hand—"he had all her credit cards and her driver's license in the other hand. She was screaming. He was too dumb to drop them."

"He mugged her?" I had never eaten breakfast with a mugger before.

I needed to find him again, if only to prove he was a hoax. Jesus, I was frightened.

"Did Wilson have a partner?" I asked.

"I think so. But he's a small-time guy," the cop said.

"Why?"

"He tried to cop a booking by giving us stuff on Mineo, but he fucked it up."

"How?" I asked.

"Lady, what did he tell you?" Casey asked.

"Oh, just something about how he had some information. But he never got to it," I said, thinking fast.

"Well, he didn't tell me," Casey said.

Like him, I didn't reveal anything. If Wilson really knew the murderer, I wanted to find out myself. If he was only a bullshit artist, I'd handle that.

"Was there a getaway car at the murder?" I asked.

"Read the press release the sheriff's office gave out."

"Somebody told me something about a yellow car," I said. I didn't want to say that somebody was Wilson. I wanted to check up on his facts without tipping my hand.

"It was in the goddamn *L.A. Times.*" Casey didn't think much of my reporting skills. "Some neighbor saw a yellow car driving away."

The cop looked at his watch. He heaved himself to his feet and looked down. One shoelace needed to be tied. He wasn't going to bother.

"Wilson doesn't know shit," he said, "but he's no playmate for you."

He was fishing in a pocket deep in the folds of his huge pants for some change. "He's nobody I'd invite to my debutante party if I was you."

"Wait." I was asleep at the switch. "Tell me about Chris Franklin."

Casey leaned down and put both palms on the tablecloth. "Nothing to tell."

"Not what I hear," I said.

"Yeah?"

"I hear you pulled him in for a lie detector test."

"I'll run you out of town in ten minutes." He was breathing hard.

"Why?"

"You're getting in the way of police procedures, and that's it. Keep away from my job. Don't obstruct the criminal justice process. You print something and some con man says he can't get a fair trial, and that makes more work for me. It ain't worth it. Correction—you ain't worth it.''

"What about Mark Loren?" I asked. "I heard you're going to arrest him.''

"Nothing doing," he said, and turned away. "I'm not choosing your friends, lady, but you got trouble coming at you from six directions.''

I put my lips together and smiled, like a debutante. I knew as much about murder as Casey knew about debutantes, but I was learning.

Chapter
Sixteen

I don't like getting hurt. The last time I had scabs I was twelve. I kept falling that summer because my dad was teaching me to ride a two-wheel bicycle and my legs grew all at once.

In Manhattan I've never been mugged. But out here that Ivy League guy smacked me back on my haunches at the airport. Jonathan broke my water glass at the bar, and I cut myself. The woman missed my skull and broke my window with a hammer. My shoulder had a green and blue bruise, a map of where she hit me. At the center of it all was Sal Mineo, in a place where people don't breathe. I pictured his orange makeup flaking like dandruff onto the pink pillow under his head.

But at the hotel that afternoon was the worst. The ground melted, a big hole opened under me, and not because of an earthquake either. It started when I pulled the gold bedspread off my pillows. I was dying for a nap. The Mexican maid shuffled across the shag carpet on straw sandals with broken heels. She was pulling open the striped curtains to the balcony, and I heard her grunt when the sun hit her eyes. I wondered if she knew people who swung hammers at other people's heads.

The phone rang. I fumbled and almost dropped it when I heard Marty Burns. It was the first time I caught an accent on him, although I tease him about the gold Phi Beta Kappa key from Brooklyn College that he wears on his belt.

"That really you?"

I laughed. He always talks like he's chewing on a lemon. This time he had a legitimate gripe. I hadn't returned his calls for two days.

"I got a wire service report here says you been kidnapped."

That's his way of saying he's glad to hear my voice.

"Yeah? Who'd kidnap me?"

"A sect of religious faggots. They get your brain?"

I love his fast talk. It was New York and I missed it. I could just see him kick his chair back, heave his legs up on the gray metal desk, and plant his heels on top of a pile of old copy.

"Not the brain," I said. "They snatch your body first."

"That's real funny," he said. "It explains why you're not sleeping at the hotel."

"Hold on a minute," I said. I yanked the curtains shut. The room was dark. I switched on the orange plastic lamp by the bed, then I switched if off.

The maid stared at me. *"Está bien?"* I nodded. She padded into the kitchenette. A second later, the room smelled of cleanser.

The clerk should have covered for me. I wondered if Marty was mad. I didn't apologize.

"You follow up on that Kate Lyons lead?"

I was relieved. "Right, turns out she's K. R. Lyons. Remember, from *Women's Wear?*"

He whistled. "You two gals make friends?"

"The impossible happened," I said. "She took a dislike to me."

"What's she like out there?"

"When she enters the room, all you see is this gray fin."

He snorted. "Like I say, you're funny. How else you been spending my money?"

Then there was a fuzzy sound. He was rubbing his palm over the mouthpiece, but then I heard him say to somebody, "It's okay. She's a pro."

"That's right," I said. "Listen, I been interviewing a lot of weird people. Why don't I start with a few profiles? There's Sal Mineo's next-door neighbor. She's a local character, part of the Hollywood underbelly, used to coach voice on 'I Love Lucy' and her father was a stunt rider—"

He cut in, "Maybe later."

"You'll be proud of me, Marty. I'm turning into a detective. It's a different world. I could write a whole book—"

"Aahm, Sara, listen—the publisher's here at my desk. He wants some teasers."

It was a compliment. They wanted headlines to tantalize readers about my series. Only I wasn't ready.

"Marty, buy me some time."

"You got nothing?" That he shouldn't be saying in front of the publisher.

"Trust me."

He covered the mouthpiece and this time I couldn't hear. Then he said, "You're out of credit."

"What's that supposed to mean?" I make my own rules about chasing down a story. But maybe the publisher was pressuring him.

He sounded guarded. "Sara, you get me any gay mafia names—agents, casting directors, stars, producers?"

My stomach tightened up and started to sink down inside my body. I looked down. There were red patches on my knees from walking on the beach. I have the kind of skin that burns and fades. It rarely tans. But then I don't work at it. I was rattled. Marty said something, but I didn't hear. I tried to bargain. "I'll give the copy desk five hundred words on Mineo's gay activism."

He yawned loud into the telephone.

"I heard that," I said. "Suppose it wasn't a sex crime?"

"Suppose the sun doesn't set tomorrow?"

"Listen, Marty, I'm miles ahead of the cops on this one." I was trying to sound confident, the way he likes.

"Nuts," he said, without changing his tone. "I need Hollywood dirt."

"That's the obvious slant." I was stalling.

"Wrong."

"How do you know what's going on in the world? You don't leave that office to change clothes." He keeps clean shirts in his desk and dirty shirts in a file cabinet. But he didn't think it was funny.

"Wire service. The L.A. County sheriff's sniffing around every star who ever parked his Mercedes on Sunset Strip. I thought you were going to dig out there. But you just dusted off the old gay rights sermon. Maybe you can sell girl scout cookies."

"But it's slander." I promised Mark. I had to be fair.

"Listen, girl scout, a year from now, two years, if you still care, you'll write it your way."

"Three more days."

"Nothing doing."

"The police are laying a trap." I was improvising.

"Nuts. Wire service says a Sergeant Casey is stuck. He'd pin that murder on anybody. I bet they got a tail on you."

"I'm so close, I'm in their way."

"Then you can name names."

"Marty, that's not the story. I got this feeling. It starts in my stomach and goes right to my brain. I'm on the track."

"I think you got sunstroke. File me five hundred words, and get the suntan oil and the stomach and the brain on an airplane."

My own editor getting in my way. "I'm too smart for this doubletalk," I said. "Nobody bosses me around like this. I'm coming home, all right, but when I finish up the job and not a minute sooner."

I gulped. I hadn't planned to say that. The blurred phone static between us made me nervous. I walked around the bed and opened the curtain again. I squinted down at the sun on the cars. I needed a strategy.

"Five hundred words or else," he said, too quietly.

I exploded again. "Nothing doing. I'm getting to the bottom of this. I'm a big girl now, and I'll go it alone."

"Before you fall on your sword, big shot, write me five hundred words."

"I'll write them, but my way."

"Name names."

"No, and Marty, I'll see you in a week. You can't pull me off this story. It's got my name on it."

"You lost your marbles?"

He was right. I was fighting him like he was an enemy. "Call it vacation," I bargained.

"Without pay," he said. He covered the mouthpiece again. Then he said, "Mr. Big here wants to know if you fell in love. I told him you ain't got the right gender for the birds on this job."

"Talk about love, Marty, you're supposed to love good journalism."

"How many times I told you," he said, "this ain't no writers' colony."

I lowered my voice. "I'll level with you. I got an eye on Chris Franklin, and he's a prime suspect."

He whistled. "With his career, he should be hiding out. A gay murder can't help him any. You know he's the centerfold in *Cosmopolitan* this month?"

"Nude?"

"Don't ask me," he said. "But what about that singer you were eyeing at the funeral—Mark Loren?"

"What about him?"

"You tell me," he said.

"No."

"Well, I hear he's been hiding for four years because he don't want anybody knowing he's a faggot."

"That's not it."

"Oh, no? Write it your way, then. But I want it five minutes ago."

"I'll write what I want," I said. I was bluffing, but I was

mad. "Take me off the payroll and you'll be bidding against every magazine in the country for the story when I'm finished."

"We're professionals," he said. "Think of that hungry son of mine at Princeton. Don't get me canned over some wild fruit-chase."

"I can get to the bottom of the whole mess, Marty. I can solve the murder."

"You and the L.A. police force."

"It's a shame you can't talk without that guy breathing down your neck." I can't stand the publisher.

He sighed. "Why's it so important to you?"

"Think about it, Marty—you taught me everything I know about this business."

There was silence in my ear, except for the static. My mind was jumping around. It landed on the Canyon Loan Company. Maybe Sal Mineo needed quick cash. I rubbed my forehead, but I couldn't come up with the name on that card that fell out of Mineo's script at his apartment. Then it hit me. Miss Chasin.

Marty was listening to somebody—the publisher—talking in the background. "Aah, Sara," Marty said, "if you're not sitting here typing at your desk on Monday morning, we're cleaning it out. We'll put your stuff downstairs in the society section."

The maid was banging pots and pans in the tiny kitchen. I was stunned. If I threatened him, that was one thing. But he knew I wouldn't write about parties and engagements. He was firing me. I swallowed hard to keep things in place. "You're kidding," I said.

"Sorry."

"Marty, I can't sit here all day and chat." I tried to take charge. "I'm working. You'll get the five hundred words."

We hung up on each other. It was a draw. I wasn't thinking straight. I did give the maid a dollar for taking away the breakfast tray. For some reason, I dug around in my suitcase and pulled out a pair of wool socks. Then I put them on and got under the covers.

I wasn't fired. That was impossible. Marty was too soft-hearted to can me for working an extra week in Los Angeles. Or was he? I felt like I'd been kicked out of a family. Marty always backed me up. I remember how he nodded sagely when I told him I was moving out on Joe. I remembered the way he flushed when he gave me my birthday bonus. Well, he'd be proud of me on this thing later. That thought lasted a split second. I knew Marty never fired anybody for insubordination. But the publisher would do it. I'm glad when he leaves me alone until my stuff is cold newsprint. The publisher strikes anywhere he wants. And I'd crossed him.

I was in trouble. I was on my own, either a crank with a hunch or, worse yet, a freelance writer. That's a euphemism reporters use when they're out of work. The idea exhausted me.

I pulled the phone onto my chest and dialed Mark. It beeped busy. I thought of something. I called room service and ordered two cheeseburgers and a Coke for an early dinner. Until I wrote the five hundred words, the *Post* was picking up the food bills. I'd have to cash a check quick with Jay. I could move to a cheaper hotel, but that would call attention to my diminished status. It had to be my secret.

I rubbed my eyes and felt my tear ducts stinging. It wasn't fair. I was doing a great job, and nobody understood that. I was never fired from anything. I do things well, with an approving teacher or editor behind me. I was going through hell out here to get the story. Did Marty think I was lounging around some pool? I made up my mind to do something really tough. Like take off my wool socks and make a phone call.

I didn't need the newspaper. It was time I gave up my nursemaid.

I called Mark again. Busy. I called room service and added coffee to my order. Two cold cheeseburgers and a watery Coke arrived. No coffee. I avoided the look in the maid's eyes and gave her two dollars. I chewed on the last supper. The roll was stale, and the burger was covered with gummy cheese. I picked off a mealy slice of tomato and some brownish lettuce. It's funny—most people think junk food is uniformly bad. But there's nothing like a rare, thick, juicy cheeseburger with the meat brown on the outside and toasted American cheese on top.

I called Mark again. Still busy. I spit out bits of meat and roll. I paced the room and looked out my balcony. The Strip looked the same. I wondered what would happen if I threw a cheeseburger into the traffic. Instead, I walked into the kitchen, opened a cabinet, and hid it behind some white cups.

I got the number of Canyon Loan Company and cleared my throat with an important harrumph when a woman answered. "Miss Chasin, I presume. This is Mrs. Diane Porter." I made my voice deep. "I'm handling probate on the Sal Mineo estate, and I need your transactions with him for the legal record."

When she asked, tremulously, I assured her that I was a lawyer.

She was dying to talk. "That was a shock. I mean one day he's in the office, a movie star, and then I see headlines on the way to work. You don't think it was a crime of passion, do you?"

"That's none of my business." I wanted her to shut up and give me the information. "Please tell me the date of your transactions."

"Well, it was about a week ago."

"Do you keep records?"

"I'll see." I heard a drawer slam. "He came to see us the day before it happened—the murder."

I thanked her but she didn't want to let it go. "Oh, right—well, he was so sweet. I'd hand him the ten thousand dollars on charm alone, but everyone says I'm easy." From the eager edge in her voice, I bet nobody'd noticed she was easy in years.

"Of course, it's always Mr. Arnold's decision, and he wants collateral."

"What collateral did Mr. Mineo offer?"

"Some health-food store his mother runs back East."

"Did he say why he needed money?"

"No, it was a secret." She paused. I waited and she started to gush. "He was willing to take our high interest rate. So I asked him why. He said it was for a friend in trouble. I think he said something about a fiancée. But he was gay, right?"

My nerves were shot. I raised my voice. "Well, don't believe everything you read."

She sniffed a little. I guessed she was around fifty and used to enduring bad temper displays, but that didn't excuse me. I asked her to read me the loan application. It was routine—name, California address, social security number—and she stopped, but then read me the information that he'd made twenty thousand dollars that year.

"Thank you," I said, and apologized for my nerves. Then I said, "Miss Chasin, what is your first name?"

"Irma," she said, "You know, first he walks in here, then the murder, then Mark Loren's on the phone—"

"Mark Loren?" I clenched my teeth and belched. This was the final blow to my digestion.

"Right. You know, the popular singer the kids are crazy for."

"No." I couldn't believe it.

"Well, everybody else knows him," she said. "He sounded Southern and sad. He told me it was like a death in the family. Said he got my name off a card."

When I hung up, everything bothered me. He kept the card from the screenplay. He lied to me. The hotel room was stifling me. It was hot and that cleanser stank. I threw myself face down on the pillows. They smelled faintly of cologne. I rolled over and looked at the ceiling. I hated the ceiling. The paint job was new, but I could see brush strokes. They had skimped on a second coat. I pulled a pillow over my face. I wished things were different.

I closed my eyes and listened to my breath. I was pulling the air through my mouth and deep into my chest. I was sweating. There were too many questions, and danger around the edges of things.

Mechanically, I got up and pulled some hotel stationery

out of the night-table drawer and put in a call to the copy desk. I told them to have somebody ready to take five hundred words in an hour. I called the hotel clerk and asked for a typewriter. He said I could have it by tomorrow. I went to the kitchen sink and threw cold water on my face. Hunched over on the bed, I scraped at the point of a pencil with my thumbnail until it was sharp, and slugged the story: "Gay Activist: Sal Mineo."

Chapter
Seventeen

I was sick of Los Angeles drivers. The black Mustang in front of me sped through one stop sign and stopped for the next. Without warning, a woman passed me in the left lane. I swung past Greenblatt's Delicatessen onto Laurel Canyon Boulevard, heading for Mark's house. When I'd finally reached him by phone this afternoon, he'd insisted on going to Kate Lyons's party too. I never mentioned the loan company and his lying.

Up in the hills, I jerked to a stop at every street sign. I punched in radio buttons. There was no news about why somebody had left Sal Mineo bleeding to death in an alley.

I snapped off the radio and fumbled through my blazer pocket in the dark for the little Sony. I couldn't go on like this. Everybody was lying to me. I was going to do some interviewing at the party tonight. That Lyons had some explaining to do. According to Mark, Kate and her husband had lived next to Sal Mineo on the beach, a little fact Kate never mentioned. I wanted to meet her mysterious husband. He was one of the last people to talk to Sal Mineo, or at least that was Nick Ray's impression.

I hesitated at the foot of Mark's hill.

I'd kept him out of my article. Jerk that I am, I keep my promises.

Watching the dark shape of the elevator swing toward me, I felt like the last person in the world. Behind and below me, thousands of city lights twinkled. The wind blew a burnt-coffee smell at me—smog.

I stepped into the elevator and closed the gate. Three days ago I was a competent reporter. Now I was scared to ask Mark questions—why he lied to me about the loan company card, why Mineo needed ten thousand dollars, why Mineo's "fiancée" had money trouble. Was Chris his fiancée? Nick Ray said Mineo was at the beach the day he was murdered because Chris was in trouble. Dammit, I hoped Mark had some answers.

I had to force Chris to talk about the murder. But he was running scared, and Mark was protecting him from me. I needed Mark's help, but he had too much power over me. I was twisting my rules. I remembered when a woman reporter was fired from the *New York Times* for having an affair with a legislator she was covering. The editor said, "I don't care if you fuck elephants, but then don't cover the circus."

Inside his house I smelled the furniture polish. It was dangerous the way he left the place open. "Mark?" I called. I felt my way along the walls. The living room glowed in the light from the aquarium. He was collapsed on the leather couch in his big dark bathrobe, staring at the fish. The air smelled of marijuana. Suddenly he irritated me. "You don't look ready for a party," I said.

He rolled on his side, away from me. He seemed mad out of nowhere. "Yeah, right," he muttered. "You think you're ready? How long you been practicing that dumb slouch?"

I was shocked. "What's wrong with you?" I asked.

"Really," he said in a tone of voice that implied the word was answer enough.

He was infuriating. I sputtered, "Next time I'll swish in here like a pretend female. You like that style, right?"

He laughed at me, his voice crackling with misery, and

pulled a small glass tube out of the folds of his bathrobe. He tapped it on the side of his wrist and inhaled something into each nostril. He bared his teeth and rubbed the leftover powder from his wrist onto his gums.

I wished we weren't fighting. He had a nasty point about my posture. He had such grace. There was something about the way he was presenting himself on the couch in his bathrobe with his collar turned up, as if he'd framed his face in black velvet.

"Too bad I don't lie around posing in candlelight," I blurted out, "but if we both did, who'd watch?"

He wiped his nose on his sleeve. He knew how to control a sloppy gesture. It made his misery look like tragedy.

"Good move," I said. "You been practicing it in front of the mirror?"

"Sara, go away, go on to your party. Leave me be." He turned away from me again. As far as I could figure out, he was engulfed in self-pity. I pawed at my pockets for my car keys, and pulled out my hand mirror.

"Take a good look." I tossed it onto his chest. "You'll feel better."

"Really," he said again, in that smug tone, and crossed his bare legs.

"What's that supposed to mean?" I asked.

"I love beauty. I love to touch pretty things. You don't get it. Maybe women can't."

"That's dumb. I like pretty things. Little girls learn that real early."

"But I'm talking about putting beauty ahead of books, money—everything."

I winced. "Yesterday you were telling me how much you love my brain."

He flopped his legs down on the couch. He seemed to have no body tension. "Today I'm a liar?" he asked softly. Then he said, "You're so uptight. You can't even get into how you look. Where does it get people like you?"

"It gets us through life with order. We don't hurt people. We don't take too much. We worry about future generations."

"You hurt people plenty. Divorces and wars aren't great."

"We keep life going."

"Too bad I got this curse," he said.

"What curse?"

"I worship beauty. It's sexy."

What was he saying? I wasn't pretty enough. Something had happened. Nobody could change this fast, or could they?

"Really," he said again.

The tone of that word. I couldn't believe how mad I was. "So that's what you inherited from Sal Mineo?"

"Sure thing," he said, wiping his nose on his sleeve again. "I'll never forget him telling me I wasn't the first person he noticed in a room, or the second. But I was the one he never did forget."

"Oh, great." I was hovering over him, my fists clenched. "Write that down and put it under your pillow." I stumbled back toward the hallway.

"What in hell does that mean?" he raised his voice.

I yelled behind me, "I don't buy your religion. Beauty isn't everything. It's superficial."

I felt the front door. When he spoke, he was standing somewhere very near me. "Don't argue with me anymore." His voice was tremulous.

"What happened to all the open California talk?" I shot back.

"Really."

"What's that supposed to mean?"

"Sal said real stuff doesn't get said." He was breathing hard. "You talk to stay away from feeling."

"Yeah?" I heard myself grunt with rage.

"Yeah," he said. "You come running over here tonight for a free party guide to gawk at sex, cheap thrills, and dopers. You don't give a flying fuck for my misery."

I don't remember that ride down to the beach. The ocean looked black. I drove eighty miles an hour along the Coast highway. At the entrance to the Lyons's estate, two uniformed guards whirled flashlights in the air. When I switched off the motor I heard the waves pounding. Another car turned onto the path, and headlights swept past a tiny dark-haired woman wearing a white fur coat.

The night air was crisp and clear. Yesterday Mark loved my brain, today he hated my slouch. I wanted to drive back and shout at him. There was no time. I had to soak up atmosphere and information.

A guard wearing sunglasses and a red satin policeman's hat stuck his head inside my car. He repeated my name into a walkie talkie and waved me to a parking space next to a Rolls Royce. The place was covered with fancy cars.

I got out of the Dodge and stretched. I was wearing my old beige wool blazer, and I smoothed down the wrinkles on my gray skirt. I had only packed work clothes.

The guard wrote my license number in a large notebook. I started to lock up. "Don't bother, lady." He poked his pencil into the hole where my back window had been.

"We're following the guest list tonight. Can't find your name," he told a young man wearing white tie and tails. He slammed his notebook shut and walked back toward the highway.

The small woman in the white fur put her hands on her hips. "Well, now what?" she asked the young man in the tuxedo. She wore her coat open to show sparkles sprinkled across her bare neck and shoulders. She clutched a large black hat under one arm. "I thought you got in anywhere in this town."

"I do." He took off after the guard. The girl held onto his sleeve with her fist, and teetered on her high-heeled sandals. She cursed when she caught a shoe in the white coat and fell against my car.

"I get in anywhere in Boston," the man said.

"This isn't Boston." The girl dropped his arm.

She seemed familiar, even in the dark. I grabbed her hand and shook it. "I saw you at the funeral." Her hand was too small, fragile, the fingers like tiny bones. She was Nell Fields, and almost as drunk as she was five days ago in the Bronx.

Her smile threatened to turn real, and she held onto me. "Honey, oh, honey," she said, her breathy voice turning sultry, "take me in there with you."

"I don't know." I was unsure of the guard.

"You got to," she said. She pointed at her friend shouting at the guard along with a small crowd of overdressed people trying to crash the party.

"He's a dud, honey, not like you," she said. She was having trouble with her *s*'s. They sounded like *sh*'s. "I need to give somebody a message in there real bad." She pointed one small forefinger across the gardens toward the house.

"I'll deliver the message," I offered.

"Nope."

"Why not?"

"It's a secret."

"Okay, okay," I said.

"You're a real one," she said. "You're Sal's type, like me." She was hustling me. She had an odd voice. It was as though she wasn't using her vocal cords. The sound she made was all whisper and seduction, something like Marilyn Monroe.

But Monroe had to be Nell Field's fantasy. Nell had been a teenage star with Mineo. Back then I wondered how it must feel to kiss your boyfriend in front of movie cameras. I thought they'd get married when I read that she followed him to a Sioux reservation and did needlepoint while he shot *Tonka* for Walt Disney. She didn't seem the needlepoint type.

Her escort came steaming over to us. "You dump me as soon as a better shot comes along?"

She crunched up her nose. "You bet, sucker." She put her small hand on mine like a teenager. "I'm with her." Something flashed through my mind. She wasn't very nice.

A moment later, a silver Rolls Royce limousine rolled slowly toward us from the direction of the sea. It stopped and the guard motioned me inside. Nell grabbed my wrist too tight.

"Hey, what's going on?" The guard indicated her. I

climbed into the car and pulled Nell after me. "I been waiting for her here," I said.

Inside the car, the motor seemed to be far away. The soft leather bucket seats were filled with goose down. The tinted windows blocked the moonlight and the sound of the surf. We were driving toward the beach house very slowly.

Nell tipped her small head back against the seat. "Made it." In profile, her eyelashes looked larger than her button nose. I heard her open and close a compact on her lap.

"Who's giving the party, her or him?" I asked.

"It's David's idea. He's got style. He gives a party every night. These limos, the guards—that's him."

"What's the party for?"

"Business anniversary." She turned on a recessed light. I watched her pull a silver flask out of the gold evening bag and swallow several loud gulps. "Brandy," she coughed. It smelled like gin.

"What business anniversary?" I asked.

"Oh, the Lyons are big producers. They make billions," she said, and peered out her window.

"What about your secret message?" I asked.

"You from New York or something?" she countered.

"Yeah."

"Why'd you make the funeral? Know Sal from New York?" Her nose was pressed against the dark gray glass. She was making a spot of mist with her breath. "Did you?" Her voice was sly. I figured a lot of people had told her a lot of lies in the past fifteen years.

"That's right," I said.

"Where from?" she asked petulantly. The spot of mist on her window was now almost as big as her face. She didn't want to look at me.

"Oh, the old neighborhood."

"Right, the parochial school and the weird nun." Her voice had respect in it. My claim on Mineo predated even hers.

"Which nun?"

"You know, what's-her-name." She looked at me for the first time.

241

"Mary Theresa."

"He loved her." Nell stretched her neck to look out the front of the car at the ocean, a black shining surface that appeared for a few seconds in front of us. "Shit, Sal had such a big fucking heart." She unscrewed her bottle of gin again, and I realized she was crying. Then she laughed a little deprived laugh. "And he had such a fucking good line. I loved the bullshit parts best of all."

"What was that?" I asked.

"Look, he was my old man. Whenever I needed help, he was there. Sal was my baby. He took care of me from the day I laid eyes on him, like it was his job. Fifteen years we loved each other."

"That sounds like a good friend." I sounded like a girl scout.

"Yeah, but it was bullshit," she said, and put a tiny fist against her front teeth. I think she hiccupped.

"Why?"

She looked at me, and her head wavered from side to side. She was really drunk. "I'll say it fast. Don't ask me again. Okay?"

I nodded.

"Because he didn't always love me that way, but he was my fiancé."

"Did he offer to lend you money?" I said stiffly.

The car stopped. She began slapping on the window as a group of people got out of the car in front of us. "There's Dougie," she said. "What a terrible haircut. I hear he's working at Fox."

"Who's that?" I asked.

"Some stiff," she said.

"What's that mean?"

She grabbed my wrist again. "Let me tell you how the old man saw it." Her voice was starlet, breathy again. The words were slow from the gin. "See, the straights, they're the guys who sit in the studios and balance budgets. They're the bank. They're steady. They could be running the goddamn Federal Reserve Bank."

"Not these people." I gestured at the house.

242

"No, no, the Lyons're independent producers. They don't answer to anybody. Sal says independents're like Mafia, only they don't got honor. That's a joke, honey."

"Is that guy David Lyons?" I asked, watching a tall man greeting the group.

"David?" and she shook her head like she remembered something funny. "Sal said he's the movie queen. He's so hot to make movies." Her words slurred, but she kept talking. "It gets him off. He's Hollywood with spats on. Sal dug him. You hear about his gun thing?"

"No. I don't know him."

"How'd you get invited, then?" She looked suspicious.

"The wife."

Nell heaved herself up and closed her coat around her tiny body. "Forget her."

"Well, what about his gun thing?"

"Well, he always gets the same clause in his contracts. If one of his pictures makes lotsa money, like forty million, the studio buys him an antique gun."

"They do that?"

"They do anything to keep him happy." She hiccupped. "He's so crazy. Sal used to tease him."

"What's that mean?"

"Oh, you know Sal. He could get the straightest stockbroker in the world wondering if he was coming or going."

"So that means David's straight?"

"People talk too much," she said, and turned the door handle. Nothing happened. The chauffeur opened the dark glass window between him and us. "Another four minutes, madam."

"Who comes to these parties?" I asked.

"All the people who want to get to stars, agents." Her voice was sweet. "That's the business, honey," she said. "Of course these're the faggots."

I tried to sound worldly. "I thought nobody cared."

"It's hard for the talent," she said. "The public doesn't buy gay stars kissing ladies. If it gets out, you're finished."

"Was that Sal Mineo's problem?"

"No," she sneered. "Sal didn't need it. He was a director, anyway. He was above it all."

"I thought a lot of actors are gay," I said.

"No—fuck no. Anybody who wants their face on a hundred million movie screens loves himself so much . . ."

"So much that—?"

"That they'd go down on themselves if they could." She laughed. "That's Sal's joke."

"Did the studio guys like him?"

"Well, he's what Hollywood people want. He's an aristocrat, you get me? He's old Hollywood, friends with Garland. He didn't have to strut."

"Why not?"

"He had a thing with Jimmy Dean."

The chauffeur released the door lock. She stepped on her ermine with one foot and almost fell out of the car. "Everybody loved him. He was the most outrageous, honey, the most elegant. They might trash him, but they all knew he was somebody."

She walked away, the back of her coat dragging the gravel path.

I slammed the car door behind me. The chauffeur had stepped out of the car. "Jesus, wait a minute," he whined.

I followed her, trying to make conversation. "That nun really loved him." Her stiletto heels kept sinking into the gravel, but she was running toward the front door of the beach estate.

"Sure, sure, she fronted for him when he lifted some money from some place."

"Nuns don't do that," I said. She shook my arm off her elbow. At the black marble steps, she straightened her shoulders to face the party.

"She took care of him good," she said.

The door opened, and the heated stream of lights and music hit me like a subway train. A harsh, irregular beat thumped in my ears. There must have been a hundred people packed into the hallway in front of me. Nell Fields put one elbow up in front of her small body, pushed between two bare backs, and disappeared without a backward glance.

Hot neon rays of pink and turquoise cut across the faces. Pretty kids dressed in what looked to me like their parents' makeup and scanty clothes.

I squeezed in and smelled thick gardenia perfume. I dodged a rhinestone earring the size of a golf ball. Nearly everybody was holding something—a glass, a joint, a cigarette. Nobody was looking at anybody else. The girl in the gigantic earrings raised her fingers, sparkling with fake gems. She looked tan, athletic, and drugged. She started dancing alone. The stones flashed and bounced. With each step she bumped into somebody else.

Suddenly I heard three quick explosions. The girl stopped dancing and fell against me. "What's going on?" I shouted. The music was pounding.

"It's him again." There were beads of sweat on her upper lip, and she reached down to her shoe. Her heel was the size of a copy pencil. "He keeps it moving."

"That was a gun," I shouted.

"Don't worry," she mouthed.

"Something's wrong."

"Him." She pointed up.

I stood on my toes and looked above the heads to an empty staircase. I pushed through the crowd, and almost stepped on a man lying across the stairs, his hands tucked under his head. He tapped my knee, smiling up. "Wait," he shouted, and pulled some sheets out from underneath him. They were pictures of his smiles, his hands, his angry look, his backside with tennis shorts, and his legs. I flipped one photograph over. The back explained that he was an actor who wanted to go to Maui and cool out for a month. So he was raffling himself off at twenty-five dollars a ticket to a hundred women. The lucky winner would have him at her mercy for a week. He didn't do faggots, and his "master" couldn't take him out of Los Angeles, since he needed all his bread to get to Hawaii.

I returned his smile. In a flash of diplomacy, I pointed to the ring finger of my left hand, and shouted, "I'm married."

* * *

At the top of the stairs the hallway carpet felt deep. I heard a man laughing. I opened a thick door and smelled bleach and fresh laundry. It was a huge linen closet filled with enough blankets and sheets to stock a department store. An explosion rang out. I ducked involuntarily inside the closet. Another door opened across the hall, and a plump-faced man beamed at me, his full-toothed smile shining through a heavy black beard. His head was shaved.

"Scared you? C'mere." He held one hand behind his back. I didn't move.

"Hurry up," he said. He seemed so cheerful that after another paranoid flash, I walked out of the closet, past him, and inside a bedroom. Then I saw he held a long antique gun behind his back. I shrank against an early-American maple highboy. He was wearing a large asbestos glove, and the gun was smoking.

"You here alone?"

"No, no, I came with a bunch of friends," I stammered. He smiled and walked over to the open window. The night sea wind blew the shade and the red velvet curtains at his face. He acted like he had been expecting me. He turned out the lamp, and it took me a minute to adjust to the moonlight. "I'm on beach patrol. Keep the damn whales away," he said genially. Then he shut one eye, took aim at something out on the beach, and fired his gun.

My ears rang and then felt stuffed with cotton. "Hey, could you stop that?" I asked. The room smelled like burning marshmallows.

"Not high yet?" he asked cheerfully, raising the gun, taking aim, and shooting again.

"No, and I'm not crazy either," I shouted. "Stop it." The gun made my ears feel useless.

He pointed the gun at the floor. "Believe me, the noise is killing me. But that rock-and-roll music they're playing down there is worse."

"Disco," I said.

"Rock-n-roll," he corrected me, leaning over to pick up something small and silver off the shag carpet. It was a bullet. When he lifted his head I saw that his eyes were small, the eyelids very tight, with no lines, pouches, or circles under them. He had the eyes of a child and the girth of a fat, middle-aged adult.

"You're a new one, right? What's your trick?" he asked. His manner was wonderful. He sounded like a young Midwestern clergyman, an interested, admiring authority.

I could have answered anything. Drugs, sexual preference, cars. But I said, "I'm a reporter."

He lifted the gun, and the skin on my back and neck contracted with terror.

"Oh, for Chrissake," he said, and pointed the gun out the window again. "Who put you on the list?"

"Your wife."

He rolled his eyes, and spoke in singsong. "My ex-wife. Ah, the shy Mrs. Lyons, ever unavailable to members of the press."

"What're you really doing?" I asked, while he braced a knee against the windowsill and took aim again.

"You won't believe me," he said, closing one eye.

"Try me."

He lowered his gun to his leg. "Two things. I'm curating my myth, and I'm shooting at moonbeams on the ocean."

I shook my head. "It's dangerous."

"I don't have to account to you," he said. "But I have ten guards keeping guests off my beach. It's private. I own it, a half-mile of it. I own the sea, the wind that blows by, and the rain that falls on it. And I'm using blanks. I'm an asshole, but I'm not a bigtime asshole."

He turned the lamp back on. I sat down on the edge of a fur-covered bed.

"What are you working on?" he asked. He pulled the silver bullet from behind his ear and threw it at me. I retrieved it from the white shag carpet. Another souvenir of Hollywood. I put it behind my ear.

"A story."

He looked at me expectantly.

"You could've told me sooner that they were blanks."

"You didn't ask," he said, "and you come into my bedroom and make me account for myself."

I asked, "What are you working on?"

"A sixty-million-dollar art movie about the life of Buddha," he said. "It's going to raise the spiritual awareness of every man, woman and child in this great country of ours. Imagine what would've happened if P. T. Barnum decided to save souls. And you?" he repeated. "What's your current assignment?"

"Sal Mineo." I watched him lean the gun against the wall and look me up and down.

"Was he your friend?" I asked.

He gave no sign of having heard my question. Instead, he asked, "You one of those righteous Americans who thinks he was killed for his sex life?"

"No, but it's a wild subculture." I sounded like an academic asshole.

"Sex doesn't make people murder." He raised his eyebrows like he was reprimanding me for debating. Then he stared out at the ocean. "You know my biggest power fantasy?" he asked as though we'd been discussing the subject for an hour.

"No, how could I?"

"You could be polite," he said, and flashed me a boyish smile. He had a sweet quality. It was the voice, the plumpness, and the young face.

"I don't want to run a studio. I turn down those joy-boys once a week. What I want is to see the whole city of Los Angeles go black when I turn off my bedroom lights at night. You follow me?"

"No. Why not run a studio?"

"A studio head answers to a board of directors, to the IRS. I answer to nobody."

"Except your wife."

"Wrong. She thinks she's going to get half because of bullshit divorce laws, but I got lawyers working on it."

"Working on what?"

"Keeping what I deserve. But you get what I mean about the city of Los Angeles?" he asked.

"Not really."

"Well, it's a joke. I grossed four million dollars last

week. That's what I read on the *Variety* charts. But I'm fat, I'm only going to make fifty more movies, and I'm still going to die someday."

"Nobody lives forever," I said.

"No shit—you got it." He crooked a finger, urging me to come close. When he smiled, his lower eyelids came up and made his small eyes twinkle at me.

"When was the last time you saw Sal Mineo?" I asked.

He averted his head and lowered his beckoning finger. "Fuck you."

He turned his back to me.

"What's wrong?" I asked.

"Oh, nothing." His voice sounded cheery. "They tell you life's all about love, money, dying with grace, saying fuck the bad stuff," and then he smiled. "Don't ask me."

"I didn't," I said. "I asked about Sal Mineo."

"Huh?" He was pulling off the asbestos glove and opening a drawer of the old highboy. He put the gun away under some blue undershorts. Then he pulled a plum-colored cowboy hat off the closet shelf and placed it on his head.

"Like it?" He patted the Stetson with his fingertips.

"Theatrical."

"You don't like me much," he said. "Believe me, worse things happen. Come on, we're going downstairs."

"Why?"

"Because you're a good audience. Maybe I'll get lucky and make the pages of your newspaper."

At the door of the room, he beckoned me again. "Hurry up."

Below him, the crowd of heads bobbed under the flashing pink and turquoise lights. The music started abruptly. Cigarette smoke curled up toward us.

I put my hand on his arm. "You saw him on the day he was killed."

"Wrong." He grabbed the banister with both fat hands. He looked like he might fall on the people packed at the foot of the staircase. The idea got me dizzy.

"When did you last see him?" I asked. I took a few steps down. I wanted to see his expression.

"On the day he was buried." He averted his face. His voice didn't sound so chipper. He sounded old.

"Before that?"

"Fuck you," he repeated dully.

"Tell me," I said.

"No."

"Tell me." We were standing on the same step.

"No." He turned and gave me another twinkly grin. He was trying to mask some terrible feeling.

"He was out here at the beach on the morning he was killed, wasn't he?" I said.

He looked at me hard. "I don't know."

"Well, when did you see him?"

"I'm going to tell you," he said. Somebody shouted his name above the music, and he waved back. "Vermin," he muttered, and then he said, "I saw him the night before. I woke him up at one-thirty. I was having a bad drunk, and he pulled on his trousers and climbed around Griffith Park with me until I relaxed. He wasn't shocked by my problem. He faced it down with me. That was Sal."

"But I heard he was out here visiting you that day."

"Who says so?"

"Nick Ray."

"I don't give two fucks for you or the things you hear."

"Why won't you admit he was here with you?"

He was walking away from me, downstairs. He shouted over his shoulder. The music was frantic. "I don't live out here anymore. I moved to Mulholland a month ago. I don't sleep in this house. I don't fuck the woman who lives here."

"What's sex have to do with it?"

"Hey, don't you know sex for people over seventeen is obsolete?" he shouted. "They look like shit doing it."

"So you weren't here that day?"

"I was sitting with my ass on my fancy chair in my fancy office at Paramount. Ask my secretary. Ask my wife. Well, she might not tell you."

"So Nick Ray was wrong?" I wanted to prolong the encounter.

"Not necessarily, scout." He raised his voice. "Maybe

Sal was out here that morning. This isn't the only house on the beach. I'd like to find out myself. Maybe he was visiting somebody else.''

"Why didn't you get him work?" I shouted.

He took a step back up and looked me in the face.

"You're a stranger," he said. "A friend of mine was murdered. The only person I met in two weeks that could get it together to murder is you."

I felt like he slapped me. "That's unfair," I said.

"Then let me alone," he shouted, and disappeared into the crowd at the bottom of the stairs. After a second I couldn't see the plum-colored cowboy hat. There was a scratch of needle on plastic record grooves, the music stopped, and lights went on. I heard his voice amplified over the buzz of party-talking. "Out front"—he sounded genial again—"and I'm going to show you something special."

For a quarter of an hour, I stood on the steps and watched the people crush through the hallway. I followed them outdoors, and eventually there were about a hundred of us standing on the front lawn, the sea wind whipping at bare arms and clothes and blowing people's hair on end. Too bad Kate Lyons's flower beds were getting trampled. Two huge floodlights went on. The faces were white against the dark that was the sea and the sky and the flowering lawns.

In front of the crowd, under lights, was the silver Rolls Royce. Lyons walked out to the Rolls, raised his arms, palms down like a minister, and addressed his guests. A tiny microphone was pinned to his blue shirt-collar. "Hallelujah!" he shouted. "I will attempt to spit on the steering wheel of a seventy-nine-thousand-dollar customized Rolls Royce Silver Cloud, owned by myself." The crowd began clapping. The sounds were flat against the deep thuds of the ocean.

He made a hoarse plugging noise in his throat and spat toward the car.

"And having failed manfully at fifty feet," he shouted, "I'll try again at thirty, praise the Lord." A few people clapped again.

"I did it!" Lyons screamed, and everybody cheered.

"Don't touch it! Let it dry!" Lyons yelled, as one girl started to wipe off the steering wheel with her sleeve.

Somebody handed me a full goblet. "Hold this," he said, and disappeared. I sipped it. Very dry champagne.

I followed a television actor with blond streaky hair into the house. His name was on the tip of my tongue—Roger somebody. He wore gold lizard boots. He positioned himself in a corner of the living room that faced the sea, turned, and smiled like he knew me. I smiled, but there was no further response. I glanced over my shoulder and saw a large projection screen. That was what he was smiling at. On the screen, I saw a closeup of Lyons spitting, and a fast zoom into the steering wheel of a Rolls Royce.

A servant offered me a huge bowl of grapes. Roger was chewing on one, his eyes glued to the movie screen.

"Who did the film?" I asked.

"Spielberg or Scorsese," he said. "Home movies. Last year's anniversary party." He tossed his hair at me and dropped a grape into my champagne glass.

Nobody else paid attention to me. It occurred to me that if Mark was at my side, everybody would stare. I'm not Hollywood beautiful. I couldn't imagine anybody looking at me instead of a buttercup like Nell Fields. Her looks were professional.

I swallowed more fizzy liquid. I hated to think of the cops bothering Mark again. I was an insensitive clod. He was lurching from one feeling to another, grieving, and scared out of his mind. That was why he hid the loan company card. It had to do with Chris; Mark just wanted to protect him.

Dammit, it was confusing.

What am I doing getting involved in it? My eyes smarted, and I swayed a little while another waiter refilled my glass. It was ridiculous to feel so much.

Lovemaking with him was incredible, but it hadn't been normal last time, all tongues and fingers. Maybe he really hated women. But then why make love so tenderly? I held the glass high and let the last drops fall on my tongue.

I had to get a grip on myself and find a bathroom. A tickle flickered inside me.

At the bathroom I joined a line of kids. Three people emerged and another three disappeared inside. I was getting uncomfortable. The girl in front of me confided, "My nose is going, you know? I shouldn't be here. My shrink says rub it on my gums, a bigger surface."

"But that way takes too long," said a guy.

The girl said, "This director I met at the Mark Taper does it with suppositories. It's fast, but your ass gets ice cold."

I was getting uncomfortable, and this line wasn't moving. I decided to give up on this bathroom. I put my head down and tried to make my way through a knot of women crowded around someone with a mustache who was wearing aviator glasses. I tried to get a better look. Then his mouth curved into the world's jauntiest smile since Gable. Burt Reynolds was wearing a blue Oxford shirt, Brooks Brothers materials, cut tight. Unbuttoned, it hugged his chest. He held a hacking jacket on a hooked finger at his shoulder.

I edged down a hallway to another line of people waiting for a bathroom under pink neon lights. Somebody was pounding on the bathroom door. I recognized Kate Lyons. Her eyelids were striped with turquoise lines and she was wearing a transparent gauzy caftan. With her opaque eyes, she looked Egyptian and menacing. Standing a foot from her and swaying in her high heels was Nell Fields. Kate turned to glare at Nell. They both looked angry. I stepped closer.

"Gate-crashing is tacky," Kate was saying.

"He wants to talk," Nell said in a slurry voice.

"Talk is free." Kate pounded the door again. "My house, my john," she shouted. A minute later, a man ran out past her.

Nell clutched her evening bag with two hands under her chin.

Kate grabbed her elbow and shouted, "Hurry up," and then they disappeared behind the bathroom door.

I stood there adding it up. Not only had I missed a chance at the bathroom, but I couldn't hear them at all. It sounded to me like Nell was the intermediary for someone who had big problems with Kate Lyons. I silently bet all the cash in my wallet that those two ladies were leaning over the bathroom sink to argue about Sal Mineo.

I ignored the line of people and blatantly pressed my ear against the door.

"They'll be a while, honey," a girl said, handing me a joint. "Try the guesthouse. Out the front door and down on the beach."

I didn't move, but I inhaled the joint. It burned my throat. I reached into my blazer pocket and pressed a button on my tape recorder. I pulled out a pencil and dropped it to the floor. I smiled a little apologetically, stooped down, and shoved the tape recorder partway under the door.

Stooped against the doorknob, I heard murmurs, and then running water. I gave it another thirty seconds, then I pulled the recorder out with two fingers. I straightened up just as the door opened, Kate Lyons leading the way. I clutched Nell's wrist. "What's it all about?"

"Don't ask me, honey." She twisted away from my grasp.

Kate Lyons was whispering something to the tuxedoed servant carrying the champagne. She ignored me and disappeared into the crowd.

I headed through the mass of party guests for the front door.

I walked around the back and took the steps down to the beach. The fresh air smelled like iodine and seaweed. Facing the waves, I realized I was drunk and stoned. A great reporter. Dark, thick clouds passed in front of the moon. I blinked and the gray ocean became bright blue. The sky was dense, hanging above me like gray absorbent cotton. I wondered what kept the ocean in place. I couldn't remember why oceans didn't surge up, destroy beaches, and then cover the earth.

Then a bunch of pebbles hit my head and shoulders. Somebody was throwing rocks near me. I heard them on all sides. Something stung my lip, and I whirled around. I held my breath and tried to blot out the noisy surf. The thumps were loud. A rock hit my bare arm.

"Stop it," I shouted at the seething ocean. Another rock hit my neck and scratched a hole in my skin. Somebody didn't mean me well. I saw a dark, square shape nestled under a small cliff. The beach cottage. I shouted, "Anybody there?"

The heavy thumps stopped. I ran blindly toward the beach house. My skirt stuck to something, and I tripped and fell backward on the sand, screaming a thin scream. I pulled cactus needles from my legs. Then, ten feet away, a door swung open and I saw the dim interior light of the beach cottage. "What's wrong?" a young voice asked.

"I'm lost," I wailed.

By the time I reached the light, the doorway was empty. Inside the foyer I locked the front door. Nobody was going to sneak up on me. My fingers ached from holding the champagne glass so tight. My thighs were tense from having to pee. I smelled marijuana smoke and cedar wood. The foyer was dim. A door was half open down a hall. Inside it, I saw a candle flickering on tile. A smell of burning incense wafted through. It was a bathroom. I relaxed; it reminded me of parties in college. But the bathroom wasn't empty.

I saw a mustached guy with his blue jeans down around his ankles, facing someone on her knees. It was a girl, whose back was toward me. I saw her mouth move away from his groin. In his right palm, he balanced a large round mirror. The girl snorted up some cocaine off the surface of the mirror, and I saw him rub flakes of cocaine on the tip of his erect cock.

I backed out of there and into another room, rattled but unable to face the dark beach again. I heard giggles. I switched on a lamp and saw three boys and two girls wrapped around each other on a sofa. They grimaced and put their hands over their eyes. I turned the lamp off.

"What's going on?" one sweet voice asked.

"That question's been on my mind all night," I said.

"Don't go barging into the john," she admonished. "He's got enough coke to go around."

"Isn't there another bathroom?" I asked.

"No, and for Chrissake, this is a line." There were a few soft murmurs of assent.

My throat closed up and I felt sick. I ran for the front door and galloped up over the path near the cactus hedge. I closed my eyes and jumped the hedge. It scratched my calves. My heels kept sinking into the sand. The beach was empty. The wind was cold.

In front of the main house I saw Kate Lyons pointing and shouting at black servants who were positioning two chrome jukeboxes and a pool table in the sand. Two of them held tall street gaslamps. She hopped around in her billowing white caftan and swore at the sweating servants.

I was tired of the hustling, the drugs, all of it. I leaned against a jukebox across from her.

One of the long gaslamps started to fall over. "Watch it," she cried, "assholes won't take any responsibility."

I grabbed the lamp and propped it up.

"What do you want?" she snapped. "You don't know what you want."

She was wrong. I wanted this story. I clutched the metal pole. "Tell me about your fight with Chris Franklin," I said. She stopped moving around in the night wind and put her sunglasses on. They were prescription, opaque mirror. I hated them. My front teeth were knocking against each other in spasms. "I've heard his version. Now I want yours."

"What the hell are you saying?"

"Obviously he wants the deal straightened out." I made my words vague, filled with hidden meaning.

"We got no deal."

"That's not what Sal Mineo thought." I suddenly realized Mineo was a mystery element. He could be evoked like God or the germ theory to hint at another reality.

"Sal didn't know what he was talking about."

But it'd worked. There was something between her and Chris. A deal, a pact.

"That got him in trouble."

"Wrong."

"Right," I said. We sounded fairly amiable, like two former schoolchums. "I heard that from Nell, you know."

Kate sneered and barked a laugh. "Nell Field is a fag-hag cokehead. She hasn't been anybody for ten years. She'll do anybody errands for a little cocaine. Sal kept her around; he dug the men she hangs out with. Sal dies and she latches onto it for her career. It's sickening."

"I thought you said you didn't know Sal Mineo."

"The things you hear about people you don't give a shit about," she said.

"She do errands for you?"

One look at her face and I knew I'd blundered onto something. Whatever we were talking about bothered her like crazy.

"Get out of here," she said, "and never come back."

I stepped back, and the long pole I was holding began to sway toward the ground. It fell behind me on the sand, and I heard the glass top break as though a wave had tossed it up on the beach.

"What's going on?" another voice asked from the steps.

It was her husband, his head chalky white in the moon-light.

"She's trying to smear me," Kate said, "for her tab-loid."

"Really? How?" David asked. "I find it hard to believe you wouldn't fight for a headline."

"Did you know Sal got a deal with her for Chris?" I asked.

"What about it?" He looked hard, angry.

"She dumped Chris," I said.

"What the fuck is she talking about? Kate, answer me."

"She's way off."

"Madam, lady of the press," he yawned, "it seems you must go."

"Well, about the cocaine—" I said.

He interrupted. "Cocaine is a banal subject. I loathe it."

He took my arm as though we were moving in a receiving

line and began steering me up the stairs and around the house to a Rolls Royce, I smelled shampoo on his beard. He reminded me of a reporter at the office who showers three times a day and complains he feels dirty. "Cocaine obliterates conscience. I hate it. Selling it. Using it. Work is the only decent thing we do out here. I believe in it, the way you believe—now, let me see . . ." he paused and kissed me on the cheek.

"Work," I said.

"No, let me think." He opened the back door of the silver car. "I believe in work the way you believe the sun will rise tomorrow."

"That's David Hume," I said.

"I don't believe him," he said quickly. "I just believe in work. Once in a while I don't even believe in that."

He pushed me politely into the interior of his car and leaned down to close the door.

He stuck his hand inside the car window. I realized with a shock that I still hadn't gone to the bathroom. I looked into his small-child eyes. "Your wife doesn't agree with you."

"But she does." I heard the cold voice again.

"She doesn't tell you the truth."

"What truth?" He couldn't help it.

"That Sal Mineo knew about her and Chris."

"What about them?"

"I think it was your wife he was visiting that last day at the beach," I said.

I smoothed my hair and felt something jammed behind one ear. I handed his silver bullet back to him. He dropped it on the sand. "Go to hell," he said, and stepped back from the car. Kate stood behind him. She took his arm. He pulled away from her grasp.

The driver steered the car slowly away from the couple. I knocked on the glass window between us. "Hurry up!" I said. But something had paid off. I punched a button of the tape recorder. After a scraping noise and silence, I heard Nell crying over some music. Water was running. "Sal

258

went to the limit for Chris. What's in it for you?" It was Kate.

I could barely make out her words over the party noises.

Nell answered, "Shut up. I know what Sal thought about your crappy deals."

The tape clicked and stopped.

Chapter
Eighteen

The air down here was awful, pure gasoline and exhaust. I blinked against the fluorescent ceiling light, but it didn't get me any answers. I was parked in the garage under my hotel, too tired to switch the lights off.

I put the Dodge in gear and drove out again past the dozing night-guard and onto Sunset where a teenage hooker was sitting on a newspaper stand brushing her hair. I needed to talk to Mark. If any living human being knew Mineo's intimate problems, he did. I had to get Mark to trust me.

Clearly, Nell Fields had crashed the party to offer Kate Lyons an olive branch from Chris. I sketched out a rough history; somehow Sal Mineo got Kate Lyons to dangle a juicy role at Chris. Maybe she even advanced him money. I wondered why Sal didn't go to her husband. It was probably her project. But Chris and Mineo fought, and Mineo got murdered. Kate backed out of the deal because she wanted to stay clear of anybody who might've murdered Sal Mineo. Chris needs to get back into her good graces in order to work. But she won't see him. Why? Kate must suspect him of murder.

I had to talk to Chris soon. He had a lot of explaining to do.

I turned into Mark's clearing and I smelled camellia and lilac blossoms. There were no cars except his old Cadillac. Mark figured in the history. I sighed aloud. Somebody, maybe the murderer, ransacked this house twice, looking for—evidence, money, Chris, drugs. I had questions for Mark about Sal Mineo's loan application. I wondered if Chris needed the ten thousand dollars to pay back Kate Lyons.

I got out of my car, yawned against the cold, and futilely locked the doors. I rang for the cable car and saw a flash of yellow eyes. A fat cat squeezed out from under the bumper of Mark's Cadillac. I reached down to pet it, and watched the cable car descend. In front of me, two date-palm trees stood like sentries against Mark's hill.

I imagined another scenario. Chris and Jonathan both had sexual motives to murder Sal Mineo—jealousy. The police were hot on this trail. Something at the back of my brain lurched forward. At the bar Mark told me Jonathan and Mineo had a date the night of the murder. He called Jonathan a trick, implying he was one of many.

And Mark lied to Chris when he said he never met Jonathan. That made me wonder. Suppose Chris, when he came out here, got jealous because his lover wasn't keeping promises. Nick Ray had opined that their relationship worked because of the distance between them.

A minute later, I stepped out of the cable car and faced the silent adobe walls.

I knocked at the door. It wasn't locked; it opened when I pushed. It was too quiet. The house was wide open. I didn't like it. Either Mark knew enough not to fear the people who broke into his house, or he was courting danger.

The cat scampered into the dark hall and I bolted the front door behind me. The house smelled of cigarettes and marijuana. I ran down the front hallway and through the living room, my sandals clattering on wood floors.

The fish swam peacefully. They're lucky. Nothing short of war outside the tank disturbs them. Mark hadn't turned the aquarium lights off. That was odd. Then I felt a vibration on the floor. I heard someone sweeping a snare with a metal brush, and I held my breath when he started singing.

And there's nothing I can say,
When death runs your life,
When you're roamin' through L.A.

He teased out a blues melody and stopped it with a percussive snap. I followed the sound through doors and down new hallways. Despite all my problems with Mark, I loved hearing him.

The melody sounded more tired than the legendary Mark Loren.

I heard him jump an octave and shriek at the top of his range. A great whoop in the middle of the mournful song. He was playing piano in stark chords as if for a church choir. He crooned in falsetto, "There's something so deep about the blues, the world can't stand it."

Then the tune went awry and I heard him picking it on a guitar. My mind switched tracks. Here I was listening to a major American singer. I was hearing something that hadn't been put on a record for the last four years. But then there was silence, and then a crash.

I found my way to a door behind the kitchen, still thinking about his career. Last spring there were rumors Mark was joining Bob Dylan's road show. Before the concert, a full-page statement welcoming him back appeared in the Sunday *New York Times*, signed by music critics. He never showed. Rumors of his death sold out an issue of *Rolling Stone* in a day. He was a pop culture mystery.

I peeked inside the room at a baby grand piano, a set of drums, and an entire wall of control boxes that looked like telephone switchboards and computers. Mark was gripping a gleaming cello, his ear to the instrument's body. A guitar lay splintered against a wall. Obviously he'd thrown it.

His special glow was gone. His shirt was wrinkled and unbuttoned, and his eyes looked red from cigarette smoke and lack of sleep. His hair hung down over his forehead in limp clumps. He looked like an ordinary tired guy in his early twenties. I felt a pang of disappointment. I wanted him to look like a star. But still Mark seemed magnetic.

He slowly pulled the bow across the strings, playing a series of Bach chords. Then he changed it to a deep moaning that reminded me of blues. I saw that he'd electrified the instrument. The notes went on and on.

I wanted to kiss him but didn't dare. I flopped down on a bed covered with an antique American quilt. He didn't look up. It was after three A.M. and I didn't want to fight anymore. My questions could wait. I just wanted to watch him make music. The sexiest thing about him was his vulnerability and the way he was always fighting to overcome it.

Up behind him, a mobile twisted slowly. It was a fragile branch that held a seashell and a crystal. The branch turned in one direction, stopped, and turned back. I felt a little stirring of wind from the open glass doors.

He started plucking the cello strings and twisting pegs.

"What's the tune?" I finally asked.

"Something I'm working on."

"What's it called?"

" 'Roaming Through L.A.,' " he said, looking down at the floor between his knees.

I knew what he was doing with that song. It was a slow-tempo Mississippi blues, F minor. "I could play chords for you."

"Forget it, babe," he said.

"Look," I said, "it's easy."

Then I heard a tapping. "What's that noise?" I asked.

He put the cello down on its side and walked over to the glass doors. I followed and pressed my nose against the glass, trying to see into the dark night. I made out a tiny bird with a long beak diving into the glass like an electric drill. "That damn bird," Mark said. "I try pretty near everything. He won't give up. I leave him peaches, dates, and nuts. All he wants is to break through that glass and get inside my house."

The bird's rhythm was steady. "He could fly in through an open window," I said.

"He doesn't like open windows."

"Why doesn't he work on trees?"

"I reckon he wants to get himself a home inside this magic invisible tree."

"Mixed up," I said.

Mark tried to brush his hair off his eyes. "Maybe not," he said. "In some parts of town, trees are obsolete, and woodpeckers'll be obsolete in a hundred years. Maybe he's trying to adjust."

He started to tap his forefinger against the windowpane.

I leaned against his side, but he walked back to the piano, and started whipping up and down octaves of scales. I sprawled out on the bed, closed my eyes, and pulled the quilt over my bare calves. I heard him walk over and switch off the lamp shining in my eyes.

"Thanks," I said.

He picked the cello off its side and began tuning the strings again. Then he began singing:

> Word I was in the house alone,
> word I was in my life alone . . .

I recognized Robert Frost and shot a look at him.

"Shit," he said. "This is a mess of sheep dung."

It made my eyes sting when he sang his feelings.

He stopped picking the melody. "One time, I used to sing my tunes because I wanted to get people going, make them cry about things that made me sad."

"What about now?" I asked.

"I don't know anymore," he said, and pressed earphones to one ear. "If it wasn't for record-company hype, I'd just be somebody who'd written a few tunes."

"I can help," I said. Then I pushed off the quilt and walked over to the baby grand piano. I sat down, adjusted the round piano stool, flexed my fingers over the Steinway keyboard, and hummed. The artist and his work. I bet nobody dared interfere with him. "I do chords, you work on melody and words," I ordered.

I couldn't make the long notes cry the way he did, but the

music sounded pretty. I had forgotten how much I liked piano. I played his chord progressions through twice, until he came in picking out the melody on the cello. Then he put down the cello. He was sitting on the edge of his chair, his spine stretched, his chin high, his eyes closed. His fingers were clasped on the top of his head. After a minute of piano chords, he was singing low and sweet:

> *But the sky turned to smoke*
> *in the heat of an L.A. night.*
> *Will it take the place of dreams?*
> *Will I ever find my way?*
> *with one stoplight after another—*
> *roamin' through L.A.*

He began setting the beat with one forefinger like a bandleader. He slowed me up. I gave it more juice, and ended it. In the silence I leaned one elbow on the piano keyboard and made funny notes. I felt sad.

"Tired?" he asked. He hugged me from behind, pulling me against him. "I know what you're feeling," he whispered.

I leaned back against his body. He was trying to end the fight. I don't think people ever really make up. They just get used to the ways they disappoint each other. "You hate my slouch?" I asked.

He buried his face in my hair.

"It sure felt like I did," he said, and leaned his elbows back onto the keyboard, coming down on the same note several octaves apart. Sometimes it seemed like he couldn't make a graceless move.

"You betrayed me," he said idly.

"How?"

"Well, this bass player calls me from New York, and tells me how your newspaper printed this snapshot I took of Sal at the beach."

That Marty Burns had no shame. I'd wring his neck. I stood up, pulling matchbooks and junk out of my pockets until I found the story on hotel stationery. "I filed a good piece."

He gave me one of his jittery looks before he read it. When he finished, he folded it a few extra times and smoothed the creases. I could see he liked it.

"You should've told me."

"I'm telling you," he said, playing three minor chords on the piano. "I'm telling you why I got mad, sugar, and that's best as I ever done."

"What's going on between us?" I asked. I wasn't ready to bring up the way he lied to me.

"I been having these sex fantasies!" His voice went up a note.

I could've cried. He was already fantasizing about other people, probably men. No wonder we hadn't had conventional sex the other night.

"Let me run it down." He made an introductory swirl of piano music. "Sara, I have been having fantasies about you. You get me hot. It's about the last thing I expected. I was playing another game entirely. I haven't dreamed about a woman in years."

He closed the piano.

"It's too confusing," I said carefully. I didn't want him seducing me away from my work.

"Don't put us down," he shot back at me. "I feel like the channels inside my heart are changing, flowing upstream when they used to flow down." He smiled to himself.

I started babbling. "Look, Sal Mineo made your whole life legitimate. No matter what happened, there was somebody who loved you."

"So, Ms. Freud?"

"You were the one who said somebody hit your life with a big hammer. You don't know what to do next. You can't trust the old things anymore."

"Like sucking cock?" he asked.

I didn't like his tone of voice. "Maybe."

"I'm not good enough for you," he said.

I widened my eyes, mute.

"Well, you're wrong," he said in a small voice.

"I don't understand you or your feelings," I said firmly.

"Sugar, I told you how I feel about you, and for a while now, I ain't been writing music and I ain't been making love." He hit his fists lightly on the keyboard.

It hit me all over again: he was a stranger. Maybe he was one of those performers who appeal to audiences on a sexual level but don't have active sex lives. They're sublimated or something. They give everything on stage and there's nothing left when they're off. Maybe he couldn't really connect to me, or to anybody.

"How do you fit in?" he asked slowly. "Tell me, smartie."

I tried to sound normal. "Well, if you were blocked, now I look like a solution."

"Shit on your theories. They're shit," he said.

I lay down on the bed. Romance is great, but reality doesn't always enhance it.

He walked stiffly across the room. He hugged me, his fingers tense against my back. "How could anything that feels so good be wrong?" he whispered. "Let's go to bed." He pulled me up off the quilt gently. I was as relaxed leaning against him as I was lying down. We fit together so well.

"How was the anniversary waltz tonight?" he asked. I told him about David Lyons spitting on the Rolls Royce.

He laughed in my ear. "The way you describe it, they sound like Martians." He leaned the two of us against the wall. "David like you?" he asked.

I shrugged. No need to mention that he kicked me out.

"Was he wearing his latest 'am-I-gay' outfit?"

"He's not gay, is he?"

"No, but he's like a lot of guys out here—sensitive; you know, a little depressed; they walk around with their hands in the pockets of their fancy linen pants. They like gays, they imitate their style. Gays got into old Hollywood before anybody. It's real hip to swish and kiss men on the mouth, even if you're as straight as Nixon."

He pursed his lips and kissed me funny. "David's like that. He wants people to wonder about him. He loves to go

267

out on a limb, and he's a compulsive gambler. He loves danger, living on the edge.''

Still leaning against him, I told him about the fight between Kate Lyons and Nell. I felt his body tense again.

"What's wrong?" I asked, pulling away.

He sat down on the side of the bed and pulled on his cheeks. I wanted to stop his hands. White fingerprints came up on his tired face.

"Drop the article," he said, his fingers covering his eyes.

"Are you serious?"

"Drop the article, please."

"Mark—"

He stood up and put his arms on my shoulders and shook me gently. "Stay with me, permanent," he said.

I pushed away. "I don't get it."

"I want you to stay out here with me," he said.

I never expected that. I had been trying to love him in the moment, the way I figured he wanted. "What does that have to do with the piece?" I asked.

"I want you to be safe. It's too dangerous," he said. "More people will die. I know it."

"Don't pull me away from my work," I said.

He grabbed me, pinning my elbows against my sides.

"Negotiate, lady," he said. "Let's put things on probation."

"Sounds like one of your games," I said.

"I'm serious," he said. "Give it three days. Don't work, just stay with me and live with me, and maybe something will change."

Somewhere I was thrilled.

"Don't think about me as work. Don't take calls from your editor, just feel stuff, and something good will happen. It's no long shot." He paused and dropped his hands from my elbows.

"I love you," he said.

My whole body flushed. I couldn't say anything.

"Three days is a beginning."

"Then what?" I croaked. It was too late at night for me to think straight.

"Hey," he said, "I'm only asking you to spare seventy-two hours for love."

Before I could protest he grabbed my wrist and pulled me, leaping over his cello. "Jump!" he said, as we ran together down the dark hallway toward his bedroom.

Inside the dark room, he dropped my arm. Suddenly he cupped my cheek in one palm. He was unbuttoning his shirt and turning slightly. I smelled him, fresh perspiration and soap. He kicked off his dungarees. I didn't want to think anything. He combed my hair from side to side with his hands, bunching it up and letting it fall until the roots tingled. I remembered his brown body arching high above the turquoise swimming pool in the sunlit flower garden. I knelt down, stroking private skin, taking possession of him with my fingertips. I felt as if ginger ale were bubbling out of my body from my pores, from between my legs. I felt I was made of bubbles, not blood, not tissue, not bone.

He pushed me down into the soft bed. The plump pillow cooled my cheek. He left me there. I heard him unlatch a glass door. Night perfumes drifted in. The air was cold.

"Hide your eyes," he commanded. I pressed my fingers against my face and saw through the thin red streams between them that he'd turned on his bedside lamp. Then the light softened. He'd thrown his shirt over the lampshade, casting a glow. He took my clothes off fast and cuddled close. "I have something to say," I whispered.

He pulled an arm languidly over his eyes. "You're going to tell me you can't give us three days."

When I was silent, he sang out, "Oh, baby, I'm a gambling man," in a cracking voice.

I struggled to sit up.

"Answer me one question," he said, tracing his fingers around my lips.

"Yes?"

"A week ago, you never dreamed you'd be working on a murder, and lying in my bed liking the sound of me asking you to stop working for love."

Before I could answer, he parted his lips and began to kiss

my face all over, light, fast, wonderful kisses. "You're close to making the deal," he said.

I raised my palm to swear. "On my honor, journalism—" He grabbed me and lay me down on my back again. In the lamplight, his face glowed and his dark hair curled down toward me. "We will begin," he interrupted, "with an orgy."

"Oh, no," I pretended to bite all my fingernails with fear. "An orgy—never."

"An orgy of tenderness," he whispered.

"Is it sexy?" I smiled despite myself.

"It's girl stuff," he said. "That's why I want to do it with you." Bending over me, he licked at my mouth. His wet tongue made me shiver.

"I wish you were feeling everything I feel and everything you feel," he said urgently.

He picked up a strand of my hair on his finger and let it float down to my face.

I rolled away.

"What's going on?" His breath made my ear tight.

"I'm thinking about you," I said.

"Doing what?"

When I didn't answer him he sang softly, "Bad sex is like white kids dancing with no music."

The night air began to warm for morning. The sunlight was close. He tickled his finger down my neck and between my breasts, singing, "I got a woman, way over town, she's good to me . . ."

He rolled me on top of him, and I balanced on my elbows. He reached around us and threw pillows off the bed. Then he flung his head from side to side, tickling himself with my wet tongue and my hair. "Silky furs," he whispered. "I been waiting."

He sucked my mouth into his, and thrust up toward me. My eyes ached like weeping, but I clenched deep inside me against tension, and pulled away from him.

He stretched an arm back and turned off the lamp. An odd blue light filled the room. I felt something land on the edge of the bed. Two yellow eyes stared at me. "Stay down,

Lucky,'' Mark mumbled. The cat purred, and made smaller and smaller circles until she curled herself up into a ball, her tail twitching against my ankle. Mark lifted his head and trailed his mouth slightly across my cheek. ''Women are great.''

I picked up some moisture from his forehead with my finger and smoothed his eyebrow. My voice came out husky. ''Why are women great?''

Mark laughed. ''Really,'' he said dryly, and the word inflected back and forth.

''Why?'' I asked again. He touched his nose to mine, and ran his tongue over my mouth. I twisted my head, and rolled to the side of the bed, shivering. He drummed his fingers on my cheek, like he was playing a tune.

''Women are different.'' He sighed. ''You have this wild red hair, fine, silky furs to hide me. The lady has these silky furs over her brain.''

He buried his face in my hair, breathing warm and damp. ''The way I feel about you is a mystery.'' He sounded irked. ''All I know is sex is the way to fight dying.

''At the funeral, it was crazy. I mean, everybody fucking their brains out all night, shouting, throwing each other around. On chairs, on airplanes, in bathrooms, in bathtubs, on lawns. Folks went crazy.''

He rolled on top of me again. His body was very heavy.

''It was like everybody felt dead, but they were forcing themselves to live.''

''What did you do?''

''Aw, babe, now wait.''

''I was there at the funeral.''

''And now you're here with me,'' he said, tightening his arm under my back. I pushed him off me. I closed my eyes, but then I heard sputtery ringing. A tiny telephone-light flashed by the bed.

''Let it alone,'' he muttered.

I reached over to the telephone and a tired English voice asked for Mark. ''Who's calling?'' I asked brazenly. Then I heard the cranky hauteur. ''Christopher.''

Mark grabbed the phone. His lips touched the receiver

and he turned his back to me. The cord stretched across my chest. "How bad?" he asked. Then he cursed and said, "Tomorrow night, as usual, and don't go anywhere else. I'll handle it."

He passed me the telephone and I hung it up. The last few days folded in on themselves and disappeared. I felt left out. Mark and Chris had too many secrets. "What's going on?"

"It's hard," Mark said. "It's hard to get into somebody's life. Give it time, sugar."

"You have to tell me."

"Chris got beat up," he said shortly.

I tried to see his facial expression in the dim light. "Who did it?"

He hesitated, and then seemed to come to a decision. "Maybe the cops, maybe some thugs at his house."

"Cops don't do that."

"They needed fast answers."

"Was it the same people who broke in here? The people who beat him up?"

He sighed and closed his eyes. "Sherlock Holmes," he said.

"Was it the same people?"

"I don't know."

I figured I could bluff. "What about him and Sal Mineo?"

"What about them?"

"Well, they broke up, didn't they?"

"How'd you know? You Joyce Haber?" He made a snorting sound in his throat.

"Well, he had a date with Jonathan the night he was murdered." I watched his nostrils tremble at the word.

"Who says?"

"You."

"When did I say that?"

"At the bar the other night."

He put his hands in front of his face and said sarcastically, "Better not close my eyes around you. I might talk in my sleep."

"And if I was a detective, I'd say Chris had a motive," I said. Mark rolled over and kissed my ear.

"Sugar, the cops don't know anything so private about my two buddies."

"You know it, and so do I."

"But I knew Sal and Chris, and it was a temporary kind of thing. Chris knew that. On a scale of ten, that spat was nothing—a three, maybe."

I didn't believe him. "I read that page of notes Sal Mineo made in the script and it sounds like Chris wasn't getting what he wanted."

"Let it alone," Mark said, his breath on my face. "You're wrong. I knew the people involved down to their toes."

"Well, I got another theory."

He gave me a sexy stare, but he couldn't stop me from asking my questions. "Why did Chris sour on the deal with Kate Lyons?"

Mark twisted his head away and folded his arms across his chest.

"You know Sal Mineo was down at the beach trying to fix things up on the morning he was murdered." I hated to watch his jaw muscle jump.

"I don't know anything."

I sat up and glared at him. "That Canyon Loan Company. Why did you hide that woman's card from me?"

He raised a hand and smacked it against the headboard. "That was my business."

"It was sneaky," I insisted. The room was getting light. I stared at a pile of my clothes next to the bed. One bird chirruped and woke up another. I felt lonely.

"You're still a member of the press, sugar. I ain't apologizing."

"Suppose I prove that card's relevant?"

He winced, "Oh, Jesus." I scanned the fine line at the edges of his eyes. This was a preview of how his face would look when he was old. "Every secret of a dead man ain't your business." He spoke slowly. "I'll make sure of it."

I kept pushing. "Why did he need ten thousand dollars?"

"Don't ask me." He looked more pained.

I hated to think about how much he was hiding from me.

273

"I need to talk to Chris," I blurted.

He was whistling something between his teeth, like he didn't want to hear me.

"Did he ask you to meet him at that bar tomorrow night?"

The whistling stopped. "Why do you want to know?"

A muscle cramped in my neck. "I want to come with you to see him."

"Nope." His mouth looked tight.

"What's so secret about that bar?"

"Nothing."

"Then take me."

"You'll get good and upset," he said. "Saturday nights are crazy."

"You're not protecting me," I said, watching him bite on his lower lip.

"I'm trying," he said softly.

"No, you're protecting yourself. You don't want me to see you there with those people, now that there's something between us."

He reached down and pulled the sheet over our bare legs. "They like me. Doesn't hurt me to be liked."

"There's more to it," I said. "Mark, it's because of who you are."

"Sara, the only reason I'm going there is Chris. I gotta help him." He yawned again.

"Why can't I help?"

"Nobody's going to read about that bar in some newspaper." He smiled with one corner of his mouth. "It ain't no place for a lady."

"I'm no lady, I'm a newsperson."

He laughed as if somebody'd told him a bad joke.

I closed my eyes and said, "I get it. You want to go there, but I can't see you there."

"Bullshit."

"What does Chris have on you, anyway?" I needed to know.

"Baby, it's cold in here," he sang suddenly.

He turned slowly toward me. I avoided the full stare. "I can give it up," he said.

I laughed, a harsh sound. The joke was on me.

Mark's breath was suddenly soft on my shoulder. "I want the murder solved more than you, babe."

"I don't believe you," I said. "I think if you had to choose between protecting your secret society and catching the murderer, you'd protect that bar."

Mark answered in a neutral monosyllable. "Wrong."

"The bar comes before me, and it always will."

"Wrong," he repeated.

"You're lying. You seduced me just to stop my work."

"But it's different now," he said sadly.

I heard several birdsongs and then a sweet warble. The sun was rising. "Mark, I can't stay with you three days."

He raised his head and blinked at me.

I had to take care of myself. He was too confusing; in five minutes he'd become a stranger again. "I got work to do, and sex isn't the same for me as it is for you."

He stretched his arms high above his head. "Don't be afraid of me," he said dully.

I couldn't trust him. "It's ugly right under the surface," I said.

"Say it," he said; his voice wasn't sweet like the South anymore. "What the hell you're talking about."

It came pouring out. "I hate gay bars, and I hate the way Chris wanted to hurt you and me in your garden."

"You hate faggots?" he asked calmly.

"No, but I don't have to love them."

"Anytime I want, I can move out of the scene," he said, his eyes still closed.

"You can't give up your whole life, and I can't live with it." He closed his eyes. "I'm going home now," I said.

"No," he murmured.

My legs were heavy. "I live in New York," I said, picking up one sandal. "I know what goes on."

"It sure don't sound like it," he said sullenly, and rolled away.

"Mark, hey," I whispered, twisting around.

He pulled the sheet tight around his body. I buckled my sandal and tried to blank out a picture of Chris sidling up to Mark's naked body. I couldn't bring myself to say goodbye.

My shirt was missing. I grabbed his off the lamp. I'd been taken in by his sexy gambits. Twenty-six and still dumb about so much stuff.

He sat up, rubbing one eye with his knuckle. "Stay the night, anyway, stay with me."

"No, I'm working on something," I said. "I'm going to find the murderer, whether it's Chris or Jonathan or the damn bartender."

He flattened a pillow with a quick smack of his hand. He spoke in a monotone. "Don't forget your bag and stuff down the hall."

Chapter Nineteen

The front bumper of Mark's white Cadillac hit the street and bounced before the whole car appeared and turned down the mountain. A station wagon passed. I released the emergency brake and slid down the sloping road shoulder after him. It was ten P.M., and I'd been staked out in my Dodge near his clearing for two hours. I'd slept away another day. Not my usual schedule. Every time I felt sad about what had happened with Mark, I forced my mind back to composing a lead about Chris Franklin's recent fight with Sal Mineo. Without Mark I couldn't get near that bar, I kept reassuring myself. Mark will lead me to Chris. If I'm wrong about Mark, he'll be able to stay away from it. If I'm right, he won't.

I stayed two cars behind Mark's wide Cadillac all the way down to Sunset where he skidded to a stop and turned right, and then left down La Cienega to Santa Monica. He wasn't doing too well. I watched his car drift from lane to lane. Driving in the cramped, smoggy flats of West Hollywood, passing car salesrooms and bars, Laurel Canyon seemed hundreds of miles away. I signaled, and hung a left into the parking lot filled with cars and shadowy men.

It was Saturday night and it felt different—tense, sexual.

Groups of men were standing still between the cars. I watched Mark get out of the car, run his fingers through his hair with that familiar comforting gesture, and take wobbling steps around the dark lot. He looked as if he'd hurt his knees or was drunk. I inhaled sharply when a guy threw both arms around his shoulders from behind. They almost fell forward. It was too far away to see, but I bet he was Chris Franklin. The two of them disappeared from sight near the bar.

Outside my car, a wind kicked leaves at my ankles. The air was dry and smelled like distant fires and electricity. I tasted metal, and a moment later something crunched under my sandals. The lot was littered with broken glass.

I turned fast when somebody pushed past me yelling something distorted, his wet tongue lolling against his bottom teeth. He was clapping his hands above his head and skipping toward the neon-lit door. His shirt was open and he was wearing unlaced tennis sneakers. Under the red light, faces were shining devilishly. The door opened for a second and music throbbed. "Telling me, baby, better come back, maybe next week, can't you see I'm on a losing streak—"

I caught a glimpse of Mark and his friend disappearing inside. Five other men slipped in after them, and the door slammed shut. The lot was quiet again except for a quick laugh, the rustling leaves of a chunky palm tree, and the sound of the motors on Santa Monica. A guy standing in front of me started dancing on the broken glass with black riding boots. I ducked past him and stared speculatively at the muscle-beach type under the entrance sign, his arms outstretched in front of the door. It was the bartender, Alvin, wearing a red silk tank top and silver shorts. He was obviously standing guard. When he turned to peek inside the bar door, I saw his silver shorts were yanked up high into his behind. Over his shoulder all I could see was darkness. I heard static and Johnny Mathis's husky crooning on the jukebox. "African Queen settles the girls down," Alvin shouted. "My poor heart's about to attack. Wind's blowing over from the high desert—desert wind makes everybody nuts."

A huge man pushed ahead of me, strutting. He looked

like a monstrous Howdy Doody. He was about six-and-a-half feet tall. His T-shirt sleeves were rolled up to display huge shoulder muscles. He had a dimple in his chin the size of the cleft in a baby's behind. "No way," Alvin said, thrusting his arms out to block the door. "Baby, it's me, Georgie," the giant implored. He had a slight lisp. "Beat it," Alvin said. "Show starts later, just before midnight. You got lotsa time."

The tall man backed off and leaned petulantly against the trunk of the nearest car.

A tin can clattered toward us and then rolled away. Alvin saw me and sighed, rolling his eyes when he recognized me.

"I'm looking for Chris Franklin," I said politely.

"The new boy in town?" he asked.

"Didn't he just walk inside?"

He ignored me and held his fingernails up to his face, checking them out. The way girls are supposed to do it. In that light they looked like polished pink seashells.

"I need to talk to him," I said, while the strange wind fanned my hair out.

Alvin put his hand on his heart. "Something wrong?"

"No, we have a date," I said, trying to stall him. A boy wearing leather pants walked between us. I jumped back. He'd cut big holes in the pants to show the curves of his buttocks. Alvin snickered, listening to him whisper into his ear, nodded, opened the door, and passed him inside. I heard Johnny Mathis reluctantly give up a sad note, and then the place was sealed off again.

Suddenly Alvin leaned down and picked up my chin. His blond handlebar mustache looked like a fun fur. He looked sad around the eyes. Then he kissed me on the mouth. Gentle. A kind of fast brush. He taunted, "Faggots understand women better than anybody."

I jerked my head away.

"Nice girl," he said in his fancy contralto with lots of operatic projection. "You're hot. *Très* hot."

I wanted to slap him. But I had to get inside.

"Tell me what you do," he continued. "How'd you score Markie? All the girls are jealous."

"I'm here as a reporter," I said. "I know what I'm doing."

Alvin widened his eyes, as if he had just understood. "Reporter. That means you get off watching. Why not interview me?" he asked, pulling on the back of his shorts. "I love your hair."

"Listen, I'm not playing. I'm trying to solve a murder."

Alvin was studying his nails again by the red light of the sign. "Darling, gimme a break. Get in your car and ride. I'm closing the back door now. Say bye-bye to momma bear."

He opened and slammed the door shut behind him with a final flash of music. Nobody in the parking lot seemed to notice. I walked back to my car, nearly slipping on an oil puddle next to a cluster of guys posing in white undershirts. I sat there waiting, my mind racing. My mouth felt glued together. I had forgotten dinner. I turned on the radio twice, but I couldn't concentrate.

Twenty minutes later, the door opened again. I squinted through the empty back window of my car at what looked like a monster silhouetted against the dim light of the bar. He lurched from one side to the other, and finally staggered a few steps and bent over. It was Alvin carrying somebody over his shoulder. He gently pushed the body into Mark's Cadillac. I sat up in my car and saw a third guy behind him. I got out of the Dodge, cursed the broken glass, and stepped toward the trio. Alvin sounded as indignant as ever. He said, "When she's that bad, we don't want to see her. You know how much we love her, but we have some rules."

I stopped dead. The guy behind Alvin had silver hair and haughty cheekbones. I was finally face to face with my chief suspect, and he looked as ratty as hell. His face was the familiar pale parchment color, but tonight there was a messy stubble on Chris Franklin's upper lip. His hair hung over his ears in tangled clumps. It looked as if his shirt was buttoned wrong. His eyes and nose were red. When he recognized me, he stumbled backward and cursed under his breath.

I knelt down and peered inside the Cadillac. Mark was

sprawled out on his back on the front seat. His eyes were closed and his arms hung limp. His beige shirt was torn, revealing his ribs and his tight pectoral muscles. A tiny muscle was moving in his bottom lip. He was giggling softly.

I straightened up and shot Alvin a strong questioning look.

"Drunk, stoned." Alvin shrugged. "He's been through it, but I couldn't let him tear the place apart. What if the vice squad nabs him?"

I looked numbly down at Mark. He was mumbling to himself, and his smile was fading. I forced myself to concentrate on Chris. "I have to talk to you."

Alvin looked from Chris to me. "Oh, oh, I love a showdown."

"I'll break your face," Chris muttered, and hiccupped. Like Mark, he wasn't exactly sober.

"Don't threaten me," I said, grabbing his wrist. I saw a large splint on two of his fingers. He pulled away weakly. Alvin shrugged and walked backward toward the bar staring at us. "My newspaper knows where I am," I told Chris. "I said I was going to be here talking to you. My story's going to name names, but it doesn't have to name all of them."

I let Chris's arm go. He blinked a few times, and I saw the purple bruise above his right cheekbone. "I thought Markie dumped you," he muttered.

"Not exactly." My throat closed funny.

"You'll ruin everything." He massaged his hurt wrist and tried to walk around the car door to get into the driver's seat. I blocked his way.

"That's flattering," I shot back, "but how could I ruin everything?"

"Well, darling, the whole point of this place is privacy," he said, trying to get around me.

"Oh, you're afraid I'll print dirty secrets?"

"You'd love the picture of Jimmy Dean sticking his thumb in Sal's bellybutton," he taunted.

"I don't believe you," I said.

"Ask Markie how Sal did it to him when *he* was fourteen." He elbowed me against the car.

I followed him a few steps. "Who hurt your fingers?"

"Tense, darling, isn't it?" He laughed sourly and slumped against the silver fender.

"Who did it?" I repeated.

"Cops, thugs." He began rubbing his eyes with the two free fingers of his hand. I noticed another cut near his scalp.

"Why are the cops after you?"

"Bugger off." He tightened his mouth into a smirk. "I hear you're one pushy bitch, always asking nasty questions. Prince Charming tell you how much comfort I am to him? I been looking after him all day."

"He never mentioned you," I said, "except to say that Sal Mineo broke up with you as soon as you moved out here."

He pressed his fist against his mouth. "Bitch, you're way out of line."

"Maybe you panicked, because without him you have no movie career."

"Sal had nothing to do with it."

I kept fishing around. "I hear he was trying to get you a deal with Kate Lyons." I could tell from the way his eyes shifted away from my face that I'd hit on something.

"The deal's mine. It's not Sal's."

"That's not what I heard. I heard you couldn't do much of anything without his help."

Two headlights swept over Mark's car and Chris's shaky hands. The horn of the car blared, but Chris didn't look up. He reached painfully into the back pocket of his jeans, his bad arm stiff and twisted. He pulled out a squashed pack of English Ovals. He put a cigarette between his front teeth, his eyes appraising me. "Sal hated nights like these—wind's weird."

It was up to me to scare him into telling me his story. "I been up to Malibu interviewing Kate Lyons about you."

He spoke while exhaling smoke. He was talking from

someplace high in his throat. "I'm not afraid of her." He kicked one of the tires of Mark's Cadillac with his sneaker.

"She wants to know where you've been."

He closed his eyes to hide his fear. His nose was rose-colored from the light of the bar sign.

"Sal Mineo protected you from her. It was like family, right?"

"Shit, Sal stayed away from drug problems. He hated that stuff."

Drugs. I inhaled and the acrid smell of spilled oil burned my throat. I had just made a giant step toward solving the puzzle.

I didn't know where to begin. "What happened to your movie deal with Kate Lyons?"

"Mark's deal," he said, leaning against the silver fender.

"But she had a deal with you." I was still missing something.

He flicked a disgusted look at me, and began picking at his splint.

"Drugs," I said. "You owe her money for drugs."

"That's her story." He dropped his eyelids while the flame burned the end of the gold cigarette.

"What's your story?" I tried to match the contempt in his voice.

"It's a long, long story," he said.

"What's that mean?"

"I can't get into it now, but maybe later," and he blew smoke toward my face.

"What about the murder? Maybe I better tell the cops how mad you were at Sal Mineo."

He bit some skin on the back of his good hand. "Well, it was foolish of me. I more or less borrowed some white stuff from dear Kate. Well, now she wants revenge."

"How much coke did you borrow?"

"Never mind."

"Well, what happened to it?"

"I sold some of it to Markie."

"And the rest of it?"

"I stashed it at his place."

"Where?"

"Behind the fish tank," he said.

Mark's ransacked bedroom flashed through my mind.

"You can't steal coke from a shark," I said. "It's crazy."

"It was only borrowed," he insisted.

"What went wrong?" I asked in a friendly voice.

He shoved his dirty splint under my nose. I smelled iodine. "This, for starters. She's a vindictive cow, and she doesn't want me setting any trends."

So maybe the cops weren't responsible for his broken fingers. Maybe Mrs. Lyons was the guilty party. But he was covering up something else. "What about Sal Mineo? How did he get involved with you in this?"

"We—he wasn't involved—we fought a lot. It was romance. We loved each other." His voice broke.

I couldn't tell if he was acting or hurting. "He knew nothing about it?"

Chris nodded.

"So what went wrong between you two?"

He bent over to look inside the open door at Mark. "I'm the best in that department, love," he said over his shoulder to me. "I could always get Sal going."

"Not enough, Chris," I said, bending down to see Mark for myself. "You broke up."

Mark had a small smile on his lips, his arms were above his head, his chest arched. It made my stomach hurt the way it does when I drink too much coffee.

Chris patted one of Mark's knees and flopped back against the silver fender again. With his good hand, he began dragging a small tortoise-shell comb through his hair. His fingers trembled. "Well, sometimes I can't keep my knickers on. But I always came dragging my tail home."

He caught the comb in his hair and dropped his hand. The comb dangled across one pale eyebrow. He yanked it loose, bumping the cut on his face. A wet film covered his eyes.

"The idiot cops asked me if I knew about his kinky adventures. I laughed in their faces, and asked them, 'Oh, you mean the jolly good boys of Sunset Strip? They were dirt.' "

I was stalking him. "At least the boys have alibis."

"They can't prove anything."

I hit my forehead. "What about the ten-thousand-dollar loan Sal was trying to get? It was supposed to buy you out of your problems with Kate Lyons."

"I don't know anything about that," he said dully.

I leaned against the open metal car door between us. "They say you murdered him."

His jaw dropped loose, like he was drowning, and two tears ran down over the bruise on his cheek. "What a nightmare." He raised one weak hand to hide his face. I felt a rush of pity. Chris Franklin didn't seem capable of violence. The cops were wrong to keep hammering at him.

He dropped his forehead against the windshield of the white Cadillac. "We were so intense," he said, making gasps through his sobs. "If Sal was here, I'd never be in this mess. It's so wrong."

I felt something pushing against the open door of the car. It was Mark, sliding his long legs forward. He raised his head and wiped his mouth on his sleeve, his eyes jumping at me. Despite myself, my body flushed. He sat up, hugging himself, and rubbed the back of his head. "Don't matter none," he mumbled.

He tried to stand up, and I reached over the door to steady his elbow, but he jerked away and stumbled back against the car. "Dirty faggots," he mumbled. "That's her story, isn't it?"

Chris patted his shoulder. "Take your time. Stars have their own clocks, and like the old man said, you're the star *del* stars."

"Gotta get back in there, apologize to my friends," Mark mumbled, and almost fell face forward. I grabbed him by the back. Mark was so narrow. He pulled away and he made a sound between a laugh and a cough.

My stomach rubbed against itself like I'd swallowed sandpaper.

They walked three slow steps toward the bar. I turned and began walking back to my Dodge. "Nobody invited you here," Mark shouted at me over his shoulder. I watched the two of them walk under the red sign and said to myself, "Everybody crashes parties in California."

Chapter Twenty

I was staring at my hotel key. It was chrome, AC-Medeco, nice. I pushed it in the lock and looked down. On the floor near my door was a food tray with what looked like the remains of a standard Chateau breakfast: chewed croissant, egg yolk, and orange rinds. Boy, this place had class. Somebody'd been eating food and left the remains in front of my door.

The dark room smelled like a dirty air conditioner. I threw the key at the empty desk and crossed the shag carpet to the balcony. I pushed aside the striped curtains and opened the doors. I thought I'd left them open. The hotel gardens and lawns beneath me smelled of cold night air and eucalyptus. I was close to the ground, compared to New York. On Sunset Strip, a flashing purple sign was doing an all-night act.

I breathed deeply, sagged against the balcony railing, and pulled my arm back in revulsion. A half-eaten turkey-and-bacon club sandwich was wedged between the iron bars. The bread felt soft and fresh. I went back inside, turned on the light above the bathroom sink, and glanced at my frightened face in the small medicine-cabinet mirror. I wrapped the sandwich in paper towels. Then I tossed it into the straw wastebasket.

The room still smelled, despite the cold air. I unbuttoned Mark's silk shirt, twisted it into a wad, and threw it as hard as I could toward the desk chair. Then I plopped down and felt my rump hit the box spring. "No emotion," I said out loud.

I unbuttoned the tight dungarees. "I will never trust anybody again, ever. Never, never never," I said.

I was alone, and I'd show them all. I was going to solve this thing. I sighed. I took my tape recorder out of my bag, threw it onto the bed, and sobbed once out loud. No job, and I felt lonely. It wouldn't be any fun to pick up the pieces of my story. I didn't have anybody to share this with anymore, and I couldn't think of one thing to look forward to, I felt weak with grief.

I turned on the small orange lamp by the bed. The gold bedspread was turned down on one side, showing starched white sheets. As soon as my head sank down into the soft pillow, I dozed off. Then I jerked up and got a spasm in my neck. There was a buzzing sound in my ears.

All I could hear was cars going by. But I was too tense. I walked to the bathroom, kicking off my dungarees and sandals. The shower had a glass door and was lined with old-fashioned aqua and yellow tiles. Inside, big-handled spigots gushed water from every angle, but the water sprayed hot and rusty brown. Terrific. Los Angeles plumbing.

I turned and felt a jet sting my back muscles. I stood still and felt it boil and scour gay bars and Mark's drunkenness out of my pores. I yawned and swallowed a few drops of hot water.

Then I heard it—a thump shook the floor. It sounded like somebody dropped a corpse in the bedroom. I turned off the faucets, shivering. I reached an arm out and tapped open the bathroom door. The cold air hit my wet body. Above the bed, the lamplight glowed in an orange circle on the dark ceiling. All I could hear were dripping spigots and distant traffic.

My brain was inventing problems. What I really needed was a good vacation for the first time in my life. It was simple. I was shaky. I turned on the shower again. Ice-cold pellets of water streamed onto the top of my head. Pissed, I ducked away, and reached for a worn towel with CHATEAU MARMONT printed inside a blue stripe. I dried my knees until they hurt.

A moment later, I sank down into the soft center of the bed, the towel wrapped around my chest. Then I grabbed my pocketbook off the night table and counted out my wad of bills. A hundred and twenty dollars wasn't going to fly me back to New York. My Visa and Master Charge cards were spent to the limit. I wondered if I had any cash left in my bank account, or if they'd even cash my check at the airport. I lay back, feeling disoriented. In the future, whatever the future was, I'd balance my checkbook.

I sat up on my elbows and tasted my dry tongue. I heard a babble of voices. The purple light from the Strip reflected on the closet door across from me. These people never sleep. I banged my head on the brass headboard, and my teeth closed on the tip of my tongue. "Shit," I said. There was practically no saliva in my mouth.

Then I heard something like a fast stream of air. My scalp shivered. I held my breath until my chest went hollow. I heard it again, but maybe not. I was panicking. I sighed and heard it again, a tiny scraping noise that sounded like metal hangers tinkling in my closet. My teeth chattered. It was Santa Ana winds. Or else my ears were hallucinating from fatigue. Christ, I was shot.

Then my ears picked up something else, a snort and a giggle. Wind was undulating the striped curtains. I looked down at my dungarees on the shag carpet. The room looked the same. I shuddered and closed my eyes.

After a minute, I opened them.

Then I heard the tittering again, and a blurry sound.

I forced myself to get up and pad across the carpet. I pulled my hair back and pressed my ear against the wall. I picked up a glass and held one end to my ear like a nut in a movie. Sure enough, I heard canned applause. It was somebody's television droning in the next room.

I flopped back into the huge bed, switched off the lamp, and found a great sleeping position on my left side with one pillow folded under my neck. I hugged another pillow for security.

A second later, I bolted upright. It was that tinkling metal noise again. I fumbled for the telephone. A strange night clerk yawned hello.

I raised my voice. "Don't you have rules about quiet? Somebody's television's blasting. They must be deaf."

He cleared his throat. I'd woken him up. "Everything else okay?" he asked.

"What's that supposed to mean?"

"Oh, nothing. You alone in 3C?" He sounded embarrassed.

I didn't need his prurient interest. "Listen, just get on the phone and tell the party people next door it's lights out," I snapped.

"Right away," and he hung up.

I lay there, tense, watching the purple light patterns on the wall. I heard a telephone. One. Two. Three. Four. Five. I counted twenty rings. I jumped. My own phone was ringing. The clerk sounded tired. "Nobody picking up," he said. "Must be one wild party."

"Sorry," I said. "I'm being a pill."

"No, listen, I get nights like that," he said.

I figured a personal appearance would do it. Those people had a lot of nerve. I padded over to the closet for my old purple velvet bathrobe. I couldn't lecture my neighbors in the middle of the night wrapped in a towel. I wasn't a native.

I felt across the closet for the velvet. My fingers touched the nubby wool blazer, my cotton shirtwaist, bare metal hangers, and then they fumbled around some soft bumps that felt like warm bananas wrapped around the steel bar. A bunch of huge fingers.

A high thumping started in my brain. I jerked my hand to my mouth. A big shoulder came at me out of the closet and hit me in the midriff. I felt stray fingers close on my neck. I clawed them away from me. Hangers clattered and clothing tumbled onto the floor. I dived back into the bed, and the towel fell off. I grabbed the chenille spread and rolled into it.

I heard him panting in the dark.

"Get out!" I yelled from the bed.

He cleared his throat and the sound went through me.

"Get out," I repeated in a scared little voice. I reached over to the night table, knocking the receiver off the phone. I groped at the orange lamp for the switch. The light hurt my eyes. I was too upset to really see him. Then I screamed again. His hair had black roots and was knotted in ugly braids with brassy ends. They looked like torn copper wires. His short skinny legs were spread apart like a defensive football player. His skin was the same ash-yellow color. Jerry Lee Johnson, a k a Cleon Wilson, started his scraping laugh: the screechy gasps sounded like a catfight. "Baby, aahm, I ain't into freaking you out." He cracked his knuckles. He loved this. It was probably the best thing he'd done in days.

I screamed, a curdling sound.

He frowned. "Shut up. I got a proposition, that's all."

I stood up, the bedspread wrapped around me. I fingered the face of the telephone behind me, trying to find nine.

Jerry rocked back and forth on his heels. I swallowed over and over. He'd loved beating his wife, or whoever she was. My fingers tugged at the base of the lamp. I could rip it out of the wall and swing it at him if he lunged at me. A low grunting noise came out of my mouth.

The room was filling up with the beery smell of his sweat.

He looked behind him, backed a few steps to my desk, and sat down on it. "It'll cost you fifty."

"What are you talking about?"

"Special information about the murder."

"No way," I sputtered.

"You fucking need me," he said in a soft voice.

I folded part of the bedspread closer to me with one hand. "Let me tell you, reporters don't pay sources."

His face dropped. "Well, I ain't sticking around." He stood up and stretched.

I got a strong whiff of him. "Tell me what you know," I demanded.

"No way." But he sat down, and that eerie laugh rang out again.

"What do you do for a living?"

He stuck out his chin. "I'm a gardener."

"Where?"

"Who wants to know?"

"Where do you work?" I repeated.

"At the beach." He curled his fists.

"Who for?"

"Nobody." His lips twisted.

I held my ground. "The cops are watching you, and I'm going to call them."

"Try anything and I'll bust your ass."

"Who do you work for?"

He kicked at my sandal on the rug. "Mr. Lyons."

He may have just remembered that I'd dropped the name at the Old World restaurant. However, *she* lived at the beach and *she* was the one with the green thumb.

"*Mrs*. Lyons," I said.

"Wrong," he said sullenly.

I switched subjects. "Somebody told me you're Cleon Wilson."

"Who's got the big mouth?" He took a step toward me, his fists raised.

I reached back and grabbed at the metal lamp. "You better keep your hands to yourself," I said, with only a small quiver in my throat.

"Don't touch that phone," he said in a mean voice. "I'll hurt you bad."

"I can hurt you worse," I said. I jabbed one finger into the palm of my other hand. "I got the cops right here, Cleon Wilson."

"You're talking hot air," he shouted. He hit me and I crashed down onto the floor, bedspread and all. I was grunting and shoving him, but he pinned me effortlessly with his fleshy fingers. His smells made my stomach turn. I was helpless and weak. I started screaming again.

"Now, listen to me—don't you be goin' around saying asshole things about me." His eyes jerked around the room in fast furtive movements. I figured he was looking for a weapon. My body was shaking. "The cops *know*," I pleaded. "They already know you're Cleon Wilson."

The huge fingers dropped my wrists, and then he pulled a knee off my calf. For a moment I was free. "Now, fuck, that's it," he said as he looked around the room again for something. I rolled away from him toward the door.

He started rubbing the back of his neck. "Look, baby, I don't mean to hurt you. I get carried away, y'know?"

I thrashed around in the bedspread.

He squatted down, his eyes glowing. "Like, no dude is perfect, and my old lady, she likes sit-down restaurants and fancy shoes."

I kept trying to get back up on my feet. He was talking in a monotone now. "Sometimes I get weird. Like whenever Ivy get mad at me, I get down on myself, and I like to go out and hurt somebody."

The words hung in the air. ". . . get down on myself, and I like to go out and hurt somebody." That was the way he described the murderer the day we ate breakfast together at the Old World.

I knew the bar crowd didn't murder Sal Mineo.

"I'm gonna find my piece and work you over," he shouted suddenly.

I started whimpering.

He knelt by my side. The bedspread made me into a helpless mummy. I saw freckles on his nose. He shouted into my face, "Look, Sal Mineo was asking for it. That cat wanted to die. Lucifer knew it. He got him so mad about drugs. He shouldn't have messed in. That's the way the dude sees it."

I struggled to sit up.

He peered into my eyes, and his face calmed. "You think you're something special. I ain't good enough to talk to you."

I pressed the bedspread tight against my body. My voice was a croak. "Why did Sal Mineo make the devil mad?"

He stood up and walked onto the balcony. "This place must be costin' you," he said. "You rich?"

I followed him, keeping the bedspread wrapped around me. "Who told you about Sal Mineo?"

Instead of answering, he asked, "What do you think about dudes who dig other things?" The sweat glistened purple on his face.

"What things?" I tried to lower my voice.

"Oh, young tricks." He turned around and looked at me. "He told me stuff—he told me a lot of stuff."

I said quickly, "David Lyons. You're talking about David Lyons?"

He turned away again, looking down over the Strip. "Sure I help the dude out at Malibu, gardening. He's a weird dude, and he sure ain't poor. He was crazy to link up with her, the bitch."

"Who?"

"His old lady."

He was a ranting maniac, but he had come up with those two producers.

"David told you about the murder?" I asked.

He whirled around. "I seen them two guys hanging out together down at the beach."

He hooked his thumbs in his dungaree pockets. "I ain't weird. I'm a straight dude. That Lyons guy's a freak, a religious nut, and a sex nut. Sal Mineo was asking for it, playing with the wrong people. I saw him and Sal walking up and down the beach, up and down, the day he got what was coming to him."

"Where?"

"At the beach, like I'm telling you."

"Prove it," I said.

"I don't got to answer to you, bitch."

He strode across the balcony. His arm came at my face, the knife tattoo shining green and blue. He pinned his wrist around my throat, squeezing my larynx. I clawed at his fleshy forearm.

Then he dropped my head, and I took long sobbing breaths. He muttered, "I never shoulda come up here to get bread."

I was bent over, hugging myself. Every muscle tensed for his next assault.

Five seconds went by. I turned around. He'd clasped his

hands high and fallen onto his knees about three feet from me. He looked like a circus midget, his overblown torso balanced over his spindly thighs. He was moving his lips, praying.

I started laughing in loud, convulsive spasms.

Without opening his eyes, he reached in his shirt pocket, pulled out a small object, and held it to his left nostril. Then he slowly licked the white surface. It looked like a pearl.

"What're you doing?" I asked him, trying to catch my breath.

He threw the thing at my face. It nicked my forehead. I picked it up. It was wet from his saliva. It was a large animal molar, hollowed out and lined with gold.

"What's this for?"

"Nose candy. Give it back to me, bitch."

The doorbell shocked me like a punch. A second later, a key turned in the lock.

Jay, the desk clerk, peered inside at us. "I just took over for the night," he said in a loud voice. "Everything okay?"

Jerry bolted for the balcony, and Jay threw open the door, shouting, "Stop! You better answer some questions!"

But Jerry had one glass door open, and a second later, he stood high on the railing. He crouched and then disappeared. I threw the bedspread up above my shoulder and strained my eyes until I spotted him, a fast shadow streaking in front of rosebushes and ivy beds, dodging the tiny garden spotlights.

"Can I help you?" Jay asked anxiously.

"I can't take any more," I said. "I'm tired of people pushing me around."

Jay sat down on the railing. "Take more what?" He was peering at me in the dark.

"Mess," I said. "I'm tired of the mess."

"Who's that guy?" He sounded more scared than me.

"Jerry Lee Johnson," I said mechanically.

Jay frowned down into the gardens. Despite the garish purple light from the Strip, he looked great. It was such a relief to see him up here. I wanted to ask him to hug me for a minute, but I didn't. People must eat well in Panama. Something gave Jay his sweet caramel skin and white teeth that glowed as if he'd swallowed a light bulb. He was saying something: ". . . been hanging around the lobby off and on for days. He looked like trouble to me."

I walked wearily back into the room and sat down on the edge of my bed.

"I threw him out twice," Jay said. "Claimed he had a date with you."

"How'd he get into my room?"

"I just came on duty," Jay said. "But I bet he didn't come in the way he left. That lawn just under here slants way down to the Strip. He probably picked your lock. The hotel's going to press charges." He replaced the dangling telephone receiver. "No wonder I couldn't get you."

"He's just a cheap con artist," I said.

"I'll say." He picked up my velvet bathrobe and hung it in the closet. "The other clerk told me some guy's been using your room number all night long, ordering room service up here. He had the continental breakfast, the Black Forest chocolate cake, the Hollywood Hills club—"

I interrupted the menu. Clearly, Jerry Johnson was costing me a fortune.

"I can't stand not knowing," I said through a yawn.

"Not knowing what?" he said, stooping down to pick up my gray wool skirt.

I shivered. "It's my work."

Jay shook his head in friendly disapproval. "What's going on?"

"I want to know who killed him."

"Sal Mineo?" Jay said.

He read surprise on my face. "That guy told me what you're working on. Who's he again?"

"He's part of my story." I swung my legs up onto the bed. My eyes closed.

Jay tiptoed to the door. He paused, "You shouldn't get into such trouble. That's what happens when you over-educate women. It overstimulates them."

The next morning I had to fight to wake myself up. I

groped for the phone to order two cups of coffee. Then I
spied the horrible white molar on the shag carpet. I picked it
up, rubbing it between my palms until the translucent
enamel surface was warm. I had to solve this murder.

It was ten-thirty and I cradled the telephone on my neck,
crushing a pillow behind my head. First I dialed Paramount.
I had a flash of doubt. It wasn't going to be easy to trick
David Lyons. I was planning the kind of elaborate maneuver
Sergeant Casey could carry off with a snap of his tired fin-
gers.

I gave the secretary my name and she said Lyons was in a
meeting. I slammed the telephone down and set the instrument on my bare stomach, dialed again, and deepened my
voice for authority. "Hello, this is Marie Ross, deputy sheriff, L.A. County." Three seconds later Lyons clicked onto
the line.

"Not a bad trick," he said, after I said my own name.
"But who the hell are you?"

"I'm one of the best reporters in New York. I met you at
your anniversary party in Malibu, remember?"

"Oh, the earnest one who didn't like me much." He
laughed.

"I'm calling," I plunged ahead, "because we have a
common interest."

"I doubt it," he said without rancor.

"Let's get together and talk," I said.

"Why, because you're such a great audience?" he asked
sarcastically.

"No, because we both want to see Sal Mineo's murderer
caught."

He didn't say anything.

"That's right, we do both care about it," I said, like I was
agreeing with him.

"Okay, let's talk," he said quietly.

"On my conditions."

"What the hell are your conditions?"

I took a deep breath. "This morning I sent a news story to
my secretary at the newspaper instructing her to publish it in
three days, unless she hears from me."

"Buying yourself an insurance policy," he said, "or else lying to me."

In fact, I was lying; his intuition was impressive. But my deviousness was coming along.

"If I get hurt, you get very famous," I said.

"Threatening me."

"Don't you want to hear what I wrote?"

"I'm all ears," he said dryly.

"I wrote that you and your wife are probably behind the murder of Sal Mineo."

"You fuck," he rasped. "You're sick and I'll sue you forever."

"I'm right," I said quietly. "Your wife employs a guy who knows too many details about the murder."

"Fuck you." He sounded as if the air'd been knocked out of him.

"He said you were on the beach with Mineo the day he was killed."

"That's a sick story."

"You're right," I said smoothly. "He was covering up for the fact that it was your wife on the beach with Sal."

"He sounds like a cheap liar. And she's not my wife anymore," Lyons sputtered.

"You're wrong," I said. "His description of the getaway car and the murder weapon are too good. Either he murdered Sal Mineo or he heard about it first hand."

"Who the hell is this schmuck?"

"His name is Jerry Johnson, and I know he works for your wife."

"You're asking for it," he muttered.

"I'm asking for your cooperation."

"No way."

"Listen to my proposition." He hadn't hung up on me. That was something. "You and I confront your wife with certain facts and see what she says."

"What facts?"

"No, I'm telling them only to your wife."

"That's crazy," he said. "What's in it for me?"

"For one, your name is cleared."

"Not enough," he said. "My name is already clear."

"But hundreds of millions of Americans will smell fire when the press yells smoke," I snapped. "I'm offering you a way to get rid of your wife."

He laughed. "The first serious deal of the year."

I was banking on his anger about dividing his estate with her. "A convicted felon can't run half your business," I said.

"Too clever for words."

I was proposing that he set up a meeting with me, him, and his wife, and that he'd have her out of the way once I published her story.

"What do I have to do, sign a contract with you in blood?"

"Just make sure I'm there when you confront your wife about Jerry Johnson."

"And what do you promise me?"

"I promise to write that you were extremely saddened and helped bring her to justice." I would've given a year of my life to hear him thinking this over.

"Maybe I should stop at your house tonight," I said after a while.

"Sorry, but I'm having a party," he said evenly. "At my place in Mulholland."

"I can't talk at a party," I said. "You're too busy shooting at moonbeams and spitting at cars."

"Maybe I'll make time for you at nine."

"Will she be there?" I asked.

"Maybe. Maybe she'll be there," he said.

"I'll come at eleven, and you better make sure she's there."

"Okay, have it your way," he said, and we hung up.

I had thirteen hours on my hands. So far he'd agreed to let me come to his house. I didn't know what he had in store for me. I sat down in front of the rented typewriter. I rolled in a piece of paper. I started with everything I knew about Kate and David Lyons.

Chapter
Twenty-one

Fourteen hours later, the Dodge was crawling like an ant over the rim of a teacup. Mulholland curved up the ridge that separated Hollywood and Beverly Hills from the San Fernando Valley. On my left were dark lawns and mansions. But if I didn't keep turning my wheel away from the drop at my right, I'd go hurtling down into the enormous sparkling grid.

Headlights came flooding at me, and the steering wheel rubbed my palms. I swerved away from the car toward the drop.

The blood was humming in my veins. As soon as I rounded the next curve, I pulled the Dodge over the white line to a driveway and rolled down my window. The huge houses were illuminated by blue spotlights. They didn't look cheap. I strained to see something with numbers. The address told me I was close to Lyons's place.

I pulled back on the road, my mind racing. The shape of the story was changing fast. I was close to something frightening. Stories always feel different once you move around inside them. Except I never imagined it like this. David Lyons had come back into the center, pulling his unhappy wife and all their greed and money in with him. There was some-

thing dark behind that couple. She could be hiding somebody—not Jerry, somebody that I didn't know, maybe the
only person who really hated Sal Mineo. I felt a spasm of
paranoia. Maybe Lyons was more involved that I thought.

Unbidden pictures of Mark flashed in my brain, his body
splashing past me at the bottom of his pool, and then the sad
way he was hugging himself outside that bar. How was he
tonight? And how was I? Not great. It was hard to believe
I'd never see him again. I'm not related to erotic politicians.

Boy, I didn't want to think about him. Instead, I tried to
concentrate on David Lyons. But my feelings were out of
control. I loved Mark before I saw him at the funeral, and
more after I touched him. It was a silly joke. The only girl
on the gay-bar scene. I squinted hard to hold back tears.
Then I pursed my lips. I couldn't exactly picture him in my
future, burping a baby at dawn or competing with my mom
on the crossword puzzles Sunday afternoons. I had to get
logical and keep my mind on what lay in store for me at Lyons's house.

One thing was sure: over the years David Lyons hadn't
made many friends out here. Sal Mineo was one. Their
friendship was David's weak spot, and I intended to use it to
trap a killer.

I looked down at the sheer drop and felt queasy, as though
my body was already falling through the air. I kept turning
my head to find another house number. All I saw were
square succulent hedges and slim cypress trees. At first I
didn't notice an old Chevy station wagon parked on the
road. Before I hit the brakes, I slammed into it.

The crash shook my body, and my car stalled. The station
wagon rolled slowly toward the sheer drop. I closed my eyes
and waited to hear it go over. I looked up. It had stopped,
and as I looked away from it, I saw an estate.

I turned the ignition off and waited. When I tried the
starter, the engine choked, and died. I pumped the gas
pedal. Flooded.

I rolled up the windows, dropped the keys in my bag, and
hopped out onto ivy as thick as moss. I was actually relieved
to be back on my feet. Walking is how I lay claim to Man-

hattan. Out here, I'd been rolling around on four wheels, except for the stroll up Sal Mineo's alley.

I started down Mulholland. Two more pieces of information were all I needed. Nobody—not the cops, not Mark—knew as much about the murder as I did.

The tall cypresses reminded me of France, and the lawns smelled freshly mowed. Ten yards down the road I saw an entrance to a wide lane flanked by Christmas lights in the shape of palm trees. I squinted at the lights outlining each long narrow leaf. It looked like a joke. There was a large sign with white light bulbs in the shape of letters: LYONS.

Before I turned into his lane, I noticed the quiet look of the sky. Dark treetops blocked the gray moonlight. I felt around in my pocket for the molar. I'd never pushed myself so hard. I never dreamed I had unknown reserves of power.

I blinked at all the Christmas lights that stretched up the lane. It was a weird sight. Two silver Rolls Royces were parked under the leaning palms. The trees looked like something out of a Dorothy Lamour movie. I wished I had my camera. Marty Burns wouldn't believe this place.

I stopped short when the lane opened up to face a huge structure illuminated by red and green spotlights. The house was as wide as a whole block of homes in Manhattan, and loomed high against the sky. I was looking at a gray castle that reminded me of mad King Ludwig of Bavaria. Wind whipped at the surface of a lake in front of the gray rock walls, spires, bulging orange turrets, and slit windows.

This was the wrong century for this monster, and California was the wrong climate. It hit me that this fantasy existed because a movie tycoon believed in his dreams and had secured the power to play them out.

I didn't approve of all this power in the hands of one person, unless he was a visionary artist. And Lyons wasn't Michelangelo.

The path was edged with geraniums and swaying, oversized petunias. Winds rustled palm fronds, and I smelled tangy pine. The lane led to a wooden bridge that spanned the moat to the huge silver entrance. The front door looked modern. It was smooth and metal, like a bank vault.

I shivered and looked around for other cars. The house seemed awfully quiet. It had to be a very intimate party. Except for one lit window on the first floor, the place looked suspiciously dark.

It suddenly seemed too late to be arriving here. But I would get to the bottom of things if I acted like I had the right to ask anybody anything at any time. For me, bravery was beginning to mean believing completely in my own position. Unfortunately, crazy people have the same point of view.

A cracking sound split the night. For one second, I was puzzled. Then I hit the ground on my hands and knees. Another shot cracked the air. I bet it was Lyons again. At the beach he'd claimed he used blanks, but I didn't want to test him.

I lay motionless in a bed of violets, about six feet away from the moat. The smell rushed up sweet and damp.

A light went on just above the moat. I raised my chin off the broken flowers. Someone trained a strong spotlight at me. I ducked and shaded my eyes, blinking away whirling spots of white.

The spotlight traveled in a jerky path around me. I tried to look up, but my eyes closed.

"Who the hell's there?" The voice was cheerful. At that distance I couldn't tell if it was him.

"I'm here to see David Lyons," I shouted back.

I heard a door slam. "What's she doing?" Another voice was shouting from the castle. It sounded like Lyons. A motor purred and then something slammed hard.

"I don't know. What's wrong with the spotlight?" I heard the other man's voice close by.

"You better check this girl out."

The front door opened and closed, and I heard a motor sound again: the drawbridge. Uneven footsteps crunched the pebbles. "So much for the Sheffield violets," Lyons said. I made out shapes of two men in the dark.

"What happened to the party?" I asked.

"The party's over."

"Why?"

"I got tired of it."

The other man laughed. "Shall I take her home?"

"She's my guest," Lyons said, and came over to me.

I saw him then for the first time, backlit by one of the green spotlights trained on his monstrous house. He was leaning on a long shotgun stuck in the ground.

He smiled, his small eyes twinkling. His thick black beard had been trimmed shorter, showing loose flesh under his jawline. He wore an elegant hacking jacket, pale blue, flared at the waist, and very English. It didn't conceal his paunchy stomach. He was wearing his asbestos glove on one hand, protecting it from the rifle.

"Maybe it's a character flaw, but I hate rifles," I said.

"You're damn lucky," he said idly. "I was shooting dewdrops on the lawn. You're in range out here." His voice was cheery.

"You shouldn't invite people to your house and then turn your lawn into a shooting gallery."

"I invited you for nine," he said.

"We agreed on eleven," I said.

"Takes two to make an appointment," he answered.

"You need me as much as I need you."

"It's okay," the other man said. "Dave's just joking. He's too guilt-ridden to shoot anybody."

"Who're you?"

"My cousin Jim," Lyons answered for him. "He works for me."

"Nepotism's big out here?"

"Sure, I only hire relatives," Lyons said. "That way you know your employees. It always pays off, except for the ex-wife."

"That's a problem you can solve," I said.

He turned back toward the castle. I was about to remind him about the story I'd claimed to have filed, but he said, "Follow me up, and I'll make you some tea. I'll lace it with my fifty-year-old Scotch."

"Thanks for the hospitality," I said.

He didn't answer, but pulled himself up the pebbled path,

sticking the gun in the ground like a cane. The blue of his coat turned purple in front of a red spotlight beam.

The drawbridge was made of wood planks like the Coney Island boardwalk, and it clattered each time he hit it with the end of the shotgun. Huge metal chains suspended it from wood columns. I followed him, watching the shotgun barrel gleam in the spotlight. At the front door, he put down the gun and slid something against the metal door. It looked like a plastic credit card. The door swung open and he motioned me ahead of him. Behind us, the drawbridge motor whirred. The bridge rose up toward the house. I stood there, feeling trapped, until he impatiently went ahead over the metal doorstep.

Inside, I found myself dwarfed by a baronial front hall. Candelabras threw a gloomy glow on wood-paneled walls. It was a huge circular space, with carved oak doors leading off in five or six directions. The house felt dank, like London. The high ceiling curved into a vaulted arch.

He opened a door on his left. I followed him into a dark kitchen that smelled of stale cigarettes, liquor, and cheese. We walked past cabinets and counters and sinks, piled high with dirty glasses and cake plates. He opened a door and I followed him into a small adjoining space.

This room was different, warm and cramped like the lair of an animal. It had barely enough area for an old teacher's desk and a single bed covered with deerskin and pillows. An antique bentwood rocking chair looked inviting. Aside from a small window, the walls were lined from floor to ceiling with white bookshelves. In niches between the books was a series of mounted oil paintings. I looked closer. The paintings were studies of people revealing lush and naked buttocks.

Next to a volume of Doris Lessing short stories was a Modern Library edition of St. Augustine's *City of God*. Beneath it, the desklight showed a work surface littered with piles of screenplays in leatherette binders. There was a silver toothbrush on the desk. The ceiling was low, about a foot above my head, and the floor was painted the immaculate glossy white of a ship's deck. Lyons laid the shotgun carefully on the floor next to the bed, tugged off the glove, and tossed it on top of the gun.

I ran my fingers across some books. "Who lives in this room?"

"Nobody lives in this godforsaken house."

"This is your room," I said, my fingernail against the Lessing volume.

He smiled his full-toothed grin, but it never reached his eyes.

"Don't you like the rest of your house?"

"I think it's unspeakably vulgar, don't you?"

I shrugged. "It's pure Disney."

He nodded. "Precisely. Disney's first production designer built it for his daughter. Her wedding present. She went broke last year."

I sat down on the bentwood rocking chair. "By all means, make yourself comfortable," he said. He sprawled onto his bed, his head resting on both hands. Under the blue jacket I saw his soft stomach flesh sag to one side. He sat up suddenly and pulled out a glass plate from under himself. It was covered with caviar and chopped onion. He rubbed at black smears on his jacket, a little embarrassed. "The maids come back tomorrow."

"That from the party?"

"Yeah."

I tried rocking to relax. "What happened to the party?"

"Oh, I got depressed," he said, locking his fingers under his neck. "I wanted to be alone." He was wearing Gucci loafers, heels together, toes pointed out. He looked like he'd just exited from an expensive boutique.

"Did your wife go back to the beach?" I asked.

He sat up on the side of the bed and brushed some spiky deerhairs off his immaculate beige pants. "Tea?" His guileless eyes didn't meet mine. "I'll make some English Breakfast Tea. I brew a mean cup. It's quite a stimulant."

"Did you keep your promise to me?" I asked, studying one of the oils. It looked like a Renoir woman with red hair cascading down to an ample pink behind.

306

"Not so fast," he said. "First we nail down terms."

"What are your terms?" I asked.

"I want to know what you know about her current drug problems."

I shrugged. One great reporter told me that the best trick is silence. I just stared at Lyons. He said hurriedly, "I hate that hippy Hollywood drug shit. I loathe decadence. It's my Jesuit background. I never touch the stuff."

I smiled encouragingly.

"Nobody I care about does it anymore," he snapped. "Sal hated that whole scene too."

"Let's wait and ask your wife about all that," I said.

"I don't think you know anything," he said, looking at me pleasantly.

"Your wife had a coke deal with Chris Franklin." I spoke slowly. "That's all I'm saying."

"But I don't know what you're talking about."

"Where is she?"

He walked out the door into the kitchen. He switched on the light and I heard him open and close cabinets. When he returned, he gave me a burning stare. "I knew every move Sal made," he said tensely. "I know he never went near Kate. Sal was my best friend. He never made a single move without me." He smiled.

I felt alarmed. How crazy was this guy?

"Why are all the people in your paintings posing like that?" I blurted.

He lay down on the bed again with a small series of grunts. "It's my dear wife's idea of a joke. She decorated my study at the beach, then brought them here and hung them. I look at them to remind myself how lucky I am to be rid of her. Think of them as my hair shirt."

He looked at his watch, and then glared at me with those small childlike eyes. "It's too late to argue. What are we really doing here?"

I stopped rocking. "We're waiting for your wife to talk about her part in the murder of your best friend."

"Maybe I don't want you to know what really happened to Sal." He grinned and began patting the fur coverlet.

He seemed freaky, too smiley for the anger I sensed in him. Why had he dragged me into this little room of his? "You can't stop me," I said. "I already know, and so does my newspaper."

"You're scared of me," he said absently. "Don't worry, I loved Sal. I wouldn't touch a hair on his head."

I was a little nervous. "Why didn't you help him with his career if you loved him so much?" I asked, rocking slightly in the chair.

He lay back on the bed and said sweetly, "Your manners can stand work, scout. Sal was one man who saw something good in me, and I loved him for it. I was on to him. He believed if he sacrificed in this life, he'd be cleansed of sin."

"How did you sacrifice for him?"

"I don't have to tell you."

My face questioned him. It was good for him to think he'd gotten me off the subject of Kate.

"In 1940, the Academy gave Judy Garland a special juvenile thing," he recited to the ceiling. "A few years ago, I got the job of producing those television specials, the Academy Awards. It hit me then that I could make Sal's career happen again." He laughed gleefully. "I get brilliant ideas out of nowhere."

It was hard to believe he was telling the truth. There was something so false about his manner.

"I decided Sal and Judy should give out a special juvenile award together. My little ploy to bring him back into the public eye. They rehearsed some jokes, but then she got real sick. She was hospitalized that month. Sal felt jinxed. He didn't have the heart to do it without her. This year I got him to promise to present it to Jodie Foster for *Taxi Driver*, and now he's dead."

He gave me an appraising look. "Sal bet me the Academy was too straight to award the kid for playing a hooker." Lyons was making eye contact whenever possible with me. It was a practiced gesture. There was an intimate flattery in the power of his attention.

I drew my eyebrows together to seem sympathetic. "But you had the power to line anything up for him," I said.

He sat up. "Think about that remark," he said, and he disappeared into the kitchen again. He returned with a steaming cup of tea and a miniature silver spoon.

The tea tasted like fresh flowers. "I didn't have the power of life and death," he said morosely. "But listen, two years ago, I tried something else. He wanted to option a novel. I took him into Fox and got some story editor to give us a development deal. If I said make Mother Goose, they'd have one word for me—'When?' " He smoothed his beige pants on his thigh. "Sal didn't know it, but it was my money, not studio money, riding on him."

I didn't buy him as a hero. "How much money?"

"Nickels and dimes," he said. "Jesus, Sal loved that story. It had him written all over it."

"What was it about?"

"A boy, a real innocent—oh, shit." He interrupted himself and started caressing the hairs between his nose and his upper lip with his thumb. He couldn't keep his hands still. "You Catholic?" he asked abruptly.

I shook my head.

"Well, *McCaffrey* is the story of a boy, a good boy who gets bruised and brutalized like Jesus." I heard anguish and pleasure in his voice.

The back of my neck twinged.

He disappeared into the kitchen again. I heard him open a refrigerator. He came back sipping yellow liquid from a crystal snifter. "Carrot," he said, licking at his mustache. "I almost poured straight vodka, but once I start I can't stop. Where was I?"

"*McCaffrey* doesn't sound like a movie," I said.

He swigged the last drop from his glass. "Everybody's in show business," he grumbled.

"What happens to him?"

"He's left bleeding in an alley," he said.

I stopped rocking and rubbed at my neck.

"Relax." He wagged his head at me. "It's just a joke. No, McCaffrey becomes a prostitute to degrade himself."

"I don't like it," I said. "Why's it Catholic?"

His eyes turned sad and he stared into his brandy glass. "Where was I?"

"You were talking about the boy and his self-degradation."

He smacked his thigh. "The boy goes crazy after he sees his father rape his mother. It's like Fellini doing Christ on the Cross."

"What's uplifting about it?"

"His suffering gets him to heaven," Lyons said happily.

"Look, there's no way that movie could be a commercial success," I said.

He looked disdainful. "Sal and I were the same. We believe money isn't everything."

"Is that right?" I asked. "There's a big difference between this place and Sal Mineo's apartment off Sunset Strip."

His eyes snapped at me. "Yeah, but you see how I live here in one room. I tried to help Sal."

I heard the insincerity in his voice. "No, David, you thought he was a fool because he didn't fight to stay rich."

"He was a good man." His voice was sad.

"Why did you have such a crush on him?"

Lyons narrowed his eyes. "You're on the wrong track."

What bothered me was that suddenly he sounded sincere.

"Forget my personality problems," he said. "God knows, they're substantial. Sal was an innocent. And I respected him. Nobody out here could take that away."

I finally saw pain in his small eyes. "He was a star. I wanted to bring him back in his own image. He was honest, pure, and he was killed. I don't know why."

He closed his eyes like he was listening to something ethereal.

The telephone rang and we both jumped. He glared at me and reached for the instrument next to his narrow bed. I started rocking again. "Too bad . . . No, no, I'm giving you nothing." He sounded like he was talking to a spoiled kid. His forehead furrowed with irritation and he stroked the flesh of his bald head. "You can cash a check tomorrow. It'll wait. Anyway, you were supposed to show up at nine."

Then his voice got loud. "Shut up—shut that mouth and use your brain. Where the hell are you?"

It had to be Kate. "Tell her to come now," I said.

He listened for a minute, sighed, sagged back on the pillow, and put an arm under his head. "Okay," he said into the telephone, "but I'm tired and I'm sick of your messes."

He threw the receiver back toward the instrument and spoke to the ceiling. His charm had vanished. "She's a lunatic. I made ten million dollars yesterday on paper, and half of it is legally hers. But she still makes me give her petty cash."

"When's she coming?" I asked.

He checked his watch, a familiar black and gold square that I see on rich people. "Ten minutes. Want another cup of tea?"

"Yes." I'd have agreed to hemlock at that point. I watched the back of his freshly shaved head as he strode, more slowly now, toward the kitchen. My voice rang with self-confidence. "Why does your wife want cash?"

When he came back, his eyes wore that genial mask again. He walked toward me and my neck throbbed. He stopped a few inches from my nose and picked up my empty china cup and saucer from the floor. "You ask her when she gets here," he said calmly. "I'll heat some milk and dilute your brew."

A minute passed and he returned with the steaming tea. It was more fragrant than ever. Then he sat down on the side of the bed again and pulled a red lizard wallet out of his blue jacket pocket. He started smoothing lots of bills and counting them, moving his lips. They were fifties and hundreds.

We looked away from each other as the motor of the drawbridge made a distant noise. The front door slammed and I stood up fast. I followed him out through the dark kitchen into the foyer.

There stood Kate Lyons, her eyes blinking accusations. The flickering candlelight made dark shadows under her eyes and around her thin mouth. She sucked her breath with anger when she saw me. "What the hell is she doing here?

That wasn't part of the bargain.'' There was something pretentious about her long black gloves. She was wearing a floor-length leopard coat.

David pulled the card that opened the door from her fingers. "I think that's mine," he said. She looked plaintively at him.

"What's yours is mine," she answered, and she kicked the door shut behind her. "You used to tell me that night and day, once upon a time."

I watched her eyes probe his face. It looked like she had a problem besides cocaine. She was still in love with her husband.

"Get rid of her, darling." Kate stuffed one glove into her coat pocket. She began rifling through her leopard evening bag.

He said nothing to explain my presence. It seemed to anger him that she'd thrown the command. "I have to ask you some things," he said.

"Yeah, sure you do," she snapped. "I get the picture." But her lower lip trembled and her eyes kept searching his face.

While Lyons jiggled some coins in his pocket, she fumbled around in her tiny bag, biting her tongue between tiny front teeth. Finally she found what she was looking for. She backed away into a corner of the round foyer, setting her purse down.

He made a guttural noise in his throat. She kept sniffing at something in her hand. "I wish you'd understand," she whined. "You hurt me so much."

I kept craning my neck to peer at what she had in her hand. It was small and shiny. I recognized it: a white molar.

I was back in the detective business. I reached into my blazer pocket, trying to contain my excitement. My voice came out loud. "You gave this tooth to Jerry Johnson," I said.

She fell back against the door. "What the hell?"

I waved the molar high in the palm of my hand. Her tooth dropped out of her hand and rolled toward me, disgorging a trail of white powder. Like Jerry's, the molar was too big to be human. It was hollowed out and lined with gold, and lacquered so it gleamed like a pearl.

She dropped and scraped at the carpet with her fingernail, pushing the faint white trail of cocaine into the tooth. Her buttocks stuck up high under the coat, like a child's.

"Jerry Johnson says you gave this tooth to him," I said to the back of her head.

"Well, he's a goddamn liar."

This much I knew. The amazing part was that she'd confirmed she knew him.

"Well, what did he do, steal it?" I tried to sound knowing.

"You figure it," she said, glaring at her husband's impassive face. "Davey, what lies is she feeding you?"

Lyons didn't seem to like what was going on in front of him. To begin with, he wasn't in charge. "Who the hell is Jerry Johnson?" he asked Kate.

"Nobody I know," she said in a husky voice.

He raised an arm above his head, like he was laying a curse on her. My provocation was finally paying off. "What did you do to Chris?" I asked her, before he could speak.

She edged behind me to the metal door, pointing an angry finger at me. "She goes or I do."

She kicked the door open and a wind teased my hair over my face. "She knows just what I'm talking about," I said, as I pointed my forefinger at her face.

"Get out," she hissed, and grabbed my hand. She pried my fingers open with long fake nails. But the molar was in my pocket.

"Davey," she said over her shoulder. "I can explain everything. Just let me talk." She shouted at me against the wind. "You got your money's worth, didn't you? My houseboy tells me every queer in town dies for Mark Loren. And he rolled back on his ass just for you this week."

I pulled my hand away from her.

Her eyes searched my face triumphantly. "Don't get me wrong—I'd take Mark any day. He's the local sex-master.

Chris says if he feels like it he gives great lessons. I bet he loosened you up good.''

It was an effort, but I smiled at her.

She was watching me closely. Then she laughed merrily, showing her tiny teeth. ''Oh, she's lovesick—how fresh, how young.''

I was enraged. I sputtered, ''Who beat up Chris Franklin?''

''None of your fucking business,'' she shouted.

Lyons reached between us and pushed us apart like a referee. ''My ex-wife—that is, my business partner—is a hysteric, a sadist, and an addict.'' He didn't look me in the eye. ''You're provoking her. I need my peace and quiet. Please go. The two of you make more noise than guns.''

I spoke right back to him. ''It's your problem. You're covering up a murder.''

Kate came at me and I ducked. She yanked my arm, pushing me back through the door and outside. I felt her breath on my neck. She swore at me, but her words got lost in the sound of the wind. Lyons held her behind himself with one arm, and started to close the door in my face with the other. ''You're very brave,'' he told me, ''but you're very wrong.'' The whir of the drawbridge vibrated in my chest. I saw a glint of desperate humor in his almond eyes before the door swung past me. He was playing close to the edge, and he liked it.

Chapter
Twenty-two

I smiled, gritting my teeth against the pain. The door was crushing my foot, but I was holding it open. I didn't understand Lyons's game. It was a dangerous situation. By not making sure the door was closed, he might be cooperating with me and setting a trap for her. My mental clock was working. I gave her ten minutes to feel alone with him. It made me impatient. I was dying to hear what he was forcing her into. Behind me, the drawbridge stretched over dark, silent water. An engine came and went. Perfect. It sounded like my Dodge exiting.

The wind died abruptly, and I smelled violets. I put both hands to the door's edge, pulled, and I stepped inside the high gothic foyer again. His voice came from the direction of the kitchen. It sounded as if they were talking inside the maid's room.

A few candles were still burning. The metal door snapped shut behind me, and my shadow jumped against one wooden wall. Shouts suddenly cut the air. Both of them were screaming.

I was closing in on danger. David could be setting a trap for me.

I took off my sandals and stuffed them into my bag, then

began to tiptoe over the wool rug. Their voices rose and fell. My bare feet quivered on the clammy kitchen tiles. I caught the faint smell of stale champagne.

I felt gleeful, sneaking in. Danger was making me high. Their shouts got louder.

". . . fucking cocksucker!"

"Shut up!" he said. The voices got low.

I pressed myself against the wall and crept close to the doorway, past cabinets and sinks. The door to the maid's room was open, throwing a rectangle of light on a high wooden cabinet against the wall. It was an elegant hutch, filled with blue willowware plates. Balled-up napkins and party glasses were jammed between them. I scrunched my body into a foot of bare wall between the cabinet and the doorway and inched my face noiselessly toward his room, breathing through my mouth. Something yellow moved in the light. Kate Lyons's leopardskin coat.

Suddenly I saw the side of her face, only three feet from my nose. Her hair was standing on end like a boy's crewcut. I strained my neck and saw her cheek, an angry patch of red.

I jumped back, hitting the cabinet with my thigh. My neck muscles went into spasms. The plates rattled like an earthquake.

"What's that noise?" She looked right at the cabinet in front of me.

"Don't change the subject," he said. I figured he had to be lying on the bed.

"It's none of your fucking business," she said. But I could hear her breathy terror.

"Tell me about Jerry Johnson."

"Look, everything's all right." She sounded ingratiating. "I just need twenty-five hundred dollars in cash. It's pocket money."

I stepped back to the doorway and peeked. She was facing me, her fists raised in front of her chest.

"I don't trust junkies," he said.

"You fuck," she spat. "What did she say about me?" Her thumb jabbed in my direction.

I jerked my head back and stared hopelessly around the kitchen for a hiding place. I felt like I had no legs.

"Who the fuck is Jerry Johnson?" His slow words dripped with anger.

I took two tiny steps back to the doorway. I really wanted to run in the opposite direction.

"Nobody, honey." She was using her kitten voice. "Just give me the cash. I'm so scared."

"What's the matter with your checkbook? Broken?"

"I can't. I don't want anybody tracing it."

"Any excuse to spend my money." He laughed, one exasperated sound. "Just tell me the truth. I got scripts to read," he said.

She made a hissing sound. "Since when you doing your own reading?"

"Don't you talk to me like that."

The bed hit the wall. Something like a slap rang out, and she wailed like a siren until a second slap sliced the air. I heard my pulse banging in my ears. "Okay, okay," she sobbed, an ugly crackling noise. It was an odd relief to hear her sound human.

"Remember who's on top here," he said softly.

It sounded like he was pushing her hard for information. I doubted he was doing it for my benefit. I wondered what he would do to me if he caught me out here. But I wasn't leaving until I had to. I was dying to get the whole damn story.

"What about the cash?" she asked.

"Talk."

She started babbling. "Honey, Sal was a busybody. He came swishing down to the beach."

"Sal never swished. What'd he want?"

"I told you—his little friend stole coke from me."

I blinked. My eyes were raw with tension. I gripped my shoulder bag. My fingers slipped down past my wallet and around the edge of a small square: the tape recorder.

"Cash value?" Lyons asked.

"Oh, about twenty grand."

A moment of silence went by. I had the machine out.

"Tell me everything Sal said." He sounded defeated. I

tapped the tape recorder behind a willowware plate, commanding it to work. Please don't break. Please don't make any noise. I crept back near the doorway.

"I already told you," she said.

"And?"

"Well, see, he got nasty with me and this gardener of mine had to rough him up." Her voice sounded subdued.

"Nasty? Not Sal."

"Don't forget, your precious Sal was in love."

"What did the gardener do to him?"

"Oh, he twisted his arm and made him get in his car."

"Then what's your problem, pet?" He sounded as if he were barely controlling his fury.

"It's not me. It's this gardener. He'll go to Mexico forever if I pay him off tonight. It's worth it."

I trembled with excitement. I knew what was coming.

"Who is this gardener?"

"Nobody."

David didn't answer her. Firecrackers exploded behind my eyeballs. My neck hurt worse. These rich jerks were talking as if somebody hadn't bled to death in a cement alley.

I grabbed for the tape recorder and checked it in the shaft of light. Tiny spools turned around and around. I shoved it back behind the plate. My story was bursting open. I knew I had to act or lose it.

I clutched the door and swung myself into the room, barely breathing. The room was small. Kate instantly shrank away from me against the rocking chair. "Get her the fuck out of here."

I felt drunk. I'd never done anything this brave in my whole life. "Jerry Johnson is your gardener," I said.

I backed up against the bookshelves in order to keep my eyes on both of them. Her small head was within reach on my right. Four feet away, on my left, David Lyons fingered a new scratch on his scalp around his right ear. "You're trespassing," he told me curtly.

"Jerry Johnson hurts people for her." I looked back longingly at the door. I had to talk fast. I had to keep them off guard.

Rage and disbelief flickered on his face.

She spat, "She's so crazy, so crazy."

"Who the hell is Jerry Johnson?" David advanced on me. "I'm tired of repeating myself."

I didn't like him at short range. His lips sprayed saliva. He grabbed my upper arm and the whole room seemed to swing around. Pain shot through my shoulder.

"Jerry Johnson told me all about Sal Mineo," I said, measuring the distance between me and the door. Seven steps and I'd be out of here. I pointed at Kate. "You better explain a few things."

He dropped my arm and I edged to the doorway. My ankles wobbled. He lunged at her and she twisted away, the rocker swinging. Then she bolted for the kitchen, bumping me hard. He tackled her and knocked her to the floor. Her forehead crashed against the curved leg of the rocking chair. I wanted to get out. Her cheek flattened against the floor. I hated the way her eyelid puffed out where it had been hit. She sat up slowly and put her hand over her eyes. She moaned, "Go back to New York and write about women's porn."

Lyons yanked her to her feet. She crashed forward again. "Don't forget your reporter," she hissed.

Before I could move, he reached back and grabbed my elbow. His fingers dug into the bone. My arm ached and my throat closed with fear. "Tell her what I mailed to the newspaper," I gasped.

He laughed. "I'll tell her about your cheap lie."

I stopped breathing and tried to jerk away. But he pinched my elbow hard. Kate was lying at my feet on her side, her coat open. I forced the words out of my mouth.

"I wrote a story saying you two were responsible for Sal Mineo's murder."

She leaped at me from the floor, but he blocked her. "You crazy girl," she shouted. "You're asking for trouble."

"But I called the *Post* this morning," he said calmly. I

kept wrenching my arm. He smiled and held it tight. "You were fired two days ago. Some guy in the entertainment section gave me the lowdown. They think you got sun on the brain, Miss New York. You don't worry me."

I flung my body toward the kitchen. He pulled me back, squeezing my elbow until I shrieked like a cat with a crushed tail. He pinched my elbow until my arm numbed down to the tips of my fingers. I tried shouting, but terror froze my voice. I forced one of his fingers backward with my free hand, and his face got livid.

"Stop it," he ordered. He rammed my knuckles into my stomach. I folded forward. My breath left my body. He had me. I felt like I was dying. He kicked the kitchen door shut and dropped my elbow. I couldn't feel anymore. He leaned against the closed door. "Talk," he said. I was bent over the wide planks of the white floor. It was hot and crowded. I had the feeling of being stuck on an elevator. Fright was hammering at me.

He peeled off his jacket and threw it toward the bed. It landed in a neat pile. I saw tears in the corners of Kate's eyes. Her teeth kneaded her lips. She finally spoke. "I'll fight her any day. But Sal Mineo fought dirty."

He was standing six feet from Kate, one hand raised like he wanted to slap her. "What the hell do you mean?"

She lifted her head. "He said he'd go to you and tell you all about my drug deals and get you so angry at me that you'd help Chris."

"As if you care how I feel," he mumbled.

"You had Chris beat up to get back your coke," I said shrilly.

"Davey, I'm an easy mark. What could I do, go to the cops and report a theft?"

"No, you're stuck. You can't go to the cops."

I straightened up and rubbed my hurt elbow. There was an ache in my gut where he'd rammed my hand. "You're in hot water," I told her. "No money can help you now."

"You're so fucking smart," she sang out, and her head turned toward him. "I'm telling you, Davey, Jerry Johnson volunteered to get Mineo off my back. It wasn't me."

"Volunteered?" I felt like punching her.

David Lyons and I locked eyes. Now we both knew what she was capable of doing. Kate and Jerry'd both thought Mineo could get Chris to return the drugs or the money he'd gotten for them. David dropped his head into his hands and sobbed once without moving. "God, this is shit. What did Johnson say about Sal? Did he say anything?"

She stood up and backed into the rocking chair.

I hated the way she was lying. My voice had no breath behind it. "What does 'volunteered' mean?"

Her chin sagged. "It means Davey's going to kill you for bothering me."

My pulse thudded in my head. Everything blurred. *Volunteer means murder.*

"You knew about Jerry that day at the beach," she said playfully. "That's why you came all the way to Malibu."

My fingers were flexing and unflexing.

Her smile came and went. "You earned your hundred bucks salary that week, dear. Dave, get rid of her." She twisted forward to see him.

I grabbed her coat collar with both hands and shook her until her teeth snapped together. "What's your story?"

She dug at my fingers with her fake nails. "Davey, do something," she wailed.

"Answer her," he ordered from behind me.

She took a long shuddering breath. "I'm telling it once, so just listen. That night Jerry drives away. I couldn't stop him, and—" She swallowed her words. "—and he sees crowds and the cops and he sees Sal's dead body." She sniffled. "Well, he drives back up to the beach and tells me he'll go straight to the cops, and—"

"I don't fucking believe you," he choked behind me. "Johnson isn't blackmailing you." I heard him smash his hands together.

I held tight to the yellow fur. "Why did he kill Sal Mineo?"

She dropped her fingers to her lap like dead things. "He heard Sal threatening me."

I was in a frenzy. "That means you had him do it. You

had him do it," I shouted, yanking her head back and forth by the collar.

She jerked back. "He's a moron," she moaned. "He was supposed to scare Sal, not kill him. I promised him half of it."

I didn't see his arm coming at me. He knocked me sideways against book spines. My knees scraped the floor. I tried to stand up, but he elbowed me down again. I crawled backward, and felt the warm adrenalin leaking from my veins. The skin on my legs burned.

His back to me, he smacked her face. He looked at his palm with surprise. Her head fell to one side, like her neck vertebrae had unlocked. She pulled her knees to her chest and kicked him in the stomach with her high heels. My own stomach clenched. He doubled over, and she jumped to her feet. I saw black circles around them. I was fainting. She was coming at me. My throat whimpered. He grabbed her thighs and threw her backward onto the narrow bed.

He picked her up by her shoulders and threw her down again.

"Sadist, you sadist," she gasped. One of her hands dangled to the floor and her long fingernails brushed his quilted gray glove. Her fingers fumbled at it. I stopped breathing. She found the silver barrel of his shotgun. I hit the floor planks on my stomach. My chin scraped a nail head. I coiled up into a ball, and a scream vibrated in my chest.

She lifted the gun high into the air, and I saw her jam the wooden handle squarely into his shoulder blade. He collapsed on top of her and she pushed him down off the bed. His calf sprawled over my leg. I scrambled to get away. He was almost senseless, a dead weight. It took all my energy to kick his leg off. I had to get out. I curled against the door and reached up for the knob.

Still lying on the bed, she pointed the gun barrel at him. I saw her mouth greedy and unhappy, a red hole in her face. The cut in her eyelid was bloating. I wanted to be invisible. I wanted to find the doorknob. I can do this, I thought. I can keep myself alive. My brain is going to get me out of this room.

She curled her fingers around the trigger. I had the knob between my fingers. He heaved himself up and grabbed the gun with both hands. She held onto it, raising it high above her head. I buried my head in my shoulder.

A second later I looked up. He had wrestled the gun down between them and was twisting it out of her hands. The explosion ripped tissue deep in my ears. I couldn't believe how the sound of the gun hurt my body. My lungs hurt from screaming. I didn't see anyone pull the trigger. My mind blanked them out.

I turned the knob behind me and fell backward into the kitchen as the door opened. I started crawling low to the floor. The skin on my back tightened, expecting pain. My legs wouldn't move. Then I was scrambling like a fleshy bug over the kitchen tiles and out toward the foyer. The metal door loomed shining and solid in front of me.

My fingernails scratched along the cold smooth surface. I beat the door with my fists and then stared at my knuckles in the dim light. Little bits of white flesh hung on them. They started to bleed.

Then I remembered my tape recorder. I started to cry. I stood up shakily, and forced my feet to take fifty slow steps back.

At the doorway, I heard a thin scream. I fumbled behind a willowware plate. It crashed to the floor and broke into two jagged pieces, and I stuffed the tape recorder into my blazer pocket.

I paused. The silence stretched out. I could feel the energy draining from my body. "Davey," she wailed.

So she was alive. I bent my head forward and peered into the doorway. I could see she was sitting on the rocker again, the gun barrel pointed directly in front of her. She wasn't wounded. I couldn't see him. But I knew he was facing her from the bed.

"Davey, dear, I'm in a fix," she said tremulously. The gun barrel shook as she sobbed. I ducked away at the sound of another explosion. I heard somebody else screaming in pain. My voice joined the animal cry. Then I heard Kate gasping.

My stomach twisted. The shot had broken flesh. The bed-springs sounded like they were alive. There was a thump, then some heavy rolling. It sounded like they were still fighting over the gun. That meant they were both alive. My skin crawled. Then I heard a long, heavy dragging. Somebody was dialing a telephone. He stopped and dialed it again.

"Doc, Lyons . . . Yeah." David's voice was a wet whisper, "No, Hank, God, listen, I need help up here fast. The old Winchester dropped and went off . . . No . . . Yeah, powder wounds, neck bleeding . . . I did, yeah . . . Kate? She's great with movie blood and practical jokes, but she's no help now, Hank." He coughed for a slow minute.

His words rattled something in my brain. I hated his control. Movie blood and practical jokes. It had been Kate Lyons who was behind that bloody condom hanging on Mark's bed. She must've sent Jerry out to look for cocaine there, too. It was her kind of signature.

Lyons's voice started up again. "Yeah, bring the drug cocktail. After she signs property papers, she's taking a long trip alone, tomorrow. Front door's open, Doc. I'm sorry. I'm passing out."

I heard something like books falling. Then another silence. Uncontrollably, I moved back to the door and peeked inside again.

I swallowed against my turning stomach when I saw him lying on the desk. He was blinking slowly like a turtle stuck on its back. Sticking up in the air between his legs was the shotgun. His throat was dark and wet and slimy, and he was breathing like his lungs were filled with fluid. The telephone wire was twisted around his fingers. I looked at his throat more closely. He'd wrapped a scarf around it; its surface and floral pattern were soaked with dark red blood. Blood was splattered on his shirt and pants. Two footprints were outlined in blood on the floor.

I moved my head so I could see more of the room. Kate was lying on the bed, her legs splayed. She looked as if she'd gone into shock. Her head was against the wall, her coat pinning her torso in an upright position. Her eye was twisted and puffed like a gargoyle's.

There was a crack in the ceiling, and several pieces of plaster were lying around her. Instinct made my neck smart. I glanced back at him. He was slowly lowering the gun. I felt pure terror. "Too bad," he whispered, and pointed the gun at my head. The gun was shaking. His small eyes flashed at me over the dark red of his throat. The gun barrel had two huge holes. It took all my strength to keep standing. Some part of the gun clicked. I watched his blinking eyes and I hated the lethal girth of his body, the naked skin on his skull. I hated his finger crooked comfortably on the trigger. His fancy shoe stuck out at me. I wanted to twist if off his foot. I hated his power. I felt as if I were falling toward him. My hate made me move.

I shrank away from the doorway, my knees sagged, and I fell down. He would shoot me like a bullying child throws a rock at a classmate, believing he's the only feeling person in the world. I heard a thump. The gun clattered to the floor. I lifted my head, peeked inside, and saw his shoe. He was sagging back on the desk. One hand was on the chrome barrel, but he'd passed out. I pulled my sandals out of my pocketbook and shoved the straps through the buckles.

I took one shaky step and then almost ran out through the kitchen again. In the foyer I saw her white molar on the antique rug. I scooped it up. I'd won. I was almost crying with relief. Then I pushed on the metal door. After a few seconds, it opened in front of me, letting in the smell of flowers and cold car fumes. My mind was racing. Sal Mineo had died so senselessly. David Lyons had tried to murder me. My eyes smarted with tears. It wasn't until I crossed the drawbridge that I felt my strength again. Wait until I get an editor to read this story.

Chapter
Twenty-three

I woke up to sun. My curtains were wide open, and I squinted at the empty blue sky over the Hollywood flats. Down on the strip, the traffic crawled like a metal snake. Horns whined under the roar of motors. I thought of thousands of people pressing gas pedals. Everybody was rushing, everybody was late. It brought me back to reality. It reminded me of Manhattan.

I dialed and listened while the telephone computer circuits crossed the Mississippi.

Jay broke in on my call. "Anyone on the line?" he asked.

"Take a message," I said.

"Sorry, but—"

"I'll call them right back." It had to be Mark calling this early. The idea of him woke up my whole body.

"It's not that." Jay hesitated. "Let's discuss it on another line."

"That's okay," I said. "What's wrong?"

His voice got blurry. "They took the elevator."

I collapsed back in bed, tired again, and frightened. An orange and black bug landed on the bedspread. "Who's coming?"

"The cops."

Jesus, I don't need them poking around now, I thought. I was ready to write the article that would rip the case apart. They couldn't stop me. I knew who killed Sal Mineo, and they didn't.

"Hang on," I said, and, carrying the phone, I grabbed my shirt, pants, and socks up off the carpet. I slid my dungarees up to my knees with one hand and kept my eyes on the door. There wasn't time for underwear.

"What do they want?" Jay asked.

"It's complicated."

The doorknob began turning before I'd buttoned the shirt. I threw the door open in a display of bravado. It was Casey. He gave no sign of recognition, but lumbered past me, his face pink and fleshy as ever, his blue eyes bloodshot.

I almost slammed the door in the face of a man behind him. He was tall and young and wore dark sunglasses, a red-and-navy-striped tie, and a navy suit. He looked dressed for a business lunch.

I couldn't stop staring at him. He twitched one shoulder and came in slowly behind Casey. It was Mr. Ivy League who'd knocked me down at the airport. I narrowed my eyes. He was probably the guy who'd chased me like a nightmare at Kate Lyons's house by the shoreline. Now he couldn't tear his eyes off me.

"You're a cop," I said. For all I knew, this guy'd been tailing me for days. The two of them stood there staring at me as though I'd walked in on them.

Casey was wearing a different jacket, but it was pulled the same way over his belly. Matching blue-plaid pants failed to hide short pink socks. His white shirt was unbuttoned at the collar to reveal an old undershirt. A wrinkled necktie hung over his lapels. He moved slowly, like he'd missed more nights of sleep.

He flipped a white antacid tablet onto his tongue. As usual, he seemed grouchy. I wondered if he suspected how much I knew. Then I almost smacked my hands together. I was in a position of power. I knew more than he did.

He stuck his head into the bathroom, then fumbled for the closet light switch. "This all your stuff?"

I watched him silently.

"I asked you something," he said, picking two of my blouses off the floor. He tossed them onto the plastic desk. I marched around him, hung them back up, and slammed the door shut.

His partner was still staring at me. He gave me the creeps. "Too busy to do a laundry?"

Casey laughed, and said, "Hey, watch your mouth, Lee." I kept quiet. Neither of them impressed me as sartorial types.

Casey closed the closet door.

"What's going on?" I asked him.

"I understand you're checking out of here," he said, rubbing his forehead. I heard a new quality in his voice.

"Maybe I am, maybe I'm not," I answered.

His eyes widened. A few white flakes stuck to his lip from the antacid tablet. "Time for you to lay your cards on the table," he said, hitting his fingertips together. He sounded tough, but careful.

"No way," I said.

"Then we'll run you to the airport." He nodded to the tall guy.

A surge of anger went through me. "I'm Sara Martin. How do you do?" I said to his partner.

"Lee Sanger," he said curtly. Then he twirled a chain of keys around his forefinger. "Bill, I'll call you from LAX."

Casey shoved back one shirtsleeve to look at a huge steel watch. Tufts of white hairs stuck out on his wrist. "You got ten—no, fifteen minutes to pack up," he ordered. But he stared at me, like he wasn't sure what I'd do.

"You're not serious."

"You bother me," he sighed.

"Why?"

"I seen it once or twice with a couple reporters. They obstruct my investigation. It's simple. You're dangerous. You don't know your place. You're making certain people nervous. It's going to blow up in my goddamn face. Suspects need to be left alone. I don't want the scumbags leaving town, burning evidence, or trying to kill each other off."

I heard the compliment. I wondered how much he knew about what had happened at the Lyonses' last night.

"We're kicking you out of Los Angeles," he said.

"What about the First Amendment? You heard of freedom of the press?"

He shook his head sourly. "I hear you ain't on assignment anymore. You're fired."

I felt like somebody punched my stomach. That lousy Marty Burns. He wasn't covering for me. "Maybe I'm investigating a book," I shot back.

Casey scratched at his scalp under the thin gray hair. "Look, collecting evidence is my job. I'm going to convict a murderer. I get county wages, taxpayers' money. I can't play your literary games."

I suddenly remembered his detective fiction. It sounded like he didn't want me horning in. "Okay, put me in jail. It'll make good headlines."

Casey peeled the wrapper off a new pack. This one had green tablets. "I'll lock you away for obstructing homicide procedures. That's the law. They'll hold you twenty days over at the detention center. You can count on a goddamn criminal record."

He threw one end of his necktie across his chest. "I'll slap a two-hundred-dollar traffic ticket on you for the car. The back window's a fucking violation."

"It's a junk heap," Lee Sanger said smugly. He rubbed one of his brown penny-loafers on the back of his pants. His glossy shoes irked me.

"That car's more practical than a convertible," I said. Casey kept on chewing the tablets. He didn't acknowledge my little joke.

"What do you really want?" I asked, as if I didn't know.

Casey curled his fingers into a fist and shook it. "I want to nail the fuck that murdered Sal Mineo."

I had a flash of sympathy. "That's what I want too."

"Sister, when I haul some psychopath to trial, the last thing I need is him claiming your article prejudiced the jury against him by calling him a murderer."

"That's not my problem," I said.

Casey shook his head. "Let me give you another example. You go to ballistics and the coroner tells you all about the murder weapon."

Sanger was adjusting his holster under his jacket. I saw a flash of black leather. He recited, "Tuesday morning, ten A.M. in the cafeteria, Dr. Candida."

I whirled around. "It's none of your business."

"Look," Casey said, "suppose I get a broad on the stand testifying the suspect bragged about owning that knife. Her testimony isn't worth spit if you already printed stuff about the murder weapon. You fuck up everything. Or suppose some juror admits they read your article—bingo, mistrial. Two years of my life down the toilet. Get it?"

"So what can I do?"

The pink skin around Casey's face wobbled. "You can make a deal. That's why we're here." He got up and walked toward the kitchenette. That was it. That was why Casey was different today. He wanted something from me. Sanger yelled, "Bill, need anything?"

Casey came back balancing three dripping glasses of water on both palms. He jabbed my elbow. "You look thirsty, sister."

I took the glass. Lee took the other and the two of them gulped water. I wondered how they'd worked up such a thirst. They reminded me of a family just come in from the beach. I pictured them hiking through desert dunes out a Malibu.

Casey was out of breath from drinking too fast. "Here's my offer," he said. "You spill everything you know."

"That's it?" I was incredulous. "What's in it for me?"

"You help bring a fucking murderer to justice."

"But my story. I have a story to write."

"Well, I better handle things," he said uneasily.

"Nobody can stop me from writing my story," I said.

He looked furtively at Sanger. "Let's hear what you got to say."

My voice went up. "Nobody stops me from writing my story."

"Suppose it kills the prosecution's case?"

"Maybe it'll get everybody going," I said.

"Look, I can keep talking to you for a year about pretrial publicity and how it hurts us. Why don't you just go home and forget it?"

I laughed on a high note. "Well, it so happens I'm broke. I can't go home. I can't buy a ticket."

Casey looked behind himself and backed his bottom down onto the plastic desk. "Amateurs kill me," he muttered.

I shook my head. "I cracked the case. You know I'm doing something right."

Casey gripped his necktie and stared at me. "Maybe the department'll spring for your ticket."

"Why do that?" I asked.

"Tradeoff," he said. He kept trying to read my face.

"Bill, you kidding?" Sanger said. "There goes your expense account for this month."

Casey waved a hand at him. "I'm handling it, Lee."

The other guy looked derisive. "Yeah? I been watching you, miss, and I figure it pays being a girl. I see how you work."

"Listen," I said. "Keep insulting me and see how far you get. I'll walk back to New York."

Casey heaved himself off the desk, fingering his coat button. He extended his right hand toward me.

"Wait, I didn't agree to hold my story," I said.

"That comes later," Casey said. "You're going to tell me what you know." My fingers pinched the fat padding around his palm.

We backed away from each other. He sat down. I smoothed my hair. I was dying to show off. "It's power," I began. "People out here in movies, they know about power and how much they want money. They figure it'll make them like themselves more. That's why they come. Then they start thinking they own the world. They start believing that they're special because they got all the power to make movies."

Casey narrowed one eye. "Cut the bullshit," he said.

331

"I'm looking for a guy who dug a hole in another guy's chest with a knife."

"Like that producer Lyons," I said, ignoring him. "He makes a hundred million in two years. But it doesn't make him happy. It turns his life upside down. He dumps his wife. She goes nuts from cocaine and a nasty personality. He gets lonely and starts believing he's got an empire to protect. He figures he's above the law."

The two sheriffs looked at each other. "But what's that got to do with anything?" Casey asked.

"This is important information," I snapped. "You don't have it. I do, so listen. You should pull Lyons in for questioning."

"Don't tell me what I should do," Casey said. "Just tell me what the hell you got."

Sanger interrupted. "She was in the Lyons's house, according to my video surveillance crew, from eleven-twenty P.M. to one-ten A.M. last night."

"You get around." I smiled sweetly. "But I got in there and you didn't."

He said, "Police officers don't do second-story work."

"Why were you watching Lyons?" I asked.

"Classified information," Sanger snapped.

"Okay, then I finished my story," I said quietly.

Casey grunted. "Sister, Lyons is a suspect. We got lots of suspects."

"Why him?" I asked.

"Well, I hear he's that type of guy who doesn't really have a sex life—repressed faggot, tight with Mineo, midnight walks by the sea, and that crap," Casey said. "I figure him to be a cold-hearted creep; you know the type. He goes crazy once and commits the crime of passion out of nowhere."

I shook my head. "It was no crime of passion. It had to do with money." I almost laughed. "Maybe that's the American passion—money.

"Last night," I continued, "when I was inside Lyons's house, I found out how the whole thing happened. It started when his wife hired Jerry Johnson to rough up Sal Mineo."

I took a step forward. "She gets this guy Jerry Johnson to do her dirty work. He helps her bully people over cocaine deals."

Casey raised his eyebrows. "The feds tell me she deals, all right."

"Back up a little." The young guy still sounded snotty. "Who's Jerry Johnson?"

I reached into my bag and threw one molar at Casey. He caught it between his palms. "That's how Johnson and Kate store cocaine. She calls him a gardener.

"He's a loser." I pointed a finger. "He's the guy you booked as Cleon Wilson, remember? He wanted to trade information about the murder and get off."

Casey looked down at the tooth. "Yeah, that was a dead end."

"No, it wasn't," I said. "I went to Watts, and you didn't. Jerry Johnson was a sick sadist. He tried to intimidate Sal Mineo, but he got carried away, and he murdered him." I stopped.

Casey asked, "What? Wait—why would Kate Lyons want to hurt Sal Mineo?"

"It's simple," I bragged. "It all started because Chris Franklin was dealing for Kate Lyons until he got big ideas and borrowed cocaine. Some he sold to Mark Loren, and the rest he hid in Mark's house. Kate sent her gardener after Chris. When Sal Mineo heard about it, he went straight to Kate and told her to lay off Chris. He said he'd see to it that she got her coke and money back. She figured Sal had the stuff. She got pissed off that he was interfering and told that sadist Jerry to get the cocaine back from Sal and scare him into keeping his mouth shut. She figured Sal was hiding it at his house, and she promised that thug half if he found it. Later, she sent Jerry to ransack Mark's house. He broke in twice looking for cocaine. Kate says she never figured there'd be a murder."

"What's your proof?" Casey asked.

My shoulder bag was lying on the brown rug on the other side of the bed. "I got proof, all right."

I pulled out the tape recorder, flipped it over, and turned

the volume way up. I set the machine gently on the bed and crossed my fingers.

It clicked, and then shouts and a thump came out. Kate Lyons was screaming something scratchy and far away. I was beside myself. I pushed the "fast-forward" button. I almost jumped up and down, pacing. More static came through. I kept pushing more buttons, trying to find a patch of audible words. The damn thing hadn't picked up anything from that distance. I hated that tape recorder. I started shaking it with both hands.

Lee Sanger made a contemptuous sound with his tongue. "This machine is worthless. You need a directional microphone. That's all we use nowadays."

"But I was in there," I said, listening to a crash. It sounded like the willowware plate.

"He let you in because you look like a harmless girl," Sanger muttered.

Casey stared at the tooth in the palm of his hand. "Maybe he thought she had the goods on his wife. How much does Lyons know?"

"Everything." I picked up the tape recorder and shook it. The spools were still turning, but nothing came out.

"I was there. I heard everything. They tried to kill each other." Suddenly I was close to tears. "They had a doctor up there, Hank somebody. Lyons has a neck wound. She shot him."

Casey stood up. "Turn it off."

I punched the button and threw the thing back on the bed.

"Tell me all about it," Casey demanded.

"Well, Lyons is going to try to cover it up. He's got a murder on her. She's in the palm of his hand. He wants her half of the business."

"Where's this Jerry Johnson?" Casey sounded hoarse.

"Johnson is probably halfway to Mexico. She was there to borrow money to pay him off. I bet Lyons figures out a way to take care of him. Nobody would miss that loser."

Casey puffed out his cheeks. "Not bad."

The other guy looked from Casey to me. "What about the doctor? He can't hide the facts. He'd lose his license."

I smiled sweetly again. "Lyons could tell him he had an accident with the gun. I bet the doctor's a friend."

Sanger drummed his fingers on his gunbelt. "How'd you get out?"

"I ran away."

"Lucky move," Casey said.

Casey raised himself off the desk and pulled out the chair. He sat down. "Now, listen to me," he said. "You had some breaks. But headlines aren't the point."

"She doesn't have a job," his partner interrupted.

"Lee, no editor's gonna turn down a story this hot."

"Really?" I was almost my old self, wanting more compliments. "You think he'll go for it?"

"Yup, and that's my problem," Casey said. "I couldn't convince a jury in the world with the story you told me."

"Why not?"

"I need six months to pin down conversations, papers, cash transactions, plane trips, receipts for purchasing a certain gun and a certain knife, drug deals."

"Reporters can help."

He shook his head. "No, once those fancy Hollywood people get wind of what we know, they'll cover it up. They'll bury the evidence so deep, it'd take an earthquake to get at it."

"What's that mean?" I asked sullenly.

"It means I'll give it everything I got." Casey raised one hand like a boy scout. "I swear it."

"But—"

"It means I'm begging you to give me a break. I need time. If I ain't wrapped it up by then, go ahead. Hell, write it—write the whole fucking story. I'll open up all my files to you. You'll have enough stuff to write a goddamn book. We could write it together. I'd like to see those fancy crooks get it in the neck. Just give me and the sheriff's office the first shot."

I didn't say anything.

Casey looked at his steel watch again. "I'm betting you want those motherfuckers punished just as much as I do."

His bloated eyes darted over and held mine.

He tried to read my face. "Sister, you're doing the right thing. Just shake on it again. Look, you got a juicy story already—on homosexual Hollywood. That'll sell newspapers. Write that one for me."

"Okay, if you stop harassing Mineo's friends," I said.

"Like who?"

"Mark and Chris."

He shrugged. "I promise you, it's a deal," and he pumped my hand.

Things were moving too fast. I'd lost my murder story because I'd done a great job of sleuthing. Punishing the murderers was too important. Sure, I could write something in six months. But that wasn't my biggest problem. I had to get Marty Burns to give me my job back without writing the whole story.

I narrowed my eyes. "If you don't help me in six months, I write a story claiming the Department abridged my First Amendment rights as a journalist."

Casey lumbered toward the door. "Slow you're not. Okay, it's still a deal." He turned to his partner. "I'm too late to make it over to Century City," he said.

He put his hand on the doorknob and paused. "You need a ride to the airport?"

"It's okay—"

New creases curved around his mouth. It was the first time I'd seen him smile since he offered me a milkshake in his office. "No, I'm keeping my word. Lee'll put you on a plane, airfare courtesy of the Department."

"I'll pay you back—"

"Skip it." He raised a fleshy palm again.

Then he was gone.

Sanger was still fiddling with his gunbelt. The stiff leather creaked. Boy, I was tired of guns. "Please wait outside," I said coldly.

In the bathroom, I brushed my teeth before I tossed my tooth brush into my bag and checked my face out in the mirror. I was surprised. I'd gotten a tan out of all this. The sun had darkened my mouth, making it look more sensual.

In the empty corridor, Sanger reached automatically for

my bag, but I held onto it. A door opened and a bare arm grabbed an *L.A. Times* from the patterned carpet. A mop of blond curls flashed at us.

On the elevator, I put my arm out fast and pressed LOBBY before Sanger could.

At the desk, Jay waved my bill at me cautiously. I smiled back and wrote a postdated check. His teeth flashed. He looked relieved. I wasn't acting like a prisoner. "Goodbye," I shouted. His counter was barricaded by a pile of luggage and two bass fiddle cases pasted with French travel stickers.

"New rock group, here from Arista." He snapped his fingers and pretended to jitterbug. "German Deco—they wear skirts on stage and say God is a sissy."

I wondered if Nietzsche'd accounted for punk.

Sheriff Sanger's Mercedes shone from water and wax. Inside, the white bucket-seats smelled like new leather. He slipped on kid gloves and drove with authority, only a thumb and forefinger guiding the wheel. He was heading west on Sunset, then down La Cienega away from the Hollywood Hills and the HOLLYWOOD sign. Someday that was what I'd remember of all this. We were two blocks from the alley where Sal Mineo was murdered.

Ahead, I saw miles of gray road sloping down into the flats. Two kids craned their necks at me from an open jeep in the next lane. I waved at them, open and friendly, California style. They pulled over to an ice machine in the 711 supermarket parking lot opposite an old sign spelled BEKINS on a boxy white warehouse.

Sanger turned down a street of quirky bungalows. I stared at them eagerly. They were a humorous hodgepodge of pure Spanish haciendas, ranch houses, and then one Eastern-developmental-style house that was mostly a pretentious door. The homes looked unreal, like fancy photographs. The lawns were tiny, with palms and vines sitting behind miniature hedges. Nothing was this green in Manhattan.

We were driving down the San Diego Freeway. "This your only case?" I asked Sanger. He nodded, flipped on his turn signal, and changed three lanes in five seconds. It made me burp funny. "What's your specialty?"

"Stakeout and surveillance."

"Was that you ringing the telephone the afternoon I went inside Sal Mineo's apartment?"

"Why don't I leave it to your imagination?" he said sarcastically.

I kept talking. I didn't want to lose touch with my story. He was the last link. "What's it like, watching that place?"

"I load the camera, monitor long-distance microphones, and joke around with the guys."

"Joke about what?"

"Nothing much."

"Tell me a joke," I said pleasantly. I tried to memorize the sloping black roof of one gingerbread house off the freeway.

"Well, one day I collect the mail, right? And I say, 'Guess what came?' Then I say, 'A box of heart candy from John Wayne.' Next day I say, 'Guess what? Heart candy from Errol Flynn.' " He glanced at me.

I kept smiling. "What really did come?"

"Magazines."

"Which ones?"

"*Playgirl, Film Quarterly, The New Yorker,* phone bills, and fan letters."

He looked at me again when he thought I wasn't looking. He didn't understand why I'd stay in gay bars until midnight and sleep over at Mark's house.

"People just start talking to you?" he asked.

I shrugged. "Sometimes."

"Well, why'd he let you into his house in the middle of the night?"

"I twisted his arm."

"Like I say, it pays to be a young girl and do what you do."

"It pays to be smart," I said. "Why'd you hit me at the airport?" I'd had this on my mind since he'd marched into my hotel room.

"You were holding me up," he said.

"From what?"

"Surveillance."

"Who were you following?"

"Classified."

"You usually hit women?"

"If I'd known who I was dealing with, I'd landed you one on the jaw," he said.

Another compliment from the L.A. County Sheriff's Department.

We whipped under a green LAX sign.

At the airport, he parked right in front of the American Airlines terminal. A man in yellow Bermuda shorts stopped to gawk at me in the sheriff's car. I stuck my chin up.

Not a bad way to exit Los Angeles. I almost wished the light on the roof of the car was flashing.

I held onto my bag and Sanger stood behind me while I waited in the ticket line. The woman in front of me wore sunglasses as big as pocket mirrors. Sanger stepped ahead of her and tossed a check on the counter. The clerk didn't bother to raise her mascara-lidded eyes.

"You should talk to Jerry Johnson soon," I said to him.

"We pulled him in yesterday for four hours," he said. "He's got an alibi. Some woman he lives with off and on, a wild woman, likes orgies."

"She's lying," I said.

We sat down on adjoining orange plastic seats looking out onto the runway. "Don't you have a guy who minds you doing this kind of thing?" he asked.

"What about you? Your work's dangerous."

"I am a guy," he said.

I yawned and watched an airplane taxi around the field.

He made that nasty clucking noise with his tongue.

I figured it was eleven-thirty. My flight was at noon. I hate waiting. I'm never early for planes.

"I got to call somebody," I said. He watched me while I walked across the lounge in search of a phone. Then he got up and started feeding change into a candy machine.

I dialed the number and when Mark answered, "Hello?" I pulled the door shut. His voice went through me. I had loved it before I knew him. "Hello?" he asked again. I pressed the receiver against my mouth and hung up fast.

But then I dialed his number again. I wasn't a dumb kid. And he didn't need more paranoia in his life. The receiver clicked. "I'm sorry," I said.

"I know, babe." His voice trailed off into the silence of the telephone.

"You okay?" I asked.

"I'm mad"—he paused—"at myself, and that's for sure."

I waited.

"I woke up with the worst hangover of my life and called you."

That felt good.

"There was a clerk answering the phone who kept going on about you. He's got something for you. He told me all about the cops."

"I'm at the airport," I blurted out. "I got to leave town."

"I hear you." He said the phrase like it was one word.

"What're you thinking about?"

"I been thinking," he murmured. "We could keep it alive, but you see limits on the things. Where you can hurt the other one worse than an enemy, and babe, I been me for a long time."

His voice was low. "Honey," he said, "you did me better than wildflowers at Christmas. I just wish you were begging me to take you back."

"I wish too," I said. Then I asked, "How long you think it'd work?"

I closed my eyes tight. I tried to picture him pacing in his living room, looking out the window at the red bougainvillea and down the green lawns toward the pool. I think I was estimating the amount of hurt I could stand.

"Not-that-long," I answered for him, like I was teaching the words to a kid.

"Not that long," he repeated.

There was a kind of relief under all my other feelings. The dream felt unfamiliar. It didn't fit.

"It's that sad," he said. "We did something new," he said, his voice trailing off.

We shared a silence.

I heard someone tapping the glass door. The sheriff jerked his thumb out toward the runway. "Plane's boarding," he said when I opened the door. "Didn't you hear the announcement?"

I turned my back to him. "Go to the police now," I said softly into the phone. "Tell them everything. It'll help."

Mark didn't answer me.

"You have to," I said.

"You told them about Chris?" he asked.

"Yes, but . . ."

"But what?"

I wanted to tell him I'd solved the case. But I was afraid I'd blow it. "It's complicated. They need proof."

He laughed a mean laugh. "I ain't proof." He cleared his throat. "But I'll try what you say. That woodpecker was working on my windowpane all night long."

"I like him," I said.

"He's reminding me," he said.

I didn't want to hang up. I didn't want to forget the spaces between his phrases when he paused for feelings.

I said, "We weren't meant to meet, Mark, but we're lucky we did."

"Don't feel bad," he said.

I wished I could reassure him about impossible things.

After he said goodbye, I pressed the telephone against my ear and listened. The disconnected wire vibrated. After a minute, the dial tone hummed. I started to dial his number again and stopped. I lingered for another three seconds waiting to hear something. But nothing happened.

I flew out of Los Angeles under the high sun that had just shed a gray shroud. Sanger had followed right behind me onto the wide empty plane, past stewardesses and to my seat in front of the silver wing. He didn't say goodbye. I was too upset to notice until he'd left.

I don't think he ever got used to talking to me instead of just following me.

First we flew northeast, low over the Pacific Ocean, and hit rolling fog. We kept diving into big balls of fluffy gray mist. I wondered if Joe was running our dog around the reservoir. The seat next to me was empty. The seatbelt sign chimed off. I told the stewardess not to wake me for meals. I was crying quietly. When the plane turned around and flew east, higher and higher over the plum-colored San Bernardino mountains and toward New York, I blew my nose and congratulated myself. I'd done my job. I'd gotten an answer. That made me feel great. I had earned the right to think about nothing at all, to take time for tears, a crying time.